'Bitch,' he said, and slapped her. His gold ring caught her mouth and she heard and felt the crack as the metal hit her front teeth. Her hands went up to protect her face till she felt the jab of the needle. The floating sensation began. Her body loosened and then the pillowcase came down over her head and she felt him tie cords around her neck.

'No, Val, I hate the dark . . .' She managed just a few words but already he'd hauled her into a sitting position against the wall and pulled her hands above her head.

'See how you like being left on your own again and again,' he said. 'I was only a kid, left in that room, and I was so frightened . . .'

The duct tape he was using on her wrists cut into her flesh. Was he going to kill her this time?

No, he'd said Glo was going to look after her, hadn't he? But what if something happened to stop Glo coming? She would be in this stinking room, bound like this, until she starved or died of thirst. Which would come first?

She passed out.

June Hampson was born in Gosport, Hampshire, where she still lives. She has had a variety of jobs including waitress, fruit picker, barmaid, shop assistant and market trader selling second-hand books. June has had many short stories published in women's magazines. *Damaged Goods* is her third novel. Her first two novels, *Trust Nobody* and *Broken Bodies*, are also available in Orion paperback.

By June Hampson

Trust Nobody
Broken Bodies
Damaged Goods

DAMAGED GOODS

JUNE HAMPSON

An Orion paperback

First published in Great Britain in 2008
by Orion
This paperback edition published in 2009
By Orion Books Ltd,
Orion House, 5 Upper St Martin's Lane,
London WC2H 9EA

An Hachette UK Company

A CIP catalogue record for this book is
available from the British Library.

Typeset at The Spartan Press Ltd,
Lymington, Hants

Printed and bound in Germany
by GGP Media GmbH, Pößneck

The Orion Publishing Group's policy is to use papers that
are natural, renewable and recyclable products and
made from wood grown in sustainable forests. The logging
and manufacturing processes are expected to conform to
the environmental regulations of the country of origin.

www.orionbooks.co.uk

For Maureen Swire and her St Vincent Singers for always being there for me, and especially for Mollie Aldred, my friend who shows me the way.

ACKNOWLEDGEMENTS

There are many people who have tirelessly believed in me and I can never thank you all enough for making my dreams come true:

Jane Wood, my editor, and my gem of an agent, Juliet Burton. Susan Lamb, my paperback editor, and Angela McMahon, my publicist. Sara O'Keeffe, Juliet Ewers, Gail Paten, Jade Chandler, Aliya Mirza, Julia Silk, Nikki Lord, Robyn Karney and the lovely Lisa Milton. You all deserve my grateful thanks. The mistake is mine if I've forgotten to put your name. I apologise, but bless you all.

Each player must accept the cards life deals him or her; but once they are in hand, he or she alone must decide how to play the cards in order to win the game.

VOLTAIRE
In Humanity

PROLOGUE

He was shit scared. Him, Valentine Waite, who'd never been afraid of any man, either in the boxing ring or out of it.

He kicked the soft peaty soil against the side of the well as he hoisted up the slight body of the girl, then set her to rest on the weather-worn circle of red brick. One small hand, fingers covered with cheap rings, swung from her lifeless form as though plucking at the dirt.

'Slag,' he muttered, lifting the rope from the ground and looping it around her body.

Remembering, he gave a small laugh that eased the tension inside him. The girl had been easily lured to Wickham Woods with the promise of more money than she'd usually get for a quick fuck. He'd picked her up, befuddled with booze, from outside the Portsmouth Guildhall. She'd recognised him almost immediately.

'You look just like that bleedin' boxer, what's 'is name,' she'd slurred. 'Valentine White, innit?'

'Lots of people tell me that.' He flicked at the

miniature black leather boxing gloves hanging from his inside mirror. 'And it's Waite, not White.' Already this dumb bitch had annoyed him. She would be easy to get rid of.

Daisy Lane might not be such easy prey.

In another couple of weeks the clocks would be going forward for British Summer Time 1966, and the protection of dark evenings would be denied him. Picking up Daisy Lane during daylight hours wasn't what he wanted at all.

The girl had asked, 'Where we goin'?'

'Does it matter?' He'd thrown a handful of notes at her and she'd scrabbled in her lap as though scared he might take the money back again. She'd shut up then, stroked the inside of his thighs, slipped her fingers inside his flies.

'Don't make me come, let's get to the woods. You deserve better than a car quickie,' he'd said, pacifying, while hating the smell of her. Body odour undisguised by perfume, and the sharp scent of gin on her breath. She'd left him alone then, lighting up a Woodbine and filling his car with smoke.

Wickham Woods was deserted; he'd guessed as much. He pulled into the parking area and a cool breeze met him as he opened the car door. The fresh air would tease the pale skin of the girl's cheeks to a pink blush, he thought, as they strolled down the dirt path.

'You must come 'ere a lot,' she said, her ridiculous heels making her stumble on the soft earth.

'I know the area. Used to be a house here but now there's only the ruins,' he'd said. 'And the well. It's the kind of place you'd pass by and not really notice.'

'It's creepy,' she gasped, stepping closer to him for comfort. A bird, a collared dove, disturbed by the noise of their presence, flew from the trees, closely followed by its mate. The girl was shivering and he pulled her close, then down onto the primrose-covered forest floor.

'Take those things off,' he'd said. She'd wriggled out of her knickers and lay back, letting her legs fall open, and he was upon her.

Afterwards, he despised himself. And her.

It hadn't taken long to choke her.

She was no match for him. He'd felt the intensity of knowing he could do as he wanted. She'd cried as she urinated, the sharp smell mingling with the sweeter evening scents.

'Don't, don't . . .' She'd continued to say the words until her breath finally left her.

Looking down at her, he thought of his mother and whispered, 'They're all the same as you. I have to put an end to their miseries like I put an end to yours. You should never have left me in the dark while you fucked your men. I was just a kid, and I was frighten-ed. But now my voices tell me every new slut offered them gives me power. And I can keep a little bit of each one, like I keep you, Mother, safe in my heart so you can never leave me again.'

He listened to the hum of the trees and it was as if

3

the woodland sounds around him were from a different world. Then he became aware of his hands, clammy, his skin sweating. His fear had returned.

He thought about Daisy. She was like his mother, a slut of the highest order, and she'd lied to him. Just like his mother had.

He'd offered himself to her and she'd turned from him as though he was dogshit on her shoe. Turned from *him* to shack up with that fucking gangster, Roy Kemp. Almost a year he'd waited, watching, learning about her movements, and keeping out of sight, away from Gosport's prying eyes, watching that house in Western Way bought for her by that thug Eddie Lane. He knew she spent every other weekend in London with her gangster. He knew the shops she used, the walks she took with her toddler, pushing him in a blue pushchair, oblivious to anyone else in the vicinity as she chased him in Stanley Park or picked seashells with him along the shore at Stokes Bay.

But most of all, imprinted on his mind, was every road she travelled from her house to Roy Kemp's terraced property in London, in that poncy little MG of hers. He knew the hours she would leave, waving goodbye to that black-haired tart, Vera, and that plump blonde slag, Susie, and Eddie Lane's kid. How old would he be now, that little boy? Two? Two and a half? The spit of his father, the dark hair and the green eyes that seemed to take in everything and give nothing away.

He should have a boy like that child.

Maybe he would. Maybe that very same little boy . . .

Daisy should be with him, not Roy Kemp. He'd been nice to her, hadn't he? Told her she reminded him of his mother, and not only with her slight body and blonde hair. He'd paid her the highest compliment, *told her she should belong to him*. He couldn't understand why she'd walked away from him at that party in Thorngate Hall. She'd been ready enough to give herself to him before, hadn't she? Then she changed her mind.

It messed his head up. He was ready to love her and she'd said it was all a *mistake*. He'd show her how much of a mistake she'd made.

And yet here he was, frightened. For at long last, this weekend, she would be his.

Valentine Waite ran his fingers through his hair and looked down at the girl's body. Momentarily he'd forgotten about her. Crouching, he extracted the money he'd given her from her grubby plastic handbag, then dropped the purse down the well. It was a long time before he heard the object hit the water. Then he took from her his usual souvenir, smiling as he slipped it and the small sharp instrument back into his wallet. He tied a rope around her body and slipped it over the supporting beams beneath the remains of the well's thatched roof. He pulled on the rope and the dead girl dangled above the dank-smelling void. He lashed the rope securely to the wooden struts.

She hung grotesquely inside the dome of

weatherbeaten thatch, her inert arms and legs swaying. She was facing downwards. He put his thumbs on her eyes, trying to close them. The lids remained open, accusing. He secured her wrists and then her ankles to the rafters with cord from his pockets and stood back, surveying his handiwork. It was exactly as he had planned: spreadeagled, she would stare forever down into the depths of the well, invisible to passersby. People stared *down* a well. He smiled. How long would it be before someone looked up?

'Why don't you marry the bleeder?'

'Don't call Roy names, Vera.' Daisy pulled at a dandelion that broke off, leaving its root in the soil. 'Sod it! Pass me the pronged thingy.' She took the small gardening fork offered by Vera and began digging furiously. 'Gotcha!' Grimy fingers dangled the root in front of Vera. 'Bloody things.'

'They're God's flowers,' Vera said, 'and I'm fed up with this weedin' lark, it'll play merry hell with me back. I'll ask you again, Missy. Why won't you at least move in with the bloke?'

Daisy sat back on her heels and sighed.

'I like this house. I don't want to live in that poky little house Roy lives in with 'is mum in London. Besides, I like me freedom. I can sleep with him then come home, or he can come down 'ere for the weekend and sleep with me, and I can send him on his way afterwards . . .'

'What you mean is you don't feel you're hurting Moira if you ain't actually living with 'im?'

'She's still in that sanatorium in Spain and she don't even know what bleedin' day it is . . .'

'He could divorce her.'

'No!'

'Said that a bit quick, didn't you, Dais?'

'We're all right as we are. I like me freedom.' Daisy pulled at a piece of toughened grass that unravelled like knitting wool. The truth was she really did cherish being her own woman, as well as having a powerful man like Roy Kemp in the background. She looked at Vera, leaning back to ease her spine. 'Don't give up on this gardening lark yet, Vera. We could have the front done before teatime. Look at these daffodils, ain't they lovely?'

Vera sniffed. Daisy smiled at her and saw Vera melt.

'Give us that bleedin' fork then.'

In companionable silence they worked the flowerbed behind the privet hedge inside the wide gravel drive that led to Western Way. Buds were on the rose bushes and already the flowering cherry was in blossom. Best of all the flowers, Daisy loved the daffs, the bright yellows making her feel winter was finally over.

'You off to 'im this weekend?'

'I am, Vera.'

'I'll take little Eddie out. You wearin' that new black minidress? The one you bought down Fleur's?'

'I am, Vera.'

7

'Is it that benefit thing Reggie and Ronnie Kray fixed up to help the Boys' Club in Kingston?'

'It is, Vera, An' now, if the bleedin' interrogation is over, can we get on with this fuckin' weeding?'

Vera's face had sunk in on itself like a week-old cabbage. Daisy was sure her friend's eyes were just a little too bright and she felt a pang of remorse at her hastiness. Vera cared about her.

Vera unpursed her lips and stared hard.

'I only likes to know where you'll be, Daisy love.'

CHAPTER 1

'Fuck it!' Pain shot up her leg. The padlock fastening the steel band shackling her ankle just would not budge. Daisy's ankle was rubbed raw and the hairgrip she had been using to pick the padlock had slipped and pierced her already angry wound.

Daisy screwed up her eyes, trying to stop the tears squeezing out, swore again, and waited for the pain to subside a little before – her fingers shaking – replacing the bent hairgrip beneath the edge of the filthy lino. She prayed it would stay hidden from his prying eyes. She stared at the wooden skirting board where the chain was securely bolted. She'd long since given up trying to force it from its mooring.

She was a fucking prisoner.

Unable to hold back her feelings any longer, she wept. Huge sobs that she knew would go unheard, ignored. The most Daisy could hope for was that her frustration and pain would be eased by her outburst.

After a while she crawled back over the linoleum, once green with pink roses and now a mish-mash of worn felt, to the stained mattress. You have to face facts, girl, she told herself. On the few times your head is reasonably clear you still ain't strong enough to free yourself.

'Bastard, bastard Valentine Waite.' Her voice sank into the dank walls of her prison.

She touched her swollen ankle and winced anew at the pain. The skin was broken and fresh blood was oozing onto the darker, dried blood. She flexed her toes and wished she hadn't, even that small sensation hurt her. And she felt suddenly ashamed of the encrusted dirt on her feet and her own musky body smell.

The chain allowed her movement to an enamelled bucket that was her lavatory. The bucket stood in the recess beneath the stained butler sink, with its small wooden draining board that was pitted with cigarette burns and clogged with unidentified grey matter in the corners. The single tap gave dribbles of cold water.

Above this was a barred window with ivy covering part of the outside glass, which, she reasoned, would make it extremely difficult for anyone to spot that a window was there. And it cut off her light. The mattress, the bucket, the sink were her islands, the chain allowed her to navigate no further.

Sometimes she could hear loud music from below, floating into the room, the popular kind, as though from a radio. Now, the Righteous Brothers were singing 'Unchained Melody'. Daisy sniffed and wiped her hand across her eyes.

Sometimes she heard voices but she'd long ago

given up screaming for help when she heard them. The penalty, if *he* was around and heard her, was another dose of the drug.

He injected it. The needle would tip her over the edge again into violent hallucinations and dreams and when she eventually came out of that haze she couldn't distinguish between reality and nightmares. She had no idea of the passing of time apart from day and night. Had she been in this room weeks or months? Logic told her it might be about four weeks and the growth of her dirty toenails seemed to agree with this. Her fingernails were torn and bloodied from hours spent trying to pick the lock, which stayed as unyielding as ever, but she had to go on hoping, didn't she? She'd lost a lot of weight. Her legs looked like white sticks. Daisy wondered if that skinny model, Twiggy, starved herself. Somehow she didn't think so, some people were naturally thin. Being slim was one thing, she thought, being starved skinny was another.

As a sort of landmark, Daisy tried to hold on to the memory of the terrible news she had heard on the radio the morning Valentine Waite had abducted her. That was her first day in this room. Those unspeakable creatures, Myra Hindley and Ian Brady, were going on trial for the appalling child murders on Saddleworth Moor. Was the trial still running or had it ended?

Thinking about her own child caused a heartache she could barely endure. To keep her sanity she knew she had to push all thoughts of little Eddie into a room inside her brain and keep it firmly locked. But when, as now, his smiling face entered her mind, all she could think of was his warm, cuddly body and his arms tight about her and her heart bled.

To dwell on whether little Eddie, too, was a prisoner of that mad bastard Valentine Waite would send her completely round the bend.

Mad bastard? Yes. For there was no doubt Valentine Waite had gone over the edge.

Daisy had read about boxers who'd become punch drunk from the battering they'd received to their heads. Sometimes this didn't happen straight away but built up gradually, causing changes of personality, often from placid to violent. But Daisy reckoned Valentine Waite was unhinged before he ever took up boxing and had somehow managed to conceal his true personality.

Daisy feared for little Eddie. Please God, she prayed, just let my son be free from harm and with my friend Vera. I don't care what happens to me if only you'll keep my son safe.

Valentine Waite rarely spoke when he visited the room. At those times, she tried to make herself as small and invisible as possible so he might leave her alone.

Whether it was the pain or the result of the needle, she welcomed sleep. And sometimes after sleeping she could, as now, gather her head and body together enough to know that she must at least try to get out of this stinking place, wherever she was, and away from *him*.

By raising herself on tiptoe and leaning across the sink she had a good view, between the bars, of the yard below and the surrounding area. Daisy was sure it was a breaker's yard. She saw a mountain of what could be rusted car parts, some dropped in puddles of rainbow-coloured oil which glittered when the sun shone. In one corner badly stacked tyres threatened to topple over.

There was some sort of crusher machine that was used regularly and noisily by an old man wearing a flat cap. The rusted and sometimes badly smashed cars which she presumed might have been involved in accidents were creakily hoisted high by a giant claw to somewhere she couldn't quite see and later returned as uneven metal squares that were dropped into an iron container.

The whole yard seemed to be surrounded by dense walls made from thick wooden railway sleepers. Beyond the sleepers Daisy could just make out some allotments that mostly seemed abandoned, and a couple of rusted air-raid shelters covered with brambles that were used as sheds. Daisy once saw a man with a small boy discarding an old pram and had shouted until her throat hurt, but of course they had neither heard nor seen her. She knew there was also a train track nearby because she sometimes heard the rattle of the carriage wheels on the lines and the shrill whistles.

The man in the yard shuffled as though he were drunk or had something wrong with his knees that meant being upright was painful for him. He kept his eyes downwards as though fearing he might slip and fall. She'd thought of breaking the window to attract his attention but the glass was beyond her reach and there was nothing in the room she could use to push through the bars. Perhaps he was deaf, or had been told to ignore her.

She'd sleep and dream. Dream and sleep. And when she was lucid she was petrified of the moment when Valentine Waite would unlock the door.

On the draining board was a threadbare towel, a flannel, a cake of Fairy soap, a round block of Gibbs dentifrice and a toothbrush. Daisy mostly kept herself clean but had chosen not to bother with the flannel, a stinking rag, preferring instead to use her hands beneath the dripping tap. The towel was no longer clean either and was starting to reek as bad as the flannel. She'd had a period and had ripped up part of the towel to use as pads, which she'd thrown in the bucket when they were soiled. She was wearing the same underwear, black skirt and black polo neck jumper she'd had on the day she had been brought to the room.

Daisy did sometimes try to fight against Waite, to escape the syringe and put off the vomiting and nausea that always followed, but he held her until her resistance evaporated. Then, terrified of his punches and unable to avoid his hands on her body, she was forced to let him do what he wanted. Sometimes she was just too confused or depressed to care.

Sometimes the dreams and vivid colours gave her a sense of weightlessness so that she could lift herself out of her body and watch as he fucked the blonde creature on the bed then wandered about the dimly lit room after he had finished with the girl. The girl, she knew, was really herself.

When he did utter the odd sentence or two, she knew it wasn't her he was speaking to, or even thinking about.

He was mad. Quite, quite mad. Daisy had read of people who were insane but able to function often as extremely clever people, until the madness took over. They showed a personality to the world that was seemingly normal yet hid an inward personality that listened to voices and believed they were chosen: chosen to restore balance to the world and those around them by doing as the voices requested. And if the voices told them to do things which normal people would never dream of, then so what? Weren't they protected by their gods, or the voices inside their heads, and convinced they heard praise and atonement?

Daisy shuddered. She couldn't deny that Valentine Waite was good-looking in a boyish way; even the broken nose only added to his charm. And he was always immaculately dressed as befitted a champion boxer, folding his clothes neatly and hanging his jacket on a padded hanger that he kept on the far side of the wall where Daisy couldn't reach.

His looks and position made him a magnet for women. She herself had fallen under his spell at a party organised for him by Ronnie and Reggie Kray. How she wished now she'd never gone with Roy Kemp to that celebration.

Waite sometimes visited the room simply to sift through drawers in a desk pushed against the wall. With his back to her, she could see him carefully examining the contents of a lacquered black box, running his fingertips over whatever was inside. To this box, kept in the top drawer, she had seen him add small items, but she couldn't reach the desk to see what they were.

He brought her food. If she didn't eat in his presence, he'd take the uneaten food away with him. It was usually tinned soup with bread rolls or sandwiches. He gave her a spoon but no sharp cutlery. Only Glo left the meals in the hope that Daisy might eat later. When this happened Daisy guessed her captor might not return for a while and Glo was instructed to make sure Daisy didn't escape.

Daisy wasn't the only one petrified of Valentine Waite.

After an injection she was sometimes given a fountain pen. Then he'd steady her hand and tell her what words to put down on the paper that blurred as the drug took effect. Afterwards she wondered if it had all been a dream.

He wasn't a careful lover. Rolling her on her back, shoving his cock into her mouth, pushing it down her throat until she gagged. And she, chained, unable to struggle against him.

Him grunting when he was inside her, grasping her like his tightened muscles might burst from his skin. Afterwards he'd slump, a dead weight on her, crying like a child and telling her she would always stay with him. That he'd keep her in his heart and in this room. And later still, he'd say, 'You made me do this.'

And he would hit her. And sometimes he called her 'Mother'.

'You awake?'

Daisy's heart leapt at the sound of the voice and the door being unlocked, then locked again after the girl had entered. Daisy opened her eyes.

Glo had a small tray with a mug and a plate of sandwiches. Daisy could smell fish. Perhaps they were bloater paste again. Daisy eyed the girl who couldn't have been more than sixteen years old.

'Help me,' she croaked. Glo's brown eyes filled with tears. She bent down, sweeping the fall of chestnut brown hair back from her eyes. She put the tray on the floor next to the mattress. Daisy saw fresh fingermarks on her skinny upper arms.

She said, 'I . . . I can't. You know that.'

Through the tangle of her own greasy hair Daisy saw the girl look away. Her eyes were like an old woman's. She was wearing jeans and a blouse. Her clothes weren't clean. Her arms were white and freckled, matching the freckles across her upturned nose set in a pale heart-shaped face. To Daisy, despite her grubbiness, Glo looked and smelled fresh and clean as washing brought in straight from the line.

'You been tryin' to pick the bleedin' lock again, ain't you?'

Daisy couldn't lie. 'Yes. Please don't tell 'im.'

'You know I won't say nothing but he'll see the fresh scratch marks on the metal casing same as I did.' She looked at Daisy's mess of an ankle. 'You better let me dab some iodine on that. Don't want it getting infected.' Always the girl seemed nervous. No wonder, Daisy thought, anyone involved with Valentine Waite had a perfect right to be scared.

The girl walked to the desk and opened an unlocked drawer, bringing out a small brown bottle and a roll of cotton wool. Daisy saw she had tried the top drawer first but of course it was locked. It was always locked.

Waite trusted Glo with keys when he wasn't around, but not all the keys. And Daisy guessed Glo only did his bidding out of fear.

'Help me.' Daisy felt the tears rise again. 'He hurts you an' all.'

'If he knew I was even 'aving a bleedin' conversation with you . . .' The girl tore off a piece of cotton wool and unscrewed the bottle, allowing a trickle of the brown liquid to soak in. 'Grit your teeth, this will 'urt but it'll do the trick.' She gently dabbed the bloodied part of Daisy's skin. Daisy stifled a cry for she knew Glo was trying to help her.

'Thank you,' she whispered.

The girl had told her her name was Gloria but he called her Glo.

'I don't know why you bother to try to get the chain off. Even if you managed it, how would you get out the room? And between 'ere and downstairs is another locked door.' Glo put the iodine and cotton wool back in the drawer.

'You could leave me the keys.'

'And if I did I'd get more than a few punches. He'd fucking kill me.' She stared at Daisy and her old woman's eyes told Daisy it was only the truth.

'We could go together. I could hide you.' Glo had reached the door, had inserted the key in the lock. She turned back.

'You couldn't 'ide yourself, could you? He found you.'

The girl let herself out of the room and relocked the door.

Daisy curled herself into a ball on the stinking mattress, listening to Glo's receding footsteps.

Yes, Valentine Waite had found her.

It must have been nearly a year since she had spoken to him at Vera's party in the Thorngate Hall. That night on the dance floor she had told him to leave her alone, that she never wanted to see him again. She remembered the look of disbelief in his eyes.

Apart from a little flirtation once when she'd been lonely, there was nothing between them. They'd never slept together. The so-called relationship was all in his twisted mind, magnified to whatever he wanted it to be.

He had told her she was like his mother, whatever that meant. But he *had* walked away from her. And she'd not seen hide nor hair of him since that day, until . . .

Don't keep going over things in your mind, Daisy, she told herself. Thinking about it won't help, all it does is depress you. Think about Vera. But Daisy's heart hurt thinking about her friend.

Vera had been one of Gosport's more successful prostitutes, then she'd opened a massage parlour, Heavenly Bodies, and become a respected member of Gosport's community. Daisy knew Vera would be out of her mind with worry about her.

She forced herself to remember as clearly as she could that final morning after they'd heard the news on the radio about the trial of the couple dubbed the Moors Murderers. Daisy was filling her car with items she'd need for a trip to London.

'You got enough bleeding stuff there for a week, not a weekend,' Vera had said, eyeing the luggage in the open boot of Daisy's red MG Midget in the gravel driveway of her house in Western Way.

'Me an' Roy are going out to a do with Violet Kray

an' 'er boys.' Daisy had stared at her friend who stood, hands on hips below a trim waist, dressed in a tight black skirt and a green satin blouse that strained across her breasts. Ruffles ran around the neck of the low-cut blouse matching the frills at her elbows. Her black high heels were sinking into the gravel. Californian Poppy, Vera's trademark perfume, wafted towards Daisy.

'Why you don't live in one bleedin' place together beats me. I've said it before and I'll say it again. All this to-ing and fro-ing. Or you could buy a house half way between London and Gosport. It ain't as though that Roy Kemp is short of a penny or two, is it?' Daisy had been cross. She'd heard it all before, and she wanted to get away, to see Roy.

'How many more times am I going to have to tell you he's still married to my mate, Moira? Besides, I like Gosport.' Daisy was looking around for her son, little Eddie. She wanted to hug him goodbye, take the memory of his little boy smell with her to London. She worried sometimes that he was too quiet, too shy for his age. But he wasn't yet two and a half and there was plenty of time for him to become a chatterbox. Daisy thought about his father, he'd been the silent type an' all.

'Humphh!' snorted Vera. 'That Moira still in the loony bin?'

Vera could be very outspoken at times. Sometimes she tried Daisy's patience. 'You know it's a sanatorium in Spain, not a loony bin. An' you also know I

want to get going. Don't keep on. Where's my boy?'
Daisy looked round the vast front garden.

Little Eddie was the son of Eddie Lane, a local toe-rag who'd got mixed up with the London mob and had been killed. He was the first great love of her life. Her child was her second. Little Eddie was a carbon copy in looks of his father and Vera was staying at Daisy's house for the weekend so she could take care of him and be company for Susie. Vera adored little Eddie and spoiled him. Not that Susie and Si, the young couple Daisy had befriended from her cafe days, didn't give in to him too.

Susie and Si had come to live with Daisy after their little girl had been killed in a road accident. And Daisy didn't want them to leave. Susie seemed to have happily taken over the role of chief cook and bottle-washer. Her husband, Si, was manager of The World's Stores, a grocery shop in Gosport's High Street.

Daisy cherished the closeness when Vera came to stay. There was plenty of room in the house and it reminded her of the days when she, Vera and Susie had lived and worked together in Bert's Cafe in the heart of Gosport.

Vera persisted. 'I still think Roy and you should live together instead of him trundling down 'ere to Gosport or you driving up to London . . .'

Daisy slammed the boot shut and turned the chrome handle.

'He has his business up there an' I won't leave you

cranky lot down here. You can set a clock by the regularity of our meetings an' that's the way we like it! Though why I don't wring your scrawny neck an' be free of you an' your nagging, I don't know!'

Daisy looked around her garden at the daffodils in full bloom.

'All this yellow after the dark days of winter is lovely, Vera. We made a good job of planting and weeding, didn't we? I'm going to get loads more bulbs off Alfie, the garden bloke down the market, about September time and plant 'em out the back garden as well. Don't you think the weather is warming up nicely?'

'Eddie!' Obviously Vera wasn't going to answer her but her voice cut through the Friday morning air like one of the ships sounding a foghorn down in Portsmouth Harbour.

'Jesus Christ, our Vera! That poor kid'll 'ave burst ear drums you keep doing that!'

'You wanted to say goodbye to 'im, didn't you?'

A front window opened and a tousled blonde head appeared. Susie put her fingers to her lips.

'He's crawled in with me and gone back to sleep. You don't want to wake 'im.' She blew Daisy a kiss and without further ado, closed the lead-paned window.

'I guess that's told me.' Daisy put her arms around Vera's small frame and hugged her tightly. 'Give 'im a kiss for me and take one for yourself.'

'Piss off!'

Daisy laughed and opened the car door. A fat tabby cat had waddled down the driveway and Vera spoke lovingly to it before picking it up.

'My Kibbles 'as come to wave you off, Dais.' She lifted the cat's paw and made a waving motion.

'You're a daft tart, Vera.' She slid inside on to the cool black leather seat. 'See you Monday morning.'

But she hadn't seen any of them since.

How could she have let herself be taken in so easily that morning?

She'd left the safety of her own driveway and driven past leafy Stanley Park and along the Browndown Road into Lee on the Solent. Trees were in blossom and the grass was emerald green. There wasn't a cloud in the sky and it promised to stay that way. She'd turned right just past Lee Tower, white and majestic against the greeny blue of the sea, past the few shops and into the quiet road that led through farmland until it reached Newgate Lane. The golf course was to the right of her with white-blossomed bushes lining the lane. She always took this route to the main road when she went to stay with Roy every fortnight.

Daisy liked to see and breathe the waters of the Solent with the Isle of Wight backdrop. She enjoyed the ships, the yachts and the ever-changing colour of the sea, sometimes muddy grey, sometimes brilliant blue, before she reached the Tower Ballroom at Lee on the Solent and turned off.

She'd braked in alarm when, rounding a corner, she'd spotted a car with its driver's door open and what appeared to be the body of a woman on the grass verge. Her heart had been beating fast as she'd got out of her car and approached the still form.

She knew it could be ages before anyone came down this rarely used road, so the poor woman could lie there hurt or worse for a long time. As she neared the body she saw it wasn't a person at all, merely bundles of rags and clothing placed there to look like one. The car was empty.

Who would do this, she'd wondered?

She didn't have to wonder for long before she was grabbed from behind and something was dropped over her head. She knew she was being thrust into the nearby car. Not her own car, she could smell and feel the difference of the car's interior.

She'd screamed and kicked out at her attacker but her wrists were already pinioned together behind her. She could smell peppermints, cologne, and feel the roughness of the man's clothes as he held her tight. And there was something familiar about him.

A sharp prick piercing her thigh was followed by a swift feeling of light-headedness, then a sweet sensation that sent her floating into a rainbow-coloured world where nothing mattered.

And when she awoke she was in this room.

She'd raised her left hand to look at the familiar gold bangle that Eddie had bought her. It had gone. She mourned its loss as painfully as she'd mourned his death until, still drugged, she'd slept again.

Daisy glanced at the mug of tea Glo had brought,

picked it up with shaking hands and sipped at it until the tepid brown liquid was gone. Then she put the mug on the lino, turned her face into the mattress and closed her eyes.

CHAPTER 2

'Pissed on or fuckin' pissed off, I don't know what's worse. Do you, Jack?'

Roy Kemp let the steady stream of his urine darken Jack McVitie's grey flannel trousers and pool into his brown brogues. 'You might pretend you ain't frightened of the twins but I know you're shitting bricks.' Roy relished the thought that Jack 'The Hat' couldn't move even if he managed to dredge up the courage, for Roy's friend Charles held him in his grip of steel.

Besides, Roy reasoned, looking around the bombsite while doing up his flies, where would the sneaky little bastard escape to that sooner or later Roy wouldn't find him?

Jack shook his head. His trademark hat didn't budge. Everyone knew the bleeder had a way of jamming his hat on so the wind wouldn't take it and expose his bald spot. Roy could see his fear in the glisten of sweat beneath the hat's brim, and along the man's top lip.

Roy's voice was glacier cold.

'You're not answering me, Jacky boy. I'm pissed off

27

and you've got pissed on. Where's Daisy Lane?' When McVitie still didn't answer, Roy nodded at Charles. The big man let go of Jack, at the same time giving him a fierce kidney punch. Winded, he fell to the ground into the piss.

'I don't know, Mr Kemp.' Roy stared down at Jack's upturned weasel face with the pain from the punch clearly etched on it. 'I been keepin' me eyes an' ears open but no one seems to know nothin'.'

'Then you're no good to me, are you, Jack? Have I given you a job you can't fucking do?' Roy bent down and flicked his fingers against the brim of McVitie's hat, which spun off into the dirt. Roy couldn't stand the bastard. He was just about to put the boot in when Charles anticipated his action and laid a beefy hand on his arm. Charles was right as usual, giving the bloke a kicking would solve nothing.

Not only could Charles Sutherland calm him down, he was the best mate Roy Kemp had ever had. And the fact that Charles was a good twenty years older than him made no difference at all. It wasn't the age of a bloke, it was what he had between his ears and in his heart that made him a good mate. Charles smiled at Roy and Roy nodded. He wasn't going to let himself boil over because of a scumbag like Jack 'The Hat' McVitie. Not yet anyway. No matter how much he was hurting inside over Daisy's disappearance.

'Get up, you fucker.'

Roy needed Jack. Jack could worm himself into any company in any situation like a maggot in an apple, when he wasn't doped up to the eyeballs that is. And with Jack running between the Richardsons and the Krays, sooner or later the sneaky bastard might hear something worth listening to. Though the Richardsons had their own problems.

An affray in Catford at Mr Smith's Club had them under scrutiny for crimes of torture and violence. Roy had had a few run-ins with the brothers but that was in the past. Roy, Charlie and Eddie Richardson went back a long way and he never really saw them as having a hand in Daisy's disappearance. But you couldn't tell. Honour among thieves was all shit. It was just possible an earlier slight had been suddenly remembered and Daisy had become a pawn in the game.

'I got contacts.' Jack had scrambled to his feet.

'What contacts?' Roy knew Jack wouldn't tell him which little bird had done a bit of singing unless he messed him up a bit, but he wouldn't need to bother about that unless it was absolutely necessary.

'Chief Superintendent Fred Gerrard of Scotland Yard is out to get the Krays. He's been out with his sidekick Nipper Read . . .'

'I know all that, you cunt.'

'Yeah, but it's bloody hilarious, Mr Kemp. Reggie and Ronnie bought a couple of snakes an' they named 'em Nipper an' Gerrard.'

Roy sighed. 'You call yourself a fucking hard man an' that's all you can come up with?'

He'd known since March, when Ronnie had killed

George Cornell in The Blind Beggar pub, that the coppers were getting fed up with the Krays being untouchable. And now they couldn't even pin that murder on Ronnie because they couldn't find a single witness from that pub full of people! Eastenders stuck together where the Krays were concerned.

The barmaid couldn't pick Ronnie out of the police line-up, and if Roy had been asked, he'd have been unable to pick the blighter out either. One thing about being in the public's eye, it made you invisible!

But he'd been there when Ronnie and his body-guard Ian Barrie had come into the bar. Barrie had let off one shot into the air and the barmaid had ducked beneath the counter for safety. George Cornell was a big bloke, he'd just ordered a pint and was totally unaware that Ronnie Kray had murder in his heart. Ron fired at close range. Cornell toppled, then the pair calmly walked out leaving Cornell on the floor. A minute later, after tossing back his brandy, Roy had decided he might like to drink at a less noisy venue. The Walker Brothers had been singing 'The Sun Ain't Gonna Shine Anymore', which was certainly true for George Cornell.

Word had got about that Cornell had called Ron a 'fat poof'. But it was common knowledge that Ronnie knew Cornell had been stirring up trouble south of the river with the Richardsons. He'd been planning on a war between the two gangs, the Richardsons trying to wipe out the Krays. Of course, if the Krays toppled so might Roy Kemp.

It hadn't escaped Roy's mind that perhaps Ronnie had abducted Daisy to teach him a lesson for the spot of long-firming she'd organised on the twins' patch. She'd sorted that, clever little bitch, as repayment for him getting rid of Eddie Lane, her first real love.

He'd had to take the blame for the long-firming fraud. It would never do to let on to anyone he'd been taken for a ride by a woman. One tough cookie was his Daisy, but with a marshmallow for a heart.

But the twins rarely went back on their word. The long-firm scam was in the past, old news, paid for, done and dusted. He dismissed the idea of a vendetta.

The streets and pubs of London were where information lay. Roy used McVitie when he needed someone of no consequence to do a bit of nosing about or roughing up for him. When Jack was off the drink he could still be a fucking bad bastard. Please, dear God, let the little shit find out something about his Daisy before it was too late, if it wasn't already.

'Get out of my sight, you fucking tosser.'

Roy watched as the man slid into the shadows caused by a burnt-out van, then scurried over tufts of coarse grass and tall weeds as quick as a rat disturbed in a sewer. He looked at Charles and laughed.

'I don't know what the fucking world is coming to. Remember when it used to be safe to walk the streets of London?'

Charles said, 'It never was, you bleeding twerp. You ready for that pint now?'

Roy grinned and pushed him in the direction of The Blind Beggar.

'What it lacks in looks on the outside it makes up for on the inside, eh, Charles?'

'You can't beat a Saturday night in this place,' the big man replied. 'Fancy a small one as well as a pint?'

Roy shrugged his large shoulders. 'Swift one.'

Charles pushed open the heavy brass-handled doors. 'Swift one for me too. Your ma needs a bit of company. She ain't herself since Daisy's been gone.'

'Is anyone?' Too late Roy regretted his sharpness. 'Sorry, mate,' he said. 'Thank God you look after my mum like you do.' Together they entered the dimly lit bar. The stench of beer and fags hit Roy. He ordered drinks from the blonde behind the bar and carried them over to where Charles had found a couple of seats. The floor was sticky with spilled beer.

'I'm very fond of your mum, you know.' Charles took a long pull on his pint. ' 'Ere, I told you I only wanted a half.' He'd suddenly noticed he was holding a pint.

'Get it down you,' said Roy. He took a pull on his own drink. On the table was a single cardboard beer mat. 'This place might be a bit of a dump but it serves an ace pint. And by the way, I know you're fond of her. I ain't blind, mate.'

Charles had been his dad's mate. They'd fought bare knuckled in fairgrounds together, and it was because of Charles that Violet his mother had met and married his dad. After all these years Roy was used to seeing him sitting in the kitchen with Violet, yacking over old times. Brawny bugger he might be, thought Roy, a bit like an oak tree that got more sinewy every year, but there was no denying Charles had been a tower of strength to Violet when Roy's father had been knocked out, never to recover from the punch he'd taken to his head.

'Roy, I've known you and Violet a long time.' Charles put his pint glass down on the table. 'I know I can't ever take your dad's place but I want to be more than a family friend to your ma. I think it's time.'

'You was a mean bastard by all accounts before I was born – and I've seen what you're capable of since – but my dad and my old lady trusted you, an' she still does.' Charles opened his mouth to speak but Roy waved him down. 'I'd like to think because of you I'm a hard bastard but a fair one. What does my old lady say?'

'Ain't asked her yet.' He frowned. 'When you get to our age it ain't always the bed bit we want, but companionship.'

'Companionship! You practically live at our 'ouse!' Roy swallowed the rest of his drink and set his glass down amid the rings on the sticky table top. He couldn't imagine his mother in bed making love, but he supposed most people would say the same thing of their parents and neither Violet nor Charles were old. His mother had been a girl when she'd had him and he was nowhere near forty yet!

'I want to look after her properly. Take 'er out and about. You're too bleeding busy.' He lowered his voice. 'You got Daisy on your mind, son. Till you get to the bottom of her disappearance it's all you can do to keep your mind on the family business. I want your mum to marry me and I want your blessing.'

Roy stared at him. It all made perfect sense.

'If it's what she wants then I'm bleeding over the moon,' he said. He saw Charles' shoulders drop with relief and decided a bit of banter wouldn't go amiss. 'As long as you don't want me to start calling you Daddy!' Charles picked up the beer mat and threw it and Roy ducked. It sailed through the air and fell on a table where two elderly blokes were playing dominoes.

'Sorry, mates, never meant to interrupt your game.' Both men had paused and were looking at him. Realisation and then fear dawned in their eyes as they recognised Roy and Charles. 'Couple of drinks for me muckers over 'ere,' he called to the barmaid. The men nodded, visibly relieved, and went back to their game. 'You want another one, mate?' Roy nodded towards the empty glasses.

Charles shook his head and rose from the seat.

'Roy, I'm off. You coming?'

'I'll walk out with you but I got a bit of business with the Maxi brothers. Them young Eyetie tosspots have been going into my clubs and mending the fucking fruit machines when there ain't nothing wrong with them.'

'You got to give 'em a bit of bleeding credit, they're only kids.'

'The family ain't over 'ere but five minutes an' the mother the only wop with a bleeding work permit. Credit is fine but they're not taking credit, they're stealing cash from the machines. My machines.'

'Want me to come along?'

'Nah, I can handle it. Go on home.' Roy grinned. 'Fucking silly chancers, them lads. Neither of 'em's out of their nappies yet.'

Outside, Charles left him and melted into the darkness. Roy breathed in the freshness of the night air, he hadn't realised how foul it was in the bar, then he began walking over to his silver Humber. With a bit of luck, after he'd sorted the lads he'd get himself an early night. Only he knew he'd never sleep. There was something about Daisy's disappearance staring him right in the face but for some reason he couldn't see it. These past weeks had been a fucking nightmare. What he didn't like was someone getting one over on him.

Never in his wildest dreams had he thought a little woman like Daisy could get under his skin, but she had. And he knew, just knew she wasn't dead. Where the fuck she was, he hadn't a clue, but he'd find her. And when he found out who was responsible, he'd kill the fucking bastard. Long and slow.

Later, Roy sat for a while outside the terraced house he shared with his mother. He hated himself for what he'd done tonight. A long-pronged carving fork pinning the boy's hand to the table and a paper screw of pills the lad would get a taste for. But he'd told the boy the truth. If Roy Kemp acted soft, he'd get shat on again and again.

He stared at the front door and then at the window where white nets stopped nosy passers-by from staring in. It had been the family home for as long as he could remember and Violet refused to leave it. Soon, he supposed, there'd be a demolition order on the street. Perhaps then and only then would his old lady move house.

He put his key in the lock and opened the door to the smell of fresh baking. Before Roy had had time to remove his hat and coat his mother called, 'I've just made sausage rolls, dear. Do you want some?'

To him Violet never seemed to change, never happier than when she could feed someone. He took off his long wool coat and slung it over the banister rail at the bottom of the stairs, perched his hat on top, then walked through the carpeted hallway into the kitchen. Violet's flowered wraparound pinny was freshly ironed. Her hands were still covered with flour and pastry was being rolled out with a milk bottle. On the top of the cooker a batch of golden-brown sausage rolls were cooling.

'You can have one of those, dear. They shouldn't burn your tongue.' The radio was on and Marvin Gaye was telling everyone just how sweet it was to be loved.

'Can't resist, can I?' He went over and helped

himself, biting into the melt-in-your-mouth pastry. His mother had made the filling herself, using choice meat from the butcher on the corner in Lydden Street. He closed his eyes then murmured his delight towards Violet, who smiled the smile of a mother besotted by her son. Then he nodded towards Charles, comfortable on a kitchen chair, a half mug of tea in front of him and crumbs down his shirt front. He was tieless and shoeless.

'How did it go?' Charles asked. Roy knew he meant the Maxi brothers.

'Taught the older one a lesson and I'm sure he'll pass it on to the younger lad. Little shits. Might have to worry about the pair of them in a few years' time though.'

'Teach 'em not to put their fingers in your tills, eh?'

'Little sods could end up with no fingers at all.' Roy put the last piece of savoury pastry into his mouth. He went over to his mother and kissed her on the back of the neck. 'These are bloody good. They're different from your usual ones though. Got something herby about them.'

'One of Daisy's recipes . . .' His mother looked at him anxiously. 'Oh, I'm sorry, lad, I shouldn't have said that.'

The rest of the sausage roll in his mouth tasted like cardboard. He forced himself to say something.

'These should put hairs on your chest, Charles.' Charles unbuttoned his shirt to show grey fuzz.

'Reckon I need 'em?'

'Put that away in my kitchen,' scolded Violet. The fondness in her tone wasn't lost on Roy.

'I won't be long before my bed.' Roy turned to Charles and with his back to his mother, mouthed, 'You asked her yet?' Charles shook his head, something like panic in his eyes. Roy smiled at him.

'Me and Charles is going to play a game of draughts, aren't we?'

'If you says so, Violet.'

Roy got up from the table and went over to the top cupboard where he took down the board and box and put it on the scrubbed table.

'You two been playing that bleeding game for years. Don't you get sick of it?'

Charles had settled himself at the table and was unfolding the draughtboard and setting out the black and white draughtsmen. Violet was washing her hands at the sink after putting the second batch of rolls in the oven.

'What else we got to do?' she said. 'Charles is better off sitting 'ere with me than going back to his poky flat. Besides,' she looked at Charles fondly, 'we got history, 'aven't we, Charles? Plenty to chunter on about you youngsters don't understand.'

Roy climbed the stairs. He knew Charles would let Violet be white. She always wanted the white pieces. And Roy knew that Violet, straight as a die Violet, would cheat Charles rotten to win. And he'd let her.

*

Alone in the bedroom he'd once shared with Moira, Roy's eyes lit on the photograph of his wife and Daisy taken years earlier at a New Year's Eve party. It was the first time he'd met Daisy. The women were smiling at each other. Firm friends they'd been then. Moira was already showing signs of the paranoia that would eventually lead to her breakdown. The dress his wife was wearing was a Fifties-style outfit. She'd had it in her head to copy Ruth Ellis, the last woman to be hanged in England for the murder of her lover.

Moira had even had a go at trying to shoot him. All because he'd had a mild fling with a hostess from one of his gaffs. The coupling meant nothing, only a few quick fucks to relieve his tension. Though he'd never admitted that to Moira because he loved her and couldn't bear to see the hurt in her eyes.

Then Moira had aborted his child in the bedroom above Daisy's Gosport cafe. God, how he'd hated her for doing that. She wasn't in her right mind, but she knew enough to understand he'd always wanted a child of his own. And the nearest he'd got to that now was little Eddie, Daisy's child.

Ironic really, that he should love the boy like a son, the kiddie of the bloke he'd killed.

Moira and Daisy had met when he was on remand at Winchester nick. Daisy was visiting her husband Kenny who was doing two years. Silly young sod hadn't kept his head down and had got raped. Then he'd got his own back on the bastard who'd raped him but in return Kenny had been strung up, hanged by the bastard. That's when Roy had stepped in. Daisy had cared for Moira, so it was only fair he sorted out her husband's killer.

Naked, Roy went into the bathroom and switched on the shower. As the water cascaded over him he tried to remember just when it was he'd fallen for Daisy, though of course he'd fancied the knickers off her the first time he'd met her.

She'd never thought of him that way, not then. Moira had been her friend and you didn't mess about with friends' husbands, well, Daisy Lane didn't. Moira, poor bitch, had tried to kill herself, the last time with a rusty razor blade she'd found on the roadway outside the villa in Spain. He'd had to commit Moira to a sanatorium for her own safety.

Roy soaped his body with the soap on a rope.

Because Daisy had befriended Moira, Roy had let Eddie take him for a ride until Roy's own credibility had been questioned, and he had to dispose of him.

Roy towelled himself dry, went back into his bedroom, took out a pair of monogrammed silk pyjamas and got into bed. Then he poured himself a large brandy from the bottle on his bedside cabinet. He shuddered as it went down in one gulp. He'd been drinking more than usual lately. It wasn't like him but then he had a lot on his mind, didn't he? He treated himself to another stiff nip.

He thought about Daisy's car abandoned in Broom Way at Lee on the Solent. She'd been on her way to visit him. Some clever bastard knew exactly what day and time that would be and had lain in wait.

Roy listened to the wind rattling the sash window. Here he was, one of the most feared blokes in London who could have his pick of most of the women he knew, and he was spending the night alone. He rubbed his hand over his aching balls.

It had to be someone who knew her, knew her movements. He thought back to the party Daisy had organised for Vera at the Thorngate Hall in Gosport. There'd been a few functions since then, of course, but that one had been the last really big bash. All the guests had been hand-picked by him, Vera or Daisy. Since then, his boys had gone round asking questions of everyone who'd been at that party but without any luck.

He'd even kept a special eye on the boxer, Valentine Waite. He'd seen the way he'd looked at Daisy across the table at one of the twins' gatherings but he'd been away from the London scene for a while. His fights took him all over the place. Six weeks ago he'd returned from South Africa and he was due to fly out soon for a match in New York, arranged by the Madison Square Garden entrepreneurs if the rumours he was hearing were right.

Roy sighed. Valentine's, Waite's nightclub, was in deep shit. He'd heard the boxer spent his money as fast as he got it. The bloke was a right fucking misfit all right.

Just to make sure Waite was in the clear he'd got a

bloke inside his Arundel country house. The boxer had a nice pile sitting in the countryside near Little-hampton. Bit sparsely furnished, so he'd been told, and remortgaged to the hilt because Waite was a naughty boy at the gambling tables. The house hadn't been lived in for quite a while.

The twins had put a bit of pressure on him for unpaid debts but Roy had told them the bloke usually paid up. Roy himself had been running several gaming clubs before the Betting and Gaming Act came into force, now he just concentrated on a couple. One club in Belgravia and another in Virginia Water, where Waite often played.

Tomorrow he was going down to Gosport.

He was looking forward to seeing little Eddie, the boy was a cracker. Daisy must be going round the bend with worry about her toddler.

Just when Roy thought he had it all and could make Daisy happy, happiness had been snatched away from the pair of them.

He would find her. Nobody takes anything or anybody away from Roy Kemp, he thought. No one.

CHAPTER 3

'What time's Roy coming?'

'How the fuckin' 'ell do I know, Suze? His mother said he'd just left so 'ow long does it take to get 'ere from bleedin' London in a fast car?'

Vera looked up from the round mirror propped against a milk bottle on the kitchen table.

'I can't never get these sodding lashes to stay stuck.' Her make-up was spread all over the table and the smell of Californian Poppy was making even Vera feel sick.

'You ain't 'alf got a lot of perfume on today,' sniffed Susie. Vera narrowed her eyes at her until they were mere slits. She saw Susie cringe.

'It'll go in a minute. They call it the first "high" note. That's in the perfume business, that is. Did I tell you one of my regulars used to be a perfume sales-man? His name was Maury and once after we'd done it he couldn't afford to pay me.'

Susie stared out of the back window for signs of rain to spoil the washing she'd just hung on the new rotary line, then asked, 'What did you do?'

Vera threw back her head and laughed. 'Well, he couldn't pay me in kind because I'd just 'ad that, so 'e opened his case – nice brown attaché, it was, with little compartments – and said, "Take your pick, Vera love."

'Inside was all these perfumes in neat boxes. Samples they was, all different, and I took the top off one with some green leaves on the label. Cor, bugger me, it stank of cat's piss. That stuff was vile! I nearly choked. Put the stopper back quick, I can tell you. Then I picked the one with a red flower on. When I 'ad a sniff, I knew it was "me". "Can I 'ave this one?" I asked. "Why," says he, "that's not been on the market long. Californian Poppy. You made a good choice there, Vera girl." The smell dazzled me. Made me think of Hollywood in America and all them Yanks an' film stars.' Vera stared into space, remembering. 'A few minutes later 'e was climbing back up the stairs with a box underneath 'is arm. "Don't let anyone ever sell you short, Vera," he said. "You're worth a bleedin' box full, not just one piddly sample bottle." Lovely man 'e was. So I been wearing Californian Poppy ever since. Daisy says it's me trademark.'

Susie was looking at her with damp eyes.

'It sure is, Vera.'

Vera wished she hadn't mentioned Daisy's name again but she'd be buggered if she'd upset Susie by crying about it, so instead she said, 'You keeping an eye on that boy?' Vera didn't mean to speak sharply.

The words just seemed to come out that way. She'd been at sixes and sevens ever since Daisy had gone. 'It's just I need to know where 'e is every minute of the day, Suze. An' for God's sake put some music on, this place is a dead an' alive 'ole.'

'Don't worry.' Susie pulled back the kitchen curtain and craned her neck. 'He's using a stick to poke the fish in the pond, 'e's all right.' Then she went over to the transistor radio on the draining board and found the Birds halfway through 'Turn, Turn, Turn'.

'That's better. A bit of music always cheers me up.' Vera got up and went to join Susie at the window. Kibbles, the big tabby, had moved outside and was sitting on the pond's raised flagstones. The child, Eddie, warmly wrapped against the morning chill, had threaded a small branch through the wire netting stretched across the fish pond and was carefully searching between the lily pads for goldfish.

'Bless 'im. He's very sharp, that boy, just like 'is father. My Kibbles is keeping an eye on 'im. Is the gate fastened?' Vera couldn't bear to think the child might get out on to the road or through the back fence and into the park.

''Course,' replied Susie.

Vera went back to her make-up. Sitting down heavily on the kitchen chair, she sighed as she looked in the mirror then began spreading green powdered eyeshadow on to her lids with her forefinger. With the Pan-Stick her face had taken on a golden glow.

She stretched her neck upwards and looked closely in the mirror to make sure she'd left no tell-tale tide line of make-up on her skin, then opened a small oblong case of mascara. She spat on the brush and began vigorously rubbing it up and down the black cake, and covered both her own and the fake lashes.

Susie came away from the window and stood behind her. Vera felt her hand on her shoulder.

'I don't 'alf miss 'er, you know.' Vera saw the reflection of Susie's face in the mirror, saw the anguish there. 'An' there's something else, isn't there, Vera? Something you don't want to tell me?'

'Sometimes I reckon I ought to 'ave you in me parlour tellin' the future instead of dozy Madame ZaZa.'

'There, I knew I was right,' said Susie, a smug smile on her face that quickly left as she asked, 'Is it something awful? To do with Daisy?'

'I'm doin' what Daisy would 'ave done. She'd 'ave kept things close to her chest until she'd worked out the right time to tell you, Suze.'

Vera remembered when Daisy had taken Susie in. She'd been a bedraggled waif then. Daisy had not only given her a place of safety where her mother's boyfriend couldn't abuse her but she'd given the girl love. To build up Susie's self-worth she'd put her to work in the cafe and when the girl fell in love with the delivery boy from The World's Stores, Daisy had helped her find a way to marry Si. But it hadn't ended there. It was Daisy who pulled Susie from the deep depression after her little girl had been killed in a Devon traffic accident. No wonder the young woman missed her.

Vera sighed. 'Still, you never know, perhaps Roy's got some news.'

'It's the not knowing, ain't it, Vera?'

Vera stopped coating her lashes and threw Susie a glance. She swept her stuff aside, dumping it into a plastic zip bag, and went to the window. The child was still happily poking the water and Vera noted her Kibbles still had one eye on his charge.

'You know that boy grows more like Eddie Lane every day.'

'Eddie's looks was the best part about him,' said Susie. 'Just so long as that little lad don't inherit 'is father's nasty nature.' She walked over to the fridge and took out a plate of sandwiches covered with a damp tea towel, which she lifted to show Vera. 'I made these earlier, just in case Roy fancied something quick to eat with a cuppa.' Vera could smell the tang of pickle.

'You got bleedin' marge on that bread?'

'I like marge. Reminds me of the caff.'

Vera gazed at her fondly. She was a nice girl was Susie. Pity she hadn't fallen for another baby yet. It was what both she and Si wanted and needed. Poor little cow, thought Vera, the girl's had more than her fair share of hard knocks in her life. She was like a second mother to little Eddie, though.

'What's in 'em, anyway?'

'Cheese an' onion an' corned beef an' pickle.'

'Well, if Roy don't eat the bleedin' lot, I'll see a few of 'em off meself.'

Susie gave her a big smile, picked up the make-up bag from the table where Vera had left it and put it on the dresser. Always tidying up was Susie. She often wondered if Susie wanted more out of life than she had.

'Suze, you ever regret marryin' Si?'

The words were out before Vera had time to check herself.

'Never! I didn't know what kindness was in a bloke 'til I met 'im. That bad patch we went through when Meggie got killed nearly split us up but we're stronger than ever now.'

'Do you miss living at the caff?'

'No. I never lived in a house as grand as this one before.'

'Me neither,' said Vera. 'Even my Kibbles likes it 'ere.'

Vera went quiet. She thought about what her life had been before Daisy had managed the caff. It had belonged to Bert, then. No one knew he was her husband Kenny's real dad. That had all come out when the caff had passed to Daisy on Kenny's death. She'd sold it to help finance the long-firm scam she'd pulled on Roy Kemp.

This posh house and her little place in Greece had been left her, mortgage free, by Eddie Lane, Kenny's brother. Most of the money from the long-firm scam

48

had been invested for little Eddie but Daisy wasn't short of a few bob in her bank account.

Before she'd disappeared Daisy had been getting restless, said she needed to be working again. She'd always worked hard, just as Vera had on the game – all her life until she'd bought the massage parlour, Heavenly Bodies. Now Vera only obliged favoured customers. Getting a bit long in the tooth for all that these days, she thought. Better to let her girls have the benefit of her experience.

Susie got up and went to the window again.

'Is 'e all right?'

Susie nodded. 'Stop worrying. Why didn't you open the massage parlour earlier?'

Vera shrugged, she went to the mirror on the wall and patted her hair.

'Time wasn't right. Everythin' depends on timing.'

'Too right. You'll have the flat empty above Heavenly Bodies, won't you?'

Vera stared at Susie's earnest face.

'You mean I won't be goin' back there to live?'

'Yeah.'

'You're right. I can't leave this 'ouse. Not when I promised if anything ever 'appened to Daisy I'd be the one to look after little Eddie and attend to all 'er affairs. Even if she was 'ere, I ain't lettin' her out of me sight ever again.'

A knock on the door startled her. 'Why is it when you're expecting someone to knock on the door or the phone to ring, an' it does, it still bleedin' makes you jump?'

'Must be Roy,' said Susie. 'Though I never 'eard his car.'

'That thing runs like grease down a warm drain. You go while I finish making meself presentable.' Vera was peering at herself in the mirror again, turning this way and that until she was satisfied she looked no different from the last time she'd looked.

When Roy came into the kitchen wafting expensive cologne that she knew didn't come off the back of no lorry, Vera realised she'd forgotten what a big bloke he was. He stepped towards her with a smile on his face. If I was twenty years younger, she thought, then dismissed the thought and squirmed girlishly when he hugged her.

Despite his welcoming smile, one look into his slate-grey eyes confirmed her worst nightmare. He had nothing to tell her.

'No Charles then?'

'No, I'm allowed out on me own today.'

'Bloody daft you are,' she said. 'Suze,' she yelled. 'Get that kettle on!'

'Don't shout, I'm only 'ere.' Susie put the kettle on.

Vera glared at her then turned back to Roy. 'Take off your coat,' she said. She leaned into Roy, speaking in a loud whisper. 'I need to talk a bit of business with you, Roy.' Susie was looking at her like she was daft, but she took an old coat from behind the kitchen door, and said, 'An' I suppose I'll be the last to know about this bit of business?' She sniffed and opened the door that led into the garden. 'I'll go out with little Eddie. Call us when you're done.'

As soon as the door closed behind her, Vera took Roy's coat and put it over the back of a kitchen chair.

'You're agitated, Vera.'

'Too bloody right I am. There's something funny going on with Daisy's bank account.' She had his full attention straight away.

'What do you mean?' His dark brows were creased and his mouth had straightened to a thin line.

'If I wasn't so worried about 'er I wouldn't tell you a dicky bird because I ain't never spoke out of turn in all me life, but there's money gone.'

'What do you mean, gone?' The kettle was boiling and Vera switched it off. It was suddenly so quiet Vera could hear the clock ticking.

'She's been cashing cheques. Her bank statements show large amounts going out. An' I got it on good authority the money's gone to someone called Gloria West. As far as I knows she don't know no Gloria West and there ain't no way she'd do anything like this without tellin' me or contacting me some-how.'

'You sure this isn't the bank's mistake?'

'I been down there. Daisy made arrangements for me to 'ave access to 'er account. *But only me*. It's a safeguard because of little Eddie.'

'This shows she's alive.' She detected pleasure in his voice.

Vera sighed. 'Of course she's bleedin' alive. I never doubted that.' This wasn't strictly the truth. Vera had forced herself to push all thoughts that Daisy might be dead from her mind. It was the only way she could face getting up in the mornings. 'I wouldn't have said anything except she ain't 'ardly got any bleedin' money left in there now. In fact there wasn't enough to pay for Eddie Lane's mum and dad's rent at The Cedars. She would never leave 'erself so short there wouldn't be money for that, nor for little Eddie neither.'

Roy picked up his coat and fumbled inside the pocket and took out a bulging black leather wallet.

'If you're short . . .' Vera pushed the wallet away.

'I got money. I paid what needs to be paid out of me own account.'

His face was expressionless. She got up and went over to the dresser drawer and after foraging around found a brown envelope. She took out a bank statement among other letters. 'I been opening her letters hoping to find out somethin'. Never expected this though.' She passed him the statement. 'Take it away with you. Maybe you can find out what's goin' on?' Roy took the paper, scanned it, then folded it and put it in his wallet. He looked at her.

'This don't make sense, Vera. This is a great deal of money paid out in a very short while. Is there any way we can find out if this really isn't just some bank mistake?'

'I already thought of that, Roy. I had to make sure, for me own peace of mind. The manager down at Lloyds is an old mate of mine, 'e used to be a client.' Vera could feel herself blushing. It was one thing speaking of her sexual exploits to Daisy or Susie but Roy was a different kettle of fish. Silly really when the bloke owned whorehouses of his own. 'Fergus told me there 'adn't been no mistake, the cheques to this Gloria West were genuine.'

Roy was drumming his fingers on the table surface. He got up, set the kettle to boil again and rinsed out the brown earthenware teapot with hot water, then spooned in tea from the flowered caddy.

'Daisy wouldn't leave you to clear up her debts without asking you first.' He stirred the boiling water in the teapot and set the knitted cosy on it.

'That's just the point, Roy. I know that and you know that. She's set money aside for little Eddie in a trust fund. That can't be touched by anyone 'til he comes of age. But the poor cow's been skint so often she wouldn't leave 'erself short like this. An' she'd never go back on 'er promise to 'er dead Eddie to take care of 'is parents in that nursing 'ome.'

Vera tried to keep her voice steady but she knew any minute she was going to cry, and crying wasn't something Vera did much of.

'I'll tell you somethin' else. I was told by one of me girls that there's a For Sale notice up in the window of what used to be Jacky's flat. Daisy bought that place when Bri and Jacky set up 'ouse together. I went round and had a look. "Under Offer" it says now. Here's the name and address of the estate agent. I want you to see if you can find out more than I could.'

Roy took the scrap of paper from Vera. She could see his knuckles were white and his fingers seemed to bore into her flesh as he suddenly grabbed her arm and turned her towards him.

'You did right, Vera. I suppose she never said she was going to sell . . .'

Vera broke away from him. 'Never! We was only looking at curtain material down the market for the windows of that flat a couple of days before she disappeared. She 'ad no intention of sellin' the place.'

'She could 'ave changed her mind.'

To stop her temper rising Vera began setting out the cups and saucers on the table, clattering the fragile china.

'You don't believe that any more than I do. One of the blokes who works in that estate agents used to be a client of mine as well, still is, actually. Only not so often nowadays . . .' She felt the warmth of another blush rising. 'I asked 'im if he could get me the contract or a copy or something and he took me into the office and showed me the papers she'd signed. I'm telling you it was her bleedin' signature—'

'Daisy's been known to forge signatures, she made a pretty good copy of mine—'

'She don't need to forge her *own* signature, does she? Anyway, that wasn't Daisy, that was Bri, her brother-in-law, that forged your name on the long-firm stuff . . .' Vera coughed and put her hand over her mouth. There I go again, she thought, putting me foot in it. Roy wasn't supposed to know that. But he grinned at her when she said, 'Don't you let on I said that, will you?'

He shook his head. 'That's all done and dusted, Vera.'

She breathed a sigh of relief.

'Who's got the deeds to Daisy's places?'

'The bank.'

He looked thoughtful. Vera knew they were in the bank's vault because she'd asked.

'Leave all this with me. I'm guessing Suze knows nothing about this?'

Vera shook her head. 'Not yet. I know what she's like. She'd 'ave been running around like an 'eadless chicken making poor Si's life and mine a misery. Now I can tell 'er you'll be sortin' this and that'll give 'er some comfort. She's a bit fragile, is our Suze.'

He leaned across her to put the bottle of sterilised milk he'd just taken from the fridge on the table. Then he rocked back on his heels. 'Whew! Vera,' he said. 'You got a lot of perfume on today.'

Vera said crossly, 'Don't you bleedin' start. Anyway you didn't come 'ere to pick on me, did you? You came to see the boy.'

He laughed. 'I came down to see the lot of you.' He

looked at the teapot. 'I could do with this cuppa, an' you got anything to eat? I'm bleedin' starving.'

She took the sandwiches from the fridge and plonked them on the table in front of him. Then she rapped sharply on the window to let Susie know she could come in and bring the child with her.

'You will let me know . . . ?'

Roy turned to her. 'You'll be the first, Vera. I wouldn't keep anything from you, I promise.'

His words made her feel better. She nodded towards the plate.

'Suze done 'em for you.'

He peeked under the tea towel. 'Good,' he said. 'Cheese and onion, my favourite.'

Roy was a good man in his way, she thought. But then he was like Eddie Lane. He looked after those he loved. As though reading her thoughts, Roy said, 'She told me she wanted you to care for the lad. You ever need anything for him you only got to ask, Vera. It's the boy that matters. She said it was to make up for you not being able to bring up your own son.'

'Sometimes that young Daisy 'as a big mouth.' Vera thought about her James, now a solicitor in London. She'd given him away to a childless couple in Gosport and paid for his keep, his schooling and, later, college and university on the understanding they never told him his real mother had prostituted herself to do it. Unfortunately his parents had died in a car crash and James, when going through their papers,

56

had discovered the sacrifice Vera had made, and her identity.

'Daisy told me your lad wanted you to go to London to live with him.'

'What would I do away from Daisy and me roots? Gosport's me 'ome.'

CHAPTER 4

Daisy heard his heavy footsteps, heard the key turn in the lock, and her heart sank. Valentine Waite entered the room then locked the door behind him. His well-shaped lips formed a smile on his handsome face but it filled her with fear.

'Say hello to Val, Daisy.'

'Hello,' she replied dutifully from her place on the mattress. She'd found to her regret it was better to agree with him and to do what he wanted. He was tall and muscular and she was no match for him, certainly not in her weakened state. He walked towards her lightly as a boxer does, and picked up the length of chain, hoisting her foot and examining the metal anklet.

Daisy gritted her teeth, trying not to cry out with the pain his callous handling caused her. He eyed the padlock then dropped her foot. Then he walked to the wall and, crouching, fingered the chain secured into the skirting board.

'Not been trying to get this off, have you, Daisy?'

She shook her head. He came back and towered

over her, bending to touch her foot. 'I see Glo's been putting some iodine on the sores. She's a good girl, is Glo.' Daisy winced with the pain as his fingers travelled over her fragile skin stained brown by the iodine.

Aware that not to answer would make him angry, Daisy said, 'Yes.'

He smiled at her again, and she gave a silent prayer of thankfulness. She could always tell what kind of a mood he was in when he visited her. A smile from him as he came through the door and she just might not get hurt. A frown and the nightmare would begin again, inflicting suffering in her mind and on her body.

'Aren't you going to ask me where I've been?'

'Yes,' said Daisy, hating herself for the lies he made come out of her mouth. 'I've missed you.'

He frowned and she could see him weighing up whether she was telling the truth or not.

'I like to hear that, Daisy. I've been to sign a contract. I'm going to New York. Ever been to a fight in New York?' He was standing over her. Even his shadow was menacing.

She shook her head. She'd only ever been to one boxing match and it had sickened her. Two men knocking the guts out of each other, their spittle and blood flying into the audience. She'd escaped before the fight was over and vowed she'd never witness another.

'I've heard it can be cold in New York. They get harsher winters than we do—'

'The winter's over, you silly bitch! But what the fuck do you know if you've never been there, cunt!' His open palm connected with the side of her face and with a crack her head swung sideways.

Her head was ringing from his sudden blow. She forced herself to speak as clearly as she could.

'I know nothing about New York.' She searched his face. But just as suddenly, he smiled again.

'Glo will look after you.'

'Yes.' She tried to sound enthusiastic. It was what he wanted her to do. Anything, she thought, anything. Just please don't touch me again.

His last rape had been followed by a beating so severe Daisy believed her arms had been broken. All the time he'd been tearing into her he'd held her arms pinioned above her head.

He'd not touched her since but had taunted her that she was a dirty whore just like his mother and if she thought she was going to leave him again she was mistaken.

'Could I have some clean clothes?' She'd been plucking up the courage to ask for days now. Her words came out in a rush.

He bent down. His breath smelled of pear drops.

'You aren't going anywhere. Why do you need to tart yourself up?' His eyes narrowed. Daisy didn't even dare to sigh. He got lightly to his feet and walked over to the desk. One day she vowed she'd find out just what it was that was so important to him in that desk drawer.

She watched as he took a key from his pocket and slipped it in the top drawer's lock. He had his back to her so Daisy couldn't see what he was doing but she saw a glimpse of the lacquered box and saw him remove something from his pocket. Then she heard him relock the drawer.

When he came to the mattress again she saw he had a needle in his hand and a small vial.

'Please don't give me that.' She'd had a long period when she'd been able to think coherently and she didn't want to go back to that nightmare state of un-reality. He shook his head.

'I have to.'

Instinct made her wriggle away from him. His other hand pulled on the chain and as the hurt shot up her leg she was stilled by the intense pain.

'Bitch,' he said, and slapped her. His gold ring caught her mouth and she heard and felt the crack as the metal hit her front teeth. Her hands went up to protect her face till she felt the jab of the needle. The floating sensation began. Her body loosened and then the pillowcase came down over her head and she felt him tie cords around her neck.

'No, Val, I hate the dark . . .' She managed just a few words but already he'd hauled her into a sitting position against the wall and pulled her hands above her head.

'See how you like being left on your own again and

again,' he said. 'I was only a kid, left in that room, and I was so frightened . . .'

The duct tape he was using on her wrists cut into her flesh. Was he going to kill her this time?

No, he'd said Glo was going to look after her, hadn't he? But what if something happened to stop Glo coming? She would be in this stinking room, bound like this, until she starved or died of thirst. Which would come first?

She passed out.

Valentine Waite sat in the corner of the Coach and Horses in Stoke Newington. Rain was lashing against the pub's windows and looked set in for the rest of the night. It was gloomy and quiet, empty apart from a blonde with hair like straw sitting at the bar drinking gin and tonic, and two young blokes at a table in the corner, heads together, talking earnestly over a couple of small beers, two folders open in front of them. The air inside the bar was stale as though the windows were never opened, but the unreal scent of green apple air freshener had been liberally used.

Every so often the blonde looked his way.

All he'd wanted at the gym was a bit of company on his own terms, but the other blokes expected him to join in with banter and bad jokes. He had, but doing what was expected always took its toll on his nerves. He ran his fingers around the rim of his glass and it made a squeaking noise. Tonic water with a slice of lemon because he was supposed to be in training. It was a boring drink and he was bored.

He wondered what was going to happen at the forthcoming fight between Cassius Clay and Henry Cooper for the world heavyweight championship. His money was on Cassius Clay, the young man was unbeatable. Good-looking bastard as well.

His own New York fight against Harry Markham was on his mind. Would the gods smile on him again? And would the race riots flare when he was there? It wasn't his country or his politics but America was awash with racial unrest, Brooklyn especially a hot spot.

He'd be glad to get away from this place for a while though. He was smarting under the threats from the Krays to pay the money he owed. That fucking Arkle, he cursed silently. Who'd have thought the horse would have strolled home on St Patrick's Day at Cheltenham, winning the bleeding Gold Cup? Thirty lengths ahead he'd been. He'd put his money on the fact that third time lucky doesn't happen. But it had, and now he was in deep shit with the twins. He took a sip of his drink.

The girl wasn't pretty but she was wearing one of the new mini-skirts. It had ridden up and she was showing a lot of leg above them high-heeled ankle-strapped shoes. Why did women flaunt themselves like that?

His own mother had been the same.

Painted and powdered and reeking of perfume,

wearing clothes that showed off her slim and shapely body. There'd only been the two of them in the terraced house and yet it wasn't possible to have even one evening alone with her. There was always some man knocking on the door and he could hear her voice now, lying. 'I won't be long, Val.'

Then he'd be left to curl up in the green velvet armchair and he'd listen to the noises that floated down from her bedroom. Even when he tried to shut the grunts and groans out of his head they came back to haunt him in the depths of the night when he was in his own bed.

Sometimes when he couldn't stand the noises in his head any longer he'd go in to her, for comfort. Occasionally the room would be empty. He was alone again and she was out on the streets. Often she'd be in bed but not alone. She'd look over at him, put her finger to her lips and wave him back to his own room to lie in the dark once more.

'You like nice clothes for school, don't you, Val? We have to eat and there's only me to put a roof over our heads.' And so it went on, his mother allowing herself to be taken away from him, time and time again.

He'd put a stop to it when he was thirteen. He'd smothered his mother while she'd slept. And no one had ever believed he could be responsible. After all, he was only a child. He'd done it at night, gone back to bed then got up and made himself some breakfast and gone to school as usual. He'd only alerted a neighbour when he came home from school.

His mother could never leave him again, he'd seen to that. She was in his heart now. Where she would always stay safe. Just as he would keep Daisy safe. Daisy looked like his mother. Small, blonde, green-eyed and a ready smile for everyone. Oh, he knew Daisy didn't prostitute herself like his mother had, but she had led him on. Then she'd spurned him. Gone off with Roy Kemp.

He'd fooled her though. He'd got her in the end. And he'd keep her.

Now he had to appease the voices that were talking inside his head, telling him they wanted their usual sacrifice. Then and only then would they allow him to fight at Madison Square Garden and win. It was unthinkable that he should offer Daisy. She was *his*.

The woman fumbled for her coat on the next stool to her. No one said goodbye to her, certainly not the barman who was out the back. She shrugged herself into her coat and looked round for her black handbag which was on the bar. She didn't remove any keys, which meant she didn't live nearby and certainly had no car. Most women driving or who lived close left a lighted place with their keys in readiness.

As she passed his table he didn't look at her but he sensed she was staring at him. He had no need to hurry himself. She'd wait in the doorway, looking at the rain. Maybe she'd pull up her collar. He hadn't seen an umbrella and she hadn't used the phone on the bar to call for a taxi. She wouldn't get far, not in this weather.

The barman came back and still Valentine waited. He finished his drink and got up slowly. No one paid any attention to him.

Once out in the rain, he looked up and down the deserted road. There she was, hovering in the doorway near the bus stop.

'Want a lift?' he asked, walking close. He grinned at her, knowing she wouldn't resist his little boy smile. The rain had flattened her hair. She put up a hand and touched it as though it could be magically transformed. Why were women so fucking stupid?

'Where's your car?'

He pointed along the road to where he knew an alleyway joined the two streets. Cars were parked on the road.

'Just up there. No parking outside the pub when I got there.'

His excuse seemed to satisfy her.

'I don't live that far, but when I get off the bus I've a fair distance across a wooded bit and I hate walking across there.'

Her cheap scent repelled him. 'You don't have to worry with me beside you,' he said. He stepped to the outside of the pavement and offered her his arm.

'You're very gentlemanly. Most men don't care which side of the pavement a woman walks.'

'But I'm not most men,' he said. She'd tucked her

arm inside his and together they walked towards the parked cars. She stumbled against him. The pavement was uneven and slippery with the rain. He tightened his grip on her arm and she giggled.

'I might have had a drop too much,' she said.

He bent his head and kissed her. It took all his willpower not to gag. Her breath stank of fags. She seemed to be enjoying his attention for her hands were already reaching into the warmth and shelter of his overcoat.

'Let's do this properly,' he said as they neared the alley. He pulled her into the darkness where the lamplight's glow didn't reach.

The closeness of the buildings either side gave sanctuary to dustbins and there was relative shelter from the rain which was easing off now.

She looked at him with surprise. 'We'd be drier in your car.'

'It's only a two-seater. Little sporty job.'

'It'll cost you.'

He knew she'd say those words sometime or other before they got down to it. Just like his mother. He laughed at her, reached into his inside pocket for his wallet and removed two ten-pound notes. He heard her gasp.

'Don't tell me you're not going to be worth it.'

She practically snatched the money away and, opening her handbag, she slipped the notes in, then perched her bag on top of the nearest bin. She began unbuttoning her coat and pulling up her short skirt.

He put his hands down to her cunt and tore away the thin film of her nylon panties.

'You eager bastard,' she murmured. He could see by the look on her face she was probably thinking about the money and didn't give a shit. She would want it over and done with so she could get home. He spread her legs wide then fumbled at his fly. He wasn't wearing underpants and she gasped as his prick forced its way out. She looked down at him and he smoothed the length of himself, encircling his hardness. Then he pushed her towards the bins.

'Fuck me, fuck me.'

Her mouth stayed open while she repeated the words and there was lipstick smeared above her lipline. He closed his eyes and squeezed his cock into her slippery softness. Her smell came up to greet him. Then he was ramming into her, eager to get the job over and done with. He was losing it, his balls slapping her arse, faster, faster as the beat changed momentum, rising to the sensation of that whiteness he wanted to reach until it burst all around him and took him far away to nothingness. 'I'm coming, you cunt, I'm coming. Feel me.'

And then it was over and he shuddered, spent, and slipped away from her. Away from the rancid sweat contained in her garments.

Something scrabbled in the darkness.

'What's that?' She pushed him away and was trying to sort out her clothing while gazing fearfully into the darkness beyond the alley. He guessed it was a rat but didn't want her scared, not yet. He did up his trousers.

'Nothing,' he replied. 'Perhaps it's a cat.'

A strong wind was blowing now. Valentine shuddered and then the excitement began. He felt for the knife in his jacket pocket.

'You're a big bloke, aren't you?' she said. He knew there was no harm now in telling her who he was.

'I'm a fighter.'

'Street?' She burped and put her hand to her mouth. 'Whoops,' she giggled.

He shook his head and realised she was much more drunk than he'd first thought. 'The ring. It's my living.'

'What's your name? Will I know you, sweetheart?'

I doubt it, he thought, you stupid bitch. 'Valentine Waite.'

She looked up at him. 'That's a funny name. Was you born on Valentine's Day?' She was looking at him as though she was the bleeding brain of Britain, he thought.

'Got it in one. You ready for the off?' She nodded and moved to exit the alleyway first. As she stepped in front of him he put one hand on her shoulder and used the other to draw the blade of his knife across her throat. He was surprised at the ease with which she fell to the ground. He stepped away from her as the blood spurted from the gaping wound. It wouldn't do for him to get messed up any more than he had to, would it?

Her eyes were open, her body twitching, the blood gushing, pooling with the puddles of rain.

Immobile, he watched her die, ignoring the look of incomprehension in her eyes.

When she was still, he stepped across her body and picked up the handbag from where it had fallen near a bin and removed his money. There was a wallet in the bag and he opened it and studied the out of date provisional driving licence.

'Well, well, so your name was Maggi Sonning, was it? You won't be needing this any more.' He slipped it into his pocket. Then he noticed a picture of a fair-haired kiddie. He studied it for a moment then tore it in two and threw it down.

He was unusually calm as he lifted the metal lid of a dustbin and set it to one side on top of the next bin. Bending, he lifted the slight form of the woman. He laid her across the bins while he took his usual souvenir. When he had placed that in his wallet, he found she fitted easily into the nearly empty container. He wiped her bag on his coat, using a handful of the woollen material to eliminate prints, and chucked it on top of her folded corpse. He replaced the lid.

It would be all right now. He had made his offering to the voices who promised him success in return for their bidding. He smiled to himself. He needn't worry any more about the forthcoming fight with Harry 'The Mark' Markham. He, Valentine Waite, would be victorious. Hadn't it always worked this way?

He waited a few moments until he was certain no one was approaching before he stepped out of the alley.

CHAPTER 5

'Can't you do anything, Charles?'

Charles shook his head. He hated to see Violet so distraught. She pushed a mug of tea across the table at him as a finale to the huge dinner they'd just eaten.

'My boy's almost losing his mind with worry,' she continued. 'And he's started drinking more than's good for him.' Her blue eyes seemed larger than ever in her pale face.

'You think I can't see that? For a bloke who can pick and choose he's certainly fallen for two women who've given him nothing but heartache.'

Violet rounded on him, tea towel flapping.

'You take that back, Charles Sutherland. Moira can't help what's happened to her. No one understands what goes on in people's heads until it makes them finally snap. A lesser bloke than my boy would have washed his hands of her a long time time ago or left her to rot in some loony bin. Instead that woman has twenty-four hour care, sunshine and the best food money can buy. Roy sees she wants for nothing. Daisy's a different kettle of fish . . .'

Charles got up from the kitchen chair and rescued the tea towel that was being wrung to pieces in her small hands. He held her close for a moment, feeling the beating of her heart like a tattoo on a war drum. Then he pushed her towards his vacant chair and went to the sink where Violet had started on the washing up. She'd made a fruit cake and it sat on a wire tray, fragrant and enticing on the scrubbed kitchen table. Charles squeezed washing-up liquid into the sink.

'I'll do this, you stay there. I know you love Daisy as if she was your own.'

He began scrubbing a cake tin with a wire scourer. He could hear Violet sniffing and turned towards her. He couldn't bear to see her cry. Her grey bubble cut had been freshly washed and set that morning by the hairdresser. That's what he liked about his Violet; she looked after herself and always smelled of violet perfume.

'Ain't there anything you can do?'

He sighed. 'Every toerag has his ear to the ground. Even the twins say they know nothing.'

'You don't think Ron and Reg are paying my boy back for the fraud on their manor?'

Charles studied her face. 'No.'

'D'you think we'll ever find her? It's just like that Maggi Sonning. No one knows who did that terrible thing to her.'

'Daisy ain't a prostitute.' Charles knew Violet was very friendly with the street girl's mother, who was now looking after Maggi's child. She was skint and

Violet often took bags of groceries round there. 'It's girls on the game who've gone missing or turned up dead. Not the likes of Daisy Lane.'

'But Daisy *is* missing. It's been nearly four weeks now.' Violet used the corner of her pinny to wipe her eyes.

Charles thought for a minute.

'There is one thing, Vi. I've been wondering if Roy ain't just a bit off centre with this.' He raised his hands in the air to show he meant no harm. 'Roy's nobody's fool. But since we're getting nowhere with the villains here and down in Gosport, I reckon it's time we involved the police.'

Hope fluttered across Violet's face, only to be replaced by worry again.

'Roy won't have *them* involved, you know that. Too much dirty linen'll be aired and not even Daisy would thank Roy for that. She won't want her picture splashed all over the papers for her kiddie to look at in years to come. Neither will Roy want it known he can't keep an eye on his own. No, that's not a good idea, Charles.'

'But the coppers informed Vera that Daisy's little red sports car had been abandoned.'

'And it was Vera being sharp as a tack didn't say Daisy had gone missing. The Gosport woodentops found out from the DVLC who the car belonged to and wanted to know why it had been left there. Vera didn't want no truck with them as by the time they got round to Western Way to inform her, someone had kindly nicked the chrome bumpers and the wheels. Vera said it had broken down. All the coppers was worried about was that it would be removed from the road. This ain't been made a police matter, Charles.'

'But listen, Vi.' He pulled up a chair opposite her and took her hands in his own. He thought how little her hands looked in his big mitts. 'There's a young detective up here who knows Daisy. He worked on the Freddie Mills case, remember, when the boxer was found dead in his car?'

Violet nodded.

'Before this copper came up to the Smoke he was down in Gosport. He knows Roy and at the moment he's doing a bit of undercover work on this missing prostitutes case. I reckon I ought to have a word with Roy and get him to chat to this bloke. Got odd-coloured eyes, good-looking though, all the women takes a fancy to 'im. He's not bent neither.'

'But if he's undercover how do you know about him?'

He tapped the side of his nose. 'It's not common knowledge, Vi. But you've met him, or rather you've seen him. He was at that party Daisy organised for Vera at the Thorngate Hall. He didn't stay above a moment but Roy recognised him straight away when he was chatting to Vera and Daisy. His real name's Vinnie something. Vinnie Endersby.'

'Any hope is better than no hope at all. If I put it to

Roy he'll go along with it. Let me talk to him first. You're a good man.'

'If you say so, Violet,' he said. He looked into her trusting eyes. In his heart he knew he wasn't a good man. He'd maimed a few and killed a few more. He didn't suffer fools gladly and to keep on top of things in London it required stamina because there was always some chancer ready to take over pole position if you let him.

But Roy was the son he'd never had. Perhaps he might have been his son if Violet's first choice hadn't been his best mate. He'd never minded being second best. Not where his Vi was concerned.

'You want a bit of cake, Charlie?'

'Violet, I thought you'd never bleedin' ask.'

'Hello, little man.' Jacky bent down and gave little Eddie a cuddle despite him trying to hide behind Vera's legs.

'Let me get in me own bleedin' salon before you starts making a fuss of 'im.' Vera knew Jacky loved the boy. More so because she couldn't have kiddies of her own due to a botched abortion when she was still a kid. Vera waited until Jacky had succeeded in making the child smile then she asked, 'All right, Jacky?' Jacky managed Heavenly Bodies.

'Got no worries, apart from Daisy.'

'I don't want to be thinking about that, and before you asks, no, there ain't no news.' She put up a hand to steady her large black hat that tended to slip down across her face. 'Bri okay?' She was deliberately changing the subject of Daisy's disappearance.

Jacky grinned back at Vera. Bri was the brother of Eddie and Kenny Lane and he'd helped Daisy with the long-firm swindle that Roy Kemp had taken the can for. Vera liked Bri.

'He's asked me to marry 'im, Vera.'

'About bleedin' time.' Vera wasn't surprised. She knew one day the big dozy bastard would wake up and realise how much he cared about Jacky, who worshipped the ground he walked on. 'You've loved him long enough.'

Vera walked through the reception area, little Eddie trotting at her side. She paused to take in the cleanliness of the blue leather sofas and the polished chrome tables. She had to admit her girls kept everything as clean as if she was still in residence wielding the whip over them. She nodded, and felt her hat slip further.

'Sod it,' she said. 'I forgot to put me 'at pin in properly.' She fingered for the spot on her head and drew out the large pin with the pearl on the end. Vera stared at herself in the mirrored wall of her massage parlour. She still felt self-conscious about the scar on the side of her face, close to her hairline. The hat made her feel better. She pushed in the long pin and this time was sure she'd made a better job of it. Little Eddie was watching her, his eyes big and wide.

'It's all right, poppet,' said Jacky, scooping him up. 'That nasty pin ain't going inside Auntie Vera's head.

Want a biccy, my pet?' Jacky looked to Vera for confirmation. Vera nodded. Hand in hand, Jacky and the solemn child made their way to the back of the salon, beyond the cubicles, to the kitchen area where the girls were drinking tea and having a crafty fag.

Madame ZaZa was smoking a Woodbine inside her small open-fronted gypsy tent. Beside her was a shelf that held her playing cards and crystal ball. She started to cough, a wracking sound that set her whole body heaving. When she finally got the coughing spell under control by taking a sip from a bottle of clear liquid, she croaked, 'All right, Vera my love?' She retied her headscarf with the coins dangling from it.

'How on earth you manages to cough and drink without removing that fag from your mouth I never can fathom.'

Madame ZaZa was Vera's resident fortune-teller. Clouds of fag smoke enveloped Vera but didn't quite disguise the smell of the gin. Since the old woman was an ex-Gosport prossie, it wasn't surprising she knew a great deal about the women who used Vera's hair and beauty salon, which was a front for prostitution. She also kept her ears sharply open for tidbits of gossip from Vera's girls after they'd serviced the men in the cubicles, so her 'visions' were usually spot on. Vera liked the old lady. When she wasn't gin-soaked she was a good laugh. Only there hadn't been many times for laughing since Daisy had been gone.

'If you was a proper fortune-teller you'd know I

wasn't all right. And you could tell me what happened to my Daisy.'

'I does me best,' Madame ZaZa said. 'I could do with a cuppa an' all.'

Vera snorted and made to follow Jacky but stopped at the door to her office. She flicked through the accounts books that Jacky kept immaculately tidy and up to date. Unfortunately, Jacky had told her she wanted to cut her hours to spend more time with Bri and his little girl, Summer, round at his bookshop. She'd got to find a replacement. She looked at the rows of figures and smiled. Thank God she was doing all right. She worried that because she was now spending so much time at Daisy's house her own livelihood was being threatened, but so far all was well. She needed every penny now she had to pay Daisy's debts as well as her own outgoings.

In the kitchen she could hear her girls cooing over little Eddie. When he gets a bit older I shall have to keep him out of here, she thought. Don't want him getting ideas. His father had enough ideas for the whole of Gosport.

Samantha had given the boy a Matchbox car and he was running it along the tabletop. Vera looked with pride at three of her girls clucking over Eddie. All had on starched white short uniforms and black high heels. She knew their frillies and black seamed stockings would tease even the most jaded palates.

'Ain't you got any clients?'

'Not 'til later,' Jacky said. 'Robin's in cubicle three doing a massage.'

Vera was glad she'd insisted on two exits for the place. There was never a problem that a bloke would be caught out while his wife was having her hair done in the salon or being entertained by Robin's magic fingers.

'I better go,' said Vera later. She'd had a good laugh and was now up to date with the town gossip. 'I gotta get the boy 'ome for 'is dinner, an' if he don't eat it all I can tell Suze she got to blame you, Jacky.'

Vera put her hand on the child's shoulder. 'Give Auntie Jacky a kiss.' The little boy obediently lifted his face.

Clutching his hand, Vera walked along the pavement towards the ferry and Woolworths. She saw the bus terminal and taxi rank ahead and remembered the many hours she'd spent there waiting for punters in all weathers. A ferry boat had pulled up at the pontoon. People were spilling off it and making their way to the waiting buses like ants trailing from dropped sugar. If it didn't have that chill to the wind it'd be a really nice day, thought Vera. She stopped and pointed as an Isle of Wight boat leaving Portsmouth dwarfed the Gosport ferry and filled the view. Little Eddie's face lit up.

'It's just like the boat's right at the end of the road, isn't it, love?'

After they'd watched it pass Vera could see the usual array of naval boats and sea craft using the

Solent channel. Ahead she could make out the tall masts of HMS *Victory*, Nelson's flagship, in the Dockyard.

Vera wished she'd dressed in something warmer than her red suit. She shivered and little Eddie looked up at her. 'You cold, pet?' He shook his head. 'I am, I must be getting old,' she said. Daisy's eyes stared back at her from the child's face.

'You getting old? Never, Vera.'

She spun round at the voice and gasped. 'Where 'ave you sprung from, Vinnie Endersby? Well, I never did.'

'I'm sure you must have done, Vera.'

Playfully she dug him in the ribs. Good-looking bastard, she thought. He was grinning at her like a Cheshire cat, his different coloured eyes twinkling.

'What you doing 'ere? I thought you was in London?'

'I'm supposed to be. Is this Daisy's lad? I don't know why I asked, he's his father to a T, isn't he?' He ruffled the lad's curls.

Vera nodded. 'How's your lad?'

'Just left him, Vera. Spent the weekend in Liss with my in-laws and I thought I'd stop off and see the old place.'

'Gosport don't change much,' she said.

'Got time for a cuppa?' He'd be sure to ask how Daisy was. To tell the truth she welcomed it. She wanted to tell him.

'Sure,' she said. Then to little Eddie, 'C'mon,

darling, let's go with the nice man down a hole in the ground, shall we?' Vinnie took her arm and they walked across the high street to the Dive cafe that had its entrance at ground level and steps leading down to a long passage-like tearoom.

It was cosy and the proprietor made the best cuppa in the whole of Gosport, so much so that it was the regular haunt of taxi and bus drivers. And Vera knew from past experience the food was beyond reproach. Especially the sticky currant buns.

Vinnie had to lift the child as the steps were too steep for the boy's chubby little legs. He set him down and turned to Vera, but she brushed his help away. 'Time I need a hand to climb down 'ere I reckon I'll be in me bleedin' box,' she said. He laughed at her. Already the warmth of the place was taking the chill off her. She eyed the huge polished tea urn and the sandwiches and buns in a big plastic case to keep them moist and clean.

'Want a bun, Vera?'

'Not for me, I 'ave to watch me figure. But the lad'll love one.'

Vinnie laughed. 'All the men in Gosport love your figure exactly the way it is.' She noted he ordered three buns. He was a nice man, she thought. Six feet tall and dark haired. If only she was twenty years younger she'd show him a thing or two, handcuffs an' all if that's what he wanted . . .

'You go through with little Eddie and I'll bring the teas.' Steam hissed from the urn and added to the heat and the tea spilled thick and brown into the white mugs. Vera licked her lips before she pushed the boy ahead of her to find a seat.

'C'mon, boy,' she said, and led her charge to a secluded table at the back. Eddie climbed into the seat opposite her and sat looking solemnly about him, the Matchbox car gripped in his hand. 'We won't tell Auntie Suze we been eating buns,' she said, pulling a face at him. Vera chided herself. She was practically enticing the boy to keep secrets and tell lies. Daisy would go mad if she knew.

'Here we are, Vera.' Vinnie had managed the perilous journey with all the plates and mugs piled up one above the other.

'You should 'ave let me help.'

'Never mind, I'm here now and I got a drop of orange squash for the boy.' Vera nodded her head. He was thoughtful as well, was Vinnie. But then having a child of his own had no doubt made him aware of kiddies' needs. His wife must have been bloody mad to have done the dirty on him. Fancy her fucking Vinnie's senior officer. What a cow! She watched as he passed the little glass of orange to Eddie and steadied it in his hands while the boy drank noisily.

'How's Daisy?' There. He'd bloody asked the one question she knew he would and she couldn't hold back the tears or the words as they tumbled from her mouth. Whether she was doing right or wrong in involving him didn't matter. This bloke cared about her Daisy and deserved to know. His face went very pale and he never interrupted her once.

'It's like she's vanished into thin air,' she concluded.

His body seemed to expand then cave in on itself with a huge sigh. For a moment he just sat, expressionless, grey-faced, staring at her. Then he picked up a teaspoon and began idly stirring his mug of tea. The smell of spice from the buns hit her and she realised she was still crying and little Eddie was cuddling into Vinnie's side, upset at seeing her cry. How could she frighten the child with her emotions? She sniffed loudly and Vinnie passed her a rather grubby handkerchief that she didn't hesitate to wipe her cheeks with. He turned to little Eddie after winking at Vera.

'Auntie Vera makes a lot of noise when she gets going, doesn't she?' The boy nodded. 'What say you eat all your bun to cheer her up?' The lad slid his free hand across the table to the golden-brown buns. 'If you finish yours you can have mine as well,' he added.

Vera blew her nose loudly into the handkerchief and saw the boy's eyes widen and a grin spread over his face. So she did it again, for effect this time, and little Eddie giggled. Then she too gave a watery laugh.

'Silly Auntie Vera,' Vinnie said. 'She don't know whether to laugh or cry.'

Vera reached across the table and squeezed his hand. 'Thank you,' she said.

'What's Roy doing about it?'

'Everything he can. He loves 'er.' Vera saw a

shadow pass across his eyes. He didn't fool her. He was as bloody upset and scared as the rest of them, but if he showed her his feelings she wouldn't have much faith in him. And she knew he wanted to help. Wanted to be relied on to do the right thing at the right time.

'I can understand him not involving the police. He's gone to the source of the problem, or so he probably thinks.' Vinnie looked deep into her eyes. 'There's no possibility she would have upped and left?'

Vera gave him what she hoped was her frostiest look then let that look linger on the child who was making short work of the bun, picking out the currants, the car momentarily cast aside on the table-top.

Vinnie glanced at the boy. 'Of course not,' he added.

Vera saw a spider's leg fall across her vision. One of her false eyelashes had come unstuck.

'I shouldn't cry. Certainly not in bleedin' public.' She reached up and pressed her forefinger against her top eyelid. 'Is that okay?' she asked. Vinnie nodded.

'I used to come in here with Daisy,' Vinnie told her.

'I know you did.'

'She tell you that?'

'Didn't need to. Daisy's mouth is tighter than a duck's arse, comes of bein' a Scorpio I guess. There was lots of things she never told me. Not big things.

We never kept big secrets, only little ones, but then we all 'ave little secrets, don't we?' Vera realised she shouldn't have said that. His wife had kept her affair secret, hadn't she? Until it had all come out in the open, and even then he'd given Clare enough rope to hang herself until she'd made her choice and it wasn't Vinnie Endersby.

'Did you ever think she'd end up with him, Vera?'

Vera didn't have to ask who he meant.

'No. I thought she was ready for a fling with that bleedin' boxer.' Vera could see by his face that he knew nothing about this, but then, why should he? 'I've said too much, haven't I?'

'Daisy is a free agent,' he said grudgingly. 'What boxer?'

'I don't know. What's 'is face? The one that's friends with the twins.'

'That's not much help. The twins court boxers because fighting is in their blood. Boxers hang around them because the twins used to box, and because they wield power. The twins knew the only way out of the gutter is crime or fighting. They chose crime.'

'He's got a funny name.'

'Who?'

'Valentine . . .'

'Valentine Waite?'

'That's 'im. He sent her some death lilies.'

'He what?' Vera thought the look on Vinnie's face was laughable.

'One Christmas he sent 'er some arum lilies. If they

ain't bleedin' death flowers I don't know what is. Why didn't he send her a nice bunch of forced spring daffs like anybody else would? Must 'ave a weird sense of 'umour, that bloke.'

'You did right to think he's a strange bloke. The twins don't trust him. How did she meet him?'

'Some get-together in London about 'im winning some fight. Roy took 'er. She was down in the dumps then about Eddie an' if you ask me she won't never get over Eddie Lane. The last time she saw that boxer was at my party when 'e just turned up. You'd gone by then.'

'What do you mean, "just turned up"?' Vera could see he was disturbed by her talk about the fighter.

Little Eddie had finished his bun except for a neat pile of currants stacked to the side of the plate. Vinnie, despite his anxiety, gave him a smile then pushed his own bun in front of the lad.

'Well, he wasn't invited.'

'You sure, Vera?' Vinnie reached across the table and took her hands in his. Vera felt his comforting warmth. It had never really occurred to her before. If she hadn't invited him and neither had Daisy, and Roy had made it perfectly plain he was only asking close family, what the bleedin' hell was Valentine Waite doing there? She stared at Vinnie.

''Course I'm sure, it was my bleedin' party, wasn't it?'

CHAPTER 6

'Leave me alone!' Angel Moore brought her leg up and with as much weight as she could muster kneed her tormentor in the balls. He staggered, doubling over and clutching his genitals.

'Bitch, bitch, fucking bitch,' he shouted, 'I'll get you for this, ooww!' Angel picked up his almost full glass of watered-down beer and slung it over his bald patch. She laughed when he stared up at her in amazement, the brownish liquid pooling in his piggy eyes. 'You won't get away with this!'

'Just fuckin' have,' she threw at him. Then, picking up the fiver from where it had fallen on the floor, she tucked it in the waistband of her suspender belt, swept her hand over her fishnet stocking tops and G-string costume and shouted to the big bloke with the ponytail who was fast approaching, 'This is where my tips go, Gordon. Not up me fuckin' fanny!'

There was a hush, before she turned in her five-inch heels and stomped off the tiny wooden square of parquet flooring that passed for a dance floor in the Soho club.

'No you don't, cunt. You know how much fucking money you just cost me?' Before she reached the door to the lavatories her shoulder was wrenched around and she was inches away from the massive frame of Gordon Kessel. He was going to hit her, she knew it. And he did. The blow sent her reeling, stumbling into a gilt-painted chair and on to the floor. 'Pick yourself up and get to the fucking dressing room.' He stood over her. Her heart was beating furiously as she waited for the boot to make contact with her almost naked body. But he simply turned and walked away. She let out a sigh of relief. To Gordon, pacifying the big spender was the priority. She could be put on hold, the punter not.

Around her the noise in the club started up again. The customers had seen their bit of entertainment for the morning and were eager to carry on with their own sordid goings-on. No one came to her aid as she held on to the chair to stand. But that's how it was. She was a fucking nobody. An exotic dancer who was expected to enjoy that fat git's fingers probing her cunt for a fiver.

Unsteadily, she walked the last few yards to the rear of the smoke-filled room towards the neon-lit sign that proclaimed 'Gents'. Beyond it was the dressing room. She focused her eyes on the door and was reaching for the handle when it opened and Wendy stood there with Benjy, her python, coiled around her body, its head held lovingly in her hand.

'You really gone an' done it now, girl,' whispered

Wendy, keeping the snake's head away from Angel. 'I saw what happened. Get out while you can. Soon as Gordy's soothed that fat slob he'll be after you.'

Angel nodded. She didn't reply because if Gordy was watching, Wendy would get a punch as well. She saw Wendy put on her customer smile, the one that said, 'How lovely to meet you wonderful men.' But Angel knew it really meant, 'I need your money, you fucking wankers who 'ave nothin' more on your minds than jacking off in the bleeding morning after I've finished dancing.'

In the flyspecked mirror Angel could see that by tomorrow the bruise would cover the side of her face. Not that she could worry about that now. She swept her make-up into her capacious bag and threw in her outdoor clothes then slung on her midi coat without buttoning it. Looking into the dim passage, her heart lifted when she saw it was empty.

She pushed down on the safety bar of the exit door and let herself out into the piss-stained alley. Then she ran, doing up the buttons on her coat as she moved, her bag slung over her shoulder bumping against her body.

The sun was bright that morning and hurt her eyes. Angel blinked, she was hardly ever out in the sunlight. She gulped at the air as she ran. It certainly felt better than the stench of farts and fags in the windowless Resort Club.

Her side began to hurt with a stitch but she daren't stop running. She crossed the Strand onto Waterloo

Bridge, where she had to stand still for a while to get her breath back. She looked about her. No one seemed to be following, but they would be. Gordy had promised the next time she stepped out of line would be her last. She was expected to do what Gordy wanted, not to have rights of her own.

A party of schoolchildren, boys and girls wearing red blazers, crocodiled past her, guided and guarded by several teachers. She wondered what the future might hold for them. She hoped their lives turned out better than hers, for there had to be somewhere she could go to escape being knocked about by Gordon Kessel.

That was when the idea hit her to go home.

At Waterloo station she descended the steps to the Ladies. No one would bother her there.

Angel had forty minutes before the train left to Portsmouth Harbour. Plenty of time to wash off her heavy make-up and change back into her ordinary clothes. She would have liked to return to the room she shared with Wendy a few streets away from the Resort Club and take more of her clothes with her. But Gordy would have thought of that and posted one of his thugs outside the place.

She thought about Sonia who worked nights. She was Angel's best friend but there was no way she'd have involved her in anything. Even going to Sonia's flat would have meant a going over for her for helping Angel.

Angel examined her face now it was clean.

'Nasty bruise you'll 'ave there, ducky.'

The old woman was using the grubby roller towel and it wound noisily as she pulled at the blue striped cotton. When Angel shrugged, she asked, 'Boyfriend trouble?'

Angel nodded. It was easier that way.

The woman clucked knowingly.

Angel coated her eyelashes with mascara and touched a lipstick to her full lips. Then she inserted a coin into the brass door-opening device and went into a cubicle where she changed her clothes.

Luckily she had her post office savings book in her handbag. A hundred and fourteen pounds wasn't a fortune but it would do until she could start earning again. And she had about eight pounds in cash left after her one-way ticket had been bought. The eight pounds included the fiver that had caused all the trouble.

When she was presentable she left the cubicle and brushed her long pale hair. Luckily the nosy woman had gone. With a parting to the left, her hair hung across her face, disguising Gordy's handiwork. Thank God his ring hadn't cut her skin.

'C'mon, girl,' she said to her reflection. 'Angela Moore, sort yourself out. It's time to get home to bleedin' Gosport.'

'Ticket please.' Angel passed the ferryman her ticket and he gave her a hand up the short wooden slope that enabled passengers to step on and off the ferry boat from the pontoon. Already she'd had to stop and pull her stiletto heel from where it had sunk and caught in the gap between the wooden planking of the pontoon. She'd forgotten about that, one of the hazards of taking the ferry from Portsmouth to Gosport.

Once on the squat boat she walked around to the far side and sat on a slatted seat. Across the stretch of water she could see Camper Nicholson's boatyard and the pontoon leading up to the bus terminal and taxi rank at the far side of the Ferry Gardens. In the distance, the red brick of Haslar Hospital guarded Stokes Bay shore. The air was sharp and clean and smelled of the sea, much easier to breathe than the fumes of London.

She'd need to use the public toilets when she got to Gosport. That cup of tea she'd drunk waiting on Waterloo Station had gone right through her.

When the boat swung in an arc to land at the Gosport pontoon, the boatman tossed and secured the rope to a bollard before allowing the passengers to disembark. Angel could smell fish and chips. She realised she was hungry, she hadn't eaten since the night before.

Beyond the bus station was the Dive cafe and opposite, the source of the gorgeous smell, the Porthole fish restaurant. Angel walked through the ferry gardens, awash with colourful bedding plants provided by the Gosport Borough Council, heading for the public toilets.

Emerging, she saw him, the big man wearing the pricey-looking coat, too warm for this time of the day, sitting with his head in his hands on the wooden seat near the tobacconists.

Angel paused for a moment, her eyes taking in the dark curls. His hat was on the seat next to him, an expensive hat. Then he looked up and he reminded her of someone. That young singer, yes, that was it. Only this man was older. And she'd seen him before, but she couldn't remember where. Certainly not Gosport, she hadn't been back here for a while now.

The man rose from the seat, picked up his hat and made his way across the road to the Victory pub. He had a long easy stride but he was unsteady on his feet. She watched him open the door and be swallowed inside.

'You don't need a meal, you need a drink, girl,' she said softly to herself.

Angel pushed open the brass-handled door of the pub. A cloud of smoke and beer fumes enveloped her, a smell she was familiar with. She searched the room and saw him at a small table at the back. The jukebox was playing a Beatles melody. At the greasy bar she ordered, pointing to the back of the bar.

'Gin and tonic for me and whatever my friend over there's drinking.'

'Brandy,' the barman said.

'A double.'

'You want to order again now? It's chucking-out time. I'm about to call last orders.'

Angel realised she was back in the real world now, not the London club scene that somehow miraculously managed to stretch opening times and closing times.

'Double up on that,' she said, taking the fiver out and laying it on the bar. Then she was moving through groups of sailors and girls until she reached him. She unloaded the glasses on to the table and sat down on the chair next to him.

He seemed to be in a trance. When he looked at her she realised he was barely holding his own against the alcohol he'd already taken before he entered the pub. But he was good-looking and by the cut of his clothes, monied.

'You're going to need someone to see you get home safely,' she said.

He narrowed his eyes and stared as though seeing her for the first time.

'I'm a long way from home and the one person I want won't be there.'

The words were slurred. She decided his wife or woman had left him and it was the old story of him drinking himself silly hoping it would dull the edge of his pain.

When Angel Moore made a pass at a bloke they never refused her. She always got what or who she wanted, even if sometimes it turned sour as it had this morning. If she wanted someone's hands on her then she should be the one calling the shots.

'Drink up,' she said. 'I'll take you home.'

She'd made a split-second decision. This bloke had money and she wouldn't mind his hands on her body one little bit. After all, her money wasn't going to last long, was it? Not when her mother got a whiff she was back in Gosport town.

Angel pushed the brandy glass into his hand.

'This one's on me,' she said. 'What's your name?'

'Don't want any more. Had 'nuff.' Angel downed half her drink. She'd forgotten what proper measures of alcohol tasted like and its strength gave her a much needed lift.

'Yes, you do.'

Angel saw the man automatically grip the glass and down the amber liquid. He's going to have one hell of a headache later, she thought. She finished her own drink then helped him to his feet. He put his hand to his head.

'My hat,' he mumbled. 'Lost my hat.'

Angel swept his hat up from the floor where it had fallen.

'I've got it,' she said. 'C'mon.'

In the doorway he blinked at the low evening sunlight and she laughed as he staggered and grabbed at her lest he stumble.

With her arm tightly through his she steered him through the market place towards the corner of North

Street. When they reached the Black Bear public house, she led him inside.

'Got a room?' she asked the landlord. 'We've just come from a wedding. Can't get me old man on a train back to London in this state. He needs to sleep it off.'

The man looked like he didn't believe a word Angel said.

'If he spews up, you clear it up.'

'You're on.'

Angel pushed her new friend into the bar. She'd already fitted his hat on his head and he simply stood, shakily, waiting to do her bidding.

'Money up front,' said the man. 'Can't be too careful nowadays.' She paid for the room, thankful she had enough cash on her, and took the key off the barman.

'Want any help getting him upstairs?'

Angel shook her head. 'This isn't the first time I've done this,' she said. 'But thanks anyway.'

'It's the room at the top of the stairs,' he said.

Angel got the man up the stairs easier than expected then propped him against the doorpost while she turned the key.

The room was cleaner and better equipped than she'd dared hope. Certainly sweeter smelling than the bloke who'd given her the key.

She hauled the man inside and with a gentle push he fell on the bed. Immediately Angel began to undress him, throwing his clothes on to the floor as she pulled them off his dead weight. When it was accomplished and he lay in an untidy heap on his side, she turned him over.

'Not bad,' she said, looking him up and down. 'Not bloody bad at all.'

Then she hauled back the feather quilt and tipped him into the bed. After a while he began to snore evenly and Angel knew he was asleep.

She picked up his shoes, which she saw were Italian leather, and placed them beneath a chair. His coat she hung in the wardrobe along with his hat and suit, made by some tailor in Savile Row, she noticed. She'd already clocked his expensive gold watch and gold pinkie ring with the black onyx initial 'R' and wondered what it stood for. She took out his wallet from his suit pocket and opened it.

'Jesus!' The wad of notes was heavy in her hands. She put it all back and laid the wallet on top of the pile of clothes.

Angel locked him in the room while she went along to the bathroom at the end of the hall. He was in no fit state to go anywhere, but she couldn't risk some petty thief chancing their arm while she was gone. In a bath of steaming hot water she contemplated her luck.

He hadn't moved when she got back to the room and in moments she was undressed again and in bed beside him. It wasn't long before his evenly paced snoring lulled her to sleep.

Angel woke to an arm encircling her nude body beneath the warm sheet. It was quite dark now. She wondered how long she'd slept. She hadn't realised how tired she'd been.

Memories set themselves into place and she turned towards the man. She stroked his strong face and her fingertips lightly brushed his closed eyelids. She breathed deeply of his warm male smell.

He opened his eyes and kissed her then, at first gently then harder, filling her mouth with his tongue. Angel decided she liked it and ran her hands over his broad back and down to the rounded part of his arse. He gave a satisfied sigh and pulled her hand away and placed it around his cock before his mouth descended on hers once more.

His penis was large and very hard and she traced her fingers along its length. As she did so, he was sighing. Fingers slid into her pubic hair, lingered for a brief moment then found the opening. Angel melted.

She let her legs fall open and he moved on top of her.

'Do you want me?' she whispered.

'Yesss . . .'

Angel raised her hips and guided his prick inside her damp warmth. Her muscles tightened and he moved rhythmically inside her. And then Angel was drowning, her body moving in time with his as her orgasm built to its peak and beyond.

'You're so wet,' he murmured. 'So wet and so open for me.'

He fucked her hard and kept fucking her, and she

held on tightly to him all the way until he was spent and fell away from her, gasping.

He was quiet then and so was she, sated.

Angel kissed him tenderly on his cheek but he didn't stir, he was already asleep again.

When Roy opened his eyes he found he was lying on his back and staring at a ceiling he hadn't seen before. He struggled to a sitting position and the room started spinning. The hammer thudding inside his skull made him raise his hands uselessly to his head. After a while the nausea subsided enough for him to look about him – and at the figure curled beside him in the bed. All he could make out was a mass of blonde hair.

He could hear street noises: market vendors. A shaft of bright sunshine had forced itself through a break in the curtains and motes of dust danced in the light.

To his left at the side of the bed was a chair on which some of his clothes lay, neatly folded and top-ped by his wallet with its comforting bulge that he hoped were the notes inside it. He looked at his wrist and saw his watch was still there. It was half past eight and wherever he was he hadn't been rolled.

His memory began to release information just as the body beside him moved and the sheet that con-cealed the blonde's face was pushed away. Her liquid eyes stared at him, then she spoke.

'You certainly tied one on. How d'you feel?'

She's beautiful, he thought, or she would be if a huge bruise wasn't marring her cheek. But what the fuck was he doing here?

'You tell me how I bleedin' look and I'll tell you if it's the way I really feel.'

She grinned at him. He saw her teeth were small and white but the effort of smiling had caused her to wince and she put a hand to her face. She struggled to a sitting position and the sheet slipped, exposing two very well-formed breasts. She was quite unself-conscious and didn't bother to cover herself.

'A shave, a bath, and you'll survive,' she said. 'And you definitely need a good toothbrush. I've known bleedin' rabbit hutches smell better.'

Automatically he cupped his hand to his mouth and breathed into it, pulling a face.

'Don't worry, I don't suppose my breath smells any sweeter.'

'Did I do that?' He nodded to her face.

She raised her hand to pull some of her hair across her cheek in an effort to cover the bruise. 'No.'

He realised then that he too was totally nude. 'Did we . . . ?'

'Yes. But you didn't ask me to marry you or pledge undying love.'

Roy shook his head as he smiled but the action caused a fresh bout of nausea and this time he couldn't contain it. He leapt from the bed, grabbed his shirt from the chair and yanked the door open.

'Down the end of the hall,' he heard her call. He made it to the lavatory just in time. After a while he rinsed out his mouth at the sink and then turned on the bath taps.

While the water, which was scaldingly hot, flooded into the old four-footed bath, he pulled back the curtain and looked down into the street below. He breathed a sigh of relief as he recognised the corner of North Street and the Lloyds bank opposite. He was still in Gosport. He opened the catch on the window and the market noises filtered in.

He'd gone into the town after visiting the boy Eddie and Vera, and because that huge black cloud of depression had fallen over him he'd indulged in a couple of drinks to ease the pain of missing Daisy. Only he hadn't stopped at a couple this time, had he? There was something that didn't tally up about her disappearance, something he should have realised sooner. But he was fucked if he could see it and getting slaughtered wasn't the answer, he knew that. The Star. He'd been in there, and the India Arms, that old coaching inn. He had a few brandies there, then he'd popped round to the George and Dragon at the end of Bemisters Lane.

He bent and turned off the taps, tested the bath then climbed in. After submerging his head in the water then sitting up and shaking his hair, Roy decided he'd felt a lot rougher at other times. He soaped himself with Imperial Leather, a fresh bar still in its cardboard wrapper he noted, then lay down as full length as the bath allowed his big frame.

The girl . . . Where did she come in?

He remembered standing on the ferry, watching the sea and the craft on the water, looking across at the Round Tower guarding Portsmouth and the two small kids on the pontoon. They were fishing with rods made from bamboo sticks, catgut and bent pins, and using bacon rinds as bait. A laugh rose in his throat.

'You'll only catch crabs with that,' he'd warned.

'Fuck off, you drunken tosser,' had been their cheery answer. So he had taken the little pissers' advice and gone for a sit-down on the wooden bench near the tobacco kiosk. Slept? He might have dozed off.

What then? Ah, yes. The Victory. And now it all became hazy. He must have picked up the girl in the pub. Well, she wasn't a prossie, if she was she'd have been long gone with his money. Anyway, if he'd felt horny enough to fuck he'd have gone down to Forton Road and screwed one of his own girls. He'd done that many times before Daisy entered his life.

But Daisy wasn't here and he missed her like fucking nobody's business.

He got up and let the water out and, after he'd dried himself, gave the bath a cursory wipe with the towel that he left on the floor beneath the sink. He could see a pile of fresh towels in the open cupboard, and found a box of cheap but unused toothbrushes.

There wasn't any toothpaste but he used soap and scrubbed vigorously, feeling better when his mouth was clean.

He knew exactly where he was now, the Black Bear.

It was time to go and have a word with the bruised beauty. He didn't even know her name.

CHAPTER 7

Angel heard his bare footsteps and saw the door open. He'd bathed and tucked a towel around his middle, his shirt flung over his shoulder. His damp hair curled crazily, slightly long but the kind of hair she liked running her fingers through.

'Bathroom's free,' he said. He had a glass of water in one hand that he placed on the table her side of the bed. 'Thought you might need this.'

Flinging off the towel and shirt he walked towards the chair to retrieve his other clothes. He was flushed with the heat of his bath and his semi-erect cock glistened long and curving towards his flat stomach. Jesus, but he had a body on him, she thought. And tanned, he hadn't got that tan in this country.

'Why don't you come back to bed?'

He paused, black socks in his hand. She knew he wanted to. His cock told her that. His eyes searched her face, her body. His lips curled into a smile.

'Thought you'd never ask,' he said. Angel smiled very sweetly, very innocently, then she licked her top lip with her tongue and knew its effect hadn't been wasted. He slid onto the sheet and pulled her towards him. His breath was sweet as he breathed warm air to the side of her face. Angel felt her entire body melt and begin to yearn for the promise his hard cock offered. He fondled her breasts, then took a nipple into his mouth. Angel felt it harden, the electricity of his touch burning her skin. She grasped his strong penis and moved her hand slowly and sensitively over its rigidity. He gasped then sought her mouth, kissing her hungrily as though he'd been starved of affection. Releasing his cock Angel squirmed below him so that he covered her. He plunged upwards and into her so she was impaled on him. And then she was moving below him, joyfully, up and down, up and down, almost struggling for breath as he responded with hard, swift thrusts. She didn't want it to end but it did. Simultaneously they came, then he collapsed on her body. He lifted himself on one elbow.

'That was nice,' he said. 'Very nice.'

She pulled her hair out of her eyes and away from her face and smiled. 'Wasn't it, just,' she replied. 'You going to tell me what this stands for?' She touched the ring on his finger, tracing the 'R'.

'Roy,' he said. 'Roy Kemp, and what do I call you?'

'Angel.' she said. 'Just Angel.'

Angel sat on the bus to Clayhall. She could have walked over Haslar Bridge, or she could have accepted a lift in that bloody great silver Humber that was miraculously still in one piece after spending the night on a spare bit of ground at the back of South Street. She didn't even know he had a car until he pointed to it as they'd left the Black Bear, saying, 'So that's where I left it.'

Angel had no idea why she she didn't take the money he'd offered her just before they'd left the pub, especially not when she'd gone to such lengths to trap him into sleeping with her. And of course, having paid for the room, she was out of pocket. It was certainly a fair wedge of notes he'd held out to her but, instead of accepting, she'd made it plain she was no whore. He'd asked for her telephone number, and she'd laughed because the telephone at her mum's prefab had been cut off ages ago. Instead she scribbled the address on a piece of paper and gave him that.

He'd never contact her. She knew that.

She'd caught him on the rebound from someone or something he wasn't willing to share with her. But then neither of them had talked intimately. It had been a mutual fuck where a good time had been had by the pair of them.

'Where to, Miss?'

'Prefabs,' she replied, going into her purse to pay him the fare. It was then she saw the roll of notes enclosed in a piece of paper. When the conductor had moved on up the bus Angel unfolded the paper.

'You paid for the room and looked after me. The best night I've had for a while. I always pay my debts – Roy.'

Silly bleeder, she thought. But she smiled at the sight of the money.

The double decker provincial bus stopped opposite the Fighting Cocks and Angel stepped down and on to the pavement opposite the pub.

She crossed the road, pausing before she turned into the pathway that ran between two lines of pre-fabricated houses. The paving stones on the pathway were broken and some of the gardens, enclosed in wire netting fencing and strewn with brambles and broken furniture, looked like they'd never seen a shovel or a fork. Yet others were kept spick and span, reflecting their tenants' neatness. She noted the small lawns bordered by flowerbeds, and windows with nets to stop nosy parkers looking in.

Angel tripped up the path, her high heels clattering, to number nineteen at the very end. She stopped before opening the gate. The place hadn't changed a bit. Those curtains could do with a damn good wash. The garden was overgrown and decorated with crisp bags and sweet wrappers blown in by the wind.

Up the concrete path she walked and grasped the metal handle of the side door. She turned it and stepped inside the kitchen.

She sighed as the smell hit her.

Opposite the door was a range of utilities: a gas boiler, cooker with an eye-level grill, clothes boiler, and the sink. Every available inch of worktop space was filled with dirty crockery. It looked as though no one had washed up for a month and Angel had never realised her mother owned so much stuff. In the sink, which had its plug in, some indescribable clothes were soaking in greasy grey water. A small kitchen table and two chairs sat in the recess near the window. One of the chairs was upturned on the grease-splattered lino. Angel's heart plummeted.

Closing the kitchen door behind her she opened the door to the living room. The smell was no better in here. Dirt, sweat, and the odour of general filth hit her. Two brown velour armchairs, their stuffing escaping from the armrests, sat either side of the fireplace. In front of one of the chairs was a coffee table with metal legs. A utility sideboard was shoved against the window next to the door that led to the overgrown back garden.

The bundle of rags was asleep on one of the armchairs with her legs splayed open. A glass was clutched tightly in one hand, on its side so that the remaining liquid had spilled unheeded down her stained skirt. An empty green gin bottle sat on the floor.

Angel stared at the shrivelled face, the stick-thin arms and legs, the bleached hair that showed inch-wide grey roots.

Angel went over to the woman and gently shook her shoulder. The woman opened her eyes.

'Hello, Ma. I see you've been putting the money I've been sending to good use.'

*

Vera slammed shut the front door of the house in Western Way.

'Suze!' she yelled up the stairs and, getting no reply, decided no one was in. Of course, she remembered, Susie had taken little Eddie to see his nan and granddad at The Cedars. They'd be a while yet. She slammed around making herself a cup of tea, then sat down at the kitchen table, her head in her hands. She wasn't sure whether she was glad she was in the house alone or cross because she had no one to share how upset she was at what she'd seen at Gosport market. Kibbles, standing on the scrubbed table, butted his head against her arm to let her know he was there.

'Hello, my little man,' she said, putting her face into his grey fur and breathing his scent. Vera wanted so much to cry but she held back the tears and comforted herself by clutching Kibbles' warm, purring body.

It had all started as she'd paid Sam the Fish for the small codling.

'I 'ope you've left the tail and 'ead on. If it's got the eyes in, it'll see my Kibbles nicely for dinners next week.'

'You get worse, you do, Vera,' Sam called after her. She put the newspaper-rolled package into her brown carrier bag, called out a greeting to Abdul on the babywear stall and was just about to turn into North Street when she saw them.

Neatly, Vera sidestepped behind the canvas sheeting of the bedding merchant.

'Sid, 'ow much is them flannelette sheets?' Her voice sounded strangled and she wasn't even looking at the bedding, for what she'd just seen had almost taken her breath away.

She had no intention of buying flannelette sheets, in fact she couldn't stand them, but surely that was Roy Kemp emerging from the side door of the Black Bear with a pretty blonde.

Vera needed somewhere to hide and Sid's stall provided it. She pushed the white sheets back towards him.

'How about them coloured ones, Siddy?' she said. 'They dearer?'

From her vantage point she saw Roy put his arm about the girl's shoulders and the girl raise her face and smile into his eyes. The tender look on his face wasn't lost on Vera. She knew that look. It was an 'after sex' look. And to come out the side door of the Black Bear instead of the saloon meant only one thing. The two of them had been there all bleedin' night!

'No, Siddy, I've changed me mind.' The couple were at the end of the street now and looked as though they were stopping to chat. 'Tea towels, Siddy. Two of them ones with the green stripe up the centre. Yes, that'll do nicely.' With one eye on the couple and one eye on her purchases, Vera didn't bother replying to Sid's cheeky repartee that she must have a tiny bed if two bleeding tea towels would cover it.

Vera saw the girl stand on tiptoe and kiss Roy's cheek before marching off towards the ferry in heels higher than Vera herself wore. Roy stood looking after her for a few moments then turned and walked back. Vera's heart was thumping fast as she hid, watching as he threaded himself through the market shoppers then walked across the spare bit of ground to where his car was parked.

'Thanks, Siddy,' she managed.

She stuffed the paper bag containing the tea towels she neither needed nor wanted into her carrier bag and, with tears clouding her eyes, walked in the opposite direction.

'That lying bleeder,' she said softly to herself. 'Told me he was going back to London yesterday.' All the way home she thought about men, about the lies they told to cover their arses and the way they were led by their dicks.

Now, burying her face into her cat's fur, she whispered, 'My poor Daisy. My poor little girly.'

CHAPTER 8

Roy knew exactly where to find the bastard, but he didn't reckon the tosser would be full of pills and booze, stripped off and dancing on a bleedin' table in the Regency.

The owners liked the eating place to be known as a club and normally Roy wouldn't bother with it. The jukebox was belting out 'Nowhere To Run' by Martha and the Vandellas and Jack McVitie, like any loner once he got tanked up, was showing off.

The club was heaving and thick with fag smoke and beer fumes but Roy didn't care about the sad state of the place or the rough clientele; after all, he and the twins were being paid protection money by the two brothers who ran it. It was full of young blokes who wanted nothing more than to look good in their girlfriends' eyes by picking fights with even sadder tossers than they were.

'Give us a brandy,' said Roy. The blonde behind the bar knew the score and pressed a double from the optic. She sat it in front of Roy on the sticky bar.

'Can't you get 'im down?' she asked. Her blue eyes

were ringed with bright blue shadow, matching the low-cut scoop top that certainly didn't hide her ample curves. For a fleeting moment he thought of Angel and her luscious breasts.

They'd parted mates. He hadn't told her he wouldn't be seeing her again but he reckoned she was wise enough to know the score. She'd done him a favour by caring for him when he'd been too drunk to look after himself, and he'd slipped enough cash into her handbag for her to buy herself a few pretty things.

'Doin' some harm, is he, up there?' McVitie's lewd movements were grotesque. His white, pimpled body glistened with sweat and Roy wondered how on earth he ever got that tiny floppy bit between his legs up to scratch. Nevertheless, Roy was glad he'd found the bastard and didn't mind waiting and drinking his brandy in relative peace while the crowd cheered McVitie on. He was weaving. Not a stitch of clothing except his socks and shoes and the ever-present brown trilby.

'Sad bastard,' said Roy. 'Put another one in there and I'll see what I can do.' He saw relief flood her face and, by way of thanks, she pressed the optic twice.

At that very moment McVitie chose to give an impressive twirl, right off the table.

'Whoops-a-daisy,' said Roy. For a moment McVitie lay on the floor stunned, staring up at Roy who nudged him with his foot before swallowing his drink straight back. Then the man at his feet began to laugh. Someone had carefully piled McVitie's clothes on the bar. Roy threw them down at him. 'Get dressed, cunt.'

McVitie, who was still laughing despite the jeers from the crowd, made sure his hat was firmly in place then scrambled up. He put his fists up and toppled sideways.

'Who you callin' a cunt?'

'Okay, you worthless lump of shit then.' Roy grabbed him before he slid to the floor again. 'Get your fucking clothes on, we're going for a walk.'

When McVitie realised it was Roy talking to him he dropped all pretence of a fighting mood.

'Out the back.' Roy pushed the half-dressed man ahead of him into the rear yard where the urinals were. The earlier rain had stopped and the sky was full of stars. 'Nice night, Jack.' Then he slammed him into the brick wall. A tin bath hanging on a nail clattered to the paved ground. Although that noise was loud, the music from inside the bar was louder and Roy knew he wouldn't be interrupted. His face was inches from McVitie's and he could smell his foetid breath. Roy pressed his arm across McVitie's neck, pinning his head against the red brick.

'What 'ave I done, Mr Kemp?' Roy could hear the fear in his voice.

'It ain't what you've done, it's what you fucking haven't done.' He tightened his grip across the man's throat. 'I asked you to find out where Daisy Lane is and you haven't bothered, have you?' The saddest thing, Roy thought, was that he'd exhausted all other avenues in discovering Daisy's whereabouts and that he, Roy Kemp, was resorting to prising information from scum like this bastard in front of him.

Roy brought up his other hand. His thumb glittered in the starlight.

'No!' McVitie tried to squirm away. Roy always marvelled at this man's capacity to drink and toss back pills like they were going out of fashion but become lucid enough when it suited him.

'You don't like my little toy, do you?' Roy laid the blade against McVitie's cheek. The man froze. One false move and his face would be peeled back like a banana skin. He'd picked up the lethal finger knife in Africa, to be worn on the thumb with the blade concealed in the palm. He dug the blade into McVitie's flesh and a pinprick line of blood oozed and rolled down the man's face.

'S . . . sorry, Mr Kemp.' Roy knew he was remembering a time less than a year back when the three and a half inch blade had sliced a man's nose. 'I . . . I been upset today. I meant to get to you but I been drowning me sorrows.' Roy relaxed his arm against the man's throat but still held the knife close to his face.

'What 'ave you got to drown your sorrows about?'

'Randolph Turpin's dead. He shot his kiddie then committed suicide.'

Roy allowed his arm to slide away. The news hit him hard just as the bastard in front of him knew it would. So the Leamington Licker was gone.

If this cunt had wanted to stop him in his tracks he'd gone the right way about it.

'You sure it was suicide or is that just talk?'

'Talk, yeah.'

He was fed up with McVitie now and the bastard stank as high as the urinals. Roy definitely wouldn't get back his share of the money he'd invested in the Great Orme Hotel in Llandudno. He should have known that had been just another of the fighter's ill-fated ventures. Roy had been there when the middle-weight boxer had won the nation's heart by beating Sugar Ray Robinson for the world title at Earl's Court in 1951.

Lately, Randy Turpin had begun to feel the pinch where money was concerned. He'd asked Roy if he wanted to buy some of his trophies but Roy didn't want anything from him. He'd slipped him some money, but to take the bloke's hard-earned prizes would have been kicking him when he was down.

He'd listened to Randy's domestic troubles though. Him and his wife Gwen were having a few difficulties, but it happened in the best of marriages, Roy had told him.

Randy wasn't himself, hadn't been for a while, but suicide? Roy sighed. This news was something that he'd take a while to get over. Mentally he shook himself. He'd think about it later after he'd sorted this stupid bastard out.

McVitie hadn't dared to move; he stood still as though he had a poker up his arse. 'So, you dancing on the fucking table in there is your way of paying respect to the great man?'

'He was a good bloke, Mr Kemp.' McVitie seemed to sag with relief as Roy stepped away from him.

'What happened?'

'Not sure yet.'

Now the fucker was going to run off at the mouth, Roy had seen it all before. 'Get the rest of your bleedin' clothes on.' He hoped Jack couldn't see how upset he was.

'It's all that punching to the 'ead. Turns boxers funny.' McVitie was doing up his shirt buttons. 'That's what I was going to tell you, Mr Kemp. That Valentine Waite 'as been acting funny.'

'What do you mean, "acting funny"?' Come to think of it, it had been a while since he'd seen the boxer out and about the town. The bloke in front of him had his full attention again. If the bastard was spinning him a line . . .

'Y'know that prossie they found in the dustbin?' Roy nodded. 'Waite was in the pub where she was, same night and everything.'

'What about it? The bloke can have a bleedin' drink.'

'It was a really filthy night so there was only a couple of salesmen in the bar and the woman. My mate the barman recognised him soon as he went in, said he left after the woman but Waite'd been watching 'er all the time. My mate said he looked over and the bloke seemed as though he was talking to someone. Not out loud or anything, just muttering now and then. I told 'im an' all, it's all that punching to the 'ead. Turns 'em funny.'

'Did your mate tell the coppers?'

McVitie laughed. 'Would you? He don't want to be mixed up in nothing. Bad enough the bint bein' in the pub in the first place.'

Roy's mind swung back to Waite's appearance at Vera's party. He'd queried his odd behaviour then but Daisy had shrugged his questions aside. Said something about Waite saying she reminded him of his mother.

Was it possible he had something to do with Daisy's disappearance? What if the bastard had hurt or even killed her? No, Daisy couldn't sign cheques and empty her bank account if she was dead. Unless there was a pretty good forger involved.

Roy stared at the man in front of him. He was breathing heavily. Perhaps, thought Roy, it was time to enlist a bit of legitimate help like Charles and his mother wanted. He thought of Vinnie Endersby. Of course him and the copper would need to come to a bit of an understanding. He'd heard the DS didn't take backhanders, but all the same . . .

'Just bought yourself a little time.' He saw the relief swim across McVitie's face. Then turn to fear once again as Roy put his hand in his breast pocket to put the knife away.

Roy smiled as he brought out his wallet and stripped a fiver from the roll. He handed it to McVitie.

'Bought yourself a drink as well,' he said. 'And by the way, you got your shirt on inside out.'

DS Vinnie Endersby left Bow Street Police Station with Sandy Yates driving the squad car, a blue and white Ford Anglia. Just lately it always seemed to be raining and today was no different with the water lashing against the windows and running down the windscreen to be swiped aside by the wipers.

'You follow boxing, Sandy?' The WPC was wearing some kind of subtle perfume. He turned his head to look at her and she gave him a look that would wither fresh chrysanthemums at a funeral.

'I don't hold with any blood sports,' she said.

Vinnie glanced at her hands on the steering wheel. Small and capable with square unpolished nails, one bearing just a hint of the red that hadn't quite escaped the polish remover. So she wasn't quite the acid drop she pretended to be, not with blood-red nails, he thought. Vinnie liked a woman who cared for her hands. Mind you, she hid her feelings well, did Sandy Yates.

He looked across at her profile. Finely arched eyebrows, blonde hair pinned above her uniform collar and tucked well beneath her cap. She'd look better with a glass of champagne in her hands, wearing a severe black dress at some high-flying party, than sitting in a cramped police car driving through the murk of a wet day in London.

'But you know where Valentine Waite lives?'

'I thought everyone knew that,' she answered, then as an afterthought, 'Sir.'

Vinnie decided to shut up. Sandy Yates wasn't an easy woman to get along with. Dedicated but difficult. Mind you, he thought, she had guts to stick the backchat and the shitty remarks some of the blokes at the station handed out. He couldn't blame her for keeping herself to herself. Most of the coppers still thought women were a waste of space in the station and only fit for making tea.

'We'll have a chat with Mr Waite about the latest girl that's turned up dead, that Maggi Sonning,' he said. 'See if he remembers seeing anyone hanging about outside the bar when he left.'

'We don't know for sure he was anywhere near Stoke Newington, Sir,' she said.

'I do,' said Vinnie. It was warm in the car and he had to admit Sandy was a better driver than he was himself so he felt quite at ease.

'Really?'

Vinnie tapped his nose. 'Ask me no questions and I'll tell you no lies.' Wonderful what a couple of fivers would do, he thought. Money always brings the creepy crawlies from the woodwork.

'He's checked out before, Sir.'

'Before isn't now. You're not the only one who's been sifting through a backlog of material. Waite might spend time abroad at boxing venues but he's been in England every time a report has come in about a missing girl. I think he needs checking out again.' What Vinnie didn't say was he wanted to get the full measure of the man. See what Daisy Lane had fancied about him. 'You haven't forgotten how many women have gone missing or been found dead over the past few years?'

'Eight, Sir.' Of course Yates hadn't forgotten. She had a memory like an elephant and what she didn't know she found out. 'You don't think that makes us look like we're chasing our own tails, Sir?'

'The cases aren't closed, Yates. If it is the same man we've got a mass murderer on our hands.'

'We don't know yet that all the prostitutes are dead. Some are classed as missing. Maybe those ones have moved on to pastures new. I've done quite a bit of research, Sir.'

'You'll have noted that a couple of the women had kiddies, then. Women don't usually leave their children. All the more reason to go over the same ground but a bit more carefully.' Vinnie thought about Daisy. She loved young Eddie to pieces. No way would she ever willingly be parted from that boy. He tried to erase her from his mind. Thinking about the job in hand was what he had to do now.

Ever since that day in Gosport when he'd talked to Vera he'd drawn blanks on every piece of information he'd followed up. He didn't believe Daisy could simply vanish off the face of the earth. His gut instinct told him Valentine Waite could provide a few answers, but unfortunately police work didn't rely on instinct. Hard facts were needed.

They were out in the country now heading towards the coast, having left behind Guildford and its cathedral with the solid brick outline set on the commanding spot on Stag Hill.

'You want to stop and look at the map, or are you familiar with the route?'

She gave him another of those withering looks. He wondered if those looks could be classed as insubordination?

'We mightn't be going the way you'd choose, Sir, but don't worry, I'll get you there safely and in half the time.'

'I believe you,' he said. He tipped his hat down over his face and moved deeper into the seat, easing his long body into a comfortable position. 'Wake me when we arrive.'

WPC Yates was shaking his knee. 'Almost there, Sir.' He rubbed a hole in the condensation on the side window and peered out. It was still raining, although less heavily now. They were on a narrow road, hardly more than a lane, and ahead he could see a double wrought-iron gate. Sandy Yates parked beneath a yew tree, leaving the lane clear and the vehicle partly concealed.

Vinnie got out of the car, grumbling about his

aching neck. Sandy looked as fresh and sparkling as she had when they'd started.

The iron gates weren't padlocked but loosely held shut by a chain. A gravel drive led straight to an imposing grey brick residence. On either side of the long drive was lawn with trees set back from it. Vinnie whistled.

'I'm in the wrong business.'

'You and me both, Sir.'

'We'll walk up under cover of the trees. No need to announce we're coming.'

The grass needed cutting, decided Vinnie. No doubt the bleeder had one of those huge new sit-on lawn mowers like the one his father-in-law owned. Probably had a gardener or gardeners to keep the place in order. Vinnie didn't need a lawn mower for the postage stamp of a garden in his Alverstoke village house.

'Are we going to ring at the front door, Sir?'

'Don't see why not. We're visitors, aren't we?'

Vinnie wasn't surprised when no one answered the oak-panelled door with its imposing black door furniture.

'You don't reckon there's a housekeeper?'

'Can't see him keeping this pile together by himself. Not when he travels.'

'He's got a couple of scrapyards as well, hasn't he, Sir? I know one of them's in Lambeth.'

'We'll get round to them in good time,' Vinnie said. He waited for what seemed to him a reasonable time, then told the WPC to stay there while he looked at the back of the house.

He'd respect Vera's wishes and not advertise Daisy's vanishing act. Trouble was, and at last he was admitting it to himself, Daisy Lane had got under his skin. If she hadn't got mixed up with Roy Kemp, who knows what might have happened between him and her?

He thought about the time he'd gone shopping with her to Chantelle's in Gosport so she could buy a dress for Reggie Kray's wedding festivities. When she'd come out of that cubicle wearing that figure-hugging frock and the shoes she'd just bought in the market, he'd taken one look and his heart had flipped over. But even then it had been Roy Kemp on her mind. He'd been her escort for the London affair.

The path continued around the building, separating the gardens from the house. He cursed as the gravel scrunched loudly beneath his feet. He passed through a kitchen garden, the smell of herbs stronger now the rain was lifting. At the back of the house French doors looked out across a lawned area. Probably have all kinds of wildlife here, even deer grazing, thought Vinnie as he caught the sight of a rabbit scampering.

To the side he could see a tennis court. There were weeds poking through the asphalt. Vinnie wondered why they hadn't been pulled. The court didn't look manicured enough for a game without it being tidied up first. He began to have misgivings about the house.

Beautiful it might be, if you were comfortable with this kind of living, but to him it seemed cold and unloved. When he got back to the front of the house again Sandy Yates grinned at him.

'Anyone home?'

'Not a soul.'

She made to walk back down the driveway.

'That's it, then, a journey for nothing. He's most probably out of the country. Isn't he fighting in New York?'

'Not yet he isn't.' Vinnie rocked on his heels. 'Thought you didn't follow the fights?'

'I can read the papers, Sir. I know Cassius Clay and Henry Cooper are getting ready for a set-to in London. Reckon our matey'll turn up for a ringside seat?'

Vinnie thought she was enjoying her dig at him. Considering himself put in his place he followed up with, 'I think we'll take a proper look around. Follow me.'

At the French doors the curtains were drawn, obscuring their sight of the room. 'We'll go in this way,' he said, peering at the lock.

'Sir, we've no reason to enter and no search warrant.'

'Nice of you to remind me but aren't we investigating a possible break-in?'

She was looking at him like he'd gone mad. A strand of her blonde hair had escaped her hat and she was trying to push it back.

'The place is secure. What break-in?'

Vinnie took his handkerchief out of his pocket and picked up an ornamental gnome from the flowerbed and tapped sharply on the glass. It shattered just above the lock, exposing the levered handle. Vinnie dropped the gnome and reached in and opened the door.

'This break-in,' he said. 'Now we don't need a warrant because upon discovering this door had been interfered with I thought it best to have a look round. Just being a good copper.' He grinned at her. 'Come on in and mind the glass,' he said, fumbling his way through the heavy damask.

The air inside was stale and dank. After a cursory glance around the large and extremely sparsely furnished room he said, 'I've got a feeling no one's been home for a while.'

His footsteps echoed on the wooden flooring as he wandered through examining the rest of the downstairs. At the foot of the stairs he paused. A thin layer of dust lay over the wooden banister rail. Upstairs the air smelled as though the place had been shut up for some time.

'I'll take the bedrooms this side, Sir.' Sandy Yates walked off to the left. Minutes later they met again at the top of the stairs.

'Well, that's a turn-up for the books,' she said. 'You'd never think anyone lived here. Not much furniture, no paintings and I'd have expected a bloke like him to have put some of his winnings into art or antiques.'

'Perhaps that's why there was no burglar alarm fitted,' Vinnie said.

'We going now, Sir?'

He nodded. 'Wasting our time here.'

When they got to the end of the lane Sandy drew to a sudden halt.

'Look, Sir. That explains a lot.' Vinnie followed her line of vision and saw the For Sale sign barely visible in the trees. It had fallen to one side in the undergrowth and brambles were covering most of it. Vinnie memorised the estate agent's number.

'Well spotted,' he said. 'It's a local property valuer. C'mon, let's give him a visit.'

Mercer and Tilbury Estate Agents, in the village of Rowington near Arundel, was manned by a tall woman in a tweed suit who introduced herself as Miss Courtney. Vinnie assumed she was around fifty but she was well preserved even without make-up. All that country air, he reckoned. He asked about Twelvetrees.

'Do you want to view?' she asked.

'We've already had a look round. There's a broken window you ought to do something about.'

She was about to protest when he showed her his warrant card. She peered at it then forced a smile.

'It's been on the market for a while now. The owner wanted a quick sale but unfortunately he's not willing to drop too much off the price.'

'Any reason why?'

It was a small village and in Vinnie's experience

usually everyone knew and participated in the local gossip. He gave Miss Courtney a dazzling smile and saw her blush.

'I really shouldn't talk about clients . . .'

'You wouldn't be talking about a client. Merely answering a couple of questions. Maybe you'll save yourself the bother of being asked the same questions later at the local station.'

He could see by her horrified look the last thing she wanted was to have anyone gossiping about her.

'The owner owes money to local people. He's run up bills and left without paying. Goes without saying he's not well liked. But celebrities can be like that, so I've been told.'

'Celebrity?'

'A boxer,' she said.

'What sort of bills?'

'The usual, butchers, grocery, wine merchants. It's rumoured he hasn't paid the help's wages. Handyman, gardener, Emily Short only has her pension to manage on and he . . .'

Vinnie stopped her. 'Okay,' he said. 'I suppose you've an address or phone number for him?' She nodded and began searching in a ledger. Then she copied down details and handed them to Sandy Yates who was waiting patiently.

'He has been seen at the property,' she said. 'Apparently returned a few times to load furniture and effects.'

Vinnie nodded his head. 'Thank you for your help.' He gave her another big smile.

When they were safely installed in the confines of the car, Sandy Yates spoke. 'If you don't mind me saying so, Sir, if I did what you've just done to that poor woman to a man I was questioning, I'd be considered a tart.'

Vinnie tipped his hat back so that some of his curly hair showed above his forehead and laughed. 'C'mon, WPC Yates, a little flirting never hurt anyone. Sorry if it got up your nose,' he said, watching her fire the engine and put her foot down. She didn't reply and he let the silence go as he wondered about the charisma of a man who could run up bills and get women to flock to him.

'Could you fancy this Valentine Waite?'

'I'm a policewoman. I don't fancy any blokes I come in contact with in the line of duty. The crims in the streets are all wankers and the coppers are even worse wankers. If you'll excuse me, Sir,' she added.

Concentration on the road ahead was etched in every line of her profile as she drove. He'd obviously upset her and he was sorry. But he had a job to do. Two jobs if the truth be known. Officially he was looking for Valentine Waite to ask him a few questions about the prostitute's murder. Unofficially he was looking for a link, however small, between Valentine Waite and Daisy's disappearance. He shook his head and glanced at Sandy.

He'd never ever understand women.

Take Clare. When she got hold of something she was like a dog with a bone, refusing to let go. Clare still blamed him for the break-up of their marriage. Told him if he'd earned more money, provided a better standard of living, she would never have entertained an affair with his, at the time, senior officer. She told him afterwards she blamed him for everything. He'd wanted to smack her pretty, petulant face. But of course, he never had.

'So we're back to London now?'

Sandy turned and gave him a glimmer of a smile.

'He never loses a fight, Sir.'

Vinnie looked at her. He could see by the softness of her face that her mood had entirely dissipated.

'So I've heard.'

'I wonder why he needs to sell his house?'

'Could be any number of reasons,' he said.

'Yes, but what would make you put your house on the market?'

'Big debts?'

'Like?'

'Buying another property. Putting money into a deal that goes wrong. Gambling debts, business failure . . .'

'What made you say gambling debts, Sir?'

'Boxers seem to suffer from an inability to manage their affairs outside the ring. Look at Turpin.'

Vinnie sat up straighter in the seat. Valentine Waite hangs around Ron and Reg Kray and they own clubs, he thought. Gambling clubs. What if he's got in a bit deep and the interest keeps on growing?

'Do you know something?' Vinnie asked.

'Only that I was in the George with you lot the other night, winding down from shift, and I overheard someone say if you said it was going to rain tomorrow Valentine Waite'd wager you a fiver it wouldn't.'

'You reckon he owes big money then?'

'It's possible,' she said. 'Anything's possible. It's even possible England might win the World Cup.'

Vinnie raised his eyes at her. She was a very surprising woman was WPC Yates.

If Valentine Waite owed money to the twins then he owed Roy Kemp too. It was time he paid Roy a visit.

CHAPTER 9

Daisy couldn't get the pillowcase off her head. Her hands were tied behind her back and she'd tried to undo the cord but her fingers were numb. A couple of times she'd been able to grip a loose end only for it to slip from her grasp.

Daisy was tired. Her concentration wasn't good. Bright colours flitted through her brain and she felt sick. She swallowed back the bile that was forcing its way up into her mouth. If she threw up it was possible she'd choke to death with this thing over her face. It was dark, so dark, and she hated the dark. If I ever get out of here I never want to be in the dark again, she thought.

But in her heart the fear grew that she'd never get away from Valentine Waite. Not until he'd killed her.

Kenny's face swam before her. Her dead husband was smiling.

'Oh, baby,' she cried. 'Is this what it felt like before you died? Am I being punished for loving your brother?' And then Kenny's face melted into Eddie's beloved face. Daisy cried out for him and somehow stumbled to her feet to stop him leaving her. She'd never hold his dear face in her hands again, ever. She fell and the pain from her ankle jolted her back to reality. Daisy heard the door being unlocked and Glo's voice.

'Oh, you poor bleedin' thing,' Glo said. 'Let me get you back on the mattress.'

'For fuck's sake, help me,' Daisy cried as Glo hauled her up and onto the bed. 'I'm going mad in this place. My baby'll have cried himself to sleep, callin' for me. I can't bear to think about it. Please, Glo, don't let him 'urt me any more. *Please.*'

'Hold still. And for Christ's sake, *shut up.*'

Daisy was being lifted and pulled and then she felt the hardness of the wall behind the bed as Glo got her into a sitting position. Her head was pushed forward and fingers were at her neck, fumbling at the pillow-case, and then it was lifted from her face. She blinked and tried to focus on the girl. Then the tears came. Glo sat down on the mattress beside her and rocked Daisy in her arms.

'Thank you, Glo.' Daisy's voice was hardly more than a whisper.

'I know, I know,' Glo said, her own voice betraying her. 'The bastard's done this to me too.'

'Help me, please,' implored Daisy. Her throat was dry from lack of water. 'Get me out of this place.' She was crying into the girl's skinny body, her bones like those of a baby bird.

'I daren't do anything.' Glo pushed her away and

Daisy saw she had a fresh mark on her face and her eye was swollen, the surrounding skin shiny where the flesh was stretched. 'I've already done more'n I should, Daisy. If he finds out . . .' The terrible truth washed over Daisy afresh. She was never going to escape from this room. Her arms and shoulders were aching from muscles pulled into unnatural positions, and her ankle was throbbing like it was on fire.

'When did the bastard hit you?' Daisy asked.

'It don't matter,' the girl said. 'You need water. I'll get you some.'

She scrambled off the mattress and filled a plastic beaker at the tap. Daisy drank noisily, greedily, water spilling on to her soiled clothes.

She gave a sigh of relief and studied the girl. She might be pretty if she was cleaned up and fed properly.

'Want some more?'

Daisy shook her head. Glo put down the beaker and looked at Daisy's leg. There was pus and the skin round the wound was red and puffy.

'That needs cleaning.'

Daisy saw she'd not relocked the door behind her. It stood open. Hope rose immediately but was dashed when the doorway was filled with the bulk of Valentine Waite. His face was flushed with anger.

'What do you think you're doing, bitch? Who said you could untie her?'

He charged into the room and lunged at Glo but his fury had made him careless.

Daisy screamed as the anklet ripped into her skin anew as he tripped over the chain. His body seemed to fly towards the sink. Daisy saw the big man go down like a ninepin. But not before she heard the cracking sound that was his head smashing against the stone of the butler sink.

'Fucking 'ell.' Daisy closed her eyes and clenched her teeth together, rocking her body to ease the pain.

When she opened them she saw Valentine Waite lying in an unmoving heap on the floor. Daisy stared at the girl.

'He'll kill me. He'll fuckin' kill me.' Glo's words were flat. 'I once saw him kick a mangy dog to death simply because it pissed against one of the cars that was ready for the crusher. He went on kicking and stamping on it long after it was dead. He'll kill me the same way.' Daisy believed her.

'Set me free,' she hissed. Her pain was now the last thing on her mind as Daisy saw the only escape route she was ever going to get. 'I'll look after you.'

'You can't even look after yourself.' Glo stood over the bulky body on the floor and peered at him. 'Do you think he's dead?'

'Unlock me chain and I'll tell you.'

Glo turned and Daisy could see from the girl's face that she was confused, terrified of the consequences if the big man regained consciousness.

'He'll kill you, Glo,' Daisy went on. 'You know he will.' This was Daisy's last chance to escape. She was praying with every fibre of her being.

'You'll take me with you?'

Daisy's heart lurched with hope.

'You know I won't leave you. I don't make promises I can't keep. But first you got to help me. Untie my hands.'

But first Glo bent closer to Waite's inert body. Daisy could hear her breathing heavily with fear as though he might suddenly open his eyes and grab her. After what seemed like minutes Glo slid her hand slowly and carefully inside his jacket pocket. Glo's eyes were big and round, filled with panic that changed to relief when she drew out his set of keys, clenched firmly in her hand lest they rattle and wake him.

The key ring that contained the padlock key to Daisy's chain was in the girl's hands.

'Hurry,' whispered Daisy. But Glo made her wait. She was less hesitant now that she had seen, as Daisy had, blood clumping Waite's hair together in matted tufts. Glo resumed her search of his pockets and came out with his wallet. She looked over at Daisy and smiled.

'We'll need this,' she said. 'Can't do nothin' without money.'

Glo knelt on the mattress and inserted the key in the steel band at Daisy's ankle. Daisy's heart was pounding so loudly she was sure it could be heard. The wide anklet snapped open. Daisy flexed her stiff foot. Her joy, despite the pain, was absolute.

'My hands,' she said quickly. 'Untie my hands.'

Glo went swiftly to the top desk drawer and unlocked it, producing a pair of scissors. From the other
drawer she stuffed cotton wool, a bandage and the
iodine into her pocket. Coming back to Daisy she
knelt on the mattress and carefully cut through the
bindings on her wrists. Once her hands were free
Daisy began rubbing the life back into them.

Daisy used Gloria's shoulders to try to stand. She
stumbled and had to clutch at Glo for support.

'I can't put any weight on my foot.' Glo slid her
arm around Daisy's waist.

'He must have twisted something when he fell over
the bleedin' chain. Don't matter. You can move your
toes and ankle so it don't seem broken. We'll sort it
out later, hold on to me. We mustn't hang about.'

But Daisy didn't move. Waite hadn't stirred and it
gave her courage.

'The desk. I want to see what's so important about
the other locked drawer. Get that box out of there.'

'Fuckin' 'ell, I thought you wanted to get away.'
Glo's eyes were wide with fear and she kept throwing
glances at the prone body on the floor. But she
propped Daisy against the wall and moved swiftly to
the desk again where she fumbled with Waite's keys
then inserted a small key into the lock. In one hand
she held the lacquered box. Daisy saw something in
the drawer had caught Glo's attention and she hesi-
tated. Then thrusting her hand back she pulled out
two small vials of liquid and a syringe.

Looking at the toxic objects Daisy felt the bile rise in her throat.

'Hurry,' she urged.

The girl seemed galvanised into action and she prepared the syringe. Daisy watched, petrified something would go wrong. What if he woke up? God only knew the torture he'd inflict on her and the girl.

Glo advanced on Waite and pulled up his sleeve, stabbing at him and releasing the plunger so that the drug entered.

'That gives us a bit more time,' she said, calmer now. She helped Daisy away from the wall she'd been leaning against. 'You wanted this bleedin' box, *you* carry it.' She shoved the box into Daisy's hands and supported her as they left the room and locked the door on Valentine Waite.

The girl looked at Daisy with a triumphant expression on her face.

'It was about time he had a taste of his own medicine,' she said. Like conspirators they grinned at each other. 'We got a flight of stairs to get down. You'll 'ave to manage, it's the only way out.' Glo held on to Daisy while she laboriously stepped on one stair then pulled her other foot to join it. The procedure had to be repeated all the way down the stairs.

'The old man's deaf as a post and 'is eyesight's shit but he could 'ave someone in the office who's brought in a scrap car. I'm going to leave you 'ere for a second and go see what's happening. Stay in the shadows. I'll be quick as I can.'

Glo walked down the passageway. She unlocked a door, pulling it back slowly. Daisy realised the door hadn't been used in a long while for bits of paint and dirt fell as it opened. Sunlight drove its way into the dim passage and Daisy took gulps of fresh air.

'We're going to need some transport,' Glo whispered. 'When you 'ear an engine, get out of this door fast. I'll be right outside. I got to take the ol' boy by surprise, see? If he's up the other end of the yard looking over the pile of remoulds, we're in luck.'

The Kinks were singing 'Sunny Afternoon' and it was turned up very loud. Glo mouthed to Daisy, 'He likes 'is radio going full blast, it's the only way 'e can 'ear it.'

Alone, Daisy stared down the gloomy passage. She was seeing the place for the first time, having no recollection of being brought to the scrapyard. She realised the room where she'd been held was well hidden. The building was old and boarded-up rooms made it easy to overlook.

But she doubted anyone *had* come looking for her here. Waite had been dead clever. By waiting so long after that little scene in the Thorngate Hall no one would have guessed he could have been involved in her disappearance.

Daisy heard the rackety sound of an engine as it shuddered and slowed. She came out of the shadows and took a peek through the door.

A battered van held a chalk-faced Glo. She leaned over and opened the passenger door.

'Bleedin' get in!'

Daisy hopped over and climbed onto the step of the ancient vehicle. She tumbled onto the seat. It had a spring showing through. Almost before Daisy had slammed the door shut the van rattled away.

'Where we going?' Daisy looked at Glo's determined face. Her chin jutted forward in concentration as she clutched the steering wheel.

Daisy said, 'I don't even know where I bleeding am.'

'London. Just south of the Thames. Lambeth.'

She could see, in the fading light, warehouses, streets and houses, lamps lit for the coming hours of darkness, and people. People. Her heart welled with joy.

'Glo,' she cried. 'Am I really out of that place?' She watched as a scruffy black dog cocked its leg against a wall and peed.

'We're both out of there. But I can't bleedin' drive if I don't know where I'm heading.'

Daisy's brain clicked into gear.

'Portsmouth. The South.'

'See if there's a pencil on the floor or in front and write it down big.'

'What?' Daisy was mystified, but she bent down and amidst the rubbish of crisp bags and sweet wrappers found a stub of pencil. 'Write what big?'

'Where we're bleedin' goin'!'

Daisy scrabbled around and came up with an old newspaper. The 'Late News' column had a wide band without any printing so Daisy licked the pencil stub and wrote PORTSMOUTH. Then as an afterthought she wrote THE SOUTH. She put it in front of Glo, careful not to obscure her vision of the road, and watched as the girl scrutinised it.

'Put it on the dashboard. I . . . I got a bad memory an' I know you'll be asleep in next to no time once we get out of London.' Daisy opened her mouth to speak but Glo continued. 'I don't want to 'ave to wake you up to ask where we're going again, do I?'

Daisy shrugged. 'S'pose not.'

'I suppose you ain't up to driving?'

'If it weren't me right ankle what I can't feel except for the pain, I might 'ave been able to share the driving. Will you be all right?' She felt guilty at having to push all the work onto Glo. 'I'll make it up to you, promise.' She had to admit she was feeling waves of tiredness sweeping over her.

'I'll 'ave to be all right, won't I?'

'You're an angel,' Daisy said.

'Yeah, I'm an angel. And we'll both be dead angels if Valentine Waite catches us.'

'If you gave him what he was giving me in that syringe he'll be in no state to do anything for a while. What was in those vials?'

'It started with a K. I've forgotten what it was.'

Daisy's mind ticked over. She didn't think there were many drugs that started with a K.

'Sounds like cats,' said Glo.

Cats, kittens, Daisy thought. Doesn't make sense.

Vera would know, she knew almost everything there was to know about drugs. But Vera wasn't here.

'You can sleep now, if you want.'

Daisy had already closed her eyes. She heard the strain of the van's engine and realised Glo was driving in second gear. Still, it wasn't surprising. The van had been taken to the yard for scrapping. Jesus, it needed a new gearbox as well as having an exhaust that seemed to be blowing fumes in from the rear.

'I never thought I'd get out of there,' she murmured. Tiredness was gaining on Daisy.

'Nor me, but we're not safe yet. If you hear this rattletrap stop, don't worry, I got to keep filling her up with oil and water. I expect I'll stop at every garage between 'ere and Portsmouth.'

'You reckon we got enough money for oil and stuff?'

'The bleeder didn't have much in 'is wallet but I think we'll be okay.'

'Well, I wouldn't know where to put in the oil or the water,' said Daisy. 'So aren't you the clever one?'

'I been around the scrapyard a long time. That's what I learnt off the old man. Didn't take me long to pick up this driving lark.'

'Must be a quick learner,' said Daisy. 'One thing I don't get though. You been able to come and go around the place so why ain't you escaped from that bastard before now?'

After a while, Glo spoke. 'Please don't laugh but I been 'urt so much, I'm scared of nearly everyone.

Where would I go? I got no money. I ain't got no confidence, Daisy. An' I was too terrified to do anything before you came along and gave me the bit of courage I needed.' She paused. 'You don't think I'm weird?'

'Weird? That bastard is the weird one. I don't think you're weird but I do think you are the bravest person I know. It took a lot of bleedin' courage to save us from that fucking maniac.'

'You really think so?'

'Yes, I do.' Daisy moved along the bench seat nearer to Glo and patted her arm. 'I think you're fucking brilliant.'

Daisy woke. Her neck ached where her head had fallen forward and her mouth tasted gritty. The van seemed to be trundling slowly along darkened lanes and Daisy was suddenly aware of the strange sound the engine was making. They were obviously off the main road.

Daisy felt the corner of the lacquered box against her foot and kicked it beneath the seat. She'd think about that later when it was light enough to study it more closely. Why was she so tired, she wondered? She'd only just woken up.

'Hello, Glo. When you gets to Portsmouth . . .'

'*If* we gets to Portsmouth in this heap,' broke in Glo. 'It's on its last legs now.'

'Well, if we get near to Portsmouth we 'ave to turn

off because we don't want to go into the 'eart of the city. We need to head for Fareham first an' then Gosport.'

'I wish you'd make up your bleedin' mind. Write it down.'

'Your memory must be absolute shit,' said Daisy. She fumbled for the scrap of pencil on the dashboard. There was enough room on the newspaper to write the names down. She shoved the piece of paper under Glo's bottom on the seat.

'There,' she said. 'It's almost too dark to read it but it won't get lost.'

'If this wasn't a scrapped vehicle it might 'ave 'ad an inside light,' said Glo.

'I reckon a bleedin' inside light is the least of our troubles.' The van was coughing and spluttering.

'You can say that again. An' the brakes on this thing are crap. That's why we're not on the main road.'

'Thanks for telling me,' said Daisy. She tried to stifle a deep yawn but suspected the weeks of anguish and the after effects of the drugs had caught up with her. Despite the pain and a throbbing head she slept again.

When she opened her eyes, the windows of the van were dripping with condensation and she realised they had stopped. It was also dark and bitterly cold. She shivered. She thought how silent it was without the rattle of the van's engine.

She was aware of soft snoring. Glo was asleep

beside her. Her head lolled against the scuffed leather seat and her mouth was open.

She's nothing more than a kid, thought Daisy. But she owed her her life.

Something knocked against her window and she jumped in alarm.

But it was merely a branch. Trees and bushes seemed to be all about them almost as though the vehicle was cocooned in leaves and twigs.

No, this wasn't a dream. She was in an old van somewhere, God knows where, with the sleeping Glo at her side. She was away from Valentine Waite. Now, she thought, the next thing I have to do is make sure my son is safe. Though I feel in my heart if he wasn't I'd have known it. Vera, my lovely Vera, she'd never let any harm come to little Eddie.

Rain began pattering softly through branches. After a short while it became more intense and fell heavily on to the metal roof. To Daisy it sounded like a lullaby . . .

The next time Daisy woke it had stopped raining. The windows of the van were steamed up and Glo was already awake.

'My mouth feels like a cat's crawled in and shit in it,' she said. 'Am I really away from him?'

Daisy nodded and smiled at her. Then she shrugged her shoulders and stretched as best she could in the cramped interior.

'Don't get too comfortable. We need to get this thing right inside these trees. To my reckoning we can be seen from the road. If Waite comes looking, 'e'll find us for sure.'

'You really are scared, aren't you?'

'Too right,' said Glo.

'Can't we just drive in a bit more?'

'Last night while you was asleep I reckon I got us as near where you wants to be as possible but then the bleedin' van conked out. I let her roll in 'ere on the grass. We're in a sort of woody bit but a broken-down ol' van is going to cause gossip. We 'ave to move it further into the trees and that means pushing it. Can you put weight on your foot?'

''Course. I'll try anyway.'

It wasn't light yet but Daisy could just make out the wide arc of tall white houses on Glo's side of the van. They were elegantly columned with long, well-tended gardens to the front of them that ran down to the pavement.

They were a far cry from the tiny terraces in the heart of Gosport.

Her heart leapt. This couldn't possibly be the Crescent, could it? She wound down the window and looked out. It *was* – the Crescent at Alverstoke! She was in Gosport!

'I'm home, aren't I?' Daisy felt the rush of emotion. 'You beautiful girl, you've got me home to Gosport.'

'I got to pee.' Glo opened her door and climbed out. Daisy could see she was embarrassed. 'You want an 'and to get out? You must be burstin' as well.' Daisy nodded.

Glo stumbled round and opened Daisy's door but as soon as she put weight on her foot the pain rushed up her leg.

'Next thing I'm doin' is look at your foot.' Glo put out her hand and helped Daisy to stand. 'I ought to find a doctor for you. Or better still contact your people, your kiddie . . .'

'No!'

Daisy shouted so loudly Glo jumped away from the van. Daisy grabbed hold of her.

'Not yet. I'll be fine. I only need to rest a while.'

Glo shook her hand away. 'Ain't they all worried enough about you? Don't you think they've a right to know you're safe?'

Daisy was ready for her. 'Ain't that the first place Valentine Waite will check? And it may not be me he 'urts next time. What if my boy is safe now and because I turn up on the doorstep that bastard punishes me by 'urting him? Or my friends I told you about. Vera? Or Suze?' She held on to Glo. 'Not yet, Glo. Please don't make me do something I'm not ready for. Of course I want to see my boy, of course I got to put Vera out of her bleedin' misery, but I got to get my head together . . .'

Glo stroked Daisy's hair. 'Shh, shh,' she said. Daisy could feel the girl's heart beating almost as fast as her own. 'I understand.'

And she knew by those two words Glo really did understand.

That she felt unworthy, dirty.

Valentine Waite had robbed her of her confidence to face even the people she loved the most. But somehow, with Glo's help, she had to find out if her boy was safe and to let them know she was out of harm's way.

After a while Glo disentangled Daisy from her arms.

'Thought you wanted a pee?' With a grubby thumb she wiped Daisy's cheeks of tears. Daisy gave a wan smile, then, holding on to the sides of the van, moved towards the bushes to relieve herself.

'Watch where you're standing.' Glo waved at the wet grass. 'There might be prickles to catch your bare feet.'

'At least they'll get washed.'

Afterwards Daisy looked about her. The van *was* almost out of sight from the road, but not quite. Nearby was a road junction and across the Crescent, a hotel. The place had a sleepy atmosphere about it. But then, Alverstoke was a village, after all.

The air smelled sweet and fresh.

'Don't hang about,' shouted Glo. She came over to her, bent down and looked at her leg. 'That's not nice. Help me with this bleedin' van, then I can get it sorted.' She patted her bulging pocket and pulled out the small brown bottle of iodine. 'Got a bandage and everything.'

'Looks like you thought of everything. You did well.'

Glo drew herself to her full height, which was

around Daisy's size of five foot three. She puffed out her skinny chest and grinned wickedly.

'Didn't I just? Especially for someone who's never driven on a proper road before.'

'What! You ain't passed your driving test then?'

'What bleedin' test? The furthest I ever drove before was to move them old cars round to the place where the crusher gets 'em. The old man let me do that when 'is knees was playing up and he couldn't get in the seats. An' I'll tell you somethin' else, I wasn't half glad we was goin' forwards all the time because I couldn't find the bleedin' reverse.'

Daisy remembered when she'd woken and found Glo driving in second gear. Now she knew why. Glo didn't understand the gearbox and the need to change the gears.

'Got you 'ere though, didn't I?'

'Fucking hell,' said Daisy, and for the first time in what seemed a lifetime she laughed. And then Glo was laughing too. And they laughed until their hysteria petered out. Daisy came down to earth with a crash when Glo said, 'You stink!'

'You don't smell of roses yourself,' said Daisy, and the laughter erupted again until Glo said, 'We still got to move this bleedin' thing.'

Glo helped Daisy to the rear of the van.

'Put your hands on that corner and bleedin' push.'

Amazingly it began to move. Just a little at first but then a little more until low pine branches smacked against the back doors.

'Never thought we'd manage that,' said Glo, wiping her hands down her jeans. She stood with her hands on her skinny hips. 'Lovely row of houses, ain't they?' She nodded towards the stately buildings.

Daisy was leaning against the side of the van for support and trying not to think about pain. She wiped her forehead with the back of her hand where a sweat had broken out.

'It's mostly the 'igh-up naval people who can afford to live here,' she said. 'They was built by a bloke called Robert Cruickshank, in the nineteenth century, I think. Anyway they're certainly in the Regency style.'

Glo was looking at her in wonderment.

'How do you know all that?'

'I read a lot,' she said. She studied Glo's face. 'If I was to ask you something, I wouldn't want you to get cross with me?'

Glo looked at her. 'Ask me what you like, I don't care.'

'I don't believe you got a bad memory.'

The girl drew in a deep breath. After staring into Daisy's eyes for a while the words came out in a rush.

'You're right, I can't read. That's what you're going to ask, ain't it?'

Daisy nodded her head. 'That's why you wanted me to write down the names of the places, weren't it? So you'd recognise them?'

'So what!'

'So nothing. Do you realise what a courageous person you are?'

Glo looked down at the earth. 'No, Daisy, I ain't. I stole an ol' van that was totally unroadworthy. I broke the law an' put both our lives at risk. I could 'ave got us killed.'

'If we'd 'ave stayed with Valentine Waite I think he would have killed us,' said Daisy. 'Maybe breaking the law was the right thing to do this time.'

Glo smiled. 'I was hopin' you'd think that. Now get back in that front seat so I can clean up your wound. Then I'm off to find some food. I'm bleedin' starving!'

CHAPTER 10

Angel awoke to the strident voice of Nancy Sinatra singing 'These Boots Are Made For Walking'. The racket was coming from their neighbour and it seemed like she had to listen at top volume because the sound bellowed out all over the Clayhall estate.

Angel groaned and pulled the pillow over her head, trying to blot out the sound, but the fucking noise would wake a dead man. A bit ironic, she thought. Hadn't she, Angel, had her own walking boots on and yet she walked right back to the mess she'd tried to escape from?

She climbed out of bed and opened the steel-framed window that faced number twenty-one, where she could see the full-breasted, middle-aged figure of Amy Short dancing about the kitchen with her baby in her arms.

'Oy! You bleedin' deaf or something? Turn that down!'

Amazingly, the side door of number twenty-one opened immediately.

Plastic curlers in bright colours adorned Amy's

dyed blonde hair. She wore a wraparound pinny and the child, who couldn't have been more than a year old, was slung across one hip. Nancy Sinatra's voice had magically faded to a whimper. Amy strode up the concrete path and paused outside Angel's bedroom window. It was said she was so nosy she could hear a whisper at twenty paces.

'Well, bless my soul if it ain't Angela. About time you came home. My Malkie'll be over like a shot when he gets in from work. How's your mum? She ain't took a poorly turn, 'as she?'

'No. She's okay.' Angel was wondering what was worse, getting caught up with Amy Short and her never-ending questions or putting up with Nancy. She was beginning to think Nancy was the safer bet.

'You back from London to stay, dear?' The baby had put a finger up its nose which rather spoiled its cherubic face.

Angel sighed. She'd better concoct some kind of story or else Amy Short would give everyone within a mile radius and down to Gosport town her own version of why the wanderer had returned. Angel stared at the weed-strewn front garden and the wire netting fence as though they might give her some inspiration.

'I'm staying for a bit. The solicitor's office I'm working in is closin' for a few weeks, maybe longer, while the building is bein' renovated. We've all been given leave, paid leave. But I shall go back as soon as the builders 'ave cleared off.'

Amy Short was hanging on to her every word. Angel pulled the collar of her mother's old nightie about her neck. She hoped Mrs Short hadn't recognised it. She'd be wondering why she wasn't wearing a nightdress of her own. But then, Angel had left London in such a hurry she'd had no time to bring any of her own clothes, had she?

'Is that so, dear?' Amy had swallowed the bait. The baby had started to grizzle and its mother fished about in her grubby apron pocket, extracting a dummy and popping it in the child's mouth.

'Sorry to have yelled at you, Mrs Short, only I didn't get much bleedin' sleep last night so I was tryin' for a lie-in this morning.'

'That's all right, dear, I understand. Now, do you want me to come round later to go to the offie to get your mum's usual half bottle of gin?' She moved her child to her other hip. 'Or are you taking charge of that now?'

So that's who was getting her mother's booze, was it? And no doubt the woman was creaming a few bob out of her mother at the same time for services rendered.

'Very kind of you, Mrs Short. I think I can see to 'er for a while. Though it'd be nice to know I could call on you if I needed any help?' It stuck in her craw to kow-tow to the woman, but it was better to have the busybody as a friend than an enemy. She wondered why Amy's son was so different to his mother.

Malcolm Short was kindness itself. Boring maybe, but ever since he'd known Angel he'd idolised her.

'Of course you can, dear. Tell you what, I'll leave you to get a bit more shut-eye, and anything you need you just holler?'

'I will. See you later.'

'Fuckin' nosy old bat,' said Angel to herself behind the safety of the closed window. She pulled the threadbare curtain across on its wire, knowing Amy would soon be back in her kitchen having a good old kite across to see what was going on.

She wouldn't be able to keep her promise about toning down the music, either. 'That kiddie'll be deaf before it's five years old,' she said to the empty hall-way as she went out of the bedroom to start her first day back in Gosport.

Her mother was asleep in the chair.

Angel looked at the once vibrant woman and a lump rose in her throat.

The photograph on the mantelpiece above her mother's chair held memories of them both in swim-suits down at Stokes Bay. Her mother, Jean, had made a packed lunch with chocolate spread sand-wiches, cake, apples and a bottle of tea. They'd laughed and splashed together in the waves. She remembered her mother helping her make a sand castle using kitchen stuff they'd brought from home. A pudding basin for a base, a cup for a turret, both of them happy and contented as they'd dug out the moat with large spoons.

Even then Angel had noticed the men staring at her mother. And why not? It wasn't only Angel who thought her mother was the most beautiful woman in the world.

Dad had been at home then. Angel hated the rows. She'd cower in her bed, hoping the raised voices would go away. Always it seemed her dad was accusing her mum of something. Usually things happened only inside his head. And when her mother denied his accusations, he'd lash out at her.

Years later Angel understood it was her father's insane jealousy that caused her mother's one brief involvement with a door-to-door salesman.

Of course it destroyed the marriage.

Jean, who had loved no one but her husband, had never got over the split.

Angel's father moved away with a younger version of Jean, and Angel and her mother were left to pick up the pieces. It made the girl grow up quickly, especially as the only way Jean seemed to cope with each new day was to go out and find friends to drink with to help ease the pain.

There were no more beach days, no more walks in Stanley Park. Not much of anything for Angel really except school, which she loved. She remembered waking up in the mornings and getting herself ready for classes while her mother lay in bed, dead to the world from the party the night before, with the man or men who'd brought her home.

It got so Angel felt as though she'd become the

mother, cleaning up after Jean, washing clothes, trying for some semblance of family life.

Then the drinking didn't stop in the pub. Bottles of gin appeared indoors. As the drinking increased the standard of living went down. Jean had worked in the local greengrocer's at Clayhall shops. But after she started turning up late, then having days off with hangovers, she was told her services were no longer required. Especially when money started going missing from the till.

And now Jean was asleep in the chair she seldom left, looking twice the age she really was.

Half a bottle of gin a day.

To some people that might not sound a lot of booze. But her mother was shot to pieces with all the alcohol she'd sunk and she'd once promised Angel and the doctor that if she couldn't give it up at least she'd stick to only half a bottle a day.

Once upon a time her mother would never have agreed to that paltry amount. Then, she'd had the will to sneak up to the Fighting Cocks and stay there until she was thrown out. She'd cadge drinks or prostitute herself for a single gin, and wake to find she'd gone home with some bloke she didn't know or found she'd slept in a garden or on the beach at Stokes Bay.

Jean would say she preferred to stay indoors but she didn't have the strength to go out now. She didn't eat. She lived only for her half bottle and the dreams that came with the drunken sleep the booze produced.

Angel put the photograph back on the mantelpiece.

The smiling child's face belied the lies, the rages and, later, the drunken beatings her mother had doled out. Angel had taken the abuse for years until one day she'd walked out and caught the train from Portsmouth Harbour station to Waterloo in search of a better life.

A fuckin' different life, that's all she'd found, certainly not a better one.

Angel looked at her mother. She knew you can't help a drunk who doesn't want to be helped. Her mother was a six-stone skeleton who would probably die in that bleeding overstuffed armchair.

But Angel loved her.

'Mornin', Mother,' she said. 'Guess what? It's clean-up day.'

She went to the back door and threw wide the door, letting in the early morning sun. Still in the misshapen nightie she stepped out into the tangle of weeds and took a deep breath of fresh air. As far as the eye could see were prefabs – prefabricated homes built to ease the housing shortage after the war.

Some of the residents kept their places like little palaces, their gardens tidy and bright with flowers. Some people, like Angel's mum, had long since given up caring.

Angel could smell the sea. Over in the distance she could see the high walls of Haslar Detention Centre, which was built at the edge of the sea wall. She wondered about the lives of the detainees inside. It was awful to be caged, for whatever reason. She looked back towards the chair that her mother seldom left. Wasn't her mother caged?

Back in the kitchen she turned on the gas to discover there wasn't any. Neither was there electric light. The electric and gas company had long ago stopped trusting her mother to pay bills. Prepayment meters had been installed. Angel found her bag and slipped in the appropriate coins and the prefab shuddered to life again. Within minutes the kettle was on, the boiler was on, and Angel was brushing her teeth with the toothbrush she'd taken from the Black Bear. As she brushed, her mind returned to the night she'd spent in the room over the pub, lying in Roy Kemp's arms. She thought of his kisses, his muscled body, his lovemaking.

Roy hadn't seen the last of her, she'd make sure of that.

CHAPTER 11

'Daisy, wake up.'

Through her dream-filled sleep Daisy became aware of Glo's voice and a hand gently shaking her shoulder. She struggled to a sitting position. God, would this thumping headache never leave her? Glo was in the driver's seat. She looked worried. In her hand was a brown paper bag and Daisy could smell fresh baking. Then it registered in her mind that the girl was wearing different clothes.

'Eat this.' Glo pushed the bag at her. Inside was a meat pie. 'Go on, eat it. I already had mine.'

Daisy blinked at her.

'Where did you get it?' Daisy's voice sounded far away and as though it didn't belong to her, but she did as Glo asked and took the bag.

'There's a little village up the road, pretty little place with a tree in the middle of it. There's a cake shop there.' Daisy realised she meant the Alverstoke Bakery. It was well known for its delicious baking. 'C'mon, eat some of it.' Daisy fumbled the pie from the brown paper and bit into it. The meat was still warm. It was steak and kidney, her favourite. She surprised herself by gobbling every last morsel. She handed back the empty bag to Glo, who looked relieved but worried again when Daisy shivered uncontrollably.

'Well, at least there's nothing wrong with your appetite.' She smiled at Daisy. 'There's some milk here.' She bent down and picked up a bottle and popped the foil top with her thumb. 'Get this down you,' she said.

Daisy accepted the milk and drank deeply.

'Where did you get the money from for all this?'

Glo coloured. 'From Valentine Waite's wallet. Anyway that ain't your problem. Are you feeling a bit better?'

'I guess,' said Daisy. She was feeling warmer now.

'Thank Christ for that. You been dead to the world for nearly a day and a half.'

Daisy stared at her, at first unwilling to believe her words, but Glo had no reason to lie.

'Where d'you get them new clothes you got on . . .'

'They ain't new. Well, they are to me, but . . . oh well, I can't tell you a lie. I stole the stuff off washing lines.'

'Glo!'

Glo stared at her defiantly. 'I can't take it back, can I? An' what's done is done. You're a silly cow. You been sweatin' and feverish an' I been out of me mind with worry . . . I need to keep you warm an' clean an' fed . . .'

Daisy pulled her into her arms.

'I'm sorry. You're right, I am a silly, selfish cow. But if someone saw you and telephoned the police . . .'

Glo shook her head. 'I was careful, Daisy. I'm not stupid.'

'But it's still stealing.'

'Only a little bit,' Glo said. 'I just wish . . .'

Daisy silenced her with a look. She knew what was coming. 'No,' she said. 'There's no way I could present meself to the questions and answers I'm going to 'ave to come up with. When I think of me little boy all pink an' clean an' smelling like talcum powder an' warm milk, I know I'm not worthy to be anywhere near 'im. Especially after what that bastard Valentine Waite made me . . .'

Daisy began to sob. She knew she was being illogical. What had happened to her wasn't her fault. She was the victim and what she wanted more than anything was to put her arms around little Eddie and to see Vera's dear face again. But logic didn't take away the feeling that she was filthy, despoiled. She wiped her face with her hand. Glo had let her cry.

'I do know 'ow you feel,' Glo told her. 'It's no good me saying each day will take you one step further away from the pain because you won't believe me. You're ill, but you'll get better. I promised I'd look after you and I will.'

163

'You're a good friend,' Daisy said quietly.

Yet all the time she had been a prisoner she'd wanted nothing more than to be back with her family.

'Let me at least get you to an 'ospital.'

Daisy gave her another withering look.

'The bleedin' 'ospital staff would want to know how I got the injuries. They'd want to examine me. I can't even bear to think about it.' And as to facing Roy Kemp? How could she even begin to tell him?

'I got some water in a Corona bottle and some clean clothes for you. I'm goin' to wash you, or you can do it yourself.' Glo bent to forage in the front of the van and came up with a small bag out of which she produced a cake of Imperial Leather soap. 'I'm going to redo your bandage and afterwards you can sleep. I've made up a bed in the back of the van. You'll be able to stretch out a bit there. The sooner you begin to feel more like your old self, the better.'

Daisy opened her mouth to speak but Glo said, 'Don't thank me, Daisy. You're the first proper friend I've 'ad.' Glo's eyes filled with tears. 'I walked up to this pub in the village. I stood outside thinking I could pick up a punter and maybe get some money off 'im for a quickie in the churchyard. You need proper medicine, Daisy, and Waite's money is nearly gone. But I couldn't do it. All those times I been man-handled and it's like something 'as bleedin' shut down inside me. I never want to 'ave to do a man again, not never. You ain't cross with me, are you, Daisy?'

Daisy put her arm out from the blanket and

enveloped the girl. When she got back home she'd make it up to Glo.

Later, Daisy lay on the makeshift bed. It was harder than the front seat in the van but bliss to be able to stretch out her legs. Glo had insisted on clearing up after her, throwing away the dirty water from the plastic bowl she'd somehow got hold of and then producing a bag of doughnuts and two bottles of Guinness for their supper.

Daisy was tired, but happier than she'd been for ages and at last it seemed her head was beginning to feel as though it belonged to her again. Even the pain of her ankle, which Glo had bathed for her and covered with strips of clean sheeting, seemed to be easing.

'Do you know you cry your little boy's name out in your sleep?'

Glo was sitting beside her. She screwed up the paper bag that had contained the doughnuts. Daisy could still smell the sugary sweetness of them.

'At least you know about my child. I know absolutely nothing about you.'

'Nothing to tell,' said Glo.

In the fast-fading light Daisy could see such sadness in the girl's eyes.

'Go on. Tell me about it,' she said. Glo sighed. She drank the last dregs from the Guinness bottle and put it down carefully as though taking her time before embarking on a journey of words she wasn't sure she wanted to share.

'I don't want you to think bad of me, Daisy. I done some terrible things.'

'More likely 'ad bad things done to you, I would think. You don't have to tell me nothing you don't want to.'

Glo gave a big sigh. 'I want to. I was about five years old when I found out the woman I called Mum wasn't me mother. She wasn't anyone's mother, just an old bag who ran the house where we all lived and sometimes cooked for us. There was eight of us. I was the youngest. The eldest, a boy, was about nine. I just thought we was a family. I never wondered why we didn't all 'ave the same colour skin. We lived in this 'ouse in London, not that I knew it was London, not then, and it was falling to bits. In one bedroom you could see the sky through the 'ole in the roof.'

She paused. Daisy put her hand on Glo's arm. The girl had guts, that was for sure, she thought.

'None of us went to school. None of us ever left the 'ouse. There was a couple of rooms where all us kids slept on the floor on mattresses. It was cool in summer and bloody freezing cold in winter. We used to pile everything we could find on to our beds to keep warm, even an old bit of carpet.'

'What about your real parents?'

'I never knew 'em. I don't think any of us remembered our real parents. Like I said, I always thought this woman we called Ma was our mum. Later I found out we was all unwanted or stolen children. And we was there to make money.'

'How?'

'How do you think, you silly cow?'

'Oh, Glo.' The penny had dropped. Glo had been forced into child prostitution.

'We all thought when we went into that room and the men played with us and got us to play with them it was normal. We didn't know any different, 'ow could we? We was told the men were "uncles", and when we was 'urt, we was given sweets afterwards.

'I 'ad a special friend, his name was Timmy. He was pretty with wispy blond hair and big blue eyes. He went into the Blue Room a lot. That's what we called that special room downstairs 'cause it had glossy blue curtains and a blue bedspread that was silky and shiny. Timmy went into the Blue Room more than any of us. The bed was made out of logs of wood, like it had come from a ship's cabin or something.' Glo's eyes glazed and Daisy could see she was remembering as though it was happening now.

'It was funny really. We all knew what was going to happen when Mum said, "Get down to the Blue Room." We daren't disobey her. There was a man there as well, his name was Uncle George. He never touched us, just shouted a lot. We was scared of 'im though. From time to time one of the kids would disappear after being in the Blue Room. We was told they'd gone on 'oliday with the "uncle" and we accepted it. Later I discovered that if a child had been accidentally killed, the child would just vanish. That was what going on holiday really meant.'

'You mentioned Timmy?'

Daisy could see, even in the dull light inside the van, that Glo's eyes were bright with tears.

'I'm sorry. I shouldn't have asked.'

'It's all right. I need to get it off me chest. Like I said, Timmy was called to spend a lot of time in the Blue Room. Afterwards he'd 'ave nightmares and I'd cuddle him, pretend he was me real brother. Especially bad they were after he was lent out.'

'What do you mean, lent out?'

'Sometimes a few of us would be smartened up, new clothes, hair washed and such, and taken in a car to a different house. A party would be going on, mostly men drinking and eating and watching dirty films, and then we'd be the bleedin' entertainment in another locked room. One after another the blokes would use us. I used to make me mind go blank. Timmy came to me one night and crawled in bed beside me, 'e was crying more than usual and he kept on fidgeting so I yelled at 'im to go to sleep. Told 'im he was a bleedin' nuisance and I was tired of 'im. After a while he got out of bed and I went back to sleep. Later, I got up to go to the lavatory. There was never any bulbs in the light fittings but luckily we could all make our way about in the dark. Anyway I crept downstairs. When I got near the bottom step this thing brushed against my 'ead. I put my hand out and felt a foot. It was cold and swinging about. Then I was screaming and the whole house woke up. Timmy had got some rope and tied it to the top banister rail and hanged 'imself. I keep thinking if I 'adn't told 'im to clear off he'd be alive today. He was eight years old.'

She buried herself in Daisy's arms and wept. After a while she disentangled herself and searched beside the makeshift bed. She found what she was searching for and flipped the top off a Corona bottle and gulped the orangeade. She passed the bottle to Daisy.

'I should never have asked,' said Daisy.

Glo took the bottle from her and replaced it beside the bed. 'You want to tell me a bit more about you?'

'We've all the time in the world to talk about me. You go on, but only if you want to,' said Daisy.

'The house was in an uproar. Mum and George cut Timmy down and we was packed off to bed again like nothing out of the ordinary had happened. I never knew what they did with Timmy's body. It was like he'd never been. Soon after, I was thirteen an' I didn't get to go to the Blue Room as much as the others by then. I was too old.'

'Too old at thirteen?'

Glo nodded. 'For blokes as likes kids. I was bein' threatened with bein' put in a proper brothel, then, one night at a gambling party, I was put up as collateral, that's what they called it. This bloke won. So he took me to this big 'ouse in the country and I thought it was the most beautiful place I'd ever seen. All I was to 'im was a servant that he knocked about and fucked any way he wanted. But I got fed. I was terrified of 'im. I still am.'

'Valentine Waite?'

Glo nodded.

'I was a prisoner. I could roam around the 'ouse and out in the grounds but I never thought to run away from 'im. Sometimes he'd get really angry with me an' beat me. All you've gone through I've gone through as well. I was properly cowed down by that bastard. And without confidence you get nothing. The only woman he ever loved was 'is mother. You look like her, Daisy. Did you know that? Of course, I've only ever seen photos. She was small and blonde. I'm sure 'e wanted to keep you close to 'im, Daisy, 'cause you remind 'im of 'is mum.'

'Well, fuck that,' said Daisy.

She could understand Glo as a prisoner of Waite accepting her fate. She'd read of this happening. There was even a name for it, the name of some foreign city, she thought. Like Belgium Syndrome or something. Stockholm, that was it. Why that place she had no idea. Glo was still talking.

'Sometimes he goes away for days on end. But sometimes he lets me go in with 'im to the scrapyards. That's 'ow I got to look after you. That old bloke who runs that place is as deaf and blind as a post. So it was easy for Waite to 'ide you away so the old man didn't know you was there.'

'He must be quite mad,' said Daisy. 'How can he do that? More to the point, why?'

'Dunno. Maybe 'is mother rejected 'im. Maybe she kept leaving 'im. Yeah, perhaps that's why he kept you locked up. Did you show an interest in 'im then change your mind?'

Daisy thought back to Vera's party when she'd told Waite she wanted nothing more to do with him.

'Sort of,' she said. 'Would he ever 'ave let me go?' Why Daisy was asking, she had no idea. She knew he would have kept her a prisoner for ever – or until he decided a worse fate for her.

'Doubt it. You've been useful to him.'

'Useful?'

'Your money, Daisy.'

Money? Daisy didn't know what Glo was on about. She'd had very little money on her when he'd abducted her from her car. She didn't know where her handbag was now, but there'd been little of value in it, apart from her chequebook. The object she mourned most was her gold bracelet that Eddie had bought her. It had never left her wrist since he had put it there.

'What money?' Daisy was frowning.

'Why do you think he's been drugging you? So you wouldn't escape? So you'd never get that bloody ankle chain off?'

Daisy's brain had been so messed up, she'd never really thought about it.

'Now you've mentioned it, why *was* I drugged?'

Glo sighed. 'I can't keep it from you any longer. Anyway, I want everything between us out in the open. Don't you remember signing things?'

And then Daisy did remember, him guiding her hand, steadying it.

'Oh God! What did I put my name to?'

'Don't be angry with me.'

'How can I be, when I don't know what to be angry about?' Daisy saw Glo take a deep breath.

'Valentine Waite made you sign cheques out to me, then 'e took me to the bank so I could collect the money.'

Daisy looked at her. Tears were glittering.

'But you'd need some form of identification before they'd give you money. You said you've no idea who you are or where you come from?'

'Grow up, Daisy. I got a birth certificate. Even got a passport. They don't necessarily belong to me but they're mine. Waite's money saw to that.'

'So you stole some of my money?'

'I didn't do it because I wanted it for meself. And he would have beat . . .' Glo was openly weeping now.

Daisy let the outburst subside a little. Then she asked, 'But surely he 'as money?'

'Had. Had money, Daisy. I told you, 'e gambles. He's up to 'is neck in debt.'

Daisy wanted to scream out loud. But what good would that have done? Alert neighbours to them living in the van? Besides, she didn't have the strength to scream.

She thought about all that Glo had told her. If she had no money in her bank account then who was paying her bills? Eddie's mum and Pappy in the retirement home for a start? That cost a fair whack a month. And what about the money to run the house in Western Way? Thank God little Eddie's money put aside for his future couldn't be touched by anyone.

Glo was crying softly now.

Would Daisy have acted the way Glo had? The answer was yes. She wouldn't have had any choice.

The girl didn't have to confess, did she? She'd done so to keep the slate clean between them. And without Glo, Daisy would still be a prisoner.

'Daisy?' Glo's voice was hardly more than a whisper.

'Yes?'

'I got something for you.' Daisy heard her fingers scrabbling against the metal floor. After a while she seemed to find what she was looking for. 'Hold your 'and out,' she said.

Daisy felt the warmth of the girl's fingers and the coldness of the metal as it slipped over her wrist.

'It's your bracelet. I stole it off 'im.'

Daisy felt the familiar shape of the gold bangle. It *was* her bracelet! She knew every pattern etched on the gold. She remembered that afternoon in Southampton when Eddy had run down to the jewellers and bought it for her. She remembered that bedroom in the pub in the New Forest where they'd made love and the room they'd shared had become their own special island.

'Thank you,' she said softly. 'This bracelet means more to me than you could ever know.'

And she knew then that nothing else mattered.

From that great love, she had little Eddie. Daisy vowed that, as soon as she could walk with Glo's help, they'd leave this van. For all Glo's denial that she'd never let another man use her body, she knew when the money was gone Glo would put her fears aside rather then let them both starve. It was time to pay Glo back. Tomorrow they'd leave this place.

Glo was crying again.

'Come 'ere,' said Daisy. 'Hush. How can I go to sleep if you keep that noise up?'

CHAPTER 12

Angel was stirring the teapot, gazing at the brown liquid, when Malkie Short pushed his bike round to the shed at number twenty-one, waving to her as he passed. Angel got out another mug. She knew he'd come to her first before he went indoors. She'd been home a fortnight but already it had become a habit.

'Good night?' she asked, passing him the steaming mug before he'd allowed his long rangy body to loop itself around one of the plastic-covered kitchen stools.

He grinned at her then put his mug on the floor. From his inside pocket he took out a box of Cadbury's chocolates and handed them to her.

'Gift for a pretty girl,' he said.

'You know you shouldn't bleedin' spoil me, Malkie,' Angel said. She took them from him and their fingers touched briefly. 'Thank you.' Somehow he always made her feel special even if he did wince every time she swore.

'They're cut price from the market.'

'It don't bloody matter,' she said. 'It's the thought that counts.' Another man wouldn't have been so honest, but that was Malkie, honest through and through, he was one of the good men. 'I bet you're tired, aren't you?' Malkie worked at the Queen's, a hotel facing The Hard at Portsmouth. He was a night porter, had been since leaving school. Angel reckoned he'd have the same job until he retired.

He left his mother's prefab around seven at night on his bike. He cycled down Clayhall Road and over Haslar Bridge then took his bike with him over on the ferry and returned the same way around seven in the mornings. You could practically set your clock by him.

'Not really. When it's quiet I can catch a bit of shut-eye. Anyway I don't need as much sleep as some.' He winked at her. It was well known that given the opportunity Angel would stay in bed all day. He pushed back the long fair hair that constantly flopped across his forehead.

'How's your mum?'

'Asleep.' Angel put her own mug down on the enamelled top and said, 'I don't know what I'd 'ave done without you these past weeks.' He coloured up. 'I . . . er . . . I . . .'

Angel put her finger on his lips. 'Shh. There's not many men would 'ave helped me scrub this place out and get it fit to live in again.' Malkie had even begged a lawn mower from someone and had pushed it up and down the back garden until the tall grass, once it had been scythed and the rubbish disposed of, now resembled a balding lawn. He'd also got hold of some cream paint and painted the bathroom walls and put down a piece of new lino. 'I couldn't 'ave done it without your 'elp,' she said.

'It's all right,' he said gruffly. Angel could see she was embarrassing him so she picked up his mug and pushed it into his hand.

'Drink it before it gets cold,' she said.

'Yeah. We still going to town this afternoon?'

Angel nodded. 'Can you get hold of the car?' She was thrilled when he'd said he could borrow his mate's car, it would make a change to get off the estate for a while. Maybe they could drive out to the beach. The sun was hot today. He finished his tea in a couple of gulps and set his mug on the tabletop.

'Picking it up at half past twelve.'

'You sure you'll have had enough sleep?'

'A couple of hours and I'll be on top of the world.'

She held the door for him as he walked past her and down the concrete path. He wouldn't be late. He was dependable, was Malkie.

Jean was stirring herself as Angel entered the living room with a cup of weak tea.

'Brought you this, Mum.'

'I don't think I fancy a cup of tea.'

Angel sighed but she put the china cup and saucer on the coffee table. Her mother had wet herself in her sleep. The smell of urine eclipsed the sweet smell of the polish Angel had used the previous day.

'The first thing I'm going to do is get you in that bleedin' bath again. Then I'm going to force a bit of toast down you.' Her mother began waving a thin arm about in protest but Angel cut her off. 'I'm going out later with Malkie. I got a day off for good behaviour,' she said. 'Amy's coming over to sit with you . . .'

'I don't need nobody . . .'

'I'm well aware of that but it'd make me feel better knowing you got a bit of company. I won't have to rush back then.' Angel picked up the cup and placed it in her mother's hands and practically forced it to her lips. Jean took a few sips then shuddered.

'Don't want it,' she said. Angel left her mother to go and run a bath.

As the steam hit the bathroom mirror she wiped a path on the glass with her hand and stared at herself. Her face had a grey tinge to it and she looked tired. Thank God she was getting away from the place for a few hours with Malkie.

Angel thought about the pile of washing she'd need to get out on the line beforehand. The pissy clothing her mother had presented her with. She'd need to turn the chair cushion and put on a clean . . .

Angel threw up in the sink.

When the nausea had passed she splashed cold water on her face then wiped the mirror again, this time with a towel. At least the colour had returned to her face.

When the water was neither too hot nor too cold and filled with scented bubbles Angel went back into the living room and practically forced her mother to relinquish her clothing. With great care she steadied Jean through to the bathroom. She had to lift her mother's almost weightless form into the bath where she soaped her frail body.

'Bloody men,' said Jean, with a strength that seemed to come from nowhere.

'What d'you mean, Mum?'

'I know I look a sight. Your father did this to me. I used to be such a pretty girl until the drink took hold of me.'

Angel wanted to say her mother had allowed the drink to take hold, that she should have been stronger and told her father to fuck off ages before he finally left the pair of them. But she couldn't. It wasn't her mother's fault that she had no willpower.

'He gave me my first drink, you know, Angie.'

'I know, Mum. It was in the Albert down Queen's Road, you was fifteen years old and he bought you a gin and orange.'

'Have I told you this before, Angie?'

Angel nodded. 'A couple of times.'

It didn't take much effort to pull her mother's bag of bones out of the water and pat her dry. Then she smoothed a little lily of the valley talcum powder over Jean's skin. Angel held her close and with difficulty slipped a cotton nightdress over her and half carried, half walked her into the second bedroom where Jean's bed was freshly made up.

'I don't want to be in bed.'

'I know you don't. But you've messed that bleedin'

chair and you can't go back until I've sorted it. I'll take you back there soon, I promise.'

Jean glared at her. 'Can I 'ave . . . ?'

'A small one? I suppose so.'

Angel lifted Jean into the clean bed and tucked her in. She was so thin, the bed looked as though it was still empty. Angel was soon back with a small glass of gin. Jean downed it shakily and laid her head on the pillow. Her mother's eyes were already closed. The effort of the bath had taken its toll.

An hour later Jean's soiled clothing and the rest of the washing was billowing on the line. When Angel had sorted the chair cushion she went back into the bedroom to check on her mother and was pleased to see she was asleep.

When Malkie opened the kitchen door, Angel was ready. She was excited. Apart from a single trip into town to the market to buy a few needed clothes she'd spent the rest of the time cleaning the prefab.

'I saw the car. Who did you get it from?' She'd seen him drive up in the black Austin A40 and park it in the layby on the road.

'I told you, a mate. He got it cheap but it's in good nick. A bit of a bugger as it's a left-hand drive. But we'll do fine. You ready?'

Angel looked down at her short green checked skirt and her white cotton top. It wasn't exactly the

London look but it was new from Bernie's market stall and she felt good.

'Don't I look bleedin' ready?' She couldn't resist teasing him because she knew he'd blush and stammer when he had to compliment her. She pulled back a wayward strand of hair and tucked it behind her ear. It refused to stay because it was freshly washed and fell back in a blonde curtain about her face.

'You look, er, you look lovely.'

Angel laughed. She grabbed her cardigan, it certainly wasn't cold but a wind could blow in from the Solent at any time.

'Mum'll be over soon, she told me to tell you.'

Angel nodded. Malkie opened the back door and once they were out on the path Angel slipped her arm through his. He smelled of fresh soap and as he turned and looked down at her Angel felt a pang of remorse. He was a nice man. Certainly too nice for her. For a fleeting moment she wished she could care about Malkie as much as he cared for her. He was an okay-looking bloke except that his rangy body meant his sleeves always seemed too short and his trouser legs needed an extra couple of inches on the bottoms. A good woman would have solved that problem, let his trouser legs down and sorted his cuffs, thought Angel, but Malkie never seemed to bother much with women. She knew she only had to say the word and he'd be her personal slave forever.

'It's nice sitting here and watching the scenery,' she said later in the car. The trees were very green and the fields seemed to stretch for miles to the sea beneath a sky that was a brilliant shade of blue. They were driving along the coast road before passing through the small village of Alverstoke where the road curved into Jellicoe Avenue and down towards Bury Road and the town.

Malkie didn't seem fazed by the car having the gears on the other side. He'd told her quite a few Austins had been made that way for export.

'Perhaps we could stop here on the way back and take a walk along the beach,' Malkie said.

'That would be lovely,' she said. 'But I don't want to make you late for work on my account.'

'That's for me to worry about.'

The sun was shining and Angel wound the window down, glad of the fresh air that blew in from the fields.

'It feels good to be away from the prefabs.'

'It can't have been easy deciding to return to your mum after the way she's treated you in the past,' he said. Angel wasn't going to tell him she'd come home because she'd nowhere else to run to. His mother had probably told him about the fictional offices where she'd said she was working and that she was on full pay. Angel decided this wasn't the time to bare her soul. Though if she ever unburdened herself it would be to Malkie. 'There's not many would have sent home money regularly like you,' he said.

'Guilt payments.'

Angel didn't add that all the time she'd been away,

part of her conscience had nagged her about the health of her mother while the other part had urged her to have a life of her own. 'It isn't that good being on your own in London.'

'Well, you're back home now.'

Angel smiled at him. He was such a nice man and she enjoyed being with him. But she couldn't produce the spark that would ignite other feelings for him; couldn't make herself feel passion. Angel knew of only one man who came close to doing that and he had been a one-night stand. Roy Kemp.

She was still thinking about him when Malkie parked the car near Walpole Park.

'It's market day,' he said. 'Fancy a look around?'

'A look is all I'm doing,' she said. 'I mustn't buy anything more than a bunch of flowers to cheer up the prefab . . .'

'Mum said you were being paid full whack while your workplace renovations were being carried out.' Angel stopped walking as he pulled her round to face him. He towered above her. 'None of that's true, is it?' Angel looked up into his worried face. She took a deep breath.

'That's the trouble with lies, they trip you up. All right, I'm not working in a posh job. I made that up—'

She didn't need to finish the sentence. 'On the spur of the moment so my old lady wouldn't go blabbing the truth all over the prefabs,' Malkie said.

Angel nodded. 'I was working as an exotic dancer.'

His eyes opened wide. 'Don't you go judging me,' she snapped. A woman loaded with bags of vegetables gave her a look of reproach as she passed by.

'Let's sit down on that bench and you can tell me about it.' Malkie pulled her towards one of the wooden benches beneath the trees.

'But that's just it, Malkie, I don't want to talk about it.' She faced him. 'I came home because I had to. Let it go at that. If I was going to talk to anyone about my life there, it would be you, but . . .'

'Okay, love. Your secret's safe with me.' He smoothed back a strand of long hair that had blown across her face, tucking it behind her ear. 'What I suggest is this. We forget about this conversation, take a walk around the market, then the shops, and end up by eating a fish dinner in that little place near the ferry. What do you think?'

Angel relaxed.

'I'd really like that,' she said.

He got up, held out his hand and pulled her to her feet.

Angel tucked her arm through his as they set off across the road, past the library towards the market.

They wandered through the gaily coloured stalls decked with materials, books, fruit and veg, every so often stopping to look at some trinket or other. They paused at the clothes stall where racks of fashion items spilled from hangers. Mini-skirts, maxi coats, crocheted waistcoats, all crying out to be loved and bought.

Fingering the clothes was torment. Angel so wanted to buy that dress, the short yellow crepe one with the orange circle on the front.

'Just your size, ducky,' said the woman stallholder. Angel dropped her hand from the dress on the hanger, smiled at the woman and began to walk away. Malkie pulled her back.

'You like that, don't you?'

Angel shrugged.

'Wrap it up,' he said quickly. He took a note out of his wallet and handed it to the woman, who gave him change from the pouch at her waist and in the blink of an eye had the dress off the rail and hanger and in a bag. Malkie presented it to Angel.

'I can't take this,' she said. She tried to push the bag back at him.

'It's paid for now and I don't think the woman wants to give a refund,' he said.

'Nah, don't give refunds,' she said, and laughed, showing blackened teeth. 'You got a good 'un there, ducky, you 'ang on to 'im.'

Malkie grabbed Angel's hand and moved through the crush of people. Angel allowed herself to be rushed away from the market and through a deep alleyway into the main street where shops beckoned from either side. She found she was almost running to keep up with his long-legged stride.

'I never expected you to buy me stuff,' she said, 'but thank you.'

'It gives me pleasure,' he said. 'And I'm not stupid.

You must 'ave left London . . .' Angel began to protest but he shouted her down. 'Let me finish. You left there in a hurry. I know because you got no clothes with you. The clobber you got on, you bought in Gosport. And you used to be the smartest girl in the prefabs, always wearing new gear because that's what you spent your money on after you saw to your mum. You can't fool me, Angel.'

'I feel as if I'm still at bleedin' school being told off,' she said.

'So you should. Sometimes people want to be nice without any ulterior motives.' He was guiding her through a small street that led to the grounds of Trinity Church. 'Want to look round inside?' He nodded towards the majestic stone building.

The last thing Angel wanted was to be enclosed in a musty-smelling church, however beautiful.

'I don't like crypts and the dead people in the churchyard,' she said. 'I'll go in if you really want to but I'd much rather sit on the grass. I need to be out in the fresh air and feel the sun on me face.'

He shrugged. 'Fine with me.'

Angel sank down on the soft short grass and lay back in the sunshine. She heard the swish, swish of the oak trees as the light wind lifted their leaves and thought how nice it was to be simply lying there and doing nothing. He sat down beside her, the package between them. After brushing back his fair hair he said, 'Me dad's coming 'ome soon.'

Angel sat up and looked at him in surprise. His dad

spent so much time away from home you could forget Amy Short had a husband. He was a brickie, a stocky man, handy with his fists but just as handy with a smile.

'Is 'e still working in Dublin?'

'Yeah. He goes where the money is. It was a good contract and there's still another six months to run.'

'Your mum must miss 'im.'

'If she does, she don't talk about it. Look what happened last time he came home? I was an only child and she believed at her age 'er days of having kiddies was over. She thought she was on the change and 'ome comes Dad and there she is, knocked up.'

'She didn't mind, did she?'

'Didn't 'ave to, did she? Our Billy's a good little soul. Our mum reckons it's all the Guinness our dad drinks over there. Gives 'im the strength of ten men.'

Angel started laughing. She sank down on one elbow and stared at him. 'You make me bloody laugh, you do, Malkie,' she said. He was busy taking his jacket off.

'Oh, funny am I?' He threw his jacket on the grass and began tickling her in the ribs and she squirmed away from him, rolling over in the warm sun, giggling. Then she sat back, leaning on him, her face to the sun again, listening to the fast beating of his heart.

'Thank you,' she said.

'What for?'

'For being you.' She closed her eyes. He lay back on the grass and she lay with him, her head still on his chest, listening to the sound of the birds and the hum of visitors' voices as they wandered around the grounds of the church.

Angel guessed she must have dozed off. Malkie was shaking her gently.

'Come on,' he said. 'Time to eat. I need to get fuelled up for work tonight and I bet you've 'ardly eaten anything today.'

'Fish and chips from the Porthole?'

He nodded and helped her to her feet, and together they set off across the green and back into the cobbled street.

The entrance and frying room of the Porthole were on the main road and at the back the customers sat and ate. The place was well known for its quality and cheap prices.

'I'm starving,' said Angel, sniffing the heavenly aroma that wafted across the road. 'Can I 'ave cod and chips and lashings of vinegar?'

'You can 'ave what you like. Go through and find a table and I'll order at the counter,' he said. 'Tea?'

'Please. And bread an' butter.'

She found a table and put her package on the seat next to her. Conversation and background music was soothing, she decided. After a little while, Malkie appeared and slid onto a chair opposite her.

'Shouldn't be long,' he said.

And within minutes a waitress placed two plates of succulent fish and chips on the table and left to reappear again with bread and butter and two teas in thick white cups and saucers.

'Salt? Pepper?' Malkie asked, pushing the condiments towards her. Those two words were all she heard before the overwhelming desire to vomit forced her to rise quickly from the table and make for the toilet.

Angel lifted her head from the bowl of the lavatory pan and with nothing at all left inside her stomach stared at the white tiles. After a while, she sat back on her haunches and wiped her mouth with the back of her hand. A similar bout of sickness had occurred last night and for no good reason she could think of. She hoped she wasn't sickening for something.

She got up and pulled the chain. She ran the tap and patted her face with cold water, then pulled some toilet paper off the roll and wiped herself. God, she could do with that cup of tea now to wash away the nasty taste in her mouth.

The sick feeling was completely gone now. She ran her hands over her stomach and up over her breasts which were a little tender. But that was because her period was due.

And then the realisation hit her.

Her period wasn't due. It was overdue.

Since she'd got back to Gosport she'd not kept a proper check on her dates. The back of her neck went icy cold and her heart started thumping.

Oh God, no! It couldn't be!

She was pregnant. And Roy Kemp must be the father.

Vera couldn't believe her eyes. There, walking arm in arm with a dozy-looking blond bloke, was that tart that had been shagging Roy!

'Bold as brass!' she muttered to herself as she slipped inside The World's Stores doorway so she could get a better look, yet be hidden if they glanced her way. She couldn't place the girl though she looked familiar, but the man, now she could study him, was a local lad, whatsisname's boy – bloke from Clayhall as came into the massage parlour when he was home from his brickie's job in Dublin. The girl was a looker all right. 'Bold as bleedin' brass,' she said to herself again.

Then it hit her. Brass. Brassy, more like. It was Angela Moore. Her mother Jean was a drunk. Not her fault, the poor woman couldn't handle the way her prick of a man had treated her. It had been put about that Angela was working for a solicitor. Solicitor my arse, she thought. *Soliciting* more like it, at that shady London open-all-hours clip joint she was working in.

Still, if she wanted it kept a secret then it was nobody's business but Angela's. But what was she doing with that Malcolm lad?

More to the point, what had the bitch been up to fucking Roy Kemp? Daisy would be right pissed off if she got to hear about that, poor little cow. Vera watched as the man pulled the girl into him, protecting her from a drunk weaving along the street. Something going on there, thought Vera. Yes, something going on there all right. 'Just as well, Angela Moore,' she whispered. 'You bleedin' stay away from Roy Kemp.'

'Vera?' Her thoughts were interrupted by a familiar voice. 'You coming inside the shop or are you just gonna block the doorway?'

'Wotcha,' she said to the gingerheaded man in the green overalls. She stepped into the coolness and sniffed the mixture of spices, loose teas, biscuits and candles. Si, the shop's manager and the son of one of her long-time clients, looked more like his dad every day. He was also Susie's husband and worshipped the ground the girl walked on.

'You come in for them broken chocolate biscuits I was telling you I'd put by, ain't you?'

'Yeah.' Vera thought quickly. 'I reckoned if I could take 'em now we could 'ave a bit of a picnic in the back garden this afternoon. You know 'ow Suze and little Eddie likes them. Got any broken Bourbons in with 'em?'

Si laughed and his freckles joined together round his eyes. He was a lovely lad, thought Vera, not a nasty bone in his body. Vera supposed he'd have freckles all over his body, just like his dad.

'For you, anything, Vera.' She walked behind him into the depths of the shop that was the best grocery store for miles around. Si was very well thought of by the management. He'd been employed there since he'd left school, starting as a delivery boy and working his way up. Vera nodded greetings to the three assistants who smiled politely and got on with their business of serving.

All the dry goods were in glass-covered tins and boxes and you could get anything you wanted, including lovely hams and cheeses that were outside in the coolroom. Vera eyed the dried fruits, their colours enticing, scoops at the ready. Nice biscuits, Garibaldi, fig rolls, custard creams, the tins tipped at an angle so you could see the contents. She knew Si liked his job there. Soon he came back with two large blue bulging sugar bags and a parcel wrapped in greaseproof. He grinned at her.

'Take these 'ome. There's a nice bit of 'am off the bone there to make some sarnies for your tea party.'

'Thanks,' she said. She knew she had a daft grin on her face but she didn't care. This kind man made her Susie a very happy girl. 'See you later, Si love.'

As Vera stepped into the hot sunshine again her thoughts flew back to Angela Moore.

'I'm keepin' an eye on you, Missy,' she promised.

CHAPTER 13

Vinnie Endersby sighed. So the big man wants to see me as much as I need to see him, does he? He looked through the window at the dirty streets. A dog was crapping on a pavement in front of a fish and chip shop. A used car lot proclaimed 'Great Deals'. He gave a wry grin. A great deal of the cars seemed to be held together with fillers. The taxi slid into the street of terraced houses.

'You can drop me here, mate. I'll walk the rest of the way.'

He paid the driver, tipped him and got out. He felt like a kid who had been summoned to another kid's house for tea after school so the mother could check him out to see if he was a suitable friend. He looked at the house numbers and paused outside the one with sparkling white net curtains and a brass doorknocker polished to within an inch of its life. He felt guilty touching its glittering surface. The air was cooler today but it was fine after the storms earlier.

'You must be Detective Sergeant Endersby.' The woman with the blue rinse gave him a warm smile. A delicious smell had followed her out to the front door and now wafted over him. Home baking. It had been a long time since he'd smelled such a heavenly aroma. His ex-wife hadn't gone in much for domestic pursuits.

'I am,' he said.

'Well, come on in. I'm Mrs Kemp. You can call me Violet,' she said over her shoulder. 'Pull the door closed behind you, dear. Do you know I've a fancy I've seen you before? Go to the fights, do you?'

She was sharp. So she'd remembered him chatting to Freddie Mills when Roy had brought Daisy Lane over to meet the great boxer.

'I do that. I saw Valentine Waite knock out Sal Widdicombe in the third round. Not a mark on Waite but Widdicombe looked like he'd gone through a potato masher . . .'

'I saw that,' she said, turning and facing him. 'Me and Vi, that's Vi Kray, we sat in the front row. We like the fights. Comes from having fighting families I expect, dear. What I say is, you can't beat a night at the fights then a slap-up meal afterwards.' She didn't wait for his answer but turned and marched down the hall. 'I think Valentine Waite is England's answer to Cassius Clay,' she threw back at him. 'Me and Vi saw Cassius Clay beat our Henry Cooper in the sixth round. It was a great shame for our 'Enry.'

'You're right.' He followed her into the kitchen where his mouth began watering at the sight of the freshly baked scones cooling on a wire tray on the draining board. He also saw a dish of cream and two pots of what looked like homemade jam. He caught sight of the labels, Raspberry and Blackberry, his favourites.

'Sit yourself down,' Violet said, waving towards a chair at the scrubbed kitchen table. 'I'll go and tell them you're here.'

Vinnie wondered who 'they' were. Had he been foolish to come to this house alone? His gut instinct after the phone call from Roy Kemp was that the bloke genuinely needed to discuss Daisy. Vinnie believed one thing and that was that Kemp cared about her. And that enabled him to agree to the visit. And besides he wanted to find Daisy just as much as Roy Kemp did.

He sat down and looked about him. This wasn't exactly the setting one imagined for a feared thug to be living in. Not with a mother who was everyone's dream mum and a little house in the backstreets of South London. He smiled at Violet as she came in from the scullery, bringing with her a shaft of cool air.

The small woman switched on the kettle.

'We'll have tea in a minute. Charles and Roy are putting me up a new clothesline. They managed to get some scaffolding poles. I was that fed up with using a prop and then the line broke again in that nasty storm the other night. Well, I mean to say, I have to get me washing done, don't I, dear?'

Vinnie decided he liked the small round woman in the wraparound pinny. He could see why Daisy liked her and all. Violet went to the back door and yelled out Roy's name.

Within moments Roy stepped into the kitchen, closely followed by the big bear of a man he knew as Charles. Both were in their shirtsleeves and Roy looked just like one of the fairground workers he'd seen at Walpole Park in Gosport on high days and holidays. Roy grinned at him, showing extremely white teeth with a small chip at the front. Far from detracting from the man's looks it added vulnerability, thought Vinnie. Roy nodded a welcome and Charles said, 'Alright, mate?' before going straight to the sink and starting to wash his hands. Roy showed Vinnie his grubby hands and shrugged. Not caring about what was obviously garden dirt, Vinnie rose and grabbed the proffered right hand and pumped it up and down.

'Cheers, mate,' said Roy. 'Glad you could come.' Then he took his turn at the sink with Charles.

'Hurry up and sit down, you lot,' said Violet. 'These scones will go 'ard if you don't eat them soon. If I'd wanted to give you rock cakes I'd have made rock cakes.' She was bustling about setting out mugs and putting food on plates. Vinnie caught Roy's eye and Roy winked at him. It was the kind of wink that said, 'You know what mothers are like!' Vinnie began to relax.

'Tell me what you know about Daisy's disappearance,' said Roy, biting into his scone.

'Let the man breathe,' said Violet. 'He's only just got in the door.'

'You want Daisy back safe and sound, don't you, Mum?'

Violet pursed her lips. 'You got to hope she's still alive, son. And don't ask such stupid questions.'

'Let's get one thing straight before we speak of Daisy,' said Vinnie. 'You going to forget I'm a copper?'

'You going to forget I'm a villain?'

Charles nearly choked on his tea as Vinnie nodded. Violet had buttered some more scones and piled them with raspberry jam and cream. She was sliding the plate towards him.

Vinnie knew they had Daisy's best interests at heart. This visit to the Kemps' home was strictly off the record and very personal to him. That was why he'd not come accompanied and in a police car.

'You and I pool resources,' he said. 'I think that's the way forward. My career's at stake, so's your liberty. How much are the Krays involved?'

Roy pushed his hand through his hair. It fell back in exactly the same place across his forehead. As he leaned forwards Vinnie could smell the fresh odour of sweat that the exertion in the garden had caused.

'Less than nothing, I 'ope. I've got a few scouts sussing out the possibilities they had something to do with it.' He laughed nervously, like he had something to hide. 'But we grew up together. I know the left hand don't always know what the right hand's doing, but this ain't their style.' He stirred his cup of tea and looked down at the table. 'Besides, Ron's a nutter,' admitted Roy. 'By now he'd 'ave wanted me to know he had the upper hand if the twins *had* abducted her.'

'All that booze and drugs don't help,' put in Charles.

Violet was filling up the kettle ready for more tea. She turned and said, 'Violet Kray's at 'er wits' end with all the rowing between them two boys since Cornell's murder. Reggie's marriage to Frances is going down the pan and 'e's drinking himself to death about it.' She stood and faced them, like a little London sparrow. 'Do you know that girl Frances has tried to top 'erself?'

Vinnie didn't know that. Poor kid, he thought.

'Mum, I don't think that's quite relevant, do you?'

'Per'aps not,' she said. 'But it shows the instability of the lads at this time. I hope this chit-chat goes no further. Violet is my best mate. If I wasn't so worried about Daisy I wouldn't say a word.'

'We keep everything said today between ourselves, right enough,' said Vinnie. 'Though Vera gave me some interesting stuff to go on.'

Roy nodded. 'Me too,' he said. 'The old tart deserves to be kept in the frame.'

Vinnie reached out, picked up his mug of tea and took a pull on it, then nodded at Roy. 'Right then, what have you got?'

Two hours later, replete with scones and jam, Vinnie realised how much all of them cared about

Daisy. He also noted that Charles was hanging around Violet like the little fireball was made of Dresden china, and Roy was determined to get to the truth. Vinnie had told Roy all he knew and was pretty sure Roy was holding nothing back from him. Roy got up from the table.

'I need a bit of help. Get your jacket off, mate.' Vinnie looked at him and frowned. Roy laughed at the expression on his face.

'Charles has cemented in a couple of blocks of wood at each end of the garden. The bloody scaffolding poles are supposed to be bolted to 'em. But he forgot to drill the holes before he started, so I'm having a bleedin' nightmare of a job tryin' to hold a pole up while he fiddles about. Give us a hand?'

Vinnie was no expert on washing lines, but he looked at Violet and decided she needed more than verbal payment for the delicious food.

'You fit to roll your sleeves up?' Roy asked. 'Won't take no more than a flicker of a gnat's eye. Then we got some people to call on, eh?'

The towel was tucked in round his collar to conserve heat and to mop the sweat that ran down his neck with the exertion of running. Valentine Waite had just left Brady's Gym in the Old Kent Road where he'd sparred with old Tommy Neil and skipped and done press-ups until he felt he needed some fresh air away from the stench of sweat that permeated the large hall.

He'd decided to run for five miles then get back to the scrapyard, which was his place of residence now the house in the country had been sold. The bank had taken the money for that in lieu of the unpaid mortgage. Still, it was one less millstone round his neck and if the bank hadn't stepped in, the twins would have. Jesus Christ, how did he let himself get in such a mess with money?

He'd go back, change and then eat out. A decent steak would set him up nicely. The chef at his club, Valentine's, used to do a grand steak. Pity Valentine's now belonged to the twins. He mourned its passing but handing it over to the Krays for part of the gambling debt he owed them had been better than ending up in an alley with a bullet in his head.

He was running easily, his breathing even. The sun was shining down on him and he took it as an omen, or part omen, that he'd win the fight in New York. If he didn't he'd be a dead man anyway. The winning purse would see him clear of his debt to Ron and Reg. Then he could start over.

He caught sight of himself in a shop window, then pulled up and stared, running on the spot. His face was heavy-jawed, his eyes had a hunger which aged him. His head was giving him gyp as well. Them cunts had wounded him. Him, Valentine Waite, who had escaped damage in the ring, had been floored by a couple of slags! And then to inject him with the Ketamine . . . Bitches! They'd pay for it, though.

Fucking Daisy Lane had put the kid up to it. Who would have thought Glo would have dared to help her escape? Just goes to show you can't trust any fucking bleeder in this world. But then, if you can't trust your own mother . . .

He should have done Daisy in, same as the others. The pair of them, her and Glo, come to that. But he rather liked the thought of keeping Daisy safe, locked up. Having Daisy in that room was almost like having his mother exactly where he wanted her. And being shackled meant Daisy could never ever say to him, like his mother used to, 'Stay there, Valentine, in the other room, close the door, I just need to go upstairs with this nice gentleman.'

He saw himself, all those years ago, when a client would knock on the door and he'd have to stop whatever he was doing and go and sit in the green velvet armchair in the other room.

Sometimes, he and his mum would have been listening to the radio and he would have to miss part of the programme. Dick Barton, Special Agent, was his favourite, and it always ended on a cliffhanger with either Dick Barton or Snowy and Jock in some perilous place. He had to make up the missing parts but they didn't quite fit the next time he heard the programme.

It was the smell, too. He could smell, on her return to him, the scent of her perfume mixed with the sex and it made him feel sick. He knew the money from the men paid the rent and put food on the table but just for once couldn't his mother have said to one of them, 'Come back another time, I'm busy with my son'?

Now, he looked both ways as he crossed the near deserted street and ran into a patch of woodland.

The demons in his head had told him how to stop all his heartache. 'Kill your mother. Once she's not on this earth in human form you can keep her safe in your heart.' He should have kept Daisy Lane safe in his heart. Not in the room over his scrapyard's office. He wouldn't be in this state if he'd kept to his part of the bargain with his demons. She'd upset him. She hadn't realised what an honour he was bestowing on her, the selfish bitch.

And to take *his* souvenirs? That box was his property. She had no right to touch what was his. No matter, he'd find her, and that cunt Glo. And when he did . . .

And then he saw *her* ahead: a slightly built girl, with a fluffy-haired dog, who'd been hanging around the gym earlier then left while he was using the rope.

She had long blonde hair teased into a beehive with curls hanging down in front of her ears. She wore a mini-skirt and a white frilled blouse. But she hadn't had the dog with her at the gym. Perhaps she'd left the hall to get home and walk the dog?

She'd stared at him in the gym, and when he'd noticed, looked away, then took a brief look back.

Perhaps he should have been more civil to the little prickteaser.

She was oblivious to him now, every so often kicking at the fresh greenery while the small animal snuffled around in the grass. Because he was running and she was walking he reached her easily.

He danced ahead of her and turned, shadow boxing. Then he stopped, barring her way, teasing her, giving her one of his special smiles. Recognition flared in her eyes. The girl held the dog's folded lead in one hand – the small animal was happily chasing leaves – and a cheap plastic handbag tightly in the other. She looked pleased to see him. Pleased that he recognised her and had taken the time to stop.

'You were in the gym earlier.'

'Yeah, and you ignored me.' Her tone was stern but she was smiling at him.

'I'm not ignoring you now, am I?' He gave her one of his little-boy grins that usually did the trick and melted women's hearts. Then he leant forward and pulled her round so she was pinned between his arms as he laid his hands, palms flat, against the rough bark of an oak tree. He could smell the scent of her hairspray. It was sharp, with an undertone of honeysuckle. The dog had got tangled up with a large branch and gave a soft yelp.

'Sweetie,' she cried, pushing his arms away and running towards the animal, which she promptly picked up and cooed over. He stood and watched her, wondering whether she'd carry on walking with the dog or come back to him.

He looked about. Couples were sunning themselves on the grass, making the most of the fine weather. Normally this part of the woodland park was deserted.

'Damn,' he said under his breath. She was fussing with the animal, examining its paws that were dark with brown dirt.

'Did you say something?' she called to him.

'Not really,' he called back. He knew he had her then. He was just about to walk towards her when she returned, carrying the animal. She set it on the earth at his feet and it scampered off. 'I'd just like to be somewhere a little more private with you.'

He was testing her to see whether she was a boxing groupie and likely to fuck for free or whether she expected him to pay for it.

'I know somewhere quiet,' she said. 'But my time will cost you money.' The disgust on his face, which he couldn't conceal, must have given him away for she added quickly, 'I can make it worth your while. And a famous man like you surely won't mind giving me some money, will you?' She stood watching him, waiting for his answer.

He sighed, and knew what had to be done.

She relaxed as he nodded. Stupid bitch. She leaned towards him. He really didn't want to kiss her, but he knew he had to make a show of wanting her so he put his hand behind her head and drew her face towards him. His tongue met hers and played around in her mouth before he pushed her away.

'We'd better find this nice quiet place then,' he said.

'You look like a naughty little boy,' she said. Her hand fumbled at the outside of his shorts, at his erection. She glanced down at his prick pushing against the material of his shorts. 'Especially in your nice running gear,' she said. She ran her cupped hand over his balls, cradling them. 'All this doesn't belong to a little boy, though.' Then she took her hand away and left him wanting.

She waved towards a building through the trees, then took hold of his hand and led him towards the cricket pavilion set back on the edge of the green. The wooden building was painted white and surrounded by a white picket fence. It looked locked and deserted.

When they reached the place, she stretched up and felt along the ledge at the top of a shuttered window.

'Got it.' She turned towards him, holding a key. The dog was scrabbling at the wood and causing splinters to fall.

'How did you know it was there?'

'No big deal,' she said. 'My dad plays cricket and my mum cleans the place. No game today means the building won't be in use. We'll be locked in, safe and snug as two bugs in a rug.'

Inside the hut it smelled musty. She locked the door behind them. Valentine wandered about while she opened cupboards and got out stuff to make up a bed. She produced two lounger mattresses and spread them on the floor. At the rear was a small kitchen with cupboards that held coffee, tea and sugar. He located clean cups and took a long drink of water. If it hadn't been such a bright day the inside would have been in complete darkness but the sunshine streaming through the shutters made it warm and light. He could see motes of dust dancing on the shafts of light.

'Take your clothes off,' she demanded.

He looked around and saw she was lying on the mattresses, already completely nude. She'd arranged the cushions so there was plenty of room for him to lie beside her. The dog was curled into a ball in the corner of the room in a pool of sunlight, asleep, tired after its run. It was a ridiculous dog, hardly bigger than a cat.

He took off his running shorts. Beneath them he was wearing a pair of Y-fronts. He left them until last. Let her see what she's got coming to her, he thought, although the enormous bulge of his hard-on gave the game away.

His cock stuck straight out and it was gigantic. He heard her gasp as he bent down on the mattresses and shoved his fingers into her wet pussy. Then he began rubbing and her legs opened wider, begging for it.

When he'd had enough of that, with one hand he raised her body and flipped her slight form over so she was face down. With his other hand he raised her arse. He knelt over her and entered her from behind, savagely. The deliberation of his movements sent shudders coursing through her body.

She was skinny beneath him and he felt as though he wanted to break her, to punish her with his prick. Ignoring the sounds she was making he went on ramming, so deep he had to pause, but only for a moment. Not because he might be hurting her but to slow himself down in case he came.

His hips began to rock again, his eyes closed and his mind floated away with his thrusts. Her cries meant nothing to him. Then the hum that had already started in the back of his throat echoed into a roaring explosion of orgasm until he fell across her body, pushing her face and head further into the musty stench of the cushions.

For a moment he was still. Then he felt her squirming beneath him, gasping for air. He raised himself so his prick slithered out of her.

'You hurt me,' she said. 'Why didn't you stop when I asked you?' He turned away from her, making himself more comfortable. 'You hurt me,' she repeated and began to cry. Why did women always cry? She looked ugly. How could he ever have thought she looked even a little like Daisy Lane, like his mother?

'Did you know that women who like being fucked are either slags or whores?' She looked at him as though she couldn't believe his words. Her face fell in on itself like a crumpled bag. It took a while, then she said, scrambling away from him, 'I didn't expect you'd be like this with me.'

But she'd enticed him, hadn't she?

'You hang around the gym because you want to be fucked. Fucked you've been. So what's the problem?'

She was huffing and trying to find her clothes from the scattering of things about them.

'I expected you to be kinder, to like me a little.'

'Like you? You make me sick. You're a filthy cunt . . .'

'You can't talk to me like that!' She rounded on him, stung by his insults, and he hit her then. One hard slap that practically lifted her off the mattresses to fall with her head banging on the wooden floor.

The dog's lead, placed neatly behind the makeshift bed, took his eye. She was trying to scramble to her feet. The dog, awake now, was barking. Short yappy yaps that grated on his nerves. While the girl was stumbling to her feet, Valentine, too quick for her, pulled at her knees and once more she was down on the cushions.

And then the lead was over her head. And he was pulling it across her throat, a strip of the leather in each of his hands.

Tighter. Tighter. Tighter.

And all the while the dog was dancing on the wooden floor, yapping, yapping, its feet making scratchy noises.

Valentine Waite rose from the girl whose face

looked grotesque in death. She had wet herself and it disgusted him.

When he'd let go of the lead and got to his feet he kicked her body to make sure she was dead. To make sure not one breath of life remained in the disgusting whore.

The dog was still barking.

Although he felt clear-headed and cleansed by his actions, he went to the sink that he found in a remarkably clean state. He inserted the plug and ran water, cold water, almost filling the square trough. Using his hands he washed himself all over, paying special attention to his cock and balls so that no trace of her remained on him, and then he dried himself on a clean terry tea towel.

The dog was still barking.

He stared down at the small, white, excitable, useless animal and then lifted it and moved towards the sink and the water . . .

CHAPTER 14

'Only a peek, that's all I need. Just to know he's safe. I can't be so near my son and not see 'im,' cried Daisy. 'It's cutting me up.'

They were sitting in the back of the van. Daisy hadn't been awake long and Glo was smearing a knob end of bread with butter straight from the packet. She broke the bread in two and handed the largest piece to Daisy, who promptly snatched at the smaller bit.

'I can go now I've got some bleedin' shoes, if you can call 'em shoes.' Daisy twisted her feet so she could admire her footwear.

'That was a bit of luck finding them propped against a step just over the road. It didn't take me long to clean off the soddin' dog's muck.'

'I expect the woman as owned them thought she'd do that later.'

'She don't 'ave to do it at all now, do she?'

Daisy laughed at Glo. She liked her leather thong sandals with the piece that went between the toes. But her laughter died quickly. This situation can't last for much longer, she thought. Sooner or later someone would realise they were living in the old van at one of the most prestigious addresses in Gosport and complain to the authorities.

Then they'd have the police round and she didn't want that because she wouldn't be able to lie to them and her whole dark story would come out. Her name and shame would be all over the *Evening News* and in due course the story handed down to her son. She'd stopped thinking little Eddie wasn't safe. She believed with all her heart he was well protected by Vera. Now she wasn't so ill she realised her head had been pretty messed up, that confusion had made her imagine all sorts of bad stuff.

'You got demons of your own to fight where Valentine Waite's concerned, Glo,' she said. 'But if that bastard's skimmed off all me money and made it look like I've done it, then Vera . . .' At the thought of her friend, tears sprang to her eyes and she hastily wiped them away with the back of her hand. 'Vera must be believing I've taken money from me account and left 'er to clear up the mess.'

Would Vera believe the truth? And what about Roy? Perhaps he'd think she'd gone off willingly with Valentine Waite? Her body shuddered at that awful thought and the memory of the pain and indignities she'd endured at the boxer's hands. Daisy was more than grateful that the bastard hadn't made her pregnant.

'Everything's such a bleeding mess,' she said, all the thoughts crowding in at once. 'I don't feel strong enough to cope with it all but I want to see my boy. *I must see him.*'

Glo put her arms around her. Daisy clung to her.

'You will come with me?'

'To see if your lad's all right?'

Daisy nodded. Her heart lifted when Glo said, 'If you want. Anyway, I don't expect you'll be able to walk very far by yourself.'

Daisy hugged Glo. 'I just want to look at him.'

She felt all fluttery inside as she wet her face with water from a bottle and scrubbed at it with a towel. Glo began tidying herself and combing her hair. She passed the comb to Daisy and she had a go at the tangles.

It had stopped raining and the air was fresh and clean as Daisy pushed the back door of the van slowly ajar. She realised how lucky they were to be so well hidden in the bushes and undergrowth. If it had been winter there would have been no leaves or greenery to disguise the van. She knew their luck couldn't hold for ever though, and Valentine Waite would never give up looking for them.

After making sure no one saw them leave the van, Daisy, with Glo's arm around her waist, began the slow walk along Crescent Road. Turning right at the end they walked into Alverstoke Village in the shadow of St Mary's Church. Daisy was shivering, not with the cold for she was warm enough. It was fear that kept her looking behind her all the time.

'He's not 'ere, you know.'

Daisy knew she was talking about Valentine Waite.

A couple of cars passed as they walked beneath the huge outspread branches of Alverstoke's oak tree that was said to have been mentioned in the Domesday Book.

Daisy smiled at the sight of the thatched cottages. They looked so pretty with the raindrops glistening on the damp blooms in the gardens. She breathed deeply of the delicious scent. The hairdresser's shop was still closed as was the little clothes shop. Only the newsagent's was open. The paperboys, Daisy could see, were inside joking and messing around while their papers were being marked up, waiting to ride off to the outreaches of Alverstoke on their bikes, which were propped against the window.

They walked arm in arm down Village Road until they came to Jellicoe Avenue and began to cross the wide road into Western Way.

'You feelin' all right, Daisy?'

She wasn't really but said, 'Don't you worry about me, I'm fine. This is the road I live in.'

'Here?' Daisy could hear the amazement in Glo's voice. It had started to drizzle again and drips fell from the willows lining the road. The substantial houses sat back in their large gardens. Glo stopped walking and stared at Daisy. 'Fuckin' 'ell,' she said.

'My Eddie bought the 'ouse for me. I never lived in such a grand place before.'

'I can't imagine a bloke ever buying an 'ouse like

one of these for me,' said Glo. 'These 'ouses are bleedin' enormous.'

Nearing her thatch-roofed home, Daisy's steps grew slower.

'What's the matter?' Glo asked.

'You need to ask?'

Glo squeezed her arm. Of course the girl understood how apprehensive she was feeling. Glo was trying to be brave for the both of them.

Daisy's heart was hammering against her ribs. At her open gate she paused, stopping Glo from going any further. The roses were in full bloom; her beloved King Alfred daffodils had long since faded, but their brown and crinkled stems were neatly bunched and tied, shrivelled back so that the goodness from the sun and rain went down into the bulbs. Vera had done that for her. A lump rose in Daisy's throat.

'I don't want anyone to see us,' she said. Her voice came out in a strangled whisper. 'Keep pressed in against the bushes, Glo.'

A wireless was playing from somewhere in the house, someone was up and about. Daisy listened hard. She pictured the little brown radio on the kitchen surface near the cooker. Once upon a time the wireless had proclaimed 'Radio de Luxe' in the top left-hand corner, but little Eddie had climbed up on a chair and picked up the wireless to see where the music came from and had dropped it, so now the wording looked as though it said 'Radio de ruxe'. The lump was growing in Daisy's throat. She glanced around the circular gravel driveway.

Then she caught a glimpse of the small figure in a red raincoat and matching sou'wester sitting on the edge of the wire-covered pond at the back of the house. He was just visible through the side fence. The boy had a stick in his hand and was stabbing at the water lilies. Beside him sat the large tabby shape of Kibbles. Every so often the cat's tail flicked as water splashed its fur.

'That's my son,' Daisy whispered.

For a while she managed to keep quite still, every fibre of her being itching to scoop Eddie up and smother him with kisses, to bury her face in his dark sweet-smelling curls. But she knew she mustn't frighten him.

Daisy was terrified the emotions that had risen to the surface were going to spill out and she'd run crying towards him, her boy.

She saw him throw down the stick and turn to pick up the huge bulk of the cat, then stagger along with the animal who seemed not to care at all that he was being manhandled. Daisy wept, then quickly stumbled away, across the gate's entrance and along the pavement, her eyes stinging with the salt from her tears.

'You goin' to eat this fried bread or not, Vera? I ain't cooking for the glory of it, you know.'

Susie was clearing the breakfast table and Vera was standing in the hallway off the kitchen, watching through the front door's tiny glass window.

'Shh!' she said. 'There's something funny going on. Someone's watching our boy.'

'Who? Who?' Susie threw the plates she'd been gathering back on the table. She dodged to Vera's side, breathing heavily.

'Who? Who? Shut up. You sound like a bleedin' owl. It's a woman. No, two women.'

'I'm going to get the boy in.' Susie turned and almost ran towards the kitchen's back door and at the same time Vera, still in her silk dressing gown and her fluffy high-heeled mules, flung herself out through the front door and across the driveway. She could see the two women running along the pavement. One was limping as she ran, both were poorly dressed.

'OY! You bleedin' stop,' she yelled. Though the women were unkempt, at that moment Vera could see there was something familiar about the limping figure.

'Stop, you bleeders.' Vera was puffing and panting. The limping woman turned. Vera knew she'd been right. *It was her Daisy, her face gaunt and filled with fear!*

Then she decided she wouldn't yell any more as it was difficult for her to run and cry out at the same time. She lunged, throwing herself forward onto the figure. They both crumpled to the pavement.

'Stop it! Stop it!' Vera had hold of Daisy but Daisy

was fighting her, fists and legs flying in all directions. 'Let me go,' Daisy was crying.

Vera could smell the unwashed odour coming from her friend. It had been a long time since she'd had to fight in the street and she'd never lost a brawl yet.

'No, you bleedin' don't get away.' Vera was fending off Daisy's fists. 'Stop it, you silly bitch.' Vera gave one almighty slap and it connected to the side of Daisy's face. Her head rocked back and a look of sheer surprise replaced Daisy's anger, which was immediately replaced by pure unadulterated terror. She fell to the pavement, curling into a tight ball, her arms covering her head.

'Please, please don't hit me, don't hurt me.'

Vera looked at her friend in silent amazement.

'Leave 'er alone! She can't be hit no more.' The other woman was at her now, pushing her away. One almighty shove from Vera sent her flying backwards.

Vera looked down at the trembling mess on the pavement and then at the other woman, who wasn't a woman at all but a skinny girl with haunted eyes, hovering over her again with her fists clenched.

'You come near me, Missy, and I'll give you some an' all,' warned Vera. She was panting, trying to get her breath back, realising the girl had the advantage of youth. Then suddenly the girl's steps faltered, like she'd thought better of it. 'I fucking warn you! Stay away from me,' Vera added for good measure.

Her words seemed to have the desired effect for the girl was standing quite still now. And then she dropped down to Daisy who was sobbing into the pavement.

Vera stared at them both. Who was this girl? And was this really her Daisy? Her lovely blonde hair was a tangle of filth and why was she unable to walk properly? The dark ragbag of a girl who was now busy stroking Daisy's hair lifted brown eyes to Vera.

'Help 'er,' she begged.

The fighting was over. Vera breathed a sigh of relief and noticed for the first time that her dressing gown had come apart and she was showing all her assets. She pulled the black silk together and tied it. Then she bent down, inching the dark-haired girl away, and put her arms around Daisy.

'It's all right, ducky,' she said, sitting down on the damp pavement with her friend. Then all three of them were sitting on the pavement. Vera lifted Daisy so she could cry into Vera's ample bosom. She felt like a baby sparrow, Vera thought. All skin and bone. 'Why 'aven't you come 'ome?'

The silence was awesome.

Then the girl said, 'I tried to get 'er to come to you.'

Vera pursed her lips and narrowed her eyes at this bit of a kid who was trying to tell her what her Daisy should have done. 'And who the fuckin' 'ell are you?'

Vera was amazed when the chit of a thing pushed her face towards hers, staring her straight in the eyes, and calmly answered back.

'When Daisy's feeling better she'll tell you all about it an' who I am, so there.'

Vera couldn't believe her ears. Who the fuck was this little madam? Still, she had to admire the girl's pluck. There weren't many who'd stand up to her.

'Look at the state of you. Who's 'urt you, Daisy love?' Daisy still didn't answer. Vera sniffed loudly. 'Come on, let's get you 'ome. I suppose you better come an' all,' she said. 'Help me get her indoors where she belongs.'

The girl helped pull Daisy to her feet.

'I don't need help,' Daisy said. So, thought Vera, she's finally got something to say for herself, has she?

'Well you ain't stayin' out 'ere all day and I ain't dressed. And let's pick up all these bleedin' shoes. We ain't walking back in bare feet.'

She bent and slipped Daisy's onto her bare feet, thinking what strange but nice little flat leather sandals they were, and put on her own wedged mules. Then she noticed the house opposite and the twitch of curtains at the downstairs window.

'The show's over, you nosy cow!' she yelled. The net magically fell straight once more. Vera looked at the girl in triumph. 'Nosy neighbours are everywhere,' she confided. The girl suddenly grinned. Then she put her arm around Daisy and the three of them stumbled back to the house. At the front door, Vera felt Daisy stiffen.

'Now what's the matter?'

'I can't let little Eddie see me like this.'

'Don't be so fuckin' stupid. It's okay for me and this skinny drink of water to see you but not your own flesh and blood? Get in that bleedin' door.'

'Stop pushing me. I didn't say I didn't want to, I said I couldn't. And you 'urt me when you gave me that rugby tackle.'

'I'll give you more than a fuckin' rugby tackle if you don't do as I tell you. And what about all the bleedin' neighbours getting to see me body for nothing?'

The girl giggled. Vera turned on her. 'And you can shut up an' all, girl.'

'Me name's not girl, it's Glo.' Vera ignored her and dragged Daisy into the hall then into the kitchen where she pushed her in front of the window.

'There 'e is! How can you say you can't look at him? He's a beautiful boy. Your own flesh and blood.'

The boy was running after Susie who suddenly stopped and turned and little Eddie flung himself into her arms and she swung him round. Vera could hear their laughter and see the joy on their faces. When she looked at Daisy again she could see the tears running silently down her face. Daisy turned to her.

'It wasn't my fault,' she said.

'Never once did I ever think it was, ducky,' Vera said. Her hand felt for Daisy's hand and she clasped it. Daisy squeezed her fingers then fell into the small woman's arms again. Vera let her cry, her own heart breaking for whatever torment had beaten her lovely

Daisy to this husk of a woman. After a while, Vera said, 'I think you better sit down and 'ave a cup of tea.'

She pushed Daisy onto a kitchen chair and looked at the girl, who was wandering around picking up things and examining them then replacing them.

'Leave that stuff alone, it don't belong to you. You come an' sit down an all, Blo.'

'Me name's not Blo, it's Glo.' Vera saw Daisy give a ghost of a smile.

'Have it your own way,' Vera said. She plugged in the kettle then heard the back door open and Susie enter.

'Fuckin 'ell,' she said, looking first at Daisy, who managed a watery smile, then at Glo. 'This is a turn-up for the books.' Then her eyes went back to Daisy, who'd got up from the chair again and was watching little Eddie from behind the safety of the yellow frilled curtain. Susie launched herself at Daisy.

'Where've you been? We been so worried. Roy's out of 'is mind . . .' Vera saw Daisy lose her balance but manage to throw her arms around Susie and bury her face in her hair. Susie wrinkled her nose at the smell coming from Daisy but she clung to her like a limpet.

'I 'ave missed you.' Susie began to cry.

After a couple of minutes Vera said, 'I can't be doin' with all this. Suze, you finish making the tea. Daisy, sit down again before you bleedin' fall down . . .'

Susie let go of Daisy and said to Vera, 'I ain't making no tea until I sees Daisy and 'er boy together.'

Vera thought she'd never seen Susie look so fierce.

'I can't let him see me like this.' Daisy covered her face with her hands.

'I don't give a flyin' fuck.' Susie went to the door and called, 'Eddie, get in 'ere. Come an' look.'

Vera heard his light footsteps then the boy peeked around the kitchen door. He entered, gazing shyly at each of them in turn. First Susie, and a smile lit his face. Then Glo, and Vera watched his little brow crease as he tried to place a new face. He caught sight of Vera anxiously watching him and turned towards her, his eyes wide open with a smile that lit his face from ear to ear. He took a step towards Vera, then stopped, looking at Daisy.

He was like a miniature statue, thought Vera, and the puzzlement on his face was plain to see. Then his eyes lit up like two beacons on bonfire night and with all the force of his toddler years he threw himself at Daisy.

'Mummy!'

'Oh, my boy,' she wept, sweeping him up into her arms and holding him tightly. 'You're safe, so safe.' Vera saw her breathing in his little-boy smell, taking great gulps of him as though she was at a banquet and eating a feast.

Not one of the other women in the room breathed a word. The sight of mother and son wrapped in each other's arms hurt Vera's heart with happiness, and she knew Susie felt the same.

Kibbles, who'd followed little Eddie indoors, took one look at all the commotion and stalked over to Vera to wind in and out of her legs. She picked him up and heard his loud purring.

'All's right with me world,' she said softly into his mackerel-coloured fur.

She watched for a while then decided action was called for.

'Stop crying, Suze. You make the place look untidy.' Susie wiped her face with her knuckles. 'And make that tea, girl, I'm gasping.' Vera knew her friend well enough to know she too was only crying with happiness. Vera went over, re-boiled the kettle and made the tea herself.

Four cups of strong tea and hours later Vera was trying to put all the bits of the jigsaw into place.

'Where's the bastard now?' she asked. She might have tempered her words but little Eddie was fast asleep in his mother's arms so it didn't matter.

'He's supposed to be fighting at Madison Square Garden in New York,' said Glo. 'Only I'm not sure of the date 'e was leaving.' Vera thought the slip of a girl looked worn out. She'd eaten a decent pile of cheese and pickle sandwiches that showed how ravenous she was and put away the best part of a pound of Bourbon biscuits.

'You got worms?' Glo had helped herself to another biscuit from the blue bag. Vera said a silent thank you to Si who regularly brought home the bags of treats for the family.

'No, Vera, but decent food ain't been easy to come by an' these are a real tonic.' Vera grinned. She was all right, was this Glo.

'Never mind about filling your bellies, that foot of yours 'as got to be properly looked at. We'd better get you up to the 'ospital, Dais.'

When Daisy had first shown her the wound caused by the shackles, Vera had almost gagged. She wanted to force Daisy into a taxi and haul her off to the Haslar there and then. On closer inspection she saw that, despite the rough rags used as bandages, Daisy's ankle was clean and actually healing over. Glo's care must have done that. Daisy certainly wouldn't have been in any fit state to look after herself. The fever and the drugs still in her body would have kept her knocked out. Vera knew all about the effects of drugs.

'I ain't going there. I'll be asked 'ow it happened and I don't want to 'ave to lie to them.' Daisy was adamant.

Vera sighed. 'If you don't want to go to the Haslar to be checked out, I'm going to get my mate, Doctor Henry Dillinger, round.'

Vera knew Daisy wouldn't object to him. Struck off he might be, but he served Vera well, looking after her girls and getting rid of unwanted little problems. She went over to the telephone. For her he'd come round straight away, even if he had to sober up on his way.

Daisy nodded. 'I don't mind him. He's a good bloke an' he won't go blabbing all over the place that I been missing. An' I really thank you for keeping things quiet, Vera. No way would I want the whole of Gosport knowing what's been happening to me. It would have been all over the *Evening News* and on file for my Eddie to read about when he gets older.' Daisy shuddered. 'Thank God you know me so well, Vera.' Vera gave her a half smile. If only the daft cow realised she knew her better than she knew herself. 'Will Doctor Dillinger look at Glo as well? If it hadn't been for her I wouldn't be 'ere, but she's been treated badly an' all.'

'I am 'ere, you know,' said Glo. 'Don't talk about me as though I don't exist.' Vera glared at her, but an idea had been forming in her mind. This girl was nobody's fool and she'd already proved her loyalty to Daisy by sticking to her through thick and thin. She could not only give the girl a job and a good wage, but her self-respect back as well.

'What if I was to give you a job in me salon?'

Glo stared at her.

'You need to be one hundred percent fit and clean and I don't allow no funny business. I got a well-respected place.'

Glo, who was clearly shaken by the request, said, 'But you don't know me.'

'You looked after Daisy. That's enough for me. I

reckon you're old enough to work. I been in this game long enough to know about girls and who's trustworthy.'

'I ain't goin' on no game! I've 'ad me fill of bein' abused by them bastards. Now I suppose you'll say if I ain't willing to open me legs the offer of a job don't stand no more?'

Vera was taken aback. The girl had guts all right. Perhaps she hadn't made herself plain when she'd talked about taking the girl on.

'I want you to work for me. Trust me, I'll make sure you don't do nothin' you don't want to.' She saw Glo's face relax. The girl gave her a watery smile.

Daisy was in a world of her own, looking down at her sleeping child. There were tears in her eyes. Vera wondered if Daisy was thinking about little Eddie's dad. Her Eddie would cut your throat if you crossed him but if he cared about you he'd give you the earth. And by God he'd loved Daisy. She was his sun, his moon and his stars. Daisy sensed her gaze and dropped her bombshell.

'I can't stay 'ere, Vera.'

'Don't be daft! Why not? This is your 'ome.'

Daisy sighed and shook her head. 'Firstly, that bastard will be looking for us. It's been nearly two weeks since we escaped after clobbering 'im.' She looked at Glo as if for confirmation and Vera saw Glo nod. 'Secondly, me money's gone and I'm not depending on your charity. And thirdly I don't want that bleeder coming after any of you if 'e can't find me.' She looked at her child. 'Especially this little one. I have to do what's best for him at all costs.'

Vera said, 'We'll worry about Mr Fuckin' Waite when the time comes. No doubt Roy'll want to sort him out . . .'

Now Vera had Daisy home again there was no way she was going to let her leave. Even if she had to break her other ankle to make her stay.

'Roy! I don't want him to know I'm back.'

Vera stared at Daisy's horror-struck face. 'Don't be so fucking stupid, the man's in shreds about you.'

'But he won't want me no more now I've been—'

'He loves you, Dais.' Vera grabbed both her hands from where they were holding on tightly to little Eddie and looked into her eyes. 'If he don't want you no more then he ain't much of a bloke, is he? But he's been moving heaven and earth to find you . . . Vinnie Endersby an' 'im are already on to that bastard. Don't forget, you're Roy Kemp's woman and when you belong to a man like that . . .'

Daisy let go of Vera's fingers and, leaning forward, put her hands around Vera's heart-shaped face, looking deep into her eyes.

'For fuck's sake, what crap, what film you been watching, our Vera, to come out with words like that? This is me! An' I don't think there'll be a bleedin' happy ending this time!'

Vera stared, then grinned. 'See, that's made a bit of your old fire come back, ain't it?'

Daisy nodded. 'Vera, you kill me, you really do.

But I got to ask. If Waite's emptied my account, who's been paying for Eddie's Pappy and Mum in their retirement home?'

Vera didn't say a word. Susie nodded towards Vera. That girl can't keep a bleeding secret to save her life, thought Vera.

'You'd 'ave done it for me.' As far as Vera was concerned, whatever she and Daisy had they could share. Susie too. 'You've 'ad the bleedin' stuffing knocked out of you, Dais. You need to rest,' she said.

Vera's hand suddenly snaked out and slapped Glo's hand away from the bag of biscuits. 'You an' all, Missy. An' they won't 'elp. But if you think you're off back to some bloody clapped-out van in the Crescent then you got another think coming. Fancy you bein' so near and me knowin' nothin' about it?'

Vera got up. Kibbles had been sprawled on her lap and Vera laid him carefully back on the warm cushion and patted his head.

She'd do what was best after she'd got Daisy into a warm bath. Not only what was best but what she, Vera, wanted; bugger what Daisy wanted. She had to make a couple of phone calls and perhaps settle Glo in her new home. That bastard would have to be bloody clever to find Glo down in her flat above Heavenly Bodies. Perhaps she ought to mention that Glo needed a bath an' all.

'Glo, go back to the van and get anything you need, will you?' Glo nodded. 'You want anyone to go with you to keep an eye out, like?'

'I think I can manage, Vera.'

'Well, I ain't taking no more crap from either of you,' Vera said to her retreating figure as she headed for the front door. 'I'm in charge now.' Then she saw Daisy's eyes had closed with weariness. Poor buggers, she thought. She could understand Daisy's reluctance to come straight to the house. What had happened to her wasn't her fault. The hard part would be getting Daisy to believe it. 'Just look at 'er, Suze.'

Susie said, 'She looks like a Madonna with her child, don't she?'

Vera gave her one of her old-fashioned looks. Sometimes that girl could come out with some funny things.

An hour later Vera had Daisy on the bathroom stool and was undressing her. The scented steam rose from the hot water.

Vera gasped. 'Jesus Christ, that bastard 'as marked you good an' proper.' Daisy tried to cover herself by sweeping up a towel and holding it in front of her. 'Ain't no use you doin' that, ducky, even a blind man could see them welts and scars and skinny ribs of yours.' Daisy dropped the towel.

'Glo's the same,' Daisy said. Her voice was flat.

Vera wished she'd kept her mouth shut. Daisy had enough on her plate without her mentioning how rough she looked, even though it broke Vera's heart to look and touch her poor body.

'Henry Dillinger'll be here soon. He'll give you a good sorting out and the girl an' all.'

Susie had taken little Eddie out to see Jacky and Bri down at the bookshop. Jacky needed to be told that Glo would be taking over Vera's flat for a while and working in the salon. Vera knew she'd be over the moon about that and soon show Glo how to take care of the bookings. Now Jacky could spend more time with Bri and his little daughter Summer like she wanted.

'How could I 'ave been so stupid?' Daisy asked. 'Valentine Waite tricked me and I fell for it, hook, line and fuckin' sinker.'

'You was wise enough to tell 'im you wanted nothing to do with him at me party and the bastard plotted 'ow to get even with you, Dais. He's a demented bugger.'

'I've got such a lot to thank you for, Vera.'

'Shut up, you silly bitch.' Vera had got her in the bath. 'You wash yourself and do your hair. Shout if you needs me. I'll only be downstairs.'

'Don't go. Don't leave me.'

Vera sighed and sat on the stool next to the bath. 'Let me wash your 'air for you then.' Vera palmed Amami shampoo into her hands. Where was Daisy's spirit gone? Where had her fierce courage disappeared to?

Daisy said, 'I don't know when I'll be able to pay you back now I'm skint . . .'

'But you ain't poor. You got riches beyond compare. You got little Eddie, me, Suze and Si, and you still got this roof over your 'ead. An' I got money from me massage parlour and the girls. We'll be fine.'

Daisy parted her wet hair and stared through its strands at Vera.

'You soon changed your tune about Glo, didn't you? How come you're offering 'er your flat?'

'Me flat's empty. You know I don't like it empty, and I don't want to go back to live there yet. Me an' Kibbles, we're all right 'ere. With you 'ome again it'll be like it was when we was living down the caff. There's room in this 'ouse for us all not to get under each other's feet, Daisy.'

'Sure, there is. But I ain't having you forking out for me. I'll soon get something, a job, you'll see.' Daisy sighed. 'Maybe I'm speaking out of turn but I need to tell you a bit about Glo. She's had a life like you couldn't believe. Well, maybe you could, our Vera.'

And when Daisy had finished Vera was stunned.

'So that's why she's such a prickly person. She ain't never been shown no kindness, 'as she?'

Daisy shook her head.

'Poor little cow,' said Vera. 'I can understand her not wanting to be left in the dark an' all. I'd better tell Jacky not to hassle her about keeping the electric lights on. Jacky's right on the ball about me girls not wasting resources. I only 'ope Glo turns out to be 'alf as good.'

When Daisy was tucked up in bed, Vera gathered

all her clothes and took them down to the rubbish heap at the bottom of the garden.

'I'll make a bonfire of you later,' she vowed. 'An' I'll make sure no bugger comes in this house as ain't supposed to.' There and then she allowed herself the release of a few tears amongst the dustbins and ashes of a previous fire.

When she went upstairs again Daisy was almost asleep. Vera bent to kiss her.

Daisy opened her eyes.

'Do you think I could 'ave a little dab of your Californian Poppy on me?' she murmured. 'If I can go to sleep smelling that, then I'll know I'm really safe again.'

CHAPTER 15

Vera made two phone calls.

She waited till balding Henry Dillinger had gone, leaving her a couple of bottles of whisky and a handful of bank notes poorer but satisfied that neither Daisy nor Glo had anything seriously wrong. Daisy's ankle was cleaned and redressed and she was dosed up with a tetanus shot, and Vera was left with what seemed like half a chemist's shop which had miraculously appeared from the doctor's black bag.

'She's 'ome,' she said to Roy. She heard the gasp at the other end of the line. And then silence as she launched into what she knew.

'Where is she now?'

'In bed. And she ain't going nowhere without me.'

The second call was to Vinnie Endersby. And almost word for word she told him what she'd told Roy.

'Thank Christ she's alive. I don't have to fear for her safety now she's back with you. I'll be there as soon as I can.'

'Thanks, Vinnie,' she said. 'You're a good man.'

She replaced the receiver and went upstairs. Daisy

233

was curled up in the bed, fast asleep. Kibbles poked his head up from the sheet and looked at Vera.

'You look after 'er, my little man.'

Downstairs she could hear Glo sorting through the stuff she'd brought back from the van and she went down to join her. Susie and little Eddie hadn't yet returned.

Vera tutted at the rubbish spread out on the kitchen table. 'That's a right lot of sorry possessions.' Immediately she regretted her words. She remembered how, long ago, she'd hitched a ride with a lorry driver carrying nothing but her baby and a bag full of similar stuff. 'Sorry,' she said. 'I'm getting above meself. When I come to Gosport years ago I only 'ad the clothes I stood up in. And me baby.'

'Really?'

'Really.' Vera sank down onto a chair. 'In fact me and me little one would 'ave died if it 'adn't been for a gypsy woman and 'er family. She took us in and nursed me. Just like you looked after Daisy.'

Glo nodded towards the kettle and Vera smiled. She was warming towards this slip of a thing by the minute. With a rattle of tea things, Glo was doing the honours. She'd also got the bag of Bourbons out again, noted Vera.

'You might as well finish 'em.'

'I wish someone cared as much about me as you and Daisy care about each other. She cried your name out in 'er sleep, you know.'

'Don't you make me cry. I don't cry.' Vera dabbed

at her eyes. If she'd had her eyelashes on they'd have been hanging off like caterpillars swinging from trapezes. 'This job I'm offering you, you don't 'ave to . . .'

'I made my stand when I said I won't go with no blokes.' Her voice fell to a whisper. 'I can work hard but you see . . . you see . . . I can't read or write very well.' Her voice tailed off and Vera reckoned it hadn't been easy for the girl to tell her that bit of news. Of course Daisy had warned her but Vera wasn't about to let on that she already knew. She tried to look surprised. 'But I'm quick to learn and I can remember stuff real good,' Glo added.

'Bloody good job I reckon you're a winner, then.'

Glo looked confused. 'You saying I *can* work for you?'

'Lots of people make fortunes and can only mark papers with an X. Because you can't read or write don't mean you're fuckin' stupid, does it? Just that somewhere along the line you gone an' slipped through the learning net.' She thought for a moment, then said, 'Mind you, reading and writing 'as its advantages. Why don't I teach you?'

'Could you?'

Vera had been thinking about it and the idea appealed to her.

'I ain't no bleeding proper teacher but I reckon I could. We could sit down with some books I got for little Eddie.'

'Won't the others laugh at me?'

235

'Do you really think so?' She could see Glo pondering her words, thinking about sitting at the kitchen table with little Eddie and the three of them working on letters.

'No. They're all too kind for that.'

'Well then,' said Vera. 'We'll start as soon as you're all settled in above Heavenly Bodies. Now, my flat's a nice place, you got to look after it. I shall ask Samantha, she's one of my girls, to keep an eye on you. You should be snug as a bug in a rug there. You'll be feelin' a bit ropey while you're finishing that course of tablets Henry gave you so you might as well be doing some schooling.'

'What! You mean I can stay there by myself? Won't you be there?'

It hadn't occurred to Vera that Glo might not want to live alone.

'Whatever for? None of the girls leave Heavenly Bodies until the last punter's done and that's usually very late or early in the mornings. Jacky's usually the last one to leave. She 'as to cash up and lock up. That'll be your job later when you got on your feet and know 'ow things work. The girls is good fun, I know you'll get on famous with them. Actually you won't really be alone. There's a kitten that seems to 'ave taken a liking to the place, a little skinny black thing. My girls have been feeding it. I don't want it 'ere because my boy gets very jealous. I don't mind if you makes a pet of it upstairs in the flat. You'll be needing some cat food.'

'I never 'ad nothing of my own before,' Glo said. 'I'd really like that.' Then she brightened even more. 'Will I be able to come and go when I want? Have a key?'

Vera was staring at her. Then she remembered what Daisy had told her about Glo being a prisoner for most of her life. She went over and put her arms around the girl. 'It'll be your 'ome. You'll be able to do whatever you likes. But no funny business, ever, with blokes in my flat! I don't allow that. Never 'ave. Downstairs is the place for men, not in me private premises.'

Even when she lived at the cafe, the only man who crossed her threshold was Kibbles.

'You got no fears on that count. You know I ain't never lived alone? I think I might like it.'

Vera gave her hand a squeeze. She looked at the girl and saw she was practically dead on her feet.

'You want to 'ave a lay down? Or a bath?'

Glo shook her head. 'I think I'd like to wait and do it all in my *own* place,' she said. 'If you can stand the sight and smell of me, I can.'

'Best get you down the flat as soon as possible then. I ain't leavin' until Suze gets back with the boy. I'll search out a few things for you to eat and a packet of tea.' Vera began stacking food on the table. She found three packets of Bourbon biscuits at the back of the cupboard. 'I can just see you dipping these in your tea while you're sitting in bed tonight,' she said.

Glo looked at her. The girl was practically dancing

about with happiness. 'I'll sort out the stuff from the van. Separate Daisy's from mine.'

Vera started rooting through the stuff as well. She thought of Daisy's nice clothes upstairs in her wardrobe, and her Chanel No. 5 perfume that she went on buying because it reminded her of Eddie. He'd bought her the first perfume she'd ever owned. Always dressed in black, Daisy did. A smart little body, hair always shining. Then she saw the box.

'What's this?' She shoved the wooden box under the girl's nose. 'What's in 'ere?'

Glo shook her head. 'Ain't got the bleedin' foggiest. It ain't ours. Daisy made me bring it because it belongs to Valentine Waite and he was forever opening the bleedin' thing and going through whatever's inside, but I don't know what's in there and I'm certain Daisy don't neither.' She shrugged. 'Thought it better not to leave anything in there that might show it was us took the van. Even though the old crate was due to be crushed in the yard.'

'Ain't you got a key?'

'Don't be bleedin' daft, Vera. He didn't leave one with it.'

'Well, I'm going to see what's inside.' She shook it. It wasn't heavy. She could hear something rustling. 'I'm going to get a screwdriver.'

Vera poked about underneath the sink where there was a toolbox with some bits in. She found a screwdriver with a large flat head.

Suddenly there was a loud knock on the door. Glo

was looking at her with large frightened eyes. Vera tied her flimsy dressing-gown belt tighter and advanced to the living room, screwdriver in hand, to where she had a good view of the front door. A sigh of relief escaped her. She went and opened the door and stared up at the tall figure of Vinnie Endersby. A whiff of piney cologne touched her nostrils and she gave him a big smile.

He stepped backwards, then calmly took the screwdriver from her hand.

'Me friend, Vera,' he said, pointing to his light-coloured gabardine mackintosh. He stepped inside then gave her back the offending weapon. 'You don't need to come at me with this.'

'Don't you mock me, DS bloody Endersby.' Her silky gown had fallen open again and for once in her life she went all shy and grabbed at it, tucking it back neatly around her curves. 'Daisy's upstairs asleep. But she's got plenty of time to make up 'er kip an' she'd like to see you.' At the bottom of the stairs Vera yelled, 'Daisy!'

'Can I go up?' Vinnie asked.

That's what she liked about him, he was courteous. Yes, that was the word, courteous. And ever since she'd seen Roy Kemp coming out of the Black Bear with that blonde trollop she'd lost all faith in him. Not that she'd ever utter a word about that. But Vinnie wasn't pushy and grabby like most coppers. And she could see, despite his joking attitude, his deep concern for Daisy. She nodded. 'Don't let the surprise show on your face. It would be bloody cruel to 'er. She's only a shadow of our Dais.' He shrugged himself out of his mac and handed it to her along with his hat. She watched his arse as he climbed the stairs then set the garments on the hall table and went back to the kitchen.

Glo was still fiddling with the box.

'You can't get into it with those bitten nails,' Vera said. 'Anyway we got a copper 'ere to help us now.' Glo looked up at her in alarm. 'It's all right, he's a mate. He's not after you for taking the van. Put the kettle on, girl. We could all do with a cuppa. Let Vinnie open the box. That's what blokes is good for, carrying heavy weights and opening boxes.'

After what seemed an eternity when Vera was longing to know what was being said between them, Daisy and Vinnie entered the kitchen. Daisy looked more rested, thought Vera. Vinnie looked strained.

'I told her Roy isn't far behind me,' he said, pulling out a chair for Daisy then one for himself. Vera saw his eyes light on Glo who was watching him warily. He jumped up again and held out his hand. 'You must be Glo? When Roy gets here we're going to need you to tell us everything. That bastard Valentine Waite has to be found.' The girl nodded and lightly touched his fingertips with her hand, unsure of him. 'Vera will have told you who I am.' He was about to say something else when he noticed the box. 'That's pretty.'

'You could do something useful and open the

bleedin' thing.' Vera pushed the screwdriver across the table.

'Why? Is it stuck?'

'It belongs to Waite.' Daisy's eyes were riveted on the lacquered box. 'I'd forgotten we 'ad that,' she said.

One quick twist beneath the rim and the lock shattered. Pieces of paper flew across the table.

'What the 'ell?' Vera picked up a twist of hair attached to a small square of paper. She read the paper, touched the hair. 'Wendy Harman November 16th 1964.' On the back was an address. 'Fuck!' said Vera, throwing the paper to the table in disgust. She looked to where Vinnie was reading a further slip of paper. He raised his eyes to hers. She had guessed immediately what these macabre keepsakes were.

'What is it?' Glo asked, stepping forward.

Vinnie touched her arm. 'Better not touch it. It's evidence,' he said. He was holding a curl of ginger hair that was tightly tied with a piece of black cotton, also with a tiny card sellotaped to it. 'Pubic hair,' he said.

Glo grabbed Vera's arm.

'But there's lots . . .'

'You don't have to tell me that.'

Glo sat down at the kitchen table and put her head in her hands.

'Vera. I know who Wendy Harman is – or was,' Vinnie said. Vera stared at him. 'Do you know what this lot represents?' he asked. Vera nodded. Thinking was one thing, knowing was another. The dirty bastard must have put together these keepsakes from every girl he fucked. And her Daisy had been with this . . . this . . . filthy animal. No, he was less than an animal, for they didn't come up with some of the ideas that men did, and Vera had known some very funny blokes in her time.

She looked at Daisy who was sitting quite still, her face as white as a freshly washed sheet.

'The police looked for Wendy Harman because she disappeared after a party at some boxer's flat. They never found her. She was a prostitute.'

'It was all over the news and the radio, wasn't it?' Vera remembered now. Vinnie nodded at her.

Glo asked, 'But why would Valentine Waite keep stuff like this?'

Vera shivered. 'Use your bleedin' noddle, Glo. Why would the deranged bugger keep Daisy and you locked up?'

'We never knew,' said Glo. She looked distraught. 'I never knew, never 'ad an inkling . . .'

Vinnie looked at her, his face grim. These scraps belonged to dead girls. It wasn't hard to figure out who had killed them. Vinnie was carefully putting the keepsakes back into the black box.

'You got a paper bag, Vera?'

She went to the cabinet drawer and handed him a brown string-handled carrier bag. Then she walked to the sink and began to scrub her hands with a nail-brush.

'You all right, Daisy? You've not said a word all this

time.' Vinnie was standing behind Daisy's chair, his hands on her shoulders. Daisy turned her head and stared up at him.

'Those poor, poor girls,' was all she said.

And Vera knew she was hoping that Valentine Waite would get everything that was coming to him.

CHAPTER 16

'Wake up, Mummy, wake up!'

Tiny fingers were prising open Daisy's eyes and she could smell the sleepy scent of her child. How silly she'd been to think she must stay away from him because she felt sullied. This was her baby from her own body and she needed him and he needed her. From downstairs came the muted sounds of the radio, a Beatles song, haunting, melodious.

She lifted the covers and little Eddie climbed into bed. She pressed him to her, so tightly he said, 'I can't breeve, Mummy. You're taking all my breff.'

Releasing him she said, 'Hello, sweet pea.'

His features were almost a carbon copy of her Eddie's. Large currant eyes stared at her, and he was so close that his nose touched hers and her vision blurred. His milky breath was warm against her lips. She wanted to eat him, he was so gorgeous.

A movement from the doorway startled her. She gasped as she saw the large figure filling the frame.

Slate-grey eyes crinkled at the sides and a smile lifted his well-shaped mouth. He looked thinner, older. Roy brushed his hands through his dark curls as he came to her and bent down, encircling the pair of them in his arms. Daisy could smell the tang of his citrus cologne.

'I've missed you so much,' he said.

The boy wriggled to free himself from the embrace. Scrambling down from the bed he ran out of the bedroom.

'Something I said?'

Daisy sat up. She clutched her nightdress to her neck. 'He'll be back. He's no doubt gone after that damned cat. I need to tell you . . .' Roy pressed his fingers across her lips.

'Later. Glo's filled me in and so 'as Vera.' She made a face as she removed his hand.

'I don't know why I put up with that woman. She's got a mouth on her like an aircraft hangar.'

His eyes twinkled. 'Thank God you've not lost some of your fire,' he said.

'Roy, I need . . .'

'Nothing,' he said, interrupting. 'You need to say nothing about that bastard Valentine Waite.'

'How did you know he was in my mind,' she said as he sat down on the edge of the bed and leaned to kiss her.

'I can read your thoughts,' he said. She could feel his warm sweet breath on her face and yet she turned away from him. His forehead creased, then he pushed himself to a standing position and dusted off his dark suit, flicking away imaginary specks before stepping back and looking at her. He looked at her for a long time. After a while he bent and kissed her chastely on her head.

Daisy saw the hurt in his eyes. This wasn't the way it was supposed to be after not seeing him for so long. He turned and walked towards the door, then took her white dressing gown from the hook on the back of the door and laid it across the bed. The dressing gown that was discoloured and well washed. The dressing gown Eddie had bought her.

'If you can come downstairs, there's something I think you need to see,' he said.

He left the door ajar and she could hear talking from downstairs and smell bacon frying. Her stomach rumbled. Daisy was reminded that she'd not eaten properly for ages, but the day before food hadn't bothered her. All she'd wanted was sleep.

She looked about the room, with its poppy wallpaper chosen by her and Vera from Bull's in Stoke Road; the dark green wardrobes, dressing table and green velvet blanket box bought from Haine's Furnishings. This was her bed, her bedroom and her green velvet curtains. In this room she felt safe. And once, a long time ago, she had felt safe in another bedroom.

A bedroom in a New Forest inn, the place where for the very first time she and Eddie had made love. Tender, experimental love, yet with a passion she'd never achieved since.

But she knew Roy loved her and she believed she loved him.

Moments ago, as he'd stepped towards her, why had her whole body recoiled with fear, with revulsion. Her sane self told her he wasn't going to hurt her. Why would he? How could she explain it wasn't *him* she didn't want touching her body. It was anyone, any man.

How could she ever let a man invade her secret places again?

Daisy got out of bed. She brushed her hair and cleaned her teeth. Every item in the bedroom and bathroom looked so clean and fresh.

She stared at herself in the bathroom mirror and saw a pathetic excuse for a woman looking back at her. Her eyes were dull, and her hair lank despite its washing. Her shoulders looked huge and bony.

She'd noticed as she got out of bed that she'd been able to put more weight on her foot. Perhaps it was Henry Dillinger's ministrations, or maybe some strength was slowly returning to her body.

She tried not to think of Valentine Waite.

Tying the belt of her dressing gown tightly around her waist, she went downstairs.

When she pushed open the door there were flowers. Store vases lined the floor and stood on every available surface. The scents of so many brightly coloured blooms were overpowering. She'd never seen so many flowers in one place in her life.

'They're for you.' Roy was sitting on a kitchen

chair. Vera, little Eddie, Susie had paused in their chattering, waiting for her reaction. Tears filled her eyes. The smell of Vera's fried bread was vying for attention but losing out to the flower scents. Before she could say a word, Roy added, 'One bloom for each moment I've missed you.'

'Oh Roy . . .' Daisy covered her face with her hands. 'I don't know what to say . . .' Vera came up to her with a fork in her hand and put her arms around her.

'Don't cry,' she said. She had on a frilled white blouse, a tight black skirt and high-heeled shoes with peep toes. The scent of her Californian Poppy fought with the blooms. 'You want some breakfast?'

'Not if you're cooking it,' Daisy said. Vera and cooking didn't mix.

'She ain't cooking, I am,' Susie said. 'She's just looking after the fried bread.' Susie took the fork out of Vera's hands, glared at her and then moved the frying pan away from the burner. Daisy could see Roy watching with amusement. She went over to him.

'The flowers are lovely,' she said. 'Thank you.' She didn't put her arms around him but looked deep into his eyes before bending and kissing him on the cheek. 'Roy, I . . .'

He gave her a small smile, then stood and walked towards the hall.

'I'll be back later, got business to see to. You take it easy this morning. Make her rest, Vera. Bye, kid.' He waved to little Eddie who was eating a bowl of cereal.

Daisy followed him out to the hall. Before he reached the front door he paused and took her in his arms. She stood quite still. She could feel Roy's heart beating. He lowered his head and kissed her cheek gently. 'It'll be all right, Daisy. I promise you.'

He opened the door and almost stepped on the wreath.

'Jesus Christ,' said Daisy. 'Shit. Shit. Shit!'

The white lilies were formed in the shape of a cross. Roy bent and extracted a card. *In Remembrance*. He showed it to Daisy. Her heart was beating fast and stabs of fear were jabbing at her spine. Vera had come to the door at the sound of Daisy's oaths.

'It's them bleedin' death flowers again. You know whose handiwork this is, don't you, Roy?' Vera bent and fingered the waxy flowers. 'The bastard thinks 'e's being clever. He must have been watching this place for ages to know you'd come 'ome.'

'He knows where I am.' Daisy was shivering. 'I should 'ave stayed in the van, I've brought trouble to you all.' Her eyes scanned the driveway but there was nothing but Roy's Humber parked on the gravel.

'Don't talk such bleedin' tripe,' Vera snapped.

'Get back inside,' said Roy, picking up the wreath, herding Daisy and Vera back inside the house then laying the flowers on the hall table.

'Chuck this fucking rubbish in the dustbin. Vera, don't let these two out of your sight.' He motioned towards Daisy and little Eddie. Susie had come to see what all the fuss was about and she had the child in her arms. 'I'll send some lads down to watch over this place.' He looked at Daisy and touched her cheek. 'You'll be safe, I promise.'

Daisy remembered he had told her once before he'd keep her safe.

And in that split second she knew she couldn't trust any man to keep her from harm. However well-meaning Roy's words, if she and little Eddie were to survive, she was the one who had to be in control of their destiny.

'Perhaps 'e sent the flowers by telephoning a florist down 'ere,' said Vera.

'No, Vera,' Roy said, tucking the card in his wallet. 'This has been made up by a florist and given to Waite and he left them himself to scare Daisy.'

Valentine Waite knew full well that Roy Kemp, hard man, was in the house when he'd laid the wreath. Roy's distinctive car was on the driveway. The fucking cheek of the bastard, thought Daisy. He thought he was untouchable.

'We'll get him,' said Roy.

Daisy knew this time he was telling the truth.

'Is she a real gypsy?' Glo was entranced by the tooth-less crone who sat in her makeshift tent in the plush waiting room of Heavenly Bodies. Glo liked the brightly coloured chiffon scarves hanging from the canvas, and the large crystal ball on the table held her spellbound. Tin coins that looked like gold jangled and swung from Madame ZaZa's headscarf, and every now and then she took a sip from the glass of clear liquid that she pulled from beneath the small circular table with the orange chenille cloth.

'Is she fuck!' Jacky said. 'About as real as a nine-bob note. Madame ZaZa is an old prossie who can't let go and be put out to grass. Vera's as soft as shit and likes 'aving her around, so she tells people's fortunes from the cards and tea leaves.

'Most of the women who get their palms read by her 'ave 'ad their life stories told her by their husbands or granddads who knew her when she was on the game, so she ain't often wrong. The rest she makes up. Mostly she tells people what they want to hear, like good fortune or a trip across the ocean. You'd be surprised at how many women *think* they've had an 'ard life. So when she tells them they 'ave, the daft old bat has got their attention straight away. Ain't that right, darlin'?'

Madame ZaZa adjusted her bright headscarf and took another swig of neat gin. She grinned at Glo.

Glo was happy. She'd spent half the previous night wandering around the flat, just touching stuff, hardly daring to believe she could live in such a nice place.

'A flat and a job! I can 'ardly believe my luck.'

Jacky grabbed hold of Glo's arm.

'You got to finish all them tablets first and rest. Vera will give the nod when you're ready to take over a bit of responsibility.' Glo looked at Jacky's starched white coat stretched over her slightly tubby body, and at her black seamed stockings and black patent high heels. Wholesome, that's the word for Jacky, Glo thought, sexy but wholesome. She'd taken a liking to her and felt the feeling was mutual.

'You got no fears on that score,' Glo said.

'Good. Because Vera told me you was to eat properly and get some decent clothes.'

Glo felt herself being scrutinised by the older woman.

'Come with me.' Jacky marched her down the passageway to a large metal locker. She opened the door and Glo could see shelves and shelves of supplies. The sweet smell of talcum powder wafted over her. Vaseline was stacked jar upon jar and rows of clothes hung from hangers. Glo rifled through them. Nuns' habits, French maids' skimpy outfits, long black leather coats, thigh-high boots with ridiculously high heels. And underwear galore, in all colours, all sizes. Bras with holes so the nipples would poke out, split-crotch knickers, platform bras, G-strings. 'All the accessories are there as well,' said Jackie. 'Not that you'll be needin' to get any out for the girls yet. They know their customers so they'll tell you what the men prefer. I might as well start as I mean to go on and get you familiar with the runnin' of the place.'

She pulled open a drawer and searched through the pile of brilliant white material, extracting a garment that she put into Glo's hands. Glo shook out the folds. It was a white cotton coat. Like the one Jacky herself was wearing, only smaller.

'You wears this over whatever you like.' Glo gave a long look at all the sexy clothes before Jacky shut the metal door. Her white coat would suit her fine. 'Don't bother about it all now. You got some shoppin' to do.' Jacky marched back to the waiting area and snapped open the till. Glo followed, the coat in her hands. 'I'm giving you this.' Into Glo's hands she pressed some notes.

'I . . . I got food.' Glo tried to give her the money back but Jacky took the coat, put it under the counter and shoved the money back at her.

'I know. This ain't for food. It's to buy yourself some decent clobber.'

Glo looked at the money. 'But there's far too much . . .'

'Not if you 'as to buy shoes and underwear as well. And toiletries.'

'But . . . But I . . .'

'But fuckin' nothing. Clear off, out into the market. An' for fuck's sake buy a litter tray for that kitten. If it shits upstairs in Vera's flat she'll go spare. Vera can't abide dirt, you know. Neither can she abide untidiness so I'll give you a little tip. Sometimes she pops down early in the morning an' if there's a dirty cup or a messy surface anywhere she gives one 'ell of a rollickin'. All you got to do is give the place a once-over before you goes to bed. I'm tellin' you, that woman is one of the straightest I know, but you don't ever want to get on the wrong side of Vera.'

Glo watched as Jacky wrote down the exact amount she'd taken from the till and given to her. Then Jacky slipped the paper down the back of the till.

'Go on then, skedaddle!' Jacky waved Glo away and was just about to open the door onto the busy street when in came a big girl wearing a pink cardigan over her white coat.

'Hello,' the girl said. 'It's a nice warm day but that wind coming off the ferry is sharp. You must be Glo?' Glo nodded. 'My name's Sam, short for Samantha but no one ever calls me that.' Glo saw that blonde Sam had the most fantastic skin, all creamy with pink cheeks. She peeled off the cardigan and stowed it beneath the counter. Her more than ample breasts were pressed against the white material of her working coat. 'I know,' she said. 'I'm a big girl and I don't wear nothing underneath this.' She smoothed her hands over her body. 'My clients don't like to see knicker or bra lines stretched into my skin.' She grinned at Jacky. 'Hello, Jack,' she said, and gave her a broad wink, then turned back to Glo. 'You done this line of work before?'

'Oh yes,' Glo lied. She wasn't going to admit she could hardly read. She was totally in awe of Sam, who was a very beautiful woman and seemed to have a nature to match. 'Daisy can vouch for that.'

'Daisy and Vera are me guardian angels,' said Jacky. 'You knows that don't you, Sam? They looked after me and set me up 'ere and now I got the bleedin' lot. A good man, a child and a job. Of course I don't turn any sort of tricks. I'm the Madam and I takes the money. But I'm groomin' you for my job, Glo, so's I can stay at home more with me man and child. We got a bookshop,' she finished proudly.

Glo looked at Jacky's face. She was alive with happiness that seemed to spill over and fill the place.

'What's all this other stuff, them crystals and chimes?'

She pointed towards the hanging wind chimes tinkling away in the corner of the shop and the crystals hanging on chains reflecting the light and making rainbow colours on the pale blue walls. Scented oils wafted exotic perfume into the reception area.

'You'll be in charge of all that later as well. I'll give you some books so you can read up on it. Can't go giving a punter a crystal meant for helping her to 'ave children if she's ninety-two and wants to heal her bunions, can you?'

Glo's heart began to beat fast. Vera had promised to help her learn to read. She wanted to do the very best for her new boss, and she was a quick learner. Thank God she'd heard a wireless programme at Daisy's about stones and their powers and had managed to memorise most of it.

'You'll meet Robin later. He does the women's body rubs – and the blokes'.' Sam laughed. 'He's a bit of a girl, if you know what I mean. An Iron Hoof, a poof.' Glo nodded, but Jacky was rattling on again. 'That's what I mean when I say he can turn 'is hand to anything. The ladies love 'im an' you won't find a kinder person – besides Vera, that is – to tell your troubles to. He's a real sweetie. Got a flat up in Beach Street.'

'So I really am the only one living 'ere?'

'We all have 'omes to go to,' Jacky said. 'You'll need to let me know about the time you needs off, so we can fit it in with the bookings.'

'You mean I can choose?'

''Course you can. Just because you're living 'ere don't mean you're on call all the time. Vera ain't no slave driver. But you'll be expected to be behind the desk at the busiest times.'

Glo couldn't believe her luck. 'What if anything goes wrong?'

'Like what?'

'Someone getting nasty?'

'Oh, I see what you mean. Most of our blokes are regulars. They pay over-the-top prices because this is a respected establishment. They 'ave to pay me first an' if I don't like the look of 'em I don't let 'em in. I refers 'em to the Forton Road brothel. Don't be fooled by Robin. He's built like a brick shithouse and 'e don't take crap from anyone. He could scare a charging rhinoceros, if 'e put his mind to it. But you'll see, it'll be all right, girl. Anyway, you can't do nothin' till you're properly on your feet and 'ave put on a bit of weight. People'll be thinking Vera's starving her employees.'

Glo gave a big sigh. She was going to like it here. She grinned at Jacky.

'Don't you give me that smarmy look.' Jacky pointed towards the market stalls outside. 'I sent you out shopping ages ago!'

CHAPTER 17

'Reggie's been round, Roy.'

Violet was washing up the tea things, Roy was going through some papers at the kitchen table. He'd not been in long and this was one job he hated. But he was filling in time, waiting for a knock on the door from Charles to say a carload of his blokes from Portsmouth had already been staked out around Daisy's house in Western Way and that Heavenly Bodies was also under surveillance.

Vinnie Endersby, too, was supposed to have been picked up by Charles from his lodgings and the pair of them should have been here by now. Gosport was only an hour and a half away but it was times like this when he wished Daisy lived with him.

Ever since Eddie Lane had pulled a fast one by muscling in on his territory, Roy had been especially vigilant of his empire. He'd taught Eddie Lane a lesson by taking his life and he hoped that might deter other toerags. Roy knew every little liberty taken against him that didn't go unchecked was another nail in his coffin. And he was nowhere near ready for the knackers' yard yet or for anybody to take over his manor.

Valentine Waite had taken liberties putting that wreath on the doorstep while Roy was inside Daisy's house. It proved he was in the area and it proved the fucker thought he was invincible. A sure sign the nutter was getting cocky. He'd lose more than that for what he'd done to Daisy when Roy got hold of the bastard.

He thought about Daisy. She'd changed, but it was only natural. She needed time to get over this thing, but it hurt him that she was terrified in case he touched her.

'Roy! I said Reggie come round. You ain't listening.'

'Sorry, Mum.' Roy gave her a smile and saw her face soften. 'I got my mind on Daisy, you know that. Was he all right?'

'Ron's not happy about some of the crap that's being kicked about by the long-firming you did on their patch. Ron don't like to feel he ain't in control.' There weren't many secrets between mother and son. 'What are you going to do?'

Roy shrugged. 'Nothing, till I've finished this bit of business. Then I'll go round to see the twins. Get Reg to pacify Ronnie. You know what he's like when he gets the hump about anything. I'll offer another lump sum.' Violet seemed satisfied by his reply.

He'd admired Daisy for her brains and her vivacity. The long-firm scam had been a hell of a risk for her to take. She done it because Eddie Lane had stitched him up and when he'd sorted Eddie out and shown him he couldn't make him a laughing stock Daisy had paid Roy back. Bloody tit for tat. Except the twins as well as himself were on the losing end. He didn't count the losses the Richardsons had taken because, with the torture gang in custody, he could worry about Charlie and Eddie Richardson later. The twins were the ones most volatile.

'I'll go round Vallance Road as soon as I get a minute,' he said. 'But Reg is all cut up at present about Frances and her overdose and depression and he's lost all control of Ronnie since the Cornell killing. You know what Ron's like, thinks he's George Raft, Humphrey Bogart and James Cagney all rolled into one. Last time he was round here he was spinning me a yarn about getting Frank Mitchell out of Dartmoor . . .'

'Not Mad Axe Mitchell?'

'The very same.'

'He's got a screw loose, that Ron. Look, I don't want no bad feeling amongst you boys, we all been friends for too long.'

'Trouble is, Mum, business and friendship don't mix.'

His mother sighed.

'My first priority is getting my hands on that bleeding boxer. Where's Charles got to?' He threw the paperwork down on the table, leaned back on the chair until it almost tipped on to its rear legs. He looked at his watch.

'You sorted out any finances for Daisy?' His mother had finished the washing-up and decided to attack the oven. She began scrubbing the inside with wire wool.

'She won't take my money, Mum.'

'What about if you was married?' His mother came out of the recesses of the oven. She pushed her hair back and transferred a smudge of grey soap to her forehead.

'And how's that going to happen with Moira still in Spain? I ain't divorcing her because she ain't right in the head. Daisy wouldn't want me to.'

Violet rinsed the grill pan in the soapy water. She was very quiet. Frank Sinatra was singing his heart out with 'Strangers In The Night' and usually Violet sang along with him. Roy knew she'd been thinking hard and long about Daisy and had had big discussions with Charles well into the early hours over their games of draughts about the right way to help Daisy back to her independence.

'I got an idea. Why don't you get Daisy to manage the Gosport brothels? That Vera knows what's what in the business. Could make a big difference to the takings, especially if Daisy and Vera cleaned them up the way Heavenly Bodies is run.'

'Rosa's doing fine on her own down at Chestnut House.'

'Rosa can't be out on the street *and* looking after the girls. Take a tip from Vera, her Heavenly Bodies salon is managed on site. Ain't she training that girly who looked after Daisy?'

'Glo? Yes she is. That kid's going to be a winner.'

Violet looked pleased with herself. 'Vera won't be happy if we take more of her trade, but what if you got another venture going and got the pair of them to manage it?'

'Just like that?'

His mother nodded. She'd dismantled the gas rings now and had dumped them in the soapy froth. She was like a bloody gasman with that fucking oven of hers, he thought. She used it so much for her baking and cooking she could take it to bits in her sleep.

'Like what kind of venture?'

'What's the one place Gosport ain't got that you got plenty of up 'ere in London?'

'That's what I admire about you, Mum. One minute you're baking and washing up and the next minute you're working out ways to make money. I suppose that's what attracted me to Daisy, she's just like you – or she was until that bastard got hold of her. I don't have the foggiest.' She was looking at him like he was a simpleton.

'An exotic dancing club. That's what Gosport town needs.'

He thought for a moment.

'You mean a strip joint?'

'If that's what you want to call it. I still think exotic dancing is classier.'

'And where do you reckon this place should be?'

'That's up to Daisy and Vera. You just buy the premises when they find them. Make it look like you

262

need the pair of 'em to work for you and give 'em a hefty wodge of the takings. We'll all be happy then. That Vera ain't stupid. She'll jump at the chance of more blokes coming into the area because it'll mean more business for her own place. And of course she'll soon put two and two together that a few rooms above the strip joint can be used as a brothel and soon the money'll be rolling in. Besides, that woman will move heaven and earth to get Daisy on her feet again. Apart from the other stuff he did to her, the cheek of that Valentine Waite swindling Daisy out of her money! I'll never get over it.'

Roy got up and swung his mother around, lifting her clean off the ground. He loved her violet smell, she always wore the scent to match her name. What she'd come up with was bloody dynamite.

She protested. 'Put me down, you big oaf!'

He knew she didn't really want to be put down, but he set her down carefully just as she asked and planted a big kiss on her permed hair.

'You're a bloody genius. There's nothing like work to help get you over a trauma. Bless you, Mum.'

Roy heard the key in the front door. Charles was back and he pushed open the kitchen door. Roy nodded to Vinnie who was close behind him.

'We fit for the off?' Vinnie asked. 'Where we looking for the bastard first?'

'Anywhere and everywhere here, then it's down to Gosport,' Roy said.

*

'Goodnight, Glo.'

Glo waved to Jacky as she walked down Gosport High Street in her grey slacks and matching lightweight grey sweater. It was a clear night with a bright moon and the stars were twinkling like diamonds on velvet. When Jacky got to Boots the chemist Glo went inside and locked the door of Heavenly Bodies. Vera was very particular about safety and it had to be double locked. Jacky was the only person besides Vera with a key. Slipping the spare key on the hook behind the counter, Glo began singing tunelessly as she gazed around the salon. It was one in the morning and she was as contented as a cat with a tin of sardines. And she knew what that was like because the tiny black kitten was wolfing down mashed sardine at this very moment up in the flat's kitchen and trying to purr at the same time. Glo had decided to call it Blackie, and already she loved it to bits.

She looked around Vera's domain. Her eyes lit on the vase of flowers on the table in the waiting area. They were well past their best. She could sort it in the morning but what if Vera came early? Glo didn't want Vera cross with her for any reason at all. It wouldn't take long to dispose of the flowers now and wash up the glass container. She could pop out early and buy fresh blooms from the market, show Vera she was concerned about the place.

With the vase in her hands she went down to the rear of the salon, slid back the bolt and opened the door. The dustbins were at the end of the cobbled yard. A gentle wind blew off the Solent and ruffled her hair in the darkness, the only light coming from a streetlamp way off. A grey cat jumped from the shadows on top of the dustbin and shot away into the blackness, the metal lid of the bin clattering to the cobbles.

'Bloody 'ell, you scared me,' she said to its retreating skinny body. Her heart was pounding like a sledgehammer. Glo wished Vera had a light out in the yard. Would she ever get over that fear, she wondered?

When Valentine Waite had left her tied to a chair with a blindfold covering her eyes, the hours had seemed like days. Indeed sometimes it *was* days before he came back and by that time she was almost a gibbering wreck.

She knew she should have tried to escape from him long ago, but she never had the bottle to do it then. Loss of confidence is a terrible thing, she thought. Yes, there had been times later, when he'd sent her from the house on errands, but as soon as she was presented with the open door and the street with people going about their everyday business, a terrible feeling would engulf her like she wasn't really there. Her heart would bang away inside her chest and she'd panic and shake so much that she needed to be back inside

Waite's house or in the scrapyard where she knew where everything was.

Glo realised now that Valentine Waite had made her so dependent on him, so totally in subjection, that she'd willingly suffered all kinds of humiliation, mental and physical, rather than find the courage to break free of him. Daisy had come along and given her strength. By witnessing the degradation of that dear woman and yes, she had to admit, by taking part in that humiliation, she had come to realise what Waite had done to herself.

Since examining the contents of that filthy box, Glo knew she was lucky to be alive. From the discussion they'd all had in the house at Western Way, it had been pointed out to her that all the victims had been blonde. Glo ran her hand through her springy dark hair. If she'd been a slight blonde like his mother, her pubic hair would be in that box along with the date of her murder and the place her body was concealed. Glo shivered. Thank Christ she was safe now.

Glo shoved the dying flowers in the rubbish bin, then clamped the lid on firmly and ran back to the salon.

Inside, she bolted the back door again, washed up the vase and after a last look around, switched off the lights and climbed the carpeted stairs to the flat.

She pushed open the door and before she had time to put on the light, he pounced on her.

Valentine Waite gave her a stinging slap that sent

her to her knees. She heard the sound of the slap against her head before she felt its intense pain. Glo put out her hands to save herself as she fell towards the floor but she couldn't escape the kick that took the breath from her body as his boot connected with her ribs.

'Think you can get away from me? I own you, cunt.'

In the darkness he was illuminated by the moonlight. She couldn't see his face and didn't want to. All she was concerned with was making herself as small as possible to deflect the next kick, when his body stiffened as though he was listening to something.

'Glo, it's only me!'

Jacky was downstairs. Glo summoned up her strength to shout out, but the sound that came from her was hardly worth the effort.

'Get away . . .'

And that was as far as she got before he was on his knees beside her with his hand clamped over her mouth. She could smell the sweat on his skin and she wanted to vomit.

'Glo!' Jacky called.

The seconds ticked by. Part of her wanted Jacky to realise she was there, that there *was* something wrong. The sensible part of her was willing Jacky to stay downstairs, to do whatever it was she'd come back for and to leave Heavenly Bodies.

Please God don't let Jacky get hurt, she begged.

'Don't you dare move, bitch,' he whispered.

'I left the takings,' sang out Jacky. 'Stupid cow I am. You know I'm supposed to put 'em in the Lloyds night safe. I'll be forgetting me head next. You all right, Glo?'

He put his wet lips to her face and whispered, 'Tell her you're all right.'

She could hear Jacky loudly moving stuff about. Please, please don't come upstairs. I don't want you hurt. The fear was making her shake. If she did what he wanted there was every possibility she could save Jacky from harm. She forced herself to keep her voice steady.

'I'm fine, I'm in bed – reading. Just tidy up for me down there before you go, will you? See you tomorrow, Jacky.'

Once more his hand was clamped over her mouth. She heard the woman at the till, familiar noises, unfamiliar noises, louder in the darkness. What the hell was Jacky doing down there, she wondered? She could hear her clattering about and muttering to herself.

'I'm off now. Cheerio, Glo.'

She heard the door slam but she didn't hear it being locked from the outside.

Glo knew then that Jacky realised something was wrong.

Glo had tried to give her clues and they'd worked.

Hadn't she told Jacky to tidy up, when the place was immaculate?

Hadn't she said she was reading when there wasn't a light on?

Please get help, Jacky. Please get help before he kills me.

How had he managed to escape being seen by Roy Kemp's men who were supposed to be keeping an eye on the place? Then the penny dropped. He'd waited for his chance at the back and when she'd taken out the dead flowers, he'd slipped inside.

'Get up, bitch,' he said. She could hear the relief in his voice that the unwanted visitor had gone. Glo got to her knees, holding on to a chair, and managed to stand upright.

God, she hated the familiar smell of him. Sickly cologne, sweat and peppermint. He grabbed her arm.

'Get in the bedroom.'

She knew better than to refuse and walked unsteadily ahead of him. Lamplight glimmered weakly through the window. She sat down on the edge of the bed. The black kitten squealed, cross at being disturbed from its sleep. It looked sleepily at her and she put out her fingers to touch the soft young fur. With amazing speed he knocked her hand away and made a grab for the animal that had started a throaty purr almost too much for its tiny frame to bear.

'Got a pet, have we?' He scooped up the kitten, holding it away from his face, watching with amusement its futile wriggling, and when its small pink mouth opened, showing minute spikes of white teeth, and it hissed at him, he laughed.

Glo's heart was pounding against her chest. She

knew if she begged him to put it down he would do the opposite. She watched him.

Glo couldn't help herself. 'Please don't . . .'

She heard the small bones crack.

He said, 'You don't have a pet no more.'

Glo closed her eyes, trying to will away the scene she'd witnessed. She swallowed back the bile that had risen.

'You took Daisy, my pet, away. It's only fair I got rid of yours.'

He was completely mad, she thought. She wanted to throw herself at him, scream, shout, and hit out at him. But what good would it do? He was far stronger than her. He could kill her as easily as he'd killed the kitten. And then a great calm enveloped her. Glo took a deep breath. If she could keep him talking, keep him from harming her, maybe, just maybe, if Jacky hadn't missed the signs, help might arrive. And then he asked, 'Where have you been?'

Glo decided to tell the truth. Daisy was safe now. Or at least she hoped she was.

'That van I took. We lived in it. Far as I know it's still in the Crescent at Alverstoke, 'idden in bushes.'

'The fuckin' van don't matter.' He sat down beside her on the bed. She wanted to move away from him but didn't want to antagonise him. 'You took something from the room above the scrapyard's office. I want it back.' Glo knew exactly what he meant, the lacquered box. Play for time, girl, she told herself. He

was staring at her, watching every flicker of movement, his eyes like pieces of flint.

'Sorry I took your wallet.'

'Not the fuckin' wallet.'

'That's all I took. We needed the money for petrol
and oil for that big leak the van had.'

He hit her again. Her ears were still ringing when
he cried out.

'Where's the fucking lacquered box?' Again he
hit her. A punch this time and she heard the bone
crack in her nose. Blood began to stream warm and
metallic-tasting to her mouth, and she tumbled from
the bed to the floor.

'Where's the box?' He'd slid from the bed and
stood over her.

'I don't know.' He was loosening his trousers. He
pulled the belt through and swung, letting her have
the full force of it as he aimed the buckle end towards
her head. She was already too dazed to try to protect
herself and screamed as the leather slapped her skin
and the metal clip tore into her hair. He yanked at it,
pulling hair out from her scalp. He was laughing now.
Another whip from the belt cut across her shoulders
and then the belt was thrown down and she felt
herself being yanked up and thrown face down across
the bed. Glo had no strength left to fight him. He
ripped clothing from her body and because she didn't
want him to hit her any more she lay, accepting the
inevitable.

He pulled her arse up and pushed in, penetrating

her with force. Glo cried, yelping with fear, but ignoring her, he squeezed in, tightly.

'It's hotter and tighter than a cunt.'

He came in seconds, his voice screaming his mother's name, and then he sank on top of her, pushing her face down onto the mattress.

Jolts of pain ran along Glo's spine. She slid from underneath him as he shrivelled, and cried into the softness of the bedding.

He moved his heavy body and she knew his moment of satiation was over. Fear engulfed her, what was he going to do next?

'Up to your tricks again, pretty boy?'

Valentine Waite was off the bed and away from his quarry in the flicker of an eyelid. Glo rolled away and hunched herself into a ball. She stared at the owner of the voice and her heart soared.

Roy stood in the doorway. Vinnie was behind him and Charles pushed his way past him into the bedroom.

Roy looked at the terrified wreck of a girl.

'You get downstairs. Jacky's there.' The air was charged with something that put the fear of God into him.

Charles said, 'You all right, little one?'

'Nothin' I can't 'andle now you're here.'

Roy saw Charles had tears in his eyes looking at the state of her. He picked up the bedspread and wrapped it around her bloodied body. He carried her to the doorway and down the stairs.

'Pleased with yourself?' Roy's voice was ice cool. Valentine Waite had calmly begun dressing himself. He showed no fear of the men in the room, even gave Roy a smile that turned his stomach. 'Don't you even think about trying to escape, bastard. You might be a fucking boxer but there's three of us, and only one of you.' He patted his breast pocket. ''Sides, what I got here'll make a nasty mess of that pretty body. Or face. Just depends where I fancies shooting, so I don't reckon your chances, 'specially not when the big man comes back upstairs. He don't like men who knock little girls about. And for God's sake do your flies up, you look pathetic.'

Roy saw the dead kitten on the carpet.

He looked at Vinnie and shook his head. The look that passed between them said they were of a single mind, that the man before them was not just a villain, but out and out evil. Then he heard Jacky's loud voice rising as she explained to Glo, 'I knew Roy was at Daisy's. His blokes were outside, so however did the fucker get past everyone?'

'I thought 'e was going to kill me,' Roy heard Glo sob. 'The bastard killed my kitten!'

'When you told me you was readin' in bed, I knew you was lying. There was no light on in your bedroom and I knows you're just like Daisy now. You can't sleep in the bleedin' dark.' Jacky's voice faded as she went further into the recesses of Heavenly Bodies.

'Not so clever, are you?' Vinnie had spoken for the first time since entering the bedroom. 'But how come you managed to evade being found? We've been looking for you for quite a while.'

Roy said, 'Ever the copper, eh, Vin?'

'I've just been going about my business.' Valentine Waite's boyish face showed no concern, as he said, 'Whatever did I do that made you want to find me?'

Roy was at boiling point. If Vinnie wasn't there, if he hadn't made a bleedin' pact with the detective, he'd have killed the fucker by now.

'You took Daisy, you bastard!' He stepped towards the boxer but Vinnie grabbed at his arm.

'Later,' he said.

Roy nodded. The detective was right.

'What if I said Daisy Lane came to me willingly?' Valentine Waite was baiting the two of them. This time Roy wasn't rising to it.

'Then I'd say you was round the fucking bend.' Mentally he thanked Vinnie for stopping him lamming into this cunt straight away. Best keep to the plan, he thought.

'Then there's the matter of Daisy's money,' Roy said. 'Not a nice thing to do, take a woman's money.'

Valentine Waite sat down on a bedroom chair, his legs straight out in front of him as though he couldn't care less. He slipped one arm along the back of the seat, his fingers plucking at the fringed velvet.

I'll give him ten out of ten for coolness, thought Roy.

'She gave it to me because she liked the way I fucked her.'

This time it was Vinnie who had to be restrained. He raised a hand and made a fist and stepped forward, but as soon as Roy caught his eye he held back, breathing in and out heavily. And in that second Roy knew Vinnie Endersby wasn't only in this for the box of hair, for the possibility of promotion. No, he wanted revenge for Daisy's sake.

Valentine Waite had missed none of this and he laughed.

'Anything else you reckon I've done that can be accounted for?'

Vinnie said, 'I've got a box of your mementos that could put you away for life. You aren't going to tell me you know nothing about missing prostitutes, are you?'

The room was filled with silence.

Then Valentine Waite pushed his hand through his hair and stood up. Charles had just entered the room and he stepped towards Waite, his hand already flying to his pocket. Roy put up an arm to still him but already the pistol was in his hand.

'Charles, put away your new toy.' Roy saw Vinnie looking at the weapon. 'It's a German Makarov, 9mm cartridge, based on the Walther. Charles loves trying out new stuff. You don't want to make it dirty using it on that fucking scumbag, do you, Charles? You know we got other plans for him.'

Waite shook his head. 'Such hastiness.' He gave

another grin. 'I only wanted to tell you there's a girly in a cricket pavilion back up in the Smoke.' He put his hand in his trouser pocket. Charles was on him again before he could withdraw it, and Waite was laughing. Laughing loudly at the three of them as though he hadn't a care in the world.

Roy watched as Charles yanked Waite's hand away. But there was no weapon held between his fingers.

Only a single curl of blonde hair with a tag attached.

'Get out of my fuckin' car.' The boxer was like a zombie, thought Roy. It was as if he now knew his run had come to an end and there was no fight left in him. Valentine Waite joined Charles in the grassy clearing in Stanley Park. Stumbling awkwardly from the back of the Humber, handcuffed to the big man, he didn't have much of a choice. It had begun to rain hard, pissing down like it was never going to end, thought Roy, as he too stepped from the car. Vinnie was turning his collar up against the elements and adjusting his hat so it would keep the worst of the rain off the back of his neck. But the good thing was rain made the ground softer, easier to work, and then if it kept on bucketing at this pace there'd be no trace of anyone ever being here. And Roy liked the thought of that.

A sound alerted his brain to the small animals scurrying in the undergrowth. Squirrels probably, or bats in the trees. Possibly rats. The leaves of the rhododendrons were slick and shiny. Overhead pine branches threw down their heavy scent. The wet earth smelled of peat.

'No one's likely to disturb us. See how easy it was for us to enter the double iron gates when normally they're kept locked?' Roy was speaking to Vinnie. Charles had dragged Waite further into the dark clearing. 'The gatekeeper's having a bit of nookie with a friend of Vera's. Hardly likely we'll be interrupted 'ere tonight.'

'If I remember correctly there are only two other entrances to Stanley Park,' said Vinnie. 'One in Western Way and the other at Stokes Bay and they're both locked. You're right, we can take our time.' He walked round to the back of the car where Roy had opened the boot and taken out two garden spades. Vinnie took one.

'This is a pact, right?' said Roy.

Vinnie nodded.

Roy had no cause to disbelieve him, he simply wanted the copper to confirm the plan. 'Come on then,' he said, slamming the boot. Carrying the second spade, he followed Charles into the driving rain.

Charles had paused at a group of gravestones. The memorials were too small to be those of a human cemetery.

'The headstones belong to pets,' Vinnie informed them. Roy could see in the dull light from the torch that Vinnie had produced that there were perhaps six graves. Trees surrounded the clearing, their branches at once shielding the men from the worst of the deluge but allowing huge drips to fall noisily.

'So what are they doin' here?'

'I can't remember if it was the Barings or the Sloane-Stanleys these animals belonged to, but see that place over there' – Vinnie pointed into the dimness where part of a building was just visible through the trees – 'that's Bay House. There's talk of making it into a school. But you got no worries, it's empty to the best of my knowledge. Quite something in its day, built in 1838 that place. All the posh nobs came down to stay. They obviously loved their pets.'

Roy nodded and thought of the kitten. He'd make Waite pay for the poor little bleeder.

'That's enough of the 'istory lesson 'cause I don't love this fuckin' pet.' He threw the spade he was carrying at Valentine Waite, who automatically stretched forward to catch it but the handcuffs stopped him. Roy laughed. 'Picked your 'eadstone yet?'

He smiled at the look that crossed the boxer's face.

'Didn't think we brought you out here for a Gosport night-time 'istory lesson, did you?' He took his own gun from his pocket and said, 'I'm not like Charles, always chopping and changing my pieces. This P38 is my little beauty. Don't mind if I keep it pointed at you while Charles unlocks the cuffs, do you? Don't want you getting any funny ideas about trying to run into the trees. That's not what I got in mind, Mr Waite.'

Valentine Waite was passive as the handcuffs were removed.

'Now pick up the spade and start digging. "Jock" shall be your 'eadstone, I think. Take off the top layer of grass so it can be set back again later.'

Roy watched him start doing exactly what he was told. Charles had his gun pointed towards the boxer again, so Roy passed his weapon to Vinnie then fumbled in his breast pocket and brought out a circular piece of steel from which he stripped a protective soft leather covering. The highly sharpened blade glittered in the rain. Lifting up his jacket sleeve he fitted the circular blade into a leather wristband already in place. The weapon stood straight out from his wrist, a lethal bracelet of razor-sharp metal.

'I got this in Africa,' Roy said, showing Vinnie. It pleased him to see Vinnie recoil slightly at the look of it. 'D'you like it? It's a tribal weapon, called an abarait. I took a fancy to it when I was in Mombasa. I never 'ad a proper chance to use it . . .'

Roy's hand flashed across Waite's face. 'Dig! You fucker!' The boxer had stopped digging to watch Roy, a puzzled look on his face. Neither Charles nor Vinnie stirred. Roy's movement had stunned them, but the one most surprised was Waite as the open seam down his face, running from cheekbone to chin, first oozed, then dripped, then ran with blood. He put up his hand and Roy could see the disbelief in his eyes as he registered the bright wetness. Then his face contorted with pain.

'. . . Until now.' Roy continued talking as though nothing out of the ordinary had happened. 'What you did to my Daisy was bad enough, but you been worse than bad with the other ladies.'

'Jesus, Roy!' Vinnie took a step forward, then thought better of it and stepped back again, all the while keeping the gun steady on Waite. Charles' face was immobile but then Charles knew what to expect when Roy decided revenge was called for.

Waite fell to the ground, a low moan escaping his lips. The sound gathered momentum and only ended when Roy kicked him away from the oblongs of turf that had begun to appear to one side of the old grave.

'Fucking shut up, get up, and dig faster, you bastard,' growled Roy. Then, in a softer voice, as the man struggled to his feet, 'Them Africans know their business, don't they? And you ain't such a pretty boy now, are you?'

Waite dug harder and deeper. Roy was right; the soft earth was yielding nicely.

Charles said, 'Don't think we're gonna need to help, he's doing fine by 'imself. I love watching people work. How about you, Vin?' Vinnie nodded, trying to ignore the rain trickling from his hat. For a while there was nothing to be heard but the rain and the steady rhythm of the spade biting into the soggy ground, until Roy resumed taunting Waite.

'If I was you, I'd be scared shitless,' he said. 'But then I expect them girls felt like that, didn't they?' Waite went on digging. The hole was sizeable now and he paused, but didn't let go of the spade. Roy motioned him to continue. 'Big, strong, fit bloke like you don't need to rest. Bet you don't get so tired dancing about the bleedin' ring. You're so fit you can kill women an' small creatures like it means nothing . . .'

Again he lunged at the man. This time the blade sliced through his wet clothing and into his chest. Roy actually amazed himself at how much damage he'd done to the bastard with so little effort.

Waite dropped the spade and clutched at his chest. Blood welled though his boxer's fingers and he hunched his shoulders forward as though expecting another blow and trying to protect himself. A strange keening sound was coming from way back in Waite's throat, reminding Roy of the cry of a wounded animal. Roy felt his skin crawl at the noise but there was no pity inside him for this fucker. His Daisy had probably cried like that when Waite had . . . was . . . was . . . And now the bastard was looking down at his chest as though it was unbelievable what was happening to him.

'You made a big mistake hurting my Daisy,' said Roy. 'No one hurts me or mine, understand?'

Waite raised his eyes and looked at Vinnie. Roy knew the copper was well used to seeing crime scenes covered with victims' blood so he wouldn't intervene. And they had a pact, didn't they? Besides, Vinnie knew what this maniac was capable of: didn't he have in his possession the evidence of the boxer's mad gratifications? Roy reckoned if Vinnie had his way, *he'd* be inflicting a few lessons on the fucker as well.

'The detective ain't goin' to help you. After all, you didn't need no help killing them girls who were only trying to make a living, did you? Oh yes, never save mementoes,' said Roy. 'Don't you agree, Vinnie?'

Vinnie nodded. The boxer looked defeated.

'You going to tell me why you kept Daisy Lane prisoner when you probably killed the other girls the same night you met them?' Vinnie asked.

Waite wiped his arm across his eyes to disperse the rain, wincing as he touched his skin, but he couldn't disperse the blood, which was oozing from his chest. He seemed to be having trouble breathing and his voice was little more than a hoarse whisper.

'Daisy reminded me of my mother. I wanted her.'

To Roy it was obvious the copper had been doing some research on the bastard when Vinnie snapped, 'Did you know his mother was on the game? That's why he picked on prossies. His mother never had time for poor little Valentine, did she? Too busy fucking her clients. Valentine had to take second place.'

Valentine Waite seemed suddenly to come to life, rage urging his body forward. His fist flashed towards the detective, but Roy caught the boxer across the forearm. Waite screamed and staggered as the abarait sliced into the flesh of his arm.

'That was a fucking stupid thing to do, wasn't it? Now you only got one good arm to dig with, that'll make things very difficult. Pick the fuckin' spade up, shut up, an' get on with it.'

Roy turned to the detective. 'Okay, Vinnie, enough of the chat,' he said. 'You got the box, I got the bloke.' He kicked against the earth. 'Finish the job.'

'Wait a minute,' said Vinnie, 'I got a couple more questions.' He turned to Waite. 'How did you know Daisy would be driving in Lee on the Solent on that day?'

Waite stood like a scarecrow, ragged, bent and ripped. He'd picked up the spade and used it now like a crutch, leaning his good arm on the handle, his other arm hanging loose at his side. 'Regular as clock-work' – he nodded towards Roy – 'them two, in their mating habits.' The spade seemed to tilt then slide on the rainslicked earth and he slipped. No one stepped forward to help him, but he managed to regain his footing.

'You're 'olding up well. Comes of bein' a fucking fit bastard, I s'pose,' Roy said. 'Well, perhaps not so fit now you got a few holes 'ere and there.'

Waite was staring at Roy. 'I got nothing to live for and I'm ready,' he said. 'Finish it now.'

'You're a cool bugger, I'll say that for you. Any other bastard would be screamin' for mercy.'

Valentine Waite let out a sigh that seemed to deflate what was left of his broken body.

'I'm supposed to fly out to New York in two days, but the demons can't let me win the fight now. I've failed them.'

Roy could see the difficulty with which the man raised his gashed arm and painfully laid it across his upper body. 'I tried to keep her in here, in my heart. My mother. I killed her. She denied me. Daisy denied me too. She didn't want me, so I had to keep her—'

He got no further for Roy's arm struck out and downwards. The blade of the abarait cut into the boxer's upper thigh, splitting the thin material of his trousers and exposing the white disconnected skin that was quickly beading dark red. Another upward slash and the blade severed his throat like wire through soft butter, leaving a gash in his neck like a second, gaping mouth.

Waite fell forward, uttering strange gurgling sounds, and sank to his knees in the mud. Feebly, and in vain, he tried to raise his hand to his neck. Roy watched the quivering boxer for a few seconds then kicked him backwards.

The metallic smell of fresh blood mingled with the peaty earth as Waite sprawled face upwards to the side of the open grave.

Roy bent down and one-handedly ripped open his victim's trousers, searching for, finding, and then stretching his genitals away from his body. The abarait flashed one last time . . .

Holding his prize, Roy moved along Waite's body and shoved the mangled mass into the man's unresisting mouth.

'You won't be needing it any more,' Roy said, getting up. 'Fucking choke on it!'

All three men stood and watched until they were sure the last spasms of death had left Valentine Waite's body.

'Bastard,' said Vinnie.

Charles, satisfied he was dead, kicked the body into the hole.

'I'll cover him up,' said Roy, removing the abarait from his wrist and carefully wiping the blade on the sleeve of his jacket. He slid the leather cover back on the blade and replaced the wrist knife in his pocket.

He turned to Vinnie. 'I know you got a soft spot for Daisy, copper, I ain't bleedin' stupid. When I ain't around no more, that's when you can move in.' He noted Vinnie's eyes narrowing. Yes, he thought, the bugger understands perfectly. 'Until then, you and her are simply *mates*.'

Vinnie shrugged and handed him back his gun in silence, barrel end first. Roy took it and stuck it in his belt.

Vinnie said, 'The deed's done. His promoters'll wonder why he's disappeared, but they'll think he's simply taken off. Everyone knows he's a peculiar bugger. On the fight scene it'll be just another mystery. Remember Freddie Mills? Was he killed or did he commit suicide? And with Waite, no body, no death.'

Roy nodded. 'If you tell it was me that killed him, I'll say you were in on it. I might go down the line, but your career'll be in fucking shit street. This way, you "find" the box of mementos in his rooms above the Lambeth scrapyard. The powers that be will probably promote you for discovering the prossies' murderer, but it will never get as far as the papers or out in the open. The name of Valentine Waite, one of England's finest fighters, will stay intact, mark my words. Like you say, it'll all blow over.'

Then he bent down and picked up one of the shovels and passed it to Vinnie. 'Changed me mind. We're partners in crime, we'll both plant him.'

CHAPTER 18

The letter was short and written on honeysuckle-scented paper. But that was her mate all over, wasn't it? Trying to be refined. Angel smiled to herself. So Sonia was coming down to Gosport for a job interview, was she? She said she was sick and tired of the pace of life in the Smoke and even more fed up with having to take shit from the bastard she was working for now.

An exotic dancing club was opening in the town. Early days yet, Sonia said, so get in before the rush starts for jobs.

And London gangster Roy Kemp was backing the club.

The penny finally dropped. To speak of the Krays was to speak of Roy Kemp. No wonder he'd worn Savile Row clothes. No wonder the bastard had never got in touch with her. It had been a one-night stand for him. One that had left her fuckin' pregnant! But if he was involved in this new club, he'd be coming down to Gosport more, wouldn't he?

It had only taken one night to make her realise she wanted him.

The gentle tap on the prefab window startled her. It was barely eight o'clock in the morning.

'All right, Angel?'

She treated Malkie to a smile and went over to the side door to let him in. For once he looked a bit half decent in his jeans and tee-shirt.

'Just come 'ome from work?' She knew he hadn't had a sleep yet after his night shift at the hotel.

'Wondered if you was all right,' he said, stepping in to the kitchen.

'Why wouldn't I be?' She plugged in the electric kettle. Going to the cupboard she brought out mugs. 'Cuppa?' He nodded. His blond floppy hair fell across his forehead and he brushed it away. He seemed full of smiles this morning. Angel liked it that he popped over every morning when he got in. It made her feel less alone.

Not that she really was alone. Not with her mother asleep in her favourite armchair in the other room.

Angel hurried to the window and stretched up to open it. The place reeked of gin and farts, the smells seemed to go right through the place.

'Let me do that.' Malkie was there like a shot. 'You shouldn't be stretching. Not in your condition.'

Angel whirled round. 'What did you say?' She'd told no one about the baby. And she knew she didn't show yet. It was her everyday ritual, as soon as she got up, to stand in front of the mirror in her bedroom and examine herself from all angles. She'd even tried on her spangly G-string that she'd been wearing when she'd left London in a hurry. And though she said it herself, she looked a dream in it with her long legs and blonde hair. She was just as slim as she'd ever been and, although there was an increase in her bust measurement, she was sure no one could tell she was pregnant. Certainly not the people who came into the vegetable shop round the corner where she was working.

He stood in the centre of the kitchen, his large feet planted firmly on her new bit of lino bought from the door-to-door salesman who called weekly for his payments.

'I ain't stupid. You got the same kind of bloom me mum 'ad when me dad come home from Ireland that time and went back and left 'er in the pudding club.'

'I . . . I . . .'

He stopped her. 'Remember when we went to Gosport, shopping, that day in me mate's car, and you threw up on the way home? I guessed then.'

She stared at him as he went over to a kitchen stool and sat down. If he'd guessed, how many other people had? Certainly not her mother, she wouldn't have been able to keep her trap shut. She'd have been yelling at her, calling her a slag. Good girls who work in solicitors' offices in London don't get caught, do they? Talk about the pot calling the kettle black.

Angel gave a huge sigh, one that seemed to rise from the bottom of her lungs and spread right through her body. She pulled out another stool from beneath the Formica table and slumped down in front of him. Malkie leaned forward, took hold of her hands and pulled her towards him. She heard the kettle switch itself off.

'The water's boiled,' she said and made to rise.

'Sod the kettle,' he said. 'Look at me.'

She turned her head up towards him and looked into his face.

'I've had a rise at work, a good one. You can escape all the pointing fingers an' wagging tongues if you want by marrying me.'

He'd stopped breathing, like he was waiting to see what came next before he decided to breathe again. A cold chill had run right through Angel's body. She didn't want to be married. Not because she didn't like Malkie, she did. He was a nice bloke, and kind, but he didn't make her heart flip upside down. He was too comfortable and he knew her too well. She didn't want to marry anyone. For fuck's sake, was this to be the end of her good times? Didn't she deserve more than looking after her mother, as well as looking after a squalling kid and being stuck indoors waiting for a bleedin' man to come in and demand his sodding dinner?

'What d'you think? You know I worship the ground you walks on.' His voice was soft, cajoling.

If only she'd had the money, or knew anyone who'd get rid of it for her, she'd have done it already. But Old Gertie who lived up the back and knew how to go about these things had gone and bleedin' died while Angel was in London. And if Angel started asking about, her condition would be out in the open. And them sodding penny royal pills and quinine tablets had been money wasted. And the hot baths and gin had been a bleedin' joke.

He was gripping her hands tightly now. She looked into his eyes. He looked as though he might burst into tears at any moment.

She thought about her job. Weighing out pounds of muddy potatoes, handing out packs of firewood and firelighters, standing on her feet all day. Being nice to nosy fuckin' people because she had to be. Putting veg and tinned stuff on tick down in a book because the poor bleeders came in straight away on paydays to pay their bills then had to start ticking up again. It wasn't her idea of a happy job.

Angel knew she was lucky to have work right on her doorstep but she was fed up with Tom the manager's wandering hands. Like a fucking octopus he was whenever no one was in the shop. Always getting her to stand on the chair to get a tin of something off the top shelf so he could look up her skirt, or getting her out in the back on some pretext or other so he could rub his fat body against hers. It was like being back in London with hands pawing at her but without the benefit of extra money tucked in her G-string. And then the electric light inside her head switched itself on.

How long before the baby made its presence felt?

What if she could get a job in Gosport town in the exotic dancing club that was due to open? She could certainly tell Tom to poke his bloody job then. Even if she only managed a month or two before anyone saw she was pregnant, at least it would give her more life than she was getting at the moment. Her heart was beating fast. And it might bring her face to face with Roy!

'Angel? Do you want more time to think it over? I know I kind of sprung it on you?'

Angel took a deep breath. Hedge your bets, girl, she told herself.

'Okay,' she said. 'But won't you care the baby's not yours?'

The look of pure joy that spread across his face before he crushed her to him was incredible.

'I don't care about that,' he said, his voice muffled against her hair. 'I guessed the baby was the reason you'd come back from London. I'll love it like it was me own, you know that. If you'd wanted to 'ave anything to do with the father you wouldn't 'ave come 'ome, would you?' Angel managed to break free long enough to shake her head. 'I love you. I always 'ave.'

'I just need a bit of time to get used to the idea.' Angel pulled away from him and stood up. She wondered if people who were caught in an earthquake felt like this, the ground opening, swallowing them up; and whether they, too, fought uselessly against the inevitable.

Automatically she reboiled the kettle and put tea leaves into the pot. Malkie had joined her, standing behind her, his arms around her waist, his face nuzzling into her neck.

'I can see it now,' he said. 'Eighteen months from now, you an' me, living 'ere together and able to care for your mum, and right opposite me own mum. A little 'un fast asleep in the front garden in one of them big navy blue Royale prams. You might even be having *my* kiddie by then. You wouldn't 'ave to give up your job at the greengrocer's unless you really wanted to, either. Mum wouldn't mind taking a hand with the kiddie.'

'Wonderful,' said Angel.

'And to think that for one brief moment I fancied him, that fucking Valentine Waite.'

'How many times 'ave I told you to stop dwelling on all that crap, Dais. It's all in the past now. Get up, love.' Vera bent to help little Eddie but he'd already got to his feet after falling over a basket of ironing on the kitchen floor. The boy had dropped Kibbles and was now stifling his sobs as he made sure the cat was all right. 'That's right, you kiss Kibbles better.' She looked from Kibbles to Daisy.

One of Vera's false eyelashes was glued higher than the other. Daisy knew Vera wasn't going out today so she decided not to say anything. She smiled to herself. It felt so good to be back amongst people she loved.

'I 'ope you ain't worried one day that cat'll turn on 'im,' said Vera. She opened the door of the oven and poked at a cake that Susie had made. The smell was heavenly, all almonds and coconut. Daisy remembered Susie saying, 'Now, Vera, for Christ's sake, leave that bleedin' oven alone. I don't want a cake that's sunk in the middle.'

'Nah.' Daisy grinned at her. 'He's got to learn that 'e can't always do what 'e wants, that other people have feelings as well. Even if it is only a bleedin' cat!'

Vera looked peeved. 'Bleedin' cat? I'll give you bleedin' cat.' She threw a scrunched-up tea towel at Daisy that caught her full in the face.

'Oww!' Daisy grabbed at it and advanced on Vera.

Her friend stood still and let her come closer. 'See, you didn't flinch. You took that smack with the tea towel and came back at me without cowering once.'

Daisy dropped the tea towel as she realised what Vera meant. 'You think I'm coming to terms with how I was treated?'

'Who knows? Time will tell about that, but at least you ain't a quivering mess no more. Glad to see you got a bit of your old sense of 'umour back an' all. I was beginning to think me best friend was a bleedin' zombie!'

Daisy walked across the kitchen in a stiff pose with her arms straight out in front of her. 'I am the un-dead, I am the undead.' She laughed and bent down and scooped up little Eddie and the cat, planted a smackeroo on little Eddie's cheek and set them down. She took a deep breath and turned to Vera.

'I'll hide the scars on the inside. Meanwhile the scars on the outside are healing nicely. Look.'

She lifted her jeans leg and showed Vera the purplish scar.

'That's fading, Dais.' Vera poked at it with a long red talon of a nail, but gently, on the healing skin. As her head was bent, Daisy lifted Vera's dark hair back from her face.

'Your scar is only a thin silver line now.' Daisy thought about the night she, Bri and Susie had found Vera in the rain in North Street. She'd been cut with a Stanley knife by Sammy, the freaky child-killer who was minding one of Roy's brothels.

'You've had a lot of scars to deal with over the years, and not just on the outside, right, Vera?'

Vera was staring at her and patting her hair back into place at the same time. 'The past makes you what you are today, girl. You can either wake up in the morning with a smile on your face or put on a bleedin' frown. Thank God you're like me, Daisy, putting on a big grin. That big grin hides the lot, don't it?'

Daisy nodded. 'I'm going to be all right now, I reckon,' she said. 'What about Glo? I ain't seen 'er for a while. How's she doing?'

'Actually, Dais, that girl's a bleedin' treasure. You know how I been teachin' 'er to read an' write?'

Daisy nodded.

'Well, she took to it like a duck to water. I made her rest up, as you know, after, after . . .'

'You can say it, Vera. We can't pretend it didn't happen. But that poor Glo . . .' Daisy realised both of them were lucky to be alive.

'Anyway,' continued Vera, 'she whizzed through them kiddies' books then started on some of my books. She takes my advice, see. Not like some people I could touch! Ain't it about time you started getting out in the fresh air?'

Daisy shivered. The house was like a cocoon, safe, but Vera was right as usual. It was time to get out and about.

'S'pose so,' she said. 'That reminds me. Where's me car?'

When Daisy had been abducted she'd been driving her red MG. She hadn't seen it since. Vera looked up from the potatoes she'd started peeling at the sink.

'Roy brought it back an' it was in the driveway. Then Vinnie took it down and put it safely in the lock-up in Seahorse Street. I said I couldn't bear to 'ave it on the premises because every time I looked at it I got all upset. Someone 'ad done some damage to it, but you don't 'ave to worry, Vinnie sorted that an' all. That Vinnie likes you. He said if your car goes wrong he can fix it anytime.'

'That's handy to know,' said Daisy. She was a bit annoyed that Vinnie hadn't been anywhere near her since him and Roy had sorted out Valentine Waite. Him and Roy had come to the house one wet and windy night and Roy had said, 'It's over, Dais. That bastard won't 'urt another living soul.' She'd known it would be no good questioning him about how he'd sorted out Valentine Waite. Not that she gave a flying fuck. She was just relieved she didn't have to look over her shoulder any more.

But she missed Vinnie.

To tell the truth she would have liked a chat with him. Maybe they could have gone down the Dive caff at the ferry and had a cuppa and a sticky currant bun together like they used to before all this . . . this . . .

'If he likes me that much why ain't he been round?'

Vera had finished peeling the spuds and was clattering about with teapot and cups.

'You belong to Roy. Vinnie knows that, Dais.'

'I don't *belong* to anyone!'

'All right then,' snapped Vera. 'He knows you're Roy's woman. For Gawd's sake stop bleedin' moaning about things. Those two blokes put their lives on the line for you, getting rid of that bastard the way they did. Would you 'ave wanted to be on the front page of the bleedin' *Evening News* and the national newspapers? Don't forget Valentine Waite was famous. A trial would 'ave dragged everything up. An' what about Glo? She didn't need reminding of bad stuff when she's tryin' to build a new life. If it's Roy you're worried about, don't be. He won't be implicated in any way. No body, no crime. And because of that lacquered box Vinnie might even get a bit of promotion out of it. That's why Roy gave Vinnie the evidence.'

'Vinnie told me he'd never compromise 'is job . . .'

'He 'asn't.' Vera thought again. 'Well, he 'as, and readin' between the lines, he didn't do it for the promotion, did he? But he 'as got the satisfaction of knowing a killer was brought to justice, street justice maybe, but justice nevertheless.'

'It just seems strange for two such different blokes to get together like that and . . .'

'They did it for you, you silly cow.'

Daisy thought for a moment. 'They can't split on each other, can they?' The thought that Vinnie could lose everything he'd ever worked for scared her to death.

'Never,' said Vera. 'One goes down, the other goes down.'

'You going to tell me where Valentine Waite is?'

'If I knew, I might. But I don't.' And Daisy knew Vera'd sooner cut out her tongue than lie.

Daisy remembered when Roy had come to the caff in North Street with the terrible news that he'd sorted her Eddie. He said then that he'd never tell her where Eddie's body was and she knew he never would. This murder would be similar, hushed up and swept under the carpet.

Daisy still had something worrying her.

'What about the people who keep them kiddies for porn? Like Glo was kept? It won't stop, will it?'

'No. Even putting bastards like Myra Hindley and

that excuse for a bloke Ian Brady in prison for life won't deter other swines from hurtin' poor innocent kiddies. Child porn is big business, always was, always will be, more's the pity. They should bring back 'anging, that's what I say. Save wasting all that good prison food and lodging on bastards like them two. You mustn't think about all that. What you should be worryin' about is bringing up little Eddie and lovin' Roy.'

Daisy began to cry. The daft tart had hit the nail right on the head. Why *couldn't* she love Roy? Vera practically slammed the two mugs of tea down on the table. Liquid bounced on to the cloth.

'Now look what you made me do. That tablecloth was clean on this morning. For Christ's sake what's the matter now? And where's the boy gone?'

'Little Eddie's in the other room. Can't you hear 'im bouncing off the sofa?' Daisy sniffed and wiped her nose with the back of her hand. Vera disappeared into the hall and within seconds she was back again, with a doll in her hand.

'An' what is this?' Vera shook the doll. 'You'll 'ave 'im growing up a nancy boy letting 'im play with dolls.'

'It's a Tiny Tears an' it belongs to Summer. She left it the last time Bri and Jacky brought her 'ere.' She took the doll from Vera and turned it upside down. 'This doll wets itself.'

'Jesus Christ, what will they think of next? You'll be tellin' me it drinks from a bottle.'

Daisy laughed through her tears. 'It bloody does. Where d'you think the wee comes from?' Vera looked pained then she too burst out laughing. Daisy put the doll on the table.

Standing in front of her, Vera raised her hand and tipped Daisy's chin towards her. 'You know I can't 'elp you if you don't tell me what's the matter?'

Daisy gulped. 'Oh, Vera. I wish I could love Roy but I can't let 'im near me.'

Vera gazed at her until the penny dropped. She removed her hand from Daisy's chin and frowned.

'You mean you ain't let him . . . ?'

'You got it. I can't bear his 'ands on me. All I see is Valentine Waite. I know Roy ain't that bleedin' boxer an' I know he won't do anything to me I don't want him to. But . . . but my body just freezes up when he comes near me.' She folded her arms on the table and laid her head on them. Daisy hadn't wanted to tell Vera. She was ashamed of turning away the man who loved her. It was like a knife slicing into her heart to see the look on his face when she froze at his touch. Would Vera understand when Daisy herself didn't know what was going on?

Vera sat down and stirred her mug of tea. 'How does he feel about it?'

'He says, when I'm ready. He says 'e understands.'

'And you?'

'I feel bad about how I'm treating him when he wants to show me how much he loves me. But it's like

I'm dirty. Like I'm not worthy of 'im. I loathe the idea of anyone, even Roy, invading my body . . .'

'You've 'ad a terrible experience, girl. If he says he understands then he does.'

'Will I get better, Vera?'

Vera nodded. 'I think so. But you got to give yourself time, lovey. And worrying about it won't help none. Your body'll tell you when you're ready to love 'im fully again, ducky.' They stayed like that, Daisy listening to the beating of Vera's heart mingling with her own, and trying to believe her.

They were interrupted by the sound of a key turning in the front door. 'That's Suze coming back. Let's get the kettle on again.'

Daisy went over to plug it in.

'Where's the boy?' Susie had shucked off her cardigan and slid off her shoes. Her short red cotton dress showed off her dimpled knees.

'He's in the front room messin' it up. You got cloth ears, or something? Can't you hear the racket?'

Susie poked her tongue out at Daisy. Then she went back into the hall to reappear moments later with little Eddie in her arms.

'Why don't we go out into the garden? It's a lovely 'ot day. You could do with a bit of colour in your cheeks, Dais.'

'Everyone's telling me what to do,' grumbled Daisy, but she was loving it.

'Tell me about it,' said Susie. 'I just popped in to Si's mum's place and all I get is, "When are you goin' to 'ave another baby? When am I going to 'old another grandchild in my arms?" I'll swing for that woman one day. "I'm doing me best, Mum," I says.' Little Eddie was tracing around her eyes and nose with his forefinger. When he got to Susie's mouth, she let his finger lie on her lips for a second then she pretended to bite it.

'Where's Si?' Vera shook more Wagon Wheels on the already overflowing plate.

'Putting up a bleedin' shelf for 'er. I thought, he can take 'er moaning, I'd 'ad enough, so I came on 'ome.'

Daisy laughed. 'Let's get out in the sunshine,' she said, carrying two chairs stacked together.

Five minutes later they were all settled outside.

Vera was kneeling on the dry grass fiddling with the tea things. Susie was sitting with her face turned towards the sun. She's such a pretty woman, thought Daisy. Blonde and cuddly, curvaceous. That was a better word, she thought, curvaceous. She *should* have another baby. That girl was a born mother. Daisy thought it was time to bring up what was on her mind.

'We got to do some serious thinking,' she said.

'About?'

'This exotic dancing club. I can't go on living on your money, Vera. Got to get out there an' sort meself out.'

'You was a bit daft telling Roy you was going to pay

'im back for buying the premises down the ferry,' said Susie.

'How do you make that out, Suze?'

'You should 'ave let him buy the place and said thank you very much. That's what he wanted and expected.'

'I don't give a flying fuck what he expected. I don't want to be beholden to any man, ever again.' Vera and Susie exchanged surprised glances. 'And don't look at each other like I'm off me bleedin' trolley. I'm taking up ownership of the place to set meself up again and I'll make sure both Vera,' she nodded at her friend, 'and Roy gets back every penny they put into it. I'm gonna make a success of that place.'

'You don't know nothing about exotic dancing.' Susie helped herself to more tea and looked enquiringly at the others.

'No. But I bleedin' do,' said Vera, 'and so does my Kirsty. That's why she's my money-spinner down me salon. Not only did she do this dancing all suggestive like but she still does a bit of it for favoured customers. You know she actually worked at that posh London place, Clive's Revue Bar?' Vera tapped the side of her nose as if to say she knew what was what. 'So that's all sorted, ain't it? And not only that, we need a couple of cages so's we can put girls in 'em. Never mind your exotic dancing, Go-Go dancing is all the rage as well.'

'Go-Go dancing's fine. Just as long as Kirsty ain't planning on doin' it in the club,' said Susie.

'Blokes likes big girls, the bigger the better. They likes their bits jiggling all over the place.'

'And she's *big*,' said Susie.

Daisy shook her head. What did she know about any of it? But she acknowledged that Kirsty was good at her job and Daisy was willing to take advice and learn.

'Is this place gonna be a knocking shop?' Susie picked up another Wagon Wheel. She unwrapped half of it and got up off the grass, brushing her skirt with her other hand. Daisy watched as she put the chocolate biscuit into little Eddie's hand. 'Ta,' she said, then grinned back at Daisy when the boy repeated the word.

'No,' said Vera. 'Definitely not. I'll get it Authority Accredited like my place. Make it legal like. Percy from the planning down the council owes me a favour.'

Daisy exchanged looks with Susie.

'A knocking shop,' they chorused.

Vera appeared not to have heard for she went on, 'An' we can have a grand opening night. Invite lots of celebrities.'

'I don't know any,' Daisy said.

'Me neither,' Susie agreed.

'I do,' Vera grinned. 'And you do so, Daisy. What about all them gangsters?'

'I ain't inviting Reggie and his brothers!'

'You'd be a bloody fool not to. Once word got round that they was interested then all sorts of

304

people'll turn up and you'll get some film stars coming as well.'

'Roy knows lots of people,' said Daisy, changing her mind and getting into the swing of things. She saw Vera wink at Susie.

'Nice to see you taking an interest, girl.'

Daisy thought for a moment. ''Course it won't hurt if a few of the girls want to sleep with the customers though, will it? Might make a bit more money that way. For them and us. Roy'll need to bung a few coppers . . .'

'My mate Judge 'Arry Withers'll know his way around a few loopholes. He used to know his way around a few of mine.' Vera grinned. 'Now you're thinking like a businesswoman, Dais.'

'But won't it take away your trade from Heavenly Bodies?'

'Nah. My girls got their regulars. I can't see that changing. But it might even bring me in a bit more trade, especially as your girls will charge a lot of dosh and my girls will be a bit cheaper. Those who can't afford either will end up in Roy's brothels. So we'll all make money.'

'Especially you, Vera, because you'll have an interest in the club as well as the massage parlour.'

Vera laughed. 'Well, fancy that,' she said. 'So you don't mind Roy and me puttin' up the money?'

'No,' said Daisy. 'Not now we've talked about it. I did think at first I was being railroaded into it and p'rhaps I was, but now I can see it's a venture that'll be good for all of us. But I'm going to pay him back every single penny, and you an' all.'

Vera shrugged.

'Do what you like.' Her eyes took on a dreamy expression. 'We'll get the punters off the ferry before they 'as a chance to sample anything else in Gosport.'

'Don't you think we might be getting into something a bit deep 'ere?' asked Susie.

'How can we? Roy Kemp is one of the most notorious blokes in London, Suze. He'll even invite the bleedin' top London coppers along. A few girly freebies and a backhander or two and we really will be running an 'ighly respected establishment.'

'I got an idea,' said Susie. 'Why don't we 'ave gaming tables upstairs and a special place where a girl can strip off her clothes to music. Only this place is like a room with lots of one-way mirrored glass around it and partitions for blokes to go in and watch the girl and you know,' she faltered, 'you know, have a wank!' This last she practically whispered. Daisy could see her looking fearfully at little Eddie in case he overheard. Vera was plainly shocked. Daisy was speechless. They both stared open-mouthed at Susie, who was blushing as red as the roses in the garden hedge.

After a while Daisy said, 'I'm seein' you in a new light.'

'Don't see why.'

'It's a bloody good idea though,' said Vera. She grinned at Daisy. 'Two bloody good ideas, eh, Dais?'

Daisy nodded.

'Together we'll be stronger,' Vera said. She'd been sitting on the grass and picking daisies that she was threading together in a long chain.

Susie said, 'You got to think of a name for the place.'

'S'pose so,' said Daisy.

'I already 'ave,' said Vera, slipping the flower necklace she'd made over Daisy's head. 'Daisychains.'

Susie clapped her hands together. 'That's brilliant.' She looked at Daisy. 'Well?'

Vera didn't give Daisy time to answer. 'It's because it's your place and one day we might even have a chain of places.' Then Vera began to laugh. A deep throaty giggle.

'What's up now?' said Daisy. Secretly she was thrilled to bits with the name. 'Daisychains,' she said out loud, trying it for sound.

'This is a naval town, and what with Portsmouth just a ferry ride away an' all, I reckon we'll get a lot of sailors in, so we'd better cater for 'em as well.'

'What d'you mean?' asked Daisy.

'Well, when sailors is away at sea for a long time and they fancies a bit of the other they often fancies each other. I've heard it called playing daisychains.'

'I guess that's settled then,' said Daisy, when her and Susie had finished laughing. 'Daisychains it's going to be.'

CHAPTER 19

'Don't you get fed up playing draughts with me?'

'Oh dear,' said Violet, 'that means I'm going to lose this game, don't it?' She pushed her grey curls off her forehead and stared at Charles, then a big sigh escaped her.

Charles knew every line, every wrinkle on her face and he loved them all. She glanced back down to the board containing the black and white pieces and said, 'Why do you bother with me? You know I always cheat.'

The kitchen still smelled of the grand roast dinner they'd eaten earlier, including the roast parsnips which Violet knew were his favourite, followed by jam roly-poly. Charles was in a mellow mood and the scotch at his elbow was giving him courage.

'If you don't know now, you never will, Violet.' He was remembering the girl he'd met all those years ago at Wickham Fair in Hampshire. And that girl sat across the table from him now. 'Remember that village fair just outside Fareham?' he said, leaning across and taking her hand. Violet wore no jewellery apart from her wedding ring and she never had. Once, he'd been with Roy inside a jeweller's shop and watched as he'd paid a Queen's ransom for a diamond brooch. The next thing he knew was that Violet had given the brooch to Daisy, telling her it looked better on her.

Violet covered his hand with hers. 'How could I forget? I loved it! Those 'orses being run up and down by the gypsies to sell to dealers outside the pub on the corner, and the smell of candyfloss and beer and the sound of the fairground. It was grand.'

'Roy's dad was alive then.'

'Yes. Been a lot of water under the bridge since then. I was a skinny little madam and you were wearing a twill shirt and moleskin trousers with that flat cap tilted back on your forehead.'

'Fancy you remembering that.'

'It was May, and all the wild flowers were out in the fields and hedgerows. The fair spread right through the village and we'd just left Roy's dad to collect 'is winnings from the boxing booth.'

'And you was the prettiest thing I'd ever seen.' And she was. Wearing a sort of cotton dress with a wide sash and black shoes with buttons on the sides.

He'd expected her to shake off his hand ages ago but she sat quite still.

'I remember you kissed me,' he went on. 'We was walking along the riverbank outside the village when I couldn't help myself and I kissed you. You didn't turn away. You kissed me right back.'

'I shouldn't 'ave.'

'I know.'

She'd cast down her eyes but he knew she wasn't really looking at the board game. He hoped she wouldn't get up and begin busying herself at the sink or the oven. Much as he loved her cooking, he only wanted a few more minutes and he might, just might pluck up the courage to ask her the question he'd been putting off for ages. It hadn't seemed right to think about himself with Daisy missing and Violet so upset, but now . . . With his free hand he took a gulp of the single malt.

'After my Roy died you practically brought up our son,' said Violet. 'You turned 'im away from the fight game because you knew I was scared he'd end up like his father. One unlucky punch and it would all be ended.'

The radio was playing 'Unchained Melody' by the Righteous Brothers and it seemed to fit Charles' mood.

'You ever wondered why I've stayed close, loving your Roy as though 'e was my own lad? The son I never had?'

Violet looked up now.

''Course. And we're getting older, ain't we? You know you're more to me than just a friend of the family. This episode with Daisy and that boxer has made me realise how vulnerable we are, how short life can be.'

Oh God, he thought, how can I say what I really

want now? His confidence plummeted and instead he said, 'I wish Roy would set up house with Daisy.'

'You know what he's like. No question of that while Moira has a breath in her body. While she's alive, Roy'll take care of her and because of the love they once 'ad there'll be no divorce. So it'll go on being Roy 'ere in London and Daisy tending to her life and son down in Gosport.'

'Do you reckon he'll spend more time down south with the new club?' Where Roy went Charles wasn't usually far behind and he hated the thought of spending even more time away from Violet.

'No more than 'e does now.' Violet looked thoughtful. 'Both Vera and Daisy have got their heads screwed on right.'

'All I want is to see Roy happy and everyone's lives neat and tidy.' He drained his glass then put it down on the table. Violet still hadn't moved her hand. He could smell, through the last of the whisky fumes, the sweet scent of her violet perfume. One, two, three, c'mon, boy, say it, he told himself. He looked at her for so long he thought it was a wonder she didn't ask what the hell he was staring at.

'If you want a tidy life, Charles, then why don't you spit it out and ask me to marry you?'

Charles couldn't believe his ears. Did she really pop the question to *him*? His heart lurched skywards.

'You mean . . . You'd *think* about it, Violet?'

'Think about it? We ain't got much time left for

thinking about things, we better get on with it. And quick. In fact as quick as they can sort the banns!'

Charles' mouth fell open and he knew he must look pretty stupid. But that lurch in his heart had done a double take and was spreading through his body leaving a wonderful hot glow. He felt absolutely bloody marvellous.

'You . . . You . . . You and me?'

Violet laughed, and to him it sounded like that girl's laugh from that May day of long ago.

'Oh, my love,' he said, hauling her from the kitchen chair and whirling her around until he was absolutely dizzy with joy.

Susie was in tears. Daisy had come down to make an early morning cup of tea and found her already in the kitchen, hankie wet enough to stick on the washing line. 'Trouble is, Daisy,' she sniffed, 'I don't want to go and live with Si's mum in Queen's Road.'

'I thought you liked his family?'

''Course I do.' Susie ran her hands through her mop of curls. 'I just don't want to live with 'em. They swallow me up. I likes egg and chips but I don't want it for every fuckin' meal, do I?'

Daisy wasn't sure about the reference to eggs and chips but she was aware that Si's mum could be demanding. She took out some slices of bread from the packet and slipped them under the grill. If she was having a cuppa she might as well make toast for the both of them. She caught a glance of Susie's red-rimmed eyes looking at her expectantly.

'What does Si say?'

'As usual he says he'll leave it up to me. You know how easy-goin' he is.' Susie paused and turned her blue eyes to Daisy, who watched as they filled with fresh tears. 'I know Vera's moved in 'ere permanently because Glo's in her flat and I don't want to be in the bleedin' way, but I love being 'ere with you. It reminds me of the caff, and 'ow close we all were there. On the other 'and, I don't want to cause a ruck between Si and his family.'

All her words had come out in a rush, like if she didn't say what was on her mind and quickly, she never would. Daisy sighed. She needed to think about this. She couldn't imagine what the house would be like without Susie and her stable influence. And Si? Daisy liked having a man about the place, especially as he didn't belong to her!

'Why does she want you both to move in with 'er?' Daisy turned the bread over on the grill.

'Because she's feeling the pinch moneywise now that Si's dad's retired.'

Daisy nodded. Susie was just soft-hearted enough to do what she didn't want to, just to please the old bat.

'Si works all day in the town at The World's Stores and you'd be at 'ome with his mum, wouldn't you?'

Susie pulled a face. 'I could get a job, I suppose. But I don't want to leave little Eddie.'

Daisy thought for a bit. That wasn't what she had in mind either; the boy loved Susie.

'What if I had a word with Si to stay on here and do odd jobs for me? He can still work full time in the town at The World's Stores. It'll be extra money for 'im.'

'But he already does all your odd jobs, Dais . . .' Susie was looking confused.

'I know, but we'll put it on a business footing and you can go on minding little Eddie. If this club is going to take off I need to know he's with someone I can trust. Besides, you know I don't like cooking and Vera burns every bloody thing she puts in a pan. What if Si gives his mum a regular backhander to 'elp out with her utility bills and such, you won't be any the worse off and his mum'll be able to manage better?'

'We don't need your money, Daisy.'

'Everyone needs money! Si's mum will realise you got a proper job here an' not just a place to live.'

Susie dabbed at her eyes and hiccuped. 'Would you really do that for us, Daisy?'

'Just said so, didn't I? Only thing is you'll have to wait 'til the place is up and running. Daisychains, I mean. I ain't got a pot to piss in yet.'

Susie laughed. 'Oh, thanks, Dais, I'm that relieved. Si's quite content 'ere. He loves to potter in the garden an' 'e's got 'is Lambretta to get into town on. He can pop in and see his mum every lunchtime if 'e wants.'

Daisy knew she wasn't telling the whole truth. There was more to her not wanting to leave than she'd offered. Susie was made to be a mum and losing little Meggie in that road accident had very nearly caused her to lose her mind. Looking after little Eddie seemed to ease the pain and there was no doubt that Susie enjoyed cooking and looking after them all. Anyway, Susie was Daisy's friend, and if it was in Daisy's power to help, she would.

'That's settled then, ain't it?'

Susie was smiling now. A smile on her pretty face meant everything to Daisy. She got up and tucked her hankie up her sleeve.

'I think I'll start me new job right away by going upstairs and getting little Eddie washed and dressed.' Daisy didn't like to say that's what Susie did most mornings anyway. Daisy settled down to another cup of tea, only to jump up again as she heard Susie wail, 'Daisy, Daisy! Little Eddie's disappeared! He's not in 'is bed!' Daisy was up the stairs like a shot.

Vera poked her head round her bedroom door. Her mascara was all smudged and she had on one solitary false eyelash.

'What's all the bleedin' noise about?' She opened the door wider and began tying the belt of her black silk dressing gown.

'Little Eddie's not in 'is bed!'

Vera stared at Susie like she'd gone mad. ''Course he ain't. He 'ad a bad dream in the night and crawled in with me. For fuck's sake stop making all this racket. Any tea going?'

'Make yer own bleedin' tea.' Daisy was on her way back down the stairs, her old white dressing gown flapping as she ran. The smell of smouldering bread rose. 'You just made me burn me bleedin' toast!'

CHAPTER 20

'I never wanted no fancy wedding. Quick, yes, fancy, no.'

Nevertheless Charles was fussing around Violet and she looked like the cat that had got the cream. For the sixth time he was pinning a spray of violets to her jacket lapel; it had kept coming adrift all morning. Violet had often said she didn't like wearing jewellery and frilly bits. To Daisy the waywardness of the violets proved why. Ever since Daisy had known Violet, her only adornment had been her wedding ring on her left hand, and she had confided to Daisy that when her and Charles decided to tie the knot he'd made it clear that if she wanted to go on wearing the wedding ring that Roy's beloved father had given her, that was fine by him. Violet had transferred that ring to her right hand and proudly showed off her new gold band.

Roy was smiling from ear to ear, watching Reggie Kray shake Charles' hand like he was pumping water. Ron was standing with his arm around his mother's shoulders and every so often passing her his hand-kerchief to blot her tears of happiness.

They'd spent a boozy couple of hours in the Grave Maurice after the Register Office wedding with Char-lie Kray as best man. He'd made sure there were eats and champagne laid on and he gave just the briefest of speeches before anyone was allowed near the bar. Daisy had enjoyed every moment.

The train was waiting at Waterloo Station bound for Bognor Regis. As Violet gave her the smile to end all smiles, Daisy knew, no matter what excuses came out of Violet's mouth, that the July wedding had all gone exactly the way she wanted it.

'I'll take that case now, son.' Charles paused at the sliding high metal barrier and took the suitcase from Roy's hand. Roy gave him a hug with just a hint of embarrassment about it then threw his arms around his mother, crushing the violets.

The ticket man looked set to bar the rest of the entourage as the couple moved away towards the long train, turning back and waving before they climbed into the carriage.

'That's that, then, mate.' Ron clapped Roy on the shoulder.

'She's in good 'ands,' said Violet Kray. 'Now what says you come back to our 'ouse and take up where we left off?'

Reg was silent, but Daisy knew his wife Frances never left his thoughts. Her breakdown consumed him to the extent that Ron seemed to have become the dominant twin.

'Thanks, Violet, but if you don't mind, me and Daisy'll take off on our own.'

Daisy froze. She gave Violet Kray a smile and a hug to disguise her reluctance at being alone with Roy. His words meant he wanted to get back to the empty house – it wasn't often they could have the place to themselves.

The twins both grinned knowingly at Roy. All three men were wearing dark blue suits and silk shirts with slim ties. They gave the dirty station a touch of old movie glamour with their slicked-back hair and carnation buttonholes. Roy put his hand protectively on Daisy's shoulder. She'd have given anything at that moment to be sitting in her own garden, gossiping with Vera in the sunshine.

'Best get back with me hubby and the boys, then,' said Violet Kray, pulling her blue silk jacket around her. 'If you changes your minds, you're both more than welcome.'

Soon Roy and Daisy were in the Humber, driving through London's busy streets. Daisy tried to take her mind off the possibility of lovemaking by watching the outside floorshow of street vendors selling souvenirs, black taxicabs picking up fares at the wave of a hand, and red buses filled with people. The heart of London scared Daisy. People rushed about like ants, not smiling, not speaking. They all looked hot and bothered in the sunshine. She was more at home in the back streets of Gosport where everyone seemed to know each other.

'Bognor Regis for a honeymoon, I ask you!' Roy slipped his hand comfortingly over Daisy's knee. Instinctively she clenched her thighs together but Roy didn't seem to notice for he carried on talking. 'Mum said they both had happy memories of that place.' Taking his eyes from the road for a brief moment, Roy smiled at her. 'Do you know, we've got the house to ourselves?'

'I certainly do.' There, he'd put her worst fears into words. She tried to feel less panicked about it.

Roy was in the shower. In the double bed, Daisy had curled herself up like a hedgehog. Oh God, she thought, I can't do this. But for Roy's sake, I must try.

Roy came into the bedroom. He was naked, and Daisy could smell the orangy scent of his cologne mixed with the freshness of his shampoo. The dampness clinging to his dark hair made it glossier and she was momentarily reminded of the shine on a raven's wing. He was one good-looking bastard and she wished with all her heart she could love him and want to make love with him, but Daisy had never been more afraid in her life.

He pushed away the candystriped sheet and climbed into the bed. Then he lay propped on one elbow staring at her nakedness. The hairs on his legs and arms glistened dark brown, matching the handful at his chest.

His fingers trailed up and down her body, running from her breasts to her stomach to the tangle of blonde pubic hairs. Daisy realised her hands were clenched into fists, her nails biting into the skin of her palms.

Relax, she told herself. He won't hurt you.

Inside her thighs, his fingers played lightly on her skin, back and forth, and she could feel he was staring at her with his slate-grey eyes. They were burning through her eyelids which were now tightly closed.

Why couldn't she touch him? Why couldn't she even smooth his hairline at the back of his neck? Daisy willed herself to stroke his body, but she couldn't move. She forced herself to open her eyes and saw him, cautious at first, bending down towards her cunt. His penis was erect with a tiny drop of milky fluid at its tip. His lips brushed her skin, moving to her inner thighs and . . .

'Roy, I can't do this.'

There was no mistaking the hurt in his eyes. He rolled from the bed and stood facing her. His prick was flagging, his balls heavy. He put out a hand and touched her face gently.

'No!' she cried, and slipped from the bed. Now the hurt and shame of refusing him had got to her. She tried to slide into his arms for comfort but he was too quick for her. He pushed her away.

'No, Daisy. I won't bother you again. Let me know

when you *do* want me.' His voice reminded Daisy of chips of ice dripping into her heart as he left the room, shutting the door behind him.

After a while, Daisy realised she'd been standing looking at the closed door for so long her naked body had chilled. She got back into bed. Every movement, every sound, every scent seemed magnified in the terraced house.

Eventually her tears ceased and she wondered how or when she would ever be normal again. Didn't Roy realise these terrible feelings were beyond her control? Each time the memory of Valentine Waite began to slip to the back of her mind, a look from a man, a glance from a passing stranger, would make her shiver, and she would be reminded of Waite's face leaning over her, his mouth murmuring obscenities, his hands touching, hurting her.

But Roy wasn't a stranger. He was supposed to be the man she loved, who certainly loved her. And yet she couldn't bear him to touch her.

Eventually Daisy slid from the bed. She listened at the door but there was no sound. She got back into bed and pulled the covers to her chin. Her heart was pounding and the loneliness was intolerable until she slept.

After waking and then tossing and turning, unable to go back to sleep, she finally crept downstairs to make a cup of tea. There was no sign of Roy. She sat at the kitchen table and wished she were at home in Gosport, but Roy had collected her in his Humber.

Daisy had yet to master the effort of getting into and driving her little MG again.

After a while she went back upstairs and got into bed.

What was she going to do? Practically, she needed Roy's money to get this Daisychains business up and running. There hadn't been the slightest hope that any of her own money could be recovered, and Daisy had insisted on Roy taking a note on her house in Western Way. In a part of Gosport that was exclusive, the property was worth a great deal. Of course Vera had chipped in with her share in the venture, borrowing on Heavenly Bodies.

The club *had* to work. Daisy *had* to make a success of it.

So she *had* to lie there and wait for Roy to return from wherever he'd gone. And until her confidence was fully restored, she accepted she had to take a lot of shit until the club was up and running and she could repay her debts and say Up Your Arse to everyone who didn't matter in her life.

'Come on, sleepyhead, I done breakfast for you.'

Daisy opened her eyes and Roy stood before her with a tray in his hands. On it was a small pot of tea, a glass of orange juice and some toast. There was also a red rose lying on the tray. She struggled to a sitting position, pulling the sheet over her naked breasts. He put the tray on her lap. Then he bent and kissed the top of her head.

'I'm sorry I was angry with you,' he said. 'Patience ain't my strong point. I do understand how you feel, Daisy, I'm just not too good at showing it. Will you forgive me?'

He was wearing a dark grey suit. Had he put it on when he got up today, she wondered, or had he worn it while he was out of the house last night and perhaps had only just come in? Either way it didn't really matter, did it? He was here now.

'Hello,' she said. 'I'm sorry, too.'

She smiled at him. He was his own man. She shouldn't want to keep tabs on him. Her own insecurity was causing these bad thoughts to surface.

Daisy picked up the rose to smell its fragrance. Glittering in the centre petals was a small round object. Daisy picked it out. It was a ring.

'Jesus,' she said, fingering the square stone. 'It's as big as an ice cube.'

'That's a lie.' He took the ring from her and slipped it on to the third finger of her left hand. 'Do you like it?' She held her hand in front of her. Her gold bangle slid down her wrist to complement the ring.

Tears welled in her eyes. 'What's not to like?'

'It means you belong to me,' he said.

'Even though I'm damaged goods?' she asked. 'And I don't want to belong to anyone except myself?'

He took the tray and set it on the floor. Then he sat on the side of the bed and held both her hands.

'Not to me you aren't damaged goods,' he said. 'And I don't mind you belonging to yourself as long as I'm in the running.'

Daisy nodded.

'It will be all right, love,' he said. 'We'll sort it together.'

CHAPTER 21

'You can do this,' said Sonia. Her dark hair swung around her face, shiny as a conker, thought Angel. Sonia was standing behind her and she too had changed into her work clothes, red high heels, a G-string and stick-on nipple tassels.

Angel's reflection in her bedroom's floor-length mirror showed long, tanned legs encased in black fishnet stockings, a tiny pair of rhinestone briefs that matched the quarter-cup bra over which her breasts were hoisted and spilled enticingly. Six-inch black patent heels added to the glamour. They were Sonia's but luckily they both took the same size shoes.

'You sure I don't show?' Angel pressed her hands over her almost flat stomach. She glanced at Sonia, who was dabbing Evening in Paris perfume on her wrists and behind her ears. Its strong smell filled the room.

''Course you don't. And unless you suddenly swell up like a barrage balloon you could be lucky and go on bein' slim for quite a while yet.'

Angel flashed her a grateful smile. 'Thank Christ

I've stopped bein' sick,' she said. 'Them Thalidomide tablets I got from the doctor works a treat. I've still got a costume from when I danced in London.' It was in the drawer and she shuddered, remembering how lucky she was to have escaped from Gordon Kessel's clutches. This costume was much nicer though. 'Shall I audition then?' She was hoping Sonia would agree. They could go down to Daisychains together.

'That's what I'm 'ere for, ain't it? If I don't get you out of this bloody prefab I think you're going to go round the bend. You're already losing confidence in how you look and I never thought it could 'appen to you, not *you*. An' you got no earthly reason to think you don't look good, you got that bloom that pregnant women get.'

Angel was grateful to her friend for driving down to see her. She glanced out of the window at the smart white Ford Anglia that was Sonia's. It was true Angel was losing her confidence. After working in the greengrocer's all day, then coming home and seeing to her mother, then cleaning and cooking, it was as though her life had been swallowed up.

'But you been working in London and I can 'ardly say I've been working in the greengrocer's at Clayhall, can I?'

'Say you've been working in the club up the Smoke with me then. I don't suppose they'll check up. Not once they've seen what we can do. I reckon we'll see off the opposition, if there is any.'

'You ain't just come down here to get me a job, I

know you too well. It's Gordon Kessel, ain't it? Have you upset 'im?'

Sonia's green eyes flashed. 'Not me. Your friend Wendy did.'

Immediately Angel was on the defensive. Wendy had helped her escape from the bully of a club owner and for that she'd be eternally grateful to the girl.

'What d'you mean? Wendy's a money-spinner.'

Sonia sighed. 'Sit down on the bed, you won't want to be standing when I tell you what happened to your mate. And I motored down 'ere not just for you but for me own peace of mind as well.'

Angel sat on the pink counterpane and Sonia sat down beside her, taking one of her hands and holding it tightly. Angel noted Sonia's long red nails and tried to ignore her own rough skin and chewed fingernails.

'Gordy was well pissed off about you leaving. He beat up on Wendy. Hit her so's she couldn't work. She was a cokehead when you was working there but she was okay, wasn't she?'

Angel nodded her head. 'We all needed a bit of a lift,' she said. 'Wendy was more fragile.' Sonia's eyes held hers.

'It was the heroin done it for 'er. He started her on that, big time. Gordy made 'er so dependent on 'im that in next to no time she didn't know what she was doing. That girl had brains and beauty, and she let 'im destroy her with that shit. He knew what 'e was doing, the vindictive bastard. He was taking it out on 'er because you showed 'im up and ran off.'

Sonia paused. 'We were all trying 'ard not to piss 'im off ourselves, so Wendy kinda slipped our minds. She'd sold her snake for dope so she couldn't do 'er act no more. Anyway, she hadn't been dancing for a while, her body was a mass of sores – and thin. No one would have paid to see that body except for novelty value. All the time she was fuckable though, he kept her locked in the room where eventually she died. Coppers broke into the filthy basement flat but she'd been dead for days.'

'Can't they do anything to Gordy?'

Sonia shrugged. 'Why? Nothing to do with him, the clever bastard.'

Angel buried her tear-stained face into Sonia's warm neck. 'I wrote 'er a letter, no wonder she didn't reply.'

Sonia patted Angel's back as though she was a child, and said, 'I 'ope you didn't put a return address on it?'

'Didn't need to, she already knew where I lived.'

Sonia sniffed. 'Well, now you know the rest of the reason I want out of the London scene where Gordon Kessel controls clubs. I don't want to end up like Wendy. Working for this Lane woman and Roy Kemp 'as surely got to be better, hasn't it?'

Angel wiped her face with the corner of the bed-spread, feeling it rough against her skin. She nodded in answer to Sonia's question. She knew for a fact Roy Kemp's London brothels were clean and well run.

'But if we get the jobs in Daisychains someone's bound to recognise us and Gordy will be after us.'

'He wouldn't dare piss Roy Kemp off, you know that.'

Angel thought for a while. Sonia was right. The both of them would be on easy street – if they got the jobs.

Sonia went over to the chair where she'd left her holdall and pulled out a short blue silk dress with long wide sleeves gathered at the wrists. 'You can borrow this for the interview, then change into what you got on for dancing.'

Angel looked at the label on the inside of the dress and whistled. Then she handed it back to Sonia. 'I can't wear that, it's got Mary Quant on the label. Must 'ave cost you a bomb.'

Sonia waved her hand away and shook out a similar dress in black and white. 'I'm wearing this one. It's another Mary Quant. We got to look the part. Harry Green came in useful with 'is money, I'll say that for 'im, daft old sod. He really thought I'd let 'im touch me. Ugh! Seventy years old and skin like old shoe leather. A kiss an' cuddle was all 'e got from me. An' I got a brand new car and some good clothes out of 'im. Why are men so stupid, Ange?'

'I can't answer that, can I? Not in the state I'm in. I'm the bleedin' stupid one to get meself knocked up.'

'You gonna tell me the bloke's name?'

Angel shook her head. She knew however close she was to Sonia she'd never tell her that Roy Kemp was the father. Not when she needed Roy Kemp and that Daisy Lane who was supposed to own the bleedin' club, Daisychains, to give her a job.

'If I knew, I would,' she lied.

'Dirty cow,' Sonia laughed. 'I just hope you 'ad a lot of fun making that baby.'

Angel smiled. How could she ever forget the night she'd spent above the Black Bear with Roy Kemp? He was some lovely bloke. Just remembering his naked, tanned body made her feel good. And who knows? He might even want her again when he saw her in action, dancing just for him. I've certainly got more going for me, she thought, than that washed-out blonde Lane woman who was giving orders left, right and centre down the nearly finished club.

Angel had gone down to Gosport on the bus to see how the renovations were going. She was surprised that a scruffy old pub opposite the ferry could be transformed so quickly into the smart new premises of Daisychains.

It was much grander than she'd envisaged. Still, Roy Kemp had the money and the clout so it was no wonder he'd got blokes working round the clock. She'd been surprised to see him with the blonde, though.

The small sparrow of a woman was pretty in a faded sort of way. But with a bit more effort, Angel decided, Daisy Lane would certainly turn a few men's heads. She looked as though she couldn't care less about her looks. Not like the mouthy dark-haired woman. Overpainted and too many frills for a woman of her age. And too much perfume! The dark-haired woman had pushed past her as she'd been passing the open doorway of the club. 'Sorry,' she'd said, then looked up into Angel's face. Recognition, then something else, Angel could have sworn it was fear, passed across the small woman's face. Angel had moved swiftly on. She'd had a headscarf over her hair and a raincoat tightly belted and with her flat shoes on she was able to scurry away.

Her heart had done a double flip when she'd spotted Roy Kemp. Thank God he hadn't noticed her. But Angel's heart was still thumping wildly all the way home on the Clayhall bus. She'd never been in love. Never saw what all the fuss was about or why they made so much of love in songs and books and films. But she knew one thing. She couldn't get Roy Kemp out of her mind.

'You sure the grand opening night is going to be on July thirtieth?'

'Sure I'm sure. There's been talk of nothing else in the city but Roy Kemp's new venture. Why?'

'Because Malkie said England's playing at Wembley that day. It's the World Cup and they're playing against West Germany. I can't see many people wanting to go along to an opening of a club on that night.'

'That football match ain't gonna take all day, is it? Whether they wins or loses, it won't matter to Daisychains, will it? If England wins, the club'll be full of people celebrating, an' if they lose, the blokes need to drown their sorrows, don't they?'

'I 'adn't thought of that.'

'Well, I 'ad,' said Sonia. She was getting changed again now, into a pair of tight jeans and an even tighter top. 'You do realise the advert in the London paper said accommodation for successful applicants was provided? You live 'ere, in Gosport. So what you gonna do?'

Angel didn't hesitate. She'd finished admiring herself and was putting her green checked skirt back on and her white V-necked jumper. Her clothes weren't as glamorous as Sonia's but there wasn't much money left over for nice things.

'I was hoping you and me could share the bleedin' accommodation, whatever it is,' she said. 'Be just like the old days, sharing. That's if we gets a job.'

'But you got a home here.' Sonia waved her arm around the sparsely furnished bedroom with its lino-covered floor and rag rug.

'But I don't want to live 'ere. Anyway I could come back every day to check on me mum, and Malkie's old lady will keep an eye on 'er.'

Sonia shrugged. 'What about Malkie? He was talking like you and 'im was getting married. Couldn't shut 'im up this morning. He really cares about you, Ange.'

'A bird in the 'and is better than two in the bush.' Angel looked defiantly at Sonia who was coating her eyelashes with more black mascara.

'And what's that supposed to mean?' Sonia stopped what she was doing and stared into Angel's eyes in the mirror. 'That you'll only marry him if you can't work out something better?'

'You got it in one.' Angel had already picked up the hairbrush and was brushing her long hair. She had her head bent forward and was sweeping vigorously from the roots to the tips.

'But won't 'e mind if you go to work in Daisy-chains? That's if we get the jobs.'

'He'll have to bleedin' not mind, if he wants to marry me.' Angel heard the click of the front gate and she stopped brushing, swung her hair back and looked through the net at the window. 'Fuck!'

'What's the matter?'

'It's Malkie's nosy cow of a mother. I'll 'ave to go and let her in. Be careful what you say to 'er or she'll 'ave your life story in five minutes. She don't know about the kid I'm carrying. Malkie was going to tell her it's his when the time's right.'

CHAPTER 22

'She wants a bleedin' pole.'

'Don't she carry her own accessories?' The words were out before Daisy realised what she'd said. She put down the notebook and pencil that all morning had seemed glued to her hands.

'Daisy, she's 'ardly likely to go around with a bleedin' twelve-foot pole in a paper bag, now is she?'

Daisy sighed. The girl needed a pole to dance. Two steel poles were being installed tomorrow, but today was today and the girl was being interviewed now and Vera was right as usual.

'Get her to do something without a pole.'

I ain't never really heard of pole dancing anyway, thought Daisy, only from Vera and her girls. Today was just one fuckin' headache after another, interviewing girls for dancing and girls for behind the bar. Thank Christ Roy had sorted out the croupiers and brought some real hard gits down from London as bouncers. He'd already told her once the place was up and running he'd stay in the background, said he had his own affairs to keep an eye on. Secretly Daisy was more than pleased about this. She reckoned she might not know a great deal now about running a club but she and Vera weren't bloody stupid and it shouldn't take long to manage things properly.

'Pole dancin' is all the rage in the States, so is lap dancin'.'

'Well, this is Gosport High Street. Does she 'op about over it like them Scottish people over those swords?' Her words were meant to lighten the escalating tension, but Vera narrowed her eyes.

'Sometimes, Daisy Lane, I think you was born yesterday. No, she makes very suggestive movements like she's about to fuck the pole. The blokes love it.'

Daisy opened her eyes wide in mock horror. 'An' you've seen her do this?'

'She wants a pole.'

'For fuck's sake, where is she? An' what's *her* name?' Vera pointed to a dark-haired girl wearing a black and white dress standing chatting to a blonde. Daisy took a double look at the two women. Two head-turners indeed, she thought. She looked around the crowded bar. The girls were certainly catching the blokes' eyes.

Even Vinnie, leaning against the bar and sipping at a pint, had the blonde in his sights. Bloody men, she thought, always eyeing up the talent, thinking with their dicks. And the moment she thought that of Vinnie Endersby she was ashamed. He was a bloody good mate to her and, what's more, she knew he cared about her, really cared. He'd been invited along, as had most of the men in the place, so she could gauge their reactions to the girls she and Vera decided to employ. Vera knew what she was looking for and, to her credit, was seldom wrong – look at the success of Heavenly Bodies. There was no stopping Gloria – as Glo was now called – with her reading and writing, and after that terrible run-in with Valentine Waite, she'd bounced back to become a top-notch manageress. But Daisy was determined that Daisychains was going to appeal to *all* men, and she reckoned the best way was to watch the men's faces and body language reacting to the assortment of females who'd come begging for work. No man wanted to spend money to watch a girl undress who they could pick up for ten bob on the Ferry Gardens.

'Which one's Sonia?'

'The dark one. Ain't she a beauty? She's been working in a London club.'

'Surely she don't want to give London up for Gosport?' Daisy wondered why anyone would leave the bright lights to come down south.

'That's where you're wrong. She's confided to me that neither of them liked the way they was bein' treated by the owner of the club they worked in so thought they'd start afresh down 'ere. I admire her honesty, Dais. Not so sure about the blonde. I . . . er . . .'

'So you like the dark one but don't trust the blonde?'

If looks were daggers, Vera would have knifed the

blonde to death, thought Daisy. She'd never seen Vera in such a mood.

'I never said that. It's just she got eyes like my Kibbles when he sits on the windowsill beggin' to be let in, all soulful like. And she's pregnant.'

'How the fuck do you know that?' Daisy couldn't believe what Vera was saying. The girl was slim, and not a sign of a thickening waistline.

'I could see it in her eyes.'

'Them soulful eyes?'

Vera snorted. 'Mark my words, that one's trouble.'

Daisy stared again at the girl across the room. Most of the men couldn't keep their eyes off her either.

'If she is in the family way, she don't show. You've just taken a dislike to her on sight, Vera, I can read you like a book.'

Vera fidgeted from one foot to the other, her eyes darting across to the blonde then back to Daisy. She put her hand on Daisy's arm.

'I got a bad feeling about her, really bad. Trouble is, Dais, they do come as a bleedin' pair.'

'Lezzies?'

'No, just good mates.'

Daisy thought for a while. 'Look, Vera, I don't have the time to sit around chatting about these girls. Let's get the bleeders to dance. Just by looking at 'em you can see they got class.'

She moved off to watch a pretty, slim girl in a minuscule knitted dress enter a metal cage that was then hoisted above the crowd. Music started up and the go-go girl began giving it her all. That girl's a winner, Daisy decided.

'You got more fuckin' front than the Ferry Gardens, Angela Moore!' Vera had pulled the blonde away from her mate and into a quiet corner.

'What are you on about?'

'Don't play the bleedin' innocent with me. I saw you coming out of the Black Bear with Roy Kemp.'

After a moment's silence the girl laughed. Vera couldn't believe it.

'I want a job. Me and Sonia, we both want jobs.'

The girl was staring at her now. Waiting for an answer.

'An' if I say to Daisy I *don't* want you workin' 'ere?'

'Then I'll spill the beans about sleeping with 'er gangster boyfriend.'

'You fuckin' little . . .' Vera could hardly believe her ears.

'Tart? That's the pot callin' the kettle black, ain't it?'

Vera had seen the look of surprise turn to pleasure on Roy's face as Angel had entered Daisychains. His gaze had lingered just a fraction too long on the leggy blonde. Vera was determined to protect her Daisy at any cost.

'Daisy could 'ave your guts for garters . . .'

'Daisy Lane would be in shreds if she found out 'er

bloke 'ad been bouncing the bedsprings with me, an' you know it.'

The pounding in Vera's ears grew louder. It was her own heart beating that this chit of a thing might hurt Daisy. Unless . . .

'I got no money an' I need a job,' Angel insisted. 'An' I'm playin' you at your own game. Money I need, aggro I don't.'

'So for a job you'll keep away from Roy?'

'I said I wouldn't let on to Daisy.' Angel sighed. Her voice had lost its hardness. 'Look, both you an' me know what blokes are like. It was a one-night stand because he was lonely. That's all it was. Anyway, I'm getting married soon.'

Vera remembered seeing her in the town with Malcolm Short.

'Not that long drink of water as lives opposite your mum?'

'He's a good man.'

Too bloody good for you, thought Vera. She softened. Perhaps it would be better if the girl was somewhere she could keep an eye on her. Daisy was still too fragile to have to cope with any more problems than those she already had.

'I don't trust you but I admire your guts in standing up to me,' said Vera. And she meant it.

'That mean me an' Sonia got jobs?'

Vera winked at her.

'Got to see you dance yet. You get the punters all hot an' bothered and the jobs are in the bag.'

'No problem. You won't regret it. Thanks, Vera.'

Angel surprised her with a quick kiss to her cheek and then swept back though the crowd to her friend.

Vera touched her cheek. Marriage wouldn't tame that one, she thought, though it'd give the baby a name on its birth certificate. Vera shook her head and sighed again. She could feel in her bones that it wasn't Malcolm's baby. Was it Roy's?

Roy was standing at the far end of the bar talking to a couple of blokes Daisy had never set eyes on before and Vinnie had joined them. Daisy waved to Kirsty and Sam who were busy doling out beers. She thought Vera was a pet to have lent out her girls for the day to do bar work, but soon they'd have their own trained bar staff. Today was special, though, none of the alcohol had been watered down.

'All them skimpy outfits and the girls showing off their bits makes the blokes thirsty. They'll be gaggin' for more booze, so after opening night we doctor the drinks.' Vera seemed to have appeared at her side from nowhere.

'You sure this is all legal, Vera?'

''Course it is. If it ain't, we grease a few palms and it's made legal.'

Daisy knew Vera was very good at greasing palms. She didn't like the idea of selling booze that wasn't the real McCoy but Vera had assured her that all the clubs did it and it was expected.

'They ain't really comin' to a place like this to drink, are they, Dais?'

'I'm not sure I can cope with all these fiddles. In the caff if someone paid me for a cuppa an' egg an' chips that's exactly what they got.'

Vera laughed. 'Never mind bleedin' egg an' chips and the watered-down booze, I'm telling you now if I could fit into some of the costumes I've seen today I'd soon show the punters what's what. So what acts we got now?'

'The girl with the ping-pong balls. Fancy being able to do that with the muscles of 'er fanny,' said Daisy, but she could see Vera wasn't listening; she was mentally adding up the talents of the girls they'd already hired.

'What about that snake girl.'

'I never saw her, what did she do?'

'You don't want to know, ducky, but them snakes 'ad smiles on their faces. Roxy, her name is. It's what I likes about the sex game, Dais, it's always changing.' Her eyes had gone misty and Daisy knew she was thinking of times gone by. She gave Vera a nudge.

'Shouldn't we start off at the gentle end of the market? I don't want us closed down before we've started.'

'Trust me, it'll be all right. The gentle end ain't where the money is. You know that big spare room upstairs 'ere?'

'What you got in mind?'

'I thought we could hold some special parties there?'

'What like?'

'Bondage, S and M, masks, dominatrix sessions with whips, thigh boots and leather clothes, or rubber . . .'

'Hang on a bit! Let's get this up and running first, you daft mare. I never said nothing but I'm not so happy about the gambling. That's one of Roy's ideas.'

Daisy had never forgotten Eddie and his flutters on the horses. He'd had a will of iron. Once they'd been at Goodwood. It was a glorious day and he'd given her money to back the horses. She'd lost it in a twinkling of an eye but the thrill that had coursed through her body as she'd cheered the horses on had stayed with her. Yet when she'd asked for just a little loan to try again, he'd refused.

'You got to learn, Dais, I'd give you the top brick off the chimney but never money to waste. The only winners are the touts and casino owners.' Daisy had gone a little way to understanding the power of a pull on a machine or the final roll of a wheel, and she hoped it would never enthral her like it had others.

She was brought back to the present by Vera's voice.

'You all right with Roy?' Daisy knew what she was asking. She lowered her eyes. These days she and Roy seemed a million miles apart even when they were in the same room. She twisted the ring he'd put on her finger. Sometimes she wondered why he'd given it to her and just what was in this club venture for him.

She was even scared to kiss him in case it led to other things. The tightness in her heart and body seemed to swallow her up until she became as rigid as one of those poles.

'I told you you would be lucky to find any real talent locally,' said Vera. 'Waste of time advertising in the *Evening News*.'

'What about that singer we saw earlier? She's local.'

'Proper lovely voice she got, Dais. I can just see her croonin' away in the background at the mike between acts or maybe upstairs in the casino. She needs a slinky black dress.'

Daisy agreed. She made some more notes and looked around the bar area. She'd had a free hand with the decorating and, with Vera's help and a mate of Ronnie Kray's, had decided to copy the decor of one of the twins' clubs in London.

Now she was looking forward to seeing their reactions when they came down with their mother and brother Charlie on the grand opening night. Ronnie especially had been very helpful, and the friend of his, a young designer, had brought samples of cloth and wallpaper for her to look at.

'Roy says Diana Dors is coming.'

'Who told you that?'

'He did. Said her mother-in-law, not sure from which hubby – oh yes, Dickie Dawson – lives in Gosport so it would be nice for Di to meet a few of her ol' mates. He also said that the twins is bringing some of their mates.'

'It is going to work, ain't it? This club, I mean.'

'Will you be still! 'Course it's goin' to bleedin' work, you silly bitch. Listen, it never entered your 'ead when you took over the caff in North Street that you wouldn't make a bleedin' go of it, did it?'

Daisy thought for a bit. 'No, but my old man, Kenny, was in prison then an' I was doing it for him so's he'd have a good start when he came out. Only that wasn't to be, was it?'

'But you made a go of that place, didn't you? And now you got little Eddie to work for an' he's your blood.'

Daisy sighed. Just lately her emotions had been all over the place. One minute she was happy and the next full of self-doubt. Be positive, girl, she said to herself. Vera was right, but Daisy knew she was gambling with a lot of money. Money she'd vowed to pay back.

'I just wish sometimes I 'ad your confidence, Vera. You go and sort them two girls out. I'm going to have a word with Vinnie then I'm going to take a breather.' Daisy walked across the red carpet and past the stage. Terracotta tiles had been laid around the bar area and the smell of new paint was everywhere. Gold-painted chairs with red velvet seats were grouped around mock-antique tables and twinkling glass chandeliers winked down at her.

The deep red theme was carried on upstairs to the

gaming tables and restaurant. Everything was fresh and clean and almost ready for the opening.

Some of the fruit machines had yet to be installed downstairs and the two-way glass mirrors in the room where the strippers were to perform hadn't been delivered. But these, and other minor delays, weren't ones to cause Daisy sleepless nights. She knew it would be all right on the night.

'Penny for 'em, Vinnie?' she asked. He gave her a lazy grin. He was leaning on the bar.

'If you're searching for Roy,' he said, 'he was here a minute ago.'

'Nah, he can look after 'imself. No doubt making deals that are no bleedin' business of mine, or yours come to that.' Why did she always forget how tall he was? She barely reached his shoulder and had to look up to him. 'Anyway, you was looking thoughtful an' I asked you what you was thinking.'

'I don't think I ought to tell you. I don't want you getting upset.'

'Tell me.'

'I was thinking about Eddie and how proud he'd be if he could see you now.' He ran his finger around the rim of his pint glass. It made a sharp squeaking sound that was soon swallowed up in the rest of the bar noise.

Daisy was momentarily stunned at his words. 'He would, wouldn't he?' She put her hand on his sleeve and willed him to look into her eyes. 'You know there ain't a day goes by when I don't think about him,

Vinnie?' Daisy looked at her gold bracelet and her heart hurt.

Vinnie nodded. 'He deserves to be remembered. I cared about him too. He fought my battles for me when I was a kid and I'm sure wherever he is, he's looking down at you and whistling "Wheel of Fortune" and saying, "That's my girl." ' He paused and a frown creased his forehead. 'I'm proud of you an' all, Dais.' The blush that had started below his collar spread over his face until it reached his hairline.

'You're blushing.' Reaching up on tiptoe she kissed him on the cheek. 'Thank you, Mr Detective,' she said, breathing in the clean smell of Imperial Leather that always seemed to be part of him. Then she grabbed his hand and said, 'Come upstairs with me. Come and look at my view across the ferry.'

The stairs, covered in deep red carpet, were of wrought iron and painted gold and black, contrasting with the red-flocked wallpaper. When they reached the top Daisy led him towards the windows where the panoramic views of Gosport Ferry, the Ferry Gardens and the strip of Solent Water across which the ferryboats sailed to Portsmouth stretched in front of them like a painting.

'It's a grand view, Dais,' he said. She was standing close to him. She felt safe, secure. But then why shouldn't she? He was a copper, but he'd helped kill a man for her. Daisy stared at the sea. Choppy white-tipped waves made the squat-bottomed ferryboats bob about like toys in a kiddie's bath. 'Can you see the

Round Tower at Portsmouth? And Gosport's submarine base?' He pointed and Daisy nodded. She felt his gaze on her.

'I love this town,' she said. Her eyes swept the taxi rank where oil spills made rainbows on the tarmac and the bus station where the Hants and Dorset and Provincial buses lay in wait for their passengers. 'And I love the people,' she added. He put his hand on her shoulder.

'Daisy, you've got to keep your wits about you now your name is above the door of this club.' She looked at him, expecting him to add something more, but he didn't. 'We'd better get downstairs,' was all he said, and she felt something collapse inside her. He walked away and she followed him downstairs, her thoughts in a whirl. Music had started up. At the bottom of the stairs Vinnie paused.

'I'm not staying any longer as I need to pop round to South Street nick, then I'm off home for a bit of shut-eye.' He put his hand on her shoulder again. 'You know where I am if ever you need me.' She nodded, though she thought it was a funny thing for him to say. After all, Roy was doing a fair job of looking after her and the club, wasn't he? Daisy stretched up and kissed him on the cheek again and watched as he left Daisychains. She walked over to Vera who was standing next to Sonia.

'Where's that Angel?' Daisy asked.

'Shh! That's who the music's for. I told her to show me what she can do and she went over to the pianist and whispered in his ear then slipped out of her dress. Just look at her.'

The girl, Angel, looked for assurance to Vera, who nodded. And as the sultry music with blues overtones continued, she moved beneath the chandeliers, her skimpy bra hardly covering her well-formed breasts. Fishnet stockings covered long legs and the tiniest G-string Daisy had ever seen glittered with sequins.

One of the men in the bar cheered, and suddenly the noise softened to a murmur as she walked sinuously to the stage then seemed to think better of it and turned in a fluid motion to move down amongst the men.

Every part of her delicious body dipped and curved like a snake. Daisy gulped.

'What do you think so far?' Vera whispered.

'Don't matter what I think, look at the blokes, they're fuckin' mesmerised by her.'

'She do ooze sex, Dais. Look, she's all over them blokes like a bleedin' rash.'

Angel knew what she was doing all right, thought Daisy. One moment she was in a man's lap then she was up and bending down so his face was almost in her arse then she was off teasing the next bloke. But she was making sure every man thought *he* was the only man in the room. She was loving the attention she was getting and the men were gagging for her.

'Look at Roy's face.' Daisy heard Vera's voice and wondered at the sudden anger in it. Angel was standing at the back of the stool he was sitting on, her fingers ruffling through Roy's hair, then she came to the side of him and put one slim leg up high, her foot resting in his crotch. Daisy was getting hot under the collar, but anyone could see Roy didn't mind the attention at all. Angel moved back, straddled him and pushed her face into Roy's so close that her long curtain of blonde tresses almost covered both their faces. Her head twisted away and up so that her fabulous breasts were in his face, and still the mournful music played.

'She's too fuckin' good at it,' said Vera. 'I wish I'd never . . .' But Daisy turned away from Vera's unfinished chatter. The girl *was* good. She'd draw men like flies round shit. She'd picked on Roy, and Daisy wasn't sure how she felt about that. Obviously he was in never-never land over all the attention, any bloke would be. But why Roy? Because Angel thought he was easily the best-looking bloke in the room?

Anger began to gnaw at Daisy. That girl knew Roy had money, and he was looking into her face as though they shared a secret. As the music stopped, the clapping and whistling was tremendous. Angel never spoke to Roy, just walked away. Daisy saw his eyes following her as she went into the room set aside for the women to change their outfits. The blokes were still mopping their foreheads.

'We'd be fools not to give her a job,' Daisy said.

'I don't like her and I don't trust her,' snapped Vera. '*And* she can cover 'erself up a bit more if you decides to take 'er on.' Daisy looked into Vera's face.

She saw the tiredness there and something more: fear. Yes, that was it, fear. Daisy thought how Vera was never wrong in her character judgements.

'Don't you be worrying about that little madam, I can handle 'er. We can't have Sonia without Angel. They come as a pair, remember?'

The door opened and out came Angel once more dressed in the blue Mary Quant dress. Daisy called her over.

'Come to the office. I need to discuss things with you.'

Daisy was suddenly conscious of the difference between them. The girl was dressed to kill, while she was wearing the same black jumper she'd had on yesterday when little Eddie had splashed her with custard. Her skirt was creased and her flat black pumps were scuffed and hadn't seen the polishing brush for weeks. She decided it wasn't any use trying to pick off Kibbles' grey hairs right now, it would only draw attention to her scruffiness. She marched towards the office, aware that Angel's perfume had been heightened by the exertions of her dance.

When Daisy opened the door she let Angel pass her. 'Sit down.' She pointed to a chair near the desk and perched herself on top of the desk. She was higher than Angel and hoped the girl would feel at a disadvantage. She looked down at her.

'I think you and Sonia will be assets to *my* club.' She stressed the word my. 'For now you can share a flat over Heavenly Bodies with Gloria, the manageress of the massage parlour, she'll keep you in line.' The girl didn't look unhappy about that news. 'I hear you might be getting married, I hope that won't interfere with work?' Angel shook her head. 'Definitely no men allowed in the flat, but as I can see you becoming a top-liner, before you even start working for *me* I'm going to up your wages.'

Angel's face was a picture. It was as though she couldn't believe her luck.

'But . . . But . . .'

'No, I'm a fair woman, Angel, and because I'm fair I'm going to do you little favours from time to time. Special favours, because *I can see through you like a bleedin' pane of glass*. You're out for all you can get. So what I'm prepared to do is this. Whenever we get a customer in the club who's got a bit of dosh I'm going to point 'im out to you. What you do with that customer and how you fleece him is up to you. But,' and here she paused, 'that bloke you've all but fucked in the bar outside belongs to me.' Daisy put her face very close to Angel's. 'You might 'ave come from the big city, but I'm a Gosport girl through and through, and you won't know what's hit you if you tangle with me. Do I make meself clear?'

Daisy could feel Angel's breath on her face and Angel narrowed her eyes. She opened her mouth to speak but thought better of it.

Daisy wondered if she was about to lose the best crowd-puller she was ever likely to have.

'I got the picture an' I reckon you an' I are going to

enjoy working together. But . . .' Angel paused and Daisy wondered what would come next. 'Only if you gets me some proper music to dance to. That ol' piano gets on my tits!'

It wasn't quite the answer Daisy had envisaged and she couldn't help laughing. Why, then, did she still feel uneasy?

'Right,' she said, with more confidence than she felt. 'Bugger off. See Vera about keys to her flat and be here for rehearsals tomorrow mornin'.'

When the door had closed Daisy checked herself in the mirror. This time, critically. The woman who stared back at her wasn't Daisy Lane. The woman in the mirror had limp blonde hair, no sparkle, sallow skin and bones that a skeleton might be proud of.

'Poor cow,' said Daisy to herself. 'You're going to get more than you bargained for if you don't liven yourself up a bit.' Angel had done her a favour. Once upon a time it had been her lighting Roy's face up like that. Oh yes, she'd seen his lust for the blonde. How could she fail to, with Angel slipping all over him like a bleedin' bar of wet soap? After all, he was only a bloke, wasn't he? Daisy ran her hand through her hair and grinned at herself. It was time to turn over a new leaf, otherwise she'd have let Valentine Waite destroy her. She opened the door, but before she stepped outside Roy came to meet her.

'Just a word, Daisy,' he said. 'Come back into the office.' He had his hand on her arm and was propelling her back through the open door.

'You're in a hurry to get me in 'ere . . .' Daisy said, realising too late Roy wasn't in a teasing mood. She'd thought he was a bit off with Vinnie earlier, but decided now wasn't the time to bring it up, though she might have done if Roy had had a smile on his face. 'I saw you with them blokes,' she said. 'I've never seen them around before.'

Roy sat down on the edge of the desk. 'They're German businessmen.' He was looking at her hard and making her feel uncomfortable. She moved over to the office chair and sat down, swinging her legs and making the seat move.

'Am I to be told what kind of business?'

'Drugs business. We've done a deal for Daisychains and my Portsmouth interests.' He tapped the floor with one foot. He was waiting for her reaction.

Daisy practically exploded. 'You know I don't want no drugs in this place!'

He was tapping his foot harder. Just when she thought she'd have to tell him to stop it, he got off the table and paced across the room. When he turned and spoke, his voice was cold.

'Listen, sweetheart. Those two blokes and me go way back. I can't use Langstone Harbour any more, the plods and coastguards have been tipped off. Farlington Marshes have been teeming with searchers with dogs. The new stuff is coming in from Germany and Amsterdam to Portsmouth, via the ferries. Don't underestimate me, Daisy, there'll be little or no risk to you.' He gave her a strange look. 'Certainly not when you've got Vinnie Endersby looking out for you.'

Daisy opened her mouth to speak but he didn't let her.

'No use you laying down the law when you ain't in a position to do so. You've forgotten, Daisy, it's my money that's backing the major part of this place.' He waved his hand at her as though telling her he wasn't going to listen no matter what she had to say. 'I know I told you I didn't want the money back. But that was then and this is now. I don't know how long I can last on the London scene. The net's closing in on Reg and Ron, and the Richardsons are already off the map. I need a decent return on my money before I retire and the drugs game down here will be my surety.'

Daisy felt as though her legs had been knocked out from under her. She'd listened carefully and taken in every word. Since he'd entered the office he'd not smiled at her once to soften the blow of what *he* wanted. She stared at him levelly.

'You promised me, Roy, that this was *my* venture. If you go back on your promise it means you lied to me. You know how I feel about lies. I can stand anything but being lied to and cheated on by someone I trust.' Daisy felt drained. How could he do this to her?

And then he began to smile. His slate-grey eyes crinkled at the corners and his mouth widened and then he threw back his head and laughed at her.

'You are so precious, Daisy. Prostitution is fine.

Gambling is fine. You don't mind if the punters drink themselves to death but you draw the line at allowing them recreational drugs.'

'It won't be recreational once they get bleedin' hooked, will it? I don't give a fuck what blokes and women do, but kids is going to get hold of this stuff. You'll have no control over where the shit ends up!'

'Daisy, Daisy, Daisy . . . Trust me. I'm a businessman, and drugs are my business.'

'I thought you loved me, cared about my feelings,' she said, rising from the chair and going to the window. She looked at the taxis waiting at the rank and wished she could be inside one of them now. Being carried away somewhere where she could leave all this bad business behind.

'I do, but love and business are two separate issues. I really don't know what's got into you. You want to play with the big boys, Daisy, you got to play big boys' games.'

As she turned and looked into his eyes she wondered where it had all gone, that special feeling, that sudden longing to touch each other, that quickening of the heart when she saw him. Now she felt only fear. Fear that he would take her and spit her out as easily as a cherry stone. He loved her, she was sure of that. But it was like loving a special possession. He simply wanted her to belong to him. She thought about the times before when Roy had told her he loved her strength of character. Now she realised Valentine Waite wasn't the only one who had tried to destroy her. Roy, in his own way, was trying to do what Waite couldn't accomplish: to mould her into someone she didn't want to be, a 'yes' woman to parade on his arm.

Daisy didn't speak. She watched with an empty heart as he took from his suit pocket a small card and gave it to her. As his fingers touched hers they felt cold.

'This is a business card, *your* business card. And it's got your name, the name and telephone number of the club, and mine and Vera's names on as well.'

Daisy took it from him. It had tiny white daisies all around the edges and writing in italics on a black background. She stared at the card. Vera had cards for Heavenly Bodies that she handed out to prospective punters and Daisy had envied her. But instead of being overjoyed, Daisy knew even this small responsibility had been taken from her. It would have been nice to have been involved in the designing of the cards, *her* cards. Or was she being petty?

'Are there more?'

'There's a bleedin' great box behind the bar counter, next to one of the tills. I'll get Vera's girls to start handing them out.'

Daisy willed her happiness to rise. This was supposed to be her special day. It was going to be all right, it really was. This club would be the making of her and Vera. As to the drugs thing, she'd sort all that out later with Roy. After all, it didn't matter where you were, Gosport or Portsmouth, if a person wanted drugs they were easy enough to come by, weren't they?

Daisy looked through the window at Old Portsmouth and, in the distance, the stone ramparts of the tower and the shingle beach where wives and sweethearts of sailors had stood since time immemorial, watching with tears in their eyes for their men to come home.

'That Angel can certainly move,' said Roy, breaking the silence. 'But I wouldn't trust 'er further than I could throw 'er.' He walked to the door and opened it. As it closed behind him, Daisy leaned her head against the window. That made three of them as didn't trust the girl. Ah well . . . Her breath misted the pane. She felt like a sheet having gone through the wringer. It was raining now and puddles had formed on the pavements and between the cobbles. The sky was a gunmetal grey, showing that worse was yet to come.

A sigh reached to every part of her. Silent tears came next, rolling down her cheeks to dampen her chin. Daisy put up her hand to wipe her face.

She could hear the noise coming from the main bar and smell the cigarette smoke blown in as Roy had left.

Stretching out her hand, she stared at her ring. It seemed to be mocking her with its huge stone and its flashiness. It seemed at odds with the plain gold bangle Eddie had slipped on her wrist all that time ago. Daisy turned and unlocked the desk drawer, then slipped the ring from her finger and dropped it inside.

She left the office and saw Vera in the doorway of Daisychains, waving goodbye to a man. Daisy collected her raincoat from the cloakroom and pushed through the crush of people to reach her friend.

'I need to get out of here,' Daisy said. 'Need to be on me bleedin' own.'

'You been crying,' said Vera. 'What's the matter?'

Daisy shook her head. 'I need to go home.'

'You won't be on your own there. Suze 'as got Bri an' Jacky round for the day. Them an' Summer an' your little Eddie won't give you no rest.'

Vera had obviously just freshly doused herself with Californian Poppy. It was such a friendly smell that Daisy wanted to cry again.

'I'll see you later, can you cope?' she said. Vera put her hands on both of Daisy's shoulders, studying her at arm's length. Daisy hated the worry she'd just etched onto Vera's face. Her friend smiled at her like a mother smiles at her kiddie.

' 'Course I can. You get off, ducky.'

She turned Daisy in the direction of the open door and pushed her through. As soon as the cool rain hit Daisy's face she felt better. Now she could cry and no one would know any different. She walked through the puddles and over the road towards the Ferry Gardens, not caring that her flat shoes weren't designed to keep out the water. In moments her hair was clinging wetly against her head.

At the rail topping the wall that separated the sea and the rocks below from the gardens, she stopped. Putting both hands on the metal she stared down into the dirty green water, then across at the ferryboat just leaving the pontoon for its journey over the narrow strip of the Solent to Portsmouth. She could smell the mud and weed, and in the distance, a few lights from Portsmouth lit up the leaden sky.

'Daisy?'

She jumped and turned at her name. Vinnie was coming towards her, practically running. In one hand he carried a briefcase.

'What on earth are you doing out in this deluge?'

'I wanted a bit of fresh air.' His eyes were full of concern. She decided she ought to say just a little more to put his mind at rest. 'It's hot and noisy in Daisychains and I had to get out.'

'But you're soaking wet.'

'So are you.' His hair, showing at the sides and front of his hat, had tightened to little curls. He was wearing a fawn mac belted around his middle.

He laughed. 'We should both get in out of the rain.'

'What are you doing 'ere anyway?'

'I had some papers to pick up from the nick but there wasn't anyone to cadge a lift home from so I decided to come down to the ferry and get a taxi from the rank. I saw you cross the road. Fancy a cuppa and a sticky bun in the Dive?'

'Nah, it'll be full of steaming people escaping from

the rain.' For a moment she'd been tempted. Vinnie and her had shared many a laugh and a tear or two over a bun in the Dive cafe.

'Share the taxi with me and I'll drop you in Western Way then.' She could hear the anxiety in his voice.

'That's the last place I want to be at present. Suze 'as the whole family round for the day. It'll be bedlam at home.'

'Come back to my house then. There isn't any room to swing a cat but it's quiet.'

'All right,' Daisy said. He grabbed her hand and made her run with him to the taxi rank where a cab had just pulled in.

Vinnie opened the rear door and pushed Daisy inside, climbing in after her.

'Alverstoke Village, mate.' He turned to Daisy. 'Where's your car?'

'I haven't had the courage to get back inside it since the day . . . that day . . .'

Vinnie put his hand over hers. His touch was warm. 'Forget I asked. Sorry, Daisy.'

'It's still in the garage,' she replied. 'At Seahorse Street. I never did thank you for taking it down there, or for fixing it.'

He gave her a rueful smile. 'Forget it. I like working on cars. I do have one of my own. When we get to my house I'll show you. It's off the road in my garage. I think it'll give you quite a laugh, and you'll understand why I'm usually in one of the station's

Triumphs.' He pointed out of the window, looking past her. 'Jesus, will you look at the rain?'

The driver had his wipers going fast but still the water streamed down the windscreen and the windows.

Daisy said, 'Never mind the bleedin' rain, what about your car?'

He gave her a boyish grin. 'You aren't the only one with an MG. Mine's a bigger model than yours, got a V8 engine. Well, it would have if it was in it, but I blew the thing up on a circuit racing with some mates who also own MGs.'

'So you belong to some sort of club?'

'Yeah, it's a vice of mine. I love the cars, so if ever you find anything else going wrong with yours, you know where to come.'

'Thanks.' Daisy thought it was exciting for him to be able to do something that was obviously a passion. She was just about to ask him more but the taxi driver spoke.

'How far in the village do you want?' The cabbie threw the words over his shoulder.

'Round near the church. The Lane'll do nicely.'

When the taxi drew to a halt at a small terrace of houses Vinnie got out first and paid the driver. After helping Daisy out, he opened a gate onto a garden that was filled with trees. She started to laugh as the rain dripped noisily through the branches.

'Don't say a thing,' he warned. 'I like my trees and I like the privacy they give me.' He stopped on the white-painted step and opened the door then waited as she passed him and stepped inside.

It was an old house. The bottom half was more or less one long room, with a breakfast bar dividing the kitchen area from the living room. Highly polished wooden flooring ran the length of it. White walls and a fireplace laid with firewood for ready lighting made the place look cosy.

'It's lovely,' said Daisy. She breathed deeply of a vanilla scent, which she supposed was polish.

'Untidy,' said Vinnie. 'Take your coat and shoes off and I'll put them in the bathroom to dry off. The airing cupboard is like an oven.'

Daisy slipped out of her coat and shoes then bent and picked them up and handed them to him. 'No,' she said, taking them back again. 'I'll put them in the bathroom while you make the tea. I could murder a cup. Give me your wet things.'

'Bathroom's through there.' Vinnie pointed to a door beyond the narrow stairs that curved up from the kitchen.

Within two minutes she was out of the bathroom and standing next to Vinnie rubbing at her hair with a pink towel.

'Sorry, Vin, I really don't think much of your choice of bathroom colour. Bit girly for a macho bloke like you.'

He clattered cups onto a tray.

'Thank Christ for that,' he said. 'I'd have worried if you'd liked it. My wife decided on the pink with all the ruffles and I bleeding hate it. Just never got around to doing anything about it.'

Daisy pulled a face at him. 'I didn't mean to belittle her colour schemes . . .'

'Come on, Daisy, she's been gone long enough for it not to hurt. It's a fucking awful bathroom!'

Daisy started to giggle. 'You're right, it is. I'll always see you shaving in that pink-painted mirror with them cherubs on.' Her giggle turned to a laugh and she realised she hadn't actually laughed properly for a long while, and this was such a silly thing to laugh about, a pink bathroom. 'Even the bleedin' ceiling's pink!' And now her eyes were wet again but from tears of a different sort. 'It's nice in here,' she said after a while, looking round at the comfortable furnishings. 'Makes me feel very calm.'

She could hear the rain pounding against the small-paned windows. It was a reassuring sound. Vinnie took a box of Swan Vestas from the mantelpiece, which was really half a tree trunk cut crossways, and hunkered down to set a match to the paper in the fireplace.

'It'll be even nicer when the fire's lit. Like the world outside doesn't matter any more,' she said.

He turned and looked at her. Daisy had finished drying her own hair and for some unknown reason she wanted to bend down and rub his hair dry as well. His wet hair was a mass of tight brown curls.

'Do you need to shut the world out?' Vinnie asked. 'Today must be a day you've longed for, your own club, right opposite the Gosport ferry. How can it not be a success?'

'Oh, I'll work me guts out to make sure it's a success all right. And I'll pay my dues to everyone who's helped in the venture. But that's just it, Vinnie. Until then, it's mine in name only. I feel, because I owe so much money, that I'm being manipulated.'

No way was she going to tell him all the ins and outs. She knew he wouldn't expect her to either.

'I just wish I'd opted for a smaller place, something like Heavenly Bodies where Vera reigns like a queen.'

The kettle began its mournful whistle. Daisy could see he was thinking about her words as he ignored the kettle, watching instead the flames take hold of the firewood and placing small pieces of coal on the flames. By the time he'd done that the kettle was wailing a sad tale. After washing his hands in the sink he made the tea.

'Do you want something to eat?' he asked.

Daisy shook her head. He went over to a transistor radio on a small oak sideboard and switched it on. The Supremes were singing 'You Can't Hurry Love'. Vinnie turned down the volume until it was background music, then he brought the tea tray over to the sofa, a brick-coloured velvet that matched the curtains. He put down the tray on the black-painted wooden box that served as a small table.

'Make yourself comfortable on the sofa. This part of the house and one of the bedrooms I did redecorate. Couldn't stand any more pink.'

He poured the tea and motioned for her to put in her own milk and sugar. She waved away the sugar. Then he sat down beside her on the two-seater. 'When you've paid back the money you owe, Daisy, you'll be able to do whatever you want with Daisy-chains. Meanwhile I'm sure you've got a free hand in much of the running of it?'

She shrugged and picked up a spoon and began to stir the milk in the cup.

'Look, Daisy,' he said, taking the spoon from her. He put it back on the tray then held on to her hand. 'Those blokes talking to Roy aren't angels. They peddle death and destruction. Some hefty backhanders for turning the other cheek have been exchanged in high places, not just down the Gosport nick. I don't like it; you won't like it either, but it's out of our hands.' He picked up her other hand as well. 'You do understand what I'm talking about?'

Daisy nodded. 'But . . .' He didn't let her get any further but put a finger over her mouth.

'Shh.' He seemed to be studying her. 'Don't take this the wrong way, Daisy, but you look worn out.' He traced his fingers over her cheek.

'I am.' Her voice sounded small, as though it didn't belong to her.

His forehead creased.

'Why don't you put your feet up on the sofa?'

Daisy looked at the size of the sofa. If it had been larger and longer she'd have willingly agreed. He saw her glancing at it.

'I'm not on duty until tonight,' he said. 'Does anyone expect you back for the next couple of hours? What about little Eddie, is he going to be all right?'

Daisy was pleased that Vinnie had thought about her child.

'No worries about my boy, Suze'll be glued to him like wallpaper on a bleedin' wall. Sometimes I worry that he'll forget who his real mum is with all the attention he gets from Vera and Suze.'

He laughed. 'Well, Vera won't leave Daisychains and I'm sure Roy can handle anything that happens there for the next few hours, so why don't you sleep upstairs? I've got paperwork that needs seeing to.' He waved a hand towards his briefcase on the floor just inside the front door. 'You'll be disturbed by nothing more than the chimes from the church clock.'

Daisy ran her hand through her hair. The idea of sleeping for a while was heavenly.

'Would I be able to have a shower first? I feel a bit mucky.'

'Only if you can face that pink bathroom.'

Daisy got up from the sofa and grinned at him.

'For a nightdress, you can borrow one of my shirts.'

She drank her tea, gulping it down in case he changed his mind and sent her home. In the bathroom she let the shower spray on her body, feeling the tension wash away and slip down the drain with the soapsuds. When she parted the violent pink shower curtain she discovered he'd left a shirt on the pink fluffy stool just inside the door. It was a blue one, police issue, she reckoned.

Moments later she was entering the kitchen and climbing the curved stairs where at the top she found two bedrooms. Vinnie was standing in the front bedroom overlooking the lane and church. He had a pillowcase in his hand and it was obvious he'd just changed the sheets for her.

'You shouldn't have bothered,' she said.

'I wanted it nice for you.' He'd folded down the covers and she went and climbed onto the bed, getting inside the flannelette sheets. The pillows were feathered as was the quilt and as Daisy felt the soft cleanness she gave a small smile of contentment. She saw him looking at her ankle. 'Is that scar left from your ordeal?'

She flexed her foot and toes and looked down at the faint mauve circle. She nodded. His face was grave but he asked no more questions. When she was properly in bed he tucked her in as though she was a child.

The rain was pattering on the window. Through the glass Daisy could see the leaves and branches of the trees swaying in the wind, and beyond them the grey stone of St Mary's Church. She looked around what was obviously Vinnie's bedroom. A pile of his clothes lay over the back of the wooden upright chair near the old-fashioned wardrobe. She could smell his cologne lingering and see the bottle beside his hairbrush and comb on top of the chest of drawers.

Books, hardbacks and paperbacks were also piled haphazardly on top of the chest.

A smile filled her heart. For the first time in a long while she felt totally at ease with herself and her surroundings.

And cared for. Yes, cared for.

Daisy knew Vera and Suze loved her, and she them. Loving little Eddie went without saying. But this was a different feeling, this one she had for Vinnie. One she hadn't experienced in a long time. There was no pressure and nothing was expected of her. She, Daisy Lane, could be herself in this small room overlooking a garden of trees with the rain battering the windows.

Vinnie grinned at her and walked to the door, where he turned.

He had his shirtsleeves rolled up, a pair of worn slippers on his feet, and his eyes as they lingered on her were like honey and hot chocolate just waiting to pour over her.

'I'll be downstairs if you want me.'

The silence that followed Daisy could have sliced with a knife. It was finally broken by her voice.

'Don't go, Vinnie,' she said. 'I don't want you to go.'

He stood there, dark hair curled with the rain, his delicious different coloured eyes held fast to hers as though he half expected her to take back her words and say she hadn't meant it. Then his familiar smile first lit his mouth then rose to meet the corners of his eyes.

He walked back to the bed and, bending, pulled her towards him, stroking her hair then kissing the nape of her neck and then her ears with soft feathery kisses. His breath was warm and sweet on her skin. Tantalisingly, his mouth travelled over her cheeks until finally finding her waiting mouth.

At long last Vinnie was going to make love to her.

And she wanted it more than anything she'd wanted in a long while.

This man had never said he loved her but she'd always sensed his longing for her. She remembered the way he'd first looked at her, carefully, as a man does a woman he desires.

'I want everything with you,' she whispered.

'Be careful, Daisy,' he replied softly. 'You may get it.'